PRAISE FOR THE C

DEBBIE M

A "wonderful, emotional and uplifting story."
—*Reader to Reader.com* on *A Cedar Cove Christmas*

"Macomber takes us back to Cedar Cove for another emotional yet amusing visit, updating readers on events large and small in the lives of favorite characters, as well as introducing some new ones."
—*Romantic Times BOOKreviews* on *8 Sandpiper Way*

"[This book's] small-town charm is virtually guaranteed to please."
—*Publishers Weekly* on *74 Seaside Avenue*

"Readers new to Macomber's considerable narrative charms will have no problem picking up the story, while loyal fans are in for a treat."
—*Booklist* on *6 Rainier Drive*

"Debbie Macomber is a skilled storyteller."
—*Publishers Weekly* on *50 Harbor Street*

"The books in Macomber's contemporary Cedar Cove series are irresistibly delicious and addictive."
—*Publishers Weekly* on *44 Cranberry Point*

"Excellent characterization will keep readers anticipating the next visit to Cedar Cove."
—*Booklist* on *311 Pelican Court*

"Macomber's endearing characters offer courage and support to one another and find hope and love in the most unexpected places."
—*Booklist* on *204 Rosewood Lane*

"Macomber is known for her honest portrayals of ordinary women in small-town America, and this tale cements her position as an icon of the genre."
—*Publishers Weekly* on *16 Lighthouse Road*

September 2009

Dear Friends,

The number nine has long held special significance for me. It all started in an algebra class when the professor said that those of us who wished to bypass the final could write an essay on anything to do with mathematics instead. I leaped at the opportunity—need I mention that working with numbers makes my blood pressure rise? An essay sounded like an easy out—until I spoke with other students in my class. One young man had decided to write about mathematics in World War II and another chose the probability of solving a complicated conjecture in our lifetime. I gulped, visited the local library and prayed for inspiration. I found it in the number nine. Yes, I wrote my entire essay on the number nine and how it's used in literature, Scripture, the classroom and daily life. Not only did I receive a top grade for the essay, the instructor asked me to share with the class everything I'd uncovered. And so you see, I have a special bond with the number nine.

Maybe that's why it's not surprising that the ninth book in the Cedar Cove series has proved to be special. Because, simultaneous with this book, my wonderful publisher is also releasing *Debbie Macomber's Cedar Cove Cookbook,* written by Charlotte Jefferson Rhodes (with my help). Charlotte has gathered her family's special recipes and those shared by her Cedar Cove friends, and put them all together for her granddaughter, Justine Gunderson, who has recently opened the Victorian Tea Room and asked her grandmother's advice. Charlotte, being Charlotte, responded with this collection—above and beyond anything Justine could have anticipated. And if you don't mind my saying so, this cookbook is incredible. It's beautiful and filled with fabulous recipes, plus Charlotte's personal comments on Cedar Cove's residents *and* on the recipes themselves.

There's more Cedar Cove news, in addition to the launch of the cookbook. The entire town of Cedar Cove (aka Port Orchard, Washington) is celebrating Cedar Cove Days from August 26 to August 30, 2009. Our little town has worked for the past two years preparing for this event. I can't begin to tell you how excited we are to welcome you to the *real* Cedar Cove.

So, as you can see, 2009 is a special year for this series. Sheriff Troy Davis has his hands full with the goings-on around town. His heart was broken after Faith decided it would be best if they didn't continue their relationship. In addition, there's the mystery of those skeletal remains in the cave outside town. Olivia's undergoing chemotherapy and doing well, and Grace has started a wonderful new program at the library.... Settle back, grab yourself a glass of iced tea and join Troy and your other friends in Cedar Cove.

Debbie Macomber

P.S. I love to hear from my readers.
You can reach me in two ways: through
my Web site (Debbie@DebbieMacomber.com)
and by mail (P.O. Box 1458, Port Orchard, WA 98366).

DEBBIE MACOMBER

92 Pacific Boulevard

ISBN-13: 978-0-7783-2669-4

92 PACIFIC BOULEVARD

www.MIRABooks.com

Printed in U.S.A.

To

Jerry Childs
and
Cindy Lucarelli
For making the dream of Cedar Cove Days
a reality

And to the board members who
worked so hard to
make it possible:

Gil and Kathy Michael
Dana Harmon and John Phillips
Gerry Harmon
Mary and Gary Johnson
Shannon Childs
and
Ron Johnson

CAST OF CHARACTERS

Some of the Residents of Cedar Cove, Washington

Olivia Lockhart Griffin: Family court judge in Cedar Cove. Mother of Justine and James. Married to **Jack Griffin,** editor of the *Cedar Cove Chronicle.* They live at 16 Lighthouse Road.

Charlotte Jefferson Rhodes: Mother of **Olivia** and of **Will Jefferson.** Now married to widower **Ben Rhodes,** who has two sons, **David** and **Steven,** neither of whom lives in Cedar Cove.

Justine (Lockhart) Gunderson: Daughter of Olivia. Mother of Leif. Married to **Seth Gunderson.** The Gundersons owned The Lighthouse restaurant, which was destroyed by fire. Justine has recently opened the Victorian Tea Room. The Gundersons live at 6 Rainier Drive.

James Lockhart: Olivia's son and Justine's younger brother. Lives in San Diego with his family.

Will Jefferson: Olivia's brother, Charlotte's son. Formerly of Atlanta. Divorced, retired and back in Cedar Cove, where he has bought the local gallery.

Grace Sherman Harding: Olivia's best friend. Librarian. Widow of **Dan Sherman.** Mother of **Maryellen Bowman** and **Kelly Jordan.** Married to **Cliff Harding,** a retired engineer who is now a horse breeder living in Olalla, near Cedar Cove. Grace's previous address is 204 Rosewood Lane (now a rental property).

Maryellen Bowman: Oldest daughter of Grace and Dan Sherman. Mother of **Katie** and **Drake.** Married to **Jon Bowman,** photographer.

Zachary Cox: Accountant, married to **Rosie.** Father of **Allison** and **Eddie Cox.** The family lives at 311 Pelican Court. **Allison** is attending university in Seattle, while her boyfriend, **Anson Butler,** has joined the military.

Rachel Pendergast: Works at the Get Nailed salon. Very recently married to widower **Bruce Peyton,** who has a daughter, **Jolene.**

Bob and Peggy Beldon: Retired. They own the Thyme and Tide B & B at 44 Cranberry Point.

Roy McAfee: Private investigator, retired from Seattle police force. Two adult children, **Mack** and **Linnette.** Married to **Corrie.** They live at 50 Harbor Street.

Linnette McAfee: Daughter of Roy and Corrie. Lived in Cedar Cove and worked as a physician's assistant in the new medical clinic. Now living in North Dakota.

Mack McAfee: A fireman and paramedic, who moved to Cedar Cove.

Gloria Ashton: Sheriff's deputy in Cedar Cove. Natural child of Roy and Corrie McAfee.

Troy Davis: Cedar Cove sheriff. Widower. Father of **Megan.**

Faith Beckwith: High school girlfriend of Troy Davis, now a widow. Has moved back to Cedar Cove, where she is renting 204 Rosewood Lane.

Bobby Polgar and **Teri Miller Polgar:** He is an international chess champion; she was a hair stylist at Get Nailed. Their home is at 74 Seaside Avenue.

Christie Levitt: Sister of Teri Polgar, living in Cedar Cove.

James Wilbur: Bobby Polgar's driver.

Pastor Dave Flemming: Local Methodist minister. Married to **Emily.**

Shirley Bliss: Widow and fabric artist, mother of **Tannith** (Tanni) Bliss.

Shaw Wilson: Friend of Anson Butler, Allison Cox and Tanni Bliss.

Mary Jo Wyse: Young woman who had her baby in Cedar Cove on the previous Christmas Eve, assisted by Mack McAfee.

Linc Wyse: Brother of Mary Jo, formerly of Seattle. Opens a car repair business in Cedar Cove.

Lori Bellamy: From a wealthy area family. Recently broke her engagement.

Louie Benson: Mayor of Cedar Cove.

One

Troy Davis had been with the sheriff's department in Cedar Cove for most of his working life. He knew this town and he knew these people; he was one of them. Four times now he'd been elected to the office of sheriff by an overwhelming majority.

Sitting at his desk on this bleak January day, he let his mind wander as he sipped stale coffee. The department stuff was never good, no matter how recently it'd been brewed. As he sat there, he thought about Sandy, his wife of more than thirty years. She'd died last year of complications related to MS. Her death had left a gaping hole in his life. He'd often discussed his cases with her and had come to appreciate her insights. She usually had opinions, carefully considered ones, on what led people to commit the crimes that brought them to his attention.

Troy would've been interested in her views on one of his current cases. A couple of local teenagers had come upon skeletal remains in a cave not far from the road leading out of town. Partial results of the autopsy were finally in, but they raised more questions than they answered. Additional tests were forthcoming, and they might provide further information. He could only hope.... Hard though it was to believe, the body had gone all this time without discovery, and no one seemed to know who it was.

Despite this perplexing—and very cold—case and, of course, the loss of his wife, Troy had reason to count his blessings. He had a comfortable life, good friends and his only child, Megan, was married to a fine young man. In fact, Troy couldn't have chosen a better husband for his daughter had he handpicked Craig himself. In a few months, Megan would give birth to his first grandchild.

As far as finances went, Troy had no complaints. His house was paid off and so was his car. He enjoyed his work and had strong ties to the community.

And yet...he was miserable.

That misery could be attributed to one source.

Faith Beckwith.

Troy had reconnected with his high-school girlfriend, and almost before he realized what was happening, he'd fallen in love with her all over again.

Neither of them possessed an impulsive personality. They were adults; they'd known what they wanted and what they were doing.

Then the relationship that had seemed so promising had come to a sudden end—thanks to his daughter's reaction and to some undeniably bad judgment on Troy's part.

When Megan learned he was dating again so soon after her mother's death, she'd been very upset. Troy understood his daughter's feelings. It *had* only been a few months since they'd buried Sandy; however, Sandy had been ill for years, and in some ways, their farewells had been said long before. But the fact that Troy had hidden his relationship with Faith from his daughter had contributed significantly to the whole mess.

On the very evening Troy had planned to ask Faith to marry him, Megan had miscarried her first pregnancy. As luck would have it, Troy, who'd been with Faith, had turned off his cell phone.

His guilt had been overwhelming. The baby had meant everything to Megan and Craig, especially so soon after Sandy's death.

In retrospect Troy saw that he'd completely mishandled the situation. Immediately after Megan's miscarriage he'd broken off the relationship with Faith. He'd acted out of remorse but he hadn't taken Faith's feelings into account; her shock and pain haunted him to this day.

He'd dedicated himself to his daughter and her needs ever since. That didn't mean he'd stopped thinking about Faith—far from it. Thoughts of her filled his every waking moment.

To complicate this already complicated situation, Faith had sold her Seattle home and moved to Cedar Cove to be closer to her son, Scott—and to Troy. Seeing her around town these days was torture. Faith had made it clear that she wanted nothing to do with him. Troy didn't blame her.

"I have that missing-persons file for you, Sheriff." Cody Woodchase stepped into his office and set the folder in Troy's in-basket.

"Thanks," Troy murmured. "You checked the appropriate dates?"

Cody nodded, dutifully efficient. "And came up blank. The only major case I can personally recall was Daniel Sherman a few years back."

Troy was well aware of the outcome. His old high-school friend had walked away from his family for no apparent reason. He'd simply vanished. The case had bothered Troy for well over a year. As it turned out, Dan had committed suicide, his body eventually found in the woods.

"That one was solved," Troy pointed out.

"I remember," Cody said. "Anyway, I pulled all the pertinent missing-persons files and printed them out for you."

"Thanks." Troy reached for the folder as soon as Cody left his office. Cedar Cove was fortunate enough to have a low crime rate. Oh, there was the occasional public disturbance, domestic violence now and then, a break-in, a drunk driver—the sort of crime common to any small town. There was a mystery every once in a while, too. The biggest that came to mind was the man who'd shown up at Thyme and Tide, the Beldons' B and B. The stranger had the misfortune to die that very night. But that case, which was actually a murder, had been solved, too.

And now…the human remains, found just before Christmas.

According to the autopsy, they were those of a young man. A teenage boy between the ages of fourteen and eighteen. Based on those bones, there was no obvious cause of death. No blunt-force trauma, for instance. He'd been dead as long as twenty-five to thirty years.

Twenty-five to thirty years!

Troy had been with the department back then, untested and eager to prove himself. Sandy was pregnant after miscarrying twice, optimistic that this time they'd have their baby.

If a missing teenager had been reported in the late '70s or early '80s, Troy was confident he would've remembered it. The files Cody had printed out indicated that he was right. Not a single case involving a missing teenager, male or female, had been left unresolved.

To be on the safe side, he checked five years before and five years after. Twelve boys, mostly runaways, had been reported missing in that time. They'd all been found, either returning of their own accord or located by friends, relatives or the authorities.

Surely this young man had family, a mother and father, who must have wondered and waited in anguish. Troy closed his eyes and tried to think of boys he'd known during that time. Random names and faces rushed through his mind.

Around 1985, he recalled, Cedar Cove High School had won the state baseball championship. He could picture the first baseman, Robbie something, and Weaver, one of his deputies now, who'd been the team's star pitcher. Troy had attended all the play-off games. Sandy had gone with him and, although she wasn't a real baseball fan, she'd clapped and yelled her heart out.

Oh, how he missed Sandy….

Troy had visited her grave a couple of times over the holidays. Even at the end, when her body had failed her and MS had stolen much of her dignity, she'd been cheerful. He missed her appreciation of life's simple joys.

At least he and Megan were over the *firsts*—the first Thanksgiving without Sandy. The first Christmas. The first birthday, wedding anniversary and Mother's Day… Those were the big ones, when her loss felt like a burden that would never grow lighter. When he and his daughter both acknowledged that nothing would ever be the same.

Troy was startled out of his reverie by someone calling his name.

"Am I interrupting anything important?" Louie Benson asked, standing in the office doorway.

"Louie." Troy rose to his feet. It wasn't every day he received a visit from the mayor of Cedar Cove. "Come on in. Good to see you." He gestured toward the chair in front of his desk.

"Happy New Year," Louie said as he slid into the seat. He rested one ankle on the opposite knee, striking a relaxed pose.

"Same to you," Troy said and sat back down. "What can I do for you?" The mayor was a busy man and didn't waste time on unnecessary visits. The fact was, Troy couldn't remember when Louie had last sought him out. Oh, they ran into each other often enough; that was unavoidable, since they worked in the same office complex. Socially they were acquaintances and he saw Louie at civic functions or the occasional party.

Louie's expression grew serious, and he leaned forward. "I've got a couple of things I want to discuss with you."

"Sure."

Louie looked down at the floor. "First, I want to remind you that I'm up for reelection this November. I was hoping for an endorsement."

"It's yours." Troy was surprised the other man felt the need to bring it up so early in the year. Besides, he'd supported Louie's previous campaigns. Nothing had changed. To the best of his knowledge, no other candidates had declared their intentions to run against him.

"I value your support," Louie said. "And of course you have mine." His gaze fell on Troy's desk. "On another matter… What can you tell me about those remains that were recently discovered?"

"I got the autopsy report a few days ago," Troy told him. "Jack Griffin ran an article about it in the *Chronicle* over the weekend. I'd hoped someone might step forward with information as a result. Dental evidence is useless because without a name we can't get a chart for comparison. To date, I have nothing."

Louie leaned back in his chair and eyed the open folder on Troy's desk. "So...no clue who that unfortunate soul might be?"

"None whatsoever."

This didn't appear to please the mayor. "The reason I'm pushing you on this is that I got a call from the Seattle paper. Apparently Jack's story aroused some interest there. They want to do a piece on those unidentified remains." The mayor's frown deepened. "I tried to steer the reporter away from the subject, but she seems determined to find out whatever she can. I gave her your contact information, so expect a call."

"Must be a slow news day." Troy appreciated getting advance notice. "Thanks for the heads-up." Over the years he'd dealt with the press many times and was accustomed to handling reporters. He had nothing against them as long as they didn't probe where they didn't belong or print misinformation.

"My fear," Louie went on to explain, "is that a negative story will hurt Cedar Cove's reputation. We want to attract tourists, not drive them away with...with ghoulish stories about our town."

"At this point there's nothing for them to report," Troy reassured him.

"Have you found out *anything?*" Louie inquired.

"Not really." Troy shrugged. "Pretty much what Jack wrote in that article. The remains are those of a male, between the ages of fourteen and eighteen. He's been dead since 1980, give or take a few years. No indication how he died."

Louie seemed uninterested in the details. "The thing is, Cedar Cove doesn't need any bad press. Our initiative this year is to attract more tourists to the area. I hate the thought of Cedar Cove becoming the center of some macabre story about unidentified remains and an unsolved mystery."

Troy nodded. "Yeah, I hear you."

"Good." Louie rose to his feet. "Do your best to solve this as quickly as possible."

Standing up, too, Troy opened his mouth to assure the mayor he was doing the best he could, but he wasn't given the opportunity.

"I'm not saying I want you to sweep anything under the rug, you understand?" the mayor said.

"Of course I won't."

"Good." Louie extended his hand and Troy shook it. "Make sure nothing sensational or misleading gets printed, okay? Like I said, I want Cedar Cove to become a tourist destination, not some freak sideshow."

"Do you remember the reporter's name?" Troy asked.

"I doubt I'd forget it. Kathleen Sadler."

"Kathleen Sadler," Troy repeated. "Not to worry, I'll set her straight."

"Thanks." Louie gave him a relieved smile. "I knew I could count on you."

When the mayor had left, Troy went back to the paperwork on his desk. The phone rang frequently that afternoon, but there was no call from the reporter. He just hoped Kathleen Sadler hadn't taken it upon herself to investigate the actual location. The cave was still taped off, but a piece of yellow crime-scene tape wasn't always a deterrent to determined reporters.

Troy had kept the names of the two teenagers who'd

discovered the body out of the *Chronicle*. However, that didn't mean Sadler wouldn't be able to track them down.

After they'd stumbled upon the remains, Troy had spoken to the teens twice. He was confident Philip "Shaw" Wilson and Tannith Bliss had told him everything they knew, which wasn't much. The conversations had been straightforward. Although Tannith—Tanni—had done a good job of pretending to shrug off the incident, Troy could tell she'd been badly shaken. He was glad to turn the sixteen-year-old over to her mother.

The last thing Tanni needed was to be questioned by the Seattle press. Shaw was a bit older and Troy felt the young man would cope admirably with a barrage of questions. It might not hurt to give the two of them some warning.

His phone rang and Troy grabbed it, prepared to talk to the elusive Kathleen Sadler. "Sheriff Davis."

"Uh, I hope I'm not disturbing you unnecessarily." It was Cody Woodchase.

Troy caught the hesitation in his voice. "You're not. What's up?"

"I just got a call from the 9-1-1 dispatcher and apparently there's been a break-and-enter at 204 Rosewood Lane."

"Faith?" Troy's reaction was immediate as he bolted to his feet. That was the address of the rental house where Faith had recently moved. She'd been there a little more than two months.

"I believe I heard she might be a…friend of yours."

"Yes," Troy said curtly, his throat muscles tight.

"I thought you'd want to know."

"I do, Cody. Thank you." Within seconds, Troy had thrown on his coat and reached for his hat. He charged out the office door, unable to think of anything but Faith. He needed to know she hadn't been hurt, that she was safe from harm.

Two

The moment Faith Beckwith approached her home she recognized that something was wrong. A sense of foreboding stopped her even before she'd unlocked the kitchen door. She shivered but it wasn't because of the damp chill of early January, although it'd been raining on and off all day, and the wind cut through her winter coat. Her indecision didn't last long; she shook it off, turned the key and stepped into—chaos.

Her kitchen floor was strewn with garbage. Someone had upended the trash bin all over the linoleum. Coffee grounds, eggshells and an empty frozen orange-juice container left a trail of grime and filth. Footprints of coffee grounds led into the living room.

Without thinking, Faith reached for the phone. She managed to restrain herself from calling Troy Davis, pausing before she hit the first number, which she'd memorized long ago. Instead, she punched out her son's work number, praying Scottie was still at the office.

The relief that cascaded through her at the sound of Scott's voice nearly buckled her knees. "Scottie…someone broke into the house."

"Mom? What do you mean?"

"Someone broke into the house," she repeated, surprised that she was able to keep her voice level, although she'd begun to tremble with shock.

"You're sure?"

"There's garbage all over the kitchen floor!"

"Mom," Scottie said calmly. "Put down the phone and dial 9-1-1, then call me back."

"Oh, of course." She should've thought of that. Normally she was a clear-thinking woman; however, stepping into this mess had completely unsettled her.

"Call me back as soon as you do."

"Okay," she promised Scottie, then pushed the disconnect button. Taking a deep breath she called emergency services and waited for the operator's voice.

"This is 9-1-1. How may I assist you?"

"My house has been broken into," Faith blurted. "I haven't gone any farther than the kitchen. Whoever was here made a terrible mess."

"Are you sure the intruder isn't still in the house?"

That hadn't even occurred to Faith. Oh, dear…

"No…" The chill she'd experienced earlier returned. It felt as if her feet were frozen to the floor. For all she knew, someone could be standing in the other room.

"Are you on a portable phone?" the operator asked, breaking into the frightening scenarios racing through her mind.

"Yes…"

"Go outside and remain on the line," the operator continued.

Faith forced herself to hurry to the door, moving as quietly as she could, which was probably ridiculous since she'd been speaking in a normal tone earlier. Surely if the person responsible was in the house, he or she would've already overheard.

"I'm outside," she whispered.

"Good," the 9-1-1 operator told her in a reassuring voice. "I have a patrol car on the way."

"Thank you."

"Deputy Weaver's estimated time of arrival is three minutes."

"I'm a friend of Sheriff Troy Davis's," she said and instantly regretted it. Troy was out of her life. Yet *he* was the person she'd wanted to contact when she realized there'd been a break-in. "I *was* a friend," she amended.

The phone beeped, indicating that there was another caller.

"I think that's my son," Faith told the operator. "He wanted me to phone him back as soon as I'd reported the...crime." She wasn't even sure how to refer to it.

"You can return the call in a moment," the operator told her. "Deputy Weaver should be there soon."

Faith sighed in relief when she saw the patrol car round the corner. "He's here now."

The phone beeped again. "I'll need to take this, otherwise Scottie will be worried." She thanked the operator and clicked off, then waited to connect with her son.

"Mom, is everything okay?"

"The officer's here," she assured her son.

"All right. I'm leaving now." Unfortunately, Scott's office was some distance from Rosewood Lane, and it would be at least fifteen minutes before he arrived.

Still, once she knew Scott was coming, she felt as though she might collapse. As though she didn't have the strength to remain upright.

The deputy parked his vehicle at the curb and after

she'd spoken with him, he stalked into the house with his weapon drawn.

Clutching her purse, Faith stood in the driveway that led to the garage. Not more than a minute passed, although it seemed much longer before Deputy Weaver reappeared.

"All clear," he told her.

Nodding, Faith started for the house, but Deputy Weaver placed a restraining hand on her arm. "Do you have family in the area?" he asked.

Faith nodded again. "My son, Scott, is on his way."

"Then I'd recommend you wait until he can accompany you inside," the deputy said.

She didn't understand. "But why? You said whoever did this isn't in the house anymore."

The deputy paused. "I don't believe this is something you'd want to see by yourself," he said. "I can go in with you, too...."

Faith had trouble taking in his words. "You mean...the damage is extensive?"

"You'll need to judge that for yourself."

"Oh." Faith didn't know how to respond to that.

"Can you think of anyone who might have a grudge against you?" the deputy asked.

"No," she said, shaking her head, taken aback by his question. "I've only been living in the area for a couple of months. This is a rental. I...I didn't want to inconvenience my son and his family by living with them while I searched for a house to buy."

Deputy Weaver nodded thoughtfully.

"Why?" she asked anxiously.

His gaze was sympathetic. "I'm sorry to say it, but this looks personal."

"*Personal?* My goodness, it can't be! I lived in Cedar Cove years and years ago, but I don't know many people here these days. I'm working at the medical clinic and, well..." Faith stopped in midsentence when she saw Troy Davis's vehicle.

He pulled up and parked behind Deputy Weaver, then climbed out of his car. It took every bit of her self-control not to rush toward him.

Troy's eyes immediately sought hers. Despite her best efforts, Faith started to tear up. She hadn't seen him since before Christmas, and in that time she'd struggled hard to cast memories of him out of her mind. Her success had been limited. Whole days would pass when she hardly thought of him. That was progress, and yet the first person she'd wanted to turn to in this crisis had been Troy.

Deputy Weaver stepped forward; he and Troy spoke briefly. Then the deputy ambled over to the house next door and Troy started walking toward her.

"Are you all right?" Troy asked, quickly assessing her.

She lowered her eyes rather than reveal how glad she was to see him. "I...I don't know yet." Somehow she managed a feeble smile that probably didn't fool him.

"Does Scott know?"

"I...I called him right away. He's the one who told me to contact emergency services. He said he was leaving the office."

"Good."

"He won't get here for another ten minutes, though."

"Would you rather wait for him or would you like me to do a walk-through of the house with you now?"

It must be bad. "Would you come with me?" she asked, her voice a whisper.

He clasped her elbow and together they headed toward

the door off the kitchen. "I guess it's a terrible mess." The deputy's reaction had implied as much.

As if touching her was a painful reminder that they'd severed their relationship, Troy dropped his hand. Trying to hide the bereft feeling that came over her, Faith opened the narrow closet next to the laundry and reached for the broom.

"I suggest we take a look at the damage before you attempt any cleanup."

"Oh, yes, of course."

He walked into the living room, and when she followed him in, Faith gasped. It was as though a cyclone had gone through, leaving its devastation behind. The furniture was toppled and yellow spray paint had been blasted across her piano and bookcase.

Most distressing of all was what they'd done to the family photos displayed along the fireplace mantel. Shocked, Faith covered her mouth with both hands.

"This has to be personal," Troy muttered. He reached for the picture of Scott and his wife and children. Each face had an X through it, drawn in bright red ink. The photo of Faith's daughter, Jay Lynn, had received the same treatment. But a photograph of her late husband, Carl, had come in for the most brutal destruction. His image had been utterly blotted out.

"Who would *do* such a thing?" Faith cried.

"Have you argued with anyone lately?" Troy asked.

That was basically the same question Deputy Weaver had asked and the answer hadn't changed. "No…"

"Think, Faith," Troy insisted. "Whoever's responsible for this—and it could be more than one person—is trying to hurt you."

"In that case," she snapped, "they've succeeded."

"I'm so sorry this happened." Troy's words were gentle, kind. For a moment it looked as if he wanted to take her in his arms.

Weak and vulnerable as she felt just then, Faith would gladly have slipped into his embrace. She would've welcomed the comfort he offered, the reassurance that, in his arms, she was safe and secure.

Thankfully he remembered that they weren't a couple anymore, and that his touch was no longer appropriate. He dropped his arm and took a small step in retreat.

"What about the bedroom?" Faith asked in an effort to disguise the uncertainty of her resolve.

"You sure you're up to this?" Troy asked.

Would anyone be? "I…I'll need to face it sooner or later."

"True." Again he led the way.

They were forced to step over drawers that had been dragged into the hallway, over chair cushions and books and lamps—and what appeared to be every piece of clothing she owned. It seemed as though the contents of her entire home had been emptied in the hallway.

When she saw her bedroom and the chaos there, tears filled her eyes and she couldn't stand to look at any more. With a sob, she turned and hurried out of the room.

Anger surged through her. She couldn't imagine who'd done this. Whoever it was wanted to disrupt the peace and serenity she'd worked so hard to achieve since moving to Cedar Cove.

"Can you tell if anything's been taken?" Troy asked. She suspected he was trying to distract her from all the wreckage.

She walked into the living room and took several deep breaths. "No…not yet." The knowledge that this might be more than vandalism upset her all over again. Whoever had broken in had probably taken whatever valuables they could find.

Why target *her?* Faith didn't own more than a few pieces of expensive jewelry, some of which she was wearing. The other pieces—her wedding band and the pearls that had been her mother's—were tucked away in a safety-deposit box at the bank.

"Is anything obvious missing?" he continued.

She shook her head.

"First thing I want you to do is get a new lock," Troy said, examining the front door. "Make it a dead bolt. Consider an alarm system, too."

"I'll look into it." His suggestion kept her from dwelling on what had happened, but not for long.

"My family," she whispered. She stared at the photographs of her children and grandchildren. "Are they safe?"

Troy shrugged uncomfortably. "My guess is this is a scare tactic."

"But why?"

Troy's face creased in a dark frown. "I can't answer that. I wish I could tell you, but I can't."

"I want to know *why...*"

"I do, too," he said, "and I promise you I'll do everything in my power to find whoever's responsible."

That was fine, but Faith's biggest concern remained her family. "Why would anyone cross out their faces? I won't be able to sleep at night if there's any chance my grandchildren might be at risk.... It's all because of me," she said in a rush. "What could I have possibly done to deserve this?"

Troy took her by the shoulders and his hold was all that kept her from collapsing.

"Faith, listen," he said, sounding stern and official. "Everything's going to be all right. I'll schedule patrol cars to drive past your place and Scott's, too. I don't want you to worry, understand?"

It was almost more than she could do to nod in simple acknowledgment.

"Mom!" She heard Scott's voice coming from the front porch.

When she didn't immediately answer, Troy spoke on her behalf. "We're inside the house," he called out. Releasing her, he moved toward the door and opened it.

Scott charged into the house and did a double take. He was struck silent, his eyes wide with shock and dismay. Once he'd recovered, he turned to Troy to supply answers, the same way Faith had moments earlier.

Faith reached out to her son. She was close to both her children and her grandchildren, too, but refused to be a burden to them. Her independence meant everything, and she was determined to preserve it. After Carl's death, she'd adjusted to being a widow, rambling around that large Seattle house on her own. Now she'd come back to Cedar Cove, but as much as possible, she still took care of whatever needed attention without calling her children for assistance.

So far she'd managed well, but this…this monster who'd invaded her home had overturned more than her furniture, he'd unsettled her entire world and destroyed her peace of mind.

"Deputy Weaver's talking to the neighbors," Troy said. "I'll check with him and see if he has any information."

"Whoever did this came through the front door?" Scott asked incredulously. He slid one arm around Faith's shoulders. She was grateful for his support.

"It appears that way," Troy answered.

"In broad *daylight?* Wasn't anyone on the street home?"

Faith looked up. "The Vesseys are in Arizona for the winter and…and—" she faltered a bit "—everyone else on the block is either at work or at school."

"Will you be okay?" Troy asked, his eyes revealing his reluctance to leave. But now that Scott had arrived, there was no reason for him to stay. He'd done his duty. No, he'd gone above and beyond anything duty required.

Calling on all her strength—and an acting ability she hadn't known she possessed—Faith reassured him with a smile. "I'll be fine. Thank you, Troy. It…it meant a great deal that you came yourself."

He touched the brim of his hat and, with a nod in Scott's direction, turned and walked out the door.

Three

Olivia Griffin spooned up the last of her soup and set the empty bowl in the kitchen sink. The homemade tomato basil was one of her favorites and her mother made sure she had an abundant supply every week. Jack would be pleased that she'd finished her lunch. She'd received her first chemotherapy treatment the previous week and it had gone better than she'd expected.

But then her expectations hadn't been optimistic. When she was diagnosed with breast cancer a few months before, Olivia had been afraid her life was almost over. To say the news had shocked her was putting it mildly. She'd always eaten properly, exercised regularly and taken all the recommended vitamins.

The important lesson she'd learned about cancer was that the disease wasn't fair; for that matter, *life* wasn't fair. And at her age, that was something she certainly should've known. Did know. Losing one of her children at thirteen, the failure of her first marriage… But somehow, she'd foolishly come to believe she could control her body, her health, if she did the right things. That loss of control was difficult to accept, yet she had no choice.

She was a woman who rigorously managed her environment—no clutter in *her* house. She realized she'd become more that way after Jordan's death.

She'd taken a leave from her position as a family court judge and was gearing up, both emotionally and physically, for the treatments scheduled during the next three months. She knew some people worked through their chemo, but everyone had urged her not to. "Give yourself a break," Jack said, and so she had.

The sound of a car door closing alerted Olivia to the fact that she had company. Glancing out the large kitchen window, she noticed that her visitor was none other than her mother. No surprise there.

Olivia frowned slightly when she saw that Charlotte was alone. Since her mother had married Ben several years ago, they were practically always together. They'd returned from a Caribbean cruise on Christmas Day and her mother had been a daily visitor ever since.

Knowing Charlotte preferred to park at the side of the house and use the back entrance, Olivia opened the door off the kitchen.

Her mother smiled as she entered the house. "I hoped I'd catch you before you had a nap," she said. She placed the basket on the table and quickly divested herself of purse and coat, hanging them on the hook by the door. Charlotte rarely stopped by without bringing some kind of treat, generally something homemade.

"Mom," Olivia joked, "I outgrew naps when I was four, remember?"

"I know, dear," Charlotte said, without taking offense, "but you need your rest, especially now."

"I slept in this morning." Olivia's normal routine had her out of bed at six and in the courthouse by eight-thirty.

The sheer luxury of not setting the alarm each night could become habit-forming, she thought.

"Slept in until what time?" Charlotte asked as she folded back the basket's red-checkered cloth and brought out a tin of cookies and an orange Bundt cake that just happened to be one of Jack's favorites.

"Nearly eight."

Her mother looked over her shoulder and pretended to gasp. "My, that's *so* late."

Olivia laughed. "Well, for me it is—and it was divine."

"Jack got ready for work on his own and didn't wake you?"

As a matter of fact, her husband *had* awakened her, but in the most romantic way. Jack had brought her a freshly brewed cup of coffee. Then he'd kissed her—repeatedly—before he'd left for the newspaper office. The memory of his kisses stirring her from a deep sleep filled her with a warm glow of happiness.

"Would you like some tea, Mom?" Olivia asked. Usually she had coffee only in the morning and tea after that.

"I'll make it," Charlotte said.

"I'm not an invalid," Olivia protested, although she knew it was pointless to argue. Without waiting for a reply, she pulled out a chair and sat down, watching as her mother bustled about the kitchen.

Olivia tended to let Jack and her mother pamper her these days. There was so little either of them could do for her, and these small indulgences—coffee in bed, some home-baked goodies—made them feel better, too.

"Where's Ben?" she asked as her mother put water on to boil and added tea bags to the pot.

"Home, in his lazy chair," Charlotte said. "He's feeling a bit under the weather."

"Did you make him some of your chicken noodle soup?" This was her mother's surefire remedy for just about anything that ailed the people she loved.

Charlotte nodded. "It's simmering in the Crock-Pot at this very moment." She took two teacups and saucers from the cupboard as she spoke. "Ben's tired out from the cruise, and then, well, this whole business with David and the baby has really upset him."

On Christmas Eve, a young pregnant woman by the name of Mary Jo Wyse had arrived in Cedar Cove looking for David Rhodes, Ben's youngest son. David was the father of her child, and he'd told the naive young woman a pack of lies. Aside from the more serious lies—like telling her he loved her and wanted the baby—he'd led Mary Jo to believe he'd be spending the holidays with Charlotte and Ben. David knew very well that his father and stepmother would be on a cruise; he'd obviously assumed that Mary Jo wouldn't try to find him.

What he hadn't expected was that she'd actually come to town, let alone that she'd go into labor and give birth to her daughter here, in Cedar Cove. It turned out to be a miraculous night, one Olivia and her best friend, Grace Harding, would long remember.

"Has Ben been in touch with David?" Olivia asked. The last she'd heard, no one had reached David to tell him Mary Jo had given birth to a daughter.

Charlotte nodded just as the kettle started to whistle. She lifted it off the burner and filled the teapot, which she covered with a cozy and carried to the kitchen table. Next, she brought over the cups and saucers. All her movements were economical and precise, Olivia thought, testament to all those years of working in the kitchen, bringing comfort to others.

"I'm afraid it wasn't a pleasant conversation," Charlotte said with a sigh. "Ben is dreadfully disappointed in his son."

Unfortunately, this wasn't the first time. Far from it...

"David tried to deny that he even knew Mary Jo."

The weasel. The jerk! Attempting to squirm his way out of responsibility was typical, of course. Olivia's first exposure to David had been when he'd attempted to swindle Charlotte out of several thousand dollars. Thankfully, Justine, Olivia's daughter, had managed to thwart him.

Charlotte released another deep sigh. "I'm afraid Ben and David argued. Ben didn't say much afterward and I didn't pressure him, but you can imagine how he feels."

"He got a beautiful granddaughter out of this mess, though," Olivia reminded her mother.

"Oh, yes, and he's thrilled about Noelle. I know he's already had his will revised."

"Have you heard from Mary Jo?" Olivia asked.

"We've talked to her a couple of times this week. She sounds well, and the baby's thriving."

"That's good news."

"And her brothers are crazy about little Noelle."

The memory of Christmas Eve produced a smile as Olivia recalled the three Wyse brothers rushing to Grace and Cliff's ranch in an effort to find their little sister. They'd fumbled and bumbled their way across the Puget Sound area and eventually arrived, just in time to see their newborn niece. Mary Jo had been staying in the apartment above Cliff's barn at the ranch, where she'd gone into labor.

"When we spoke yesterday, Mary Jo said Mack McAfee had stopped by to see the baby," Charlotte told her.

"He went over to Seattle, then?" The young firefighter

had been with Mary Jo during much of her labor and had delivered the baby. It was his first birth. Olivia could clearly recall how excited he'd been. Mack's face had shone with such joy, you'd almost think *he'd* been the child's father.

"Yes, and Mary Jo said he brought Noelle another stuffed animal." Charlotte removed the cozy and picked up the pot, pouring them each a cup of steaming green tea. Shaking her head in amusement, she looked up at Olivia. "Between Mack and Mary Jo's brothers, that baby has enough toys to last her whole childhood."

"That's so nice," Olivia said, reaching for her cup.

"Did you hear about Faith Beckwith?" Charlotte opened the tin and offered Olivia an oatmeal-raisin cookie.

"That she moved back to town, you mean?" This was old news as far as Olivia was concerned. She bit into her cookie, which as always was just right.

"No." Charlotte took a sip of tea. "That her home was vandalized."

"No!" Olivia was horrified. "Oh, dear, does Grace know?"

The rental belonged to her best friend, who'd agonized over whether to sell the house or keep it. Her first tenants, a young navy couple, Ian and Cecilia Randall, had barely settled in when Ian was transferred to another duty station. The next tenants had gotten months behind in their rent and seemed determined to work the system and live there rent-free as long as possible. Apparently the couple and the hangers-on who lived with them knew exactly what they were doing.

The experience had been terrible for poor Grace. Fortunately, the renters had moved of their own accord—with a little help from Jack and Grace's husband, Cliff, who'd come up with a rather inventive means of persuading the gang of deadbeats to vacate the house quickly.

"Oh, dear," Charlotte murmured as she set aside her cup. "I forgot. Grace asked me not to tell you."

"Why ever not?"

"She didn't want you to worry."

The one thing Olivia wished was that her family and friends would stop treating her as if she'd faint at the smallest hint of bad news.

"I'll talk to Grace later, but first tell me about Faith."

Her mother held her teacup in both hands. "Oh, she's fine. The minute I heard about the break-in, I went over to help her clean up. So did Grace and Cliff, of course, and Corrie and Peggy and a bunch of others. The place was a mess." Charlotte grimaced. "An *awful* mess."

"How's Faith handling all this?"

Her mother leaned against the back of her chair. "You know Faith. She's a strong woman, but this break and enter rattled her. Thank goodness the vandal was gone by the time she got home."

Olivia could easily guess how unsettling this must have been for Faith. "Was anything taken?" she asked.

"When I saw her, she wasn't sure, and we were all so busy cleaning up the house it was hard to tell. I don't think she'll know until she has a chance to go through everything."

"Who else came to help?" This was something Olivia loved about Cedar Cove. Neighbors were more than neighbors—they were friends who willingly pitched in when needed.

"Well, naturally, her son and his wife."

"Of course."

"Megan Bloomquist was there, too."

"Troy's daughter?"

"Yes. Faith and Megan have struck up quite a friendship."

This was surprising. "What about the sheriff and Faith?"

Charlotte set her teacup in its saucer, her frown thoughtful. "That, unfortunately, is a delicate situation. I hear they've decided not to see each other anymore."

"Really?" Olivia was sorry about that. She remembered that the two of them had dated in high school. Recently there'd been rumors that they'd reconnected, which seemed like such a satisfying idea. It saddened her to think that everything wasn't going to fall neatly into place. But, as she very well knew, not every romance had a happy ending.

Both were silent for several seconds. "The locksmith showed up while I was there," Charlotte said. "Troy suggested a dead-bolt system for the house, and Grace got it installed immediately."

"Good."

"Front and back doors, and the garage, as well." Her mother grinned. "Lloyd said he'd defy anyone to get into that house again."

Lloyd Copeland was the town's locksmith and had twenty years' experience. If he said the house was secure, then it was secure. The only way in would be through a window, but Olivia recalled that Grace had installed extrastrong glass in the downstairs panes.

"I'm glad," Olivia said. "Faith needs the peace of mind."

"Amen to that." Charlotte finished her tea and stood to bring her cup to the sink. "Anything more I can do for you, Olivia?"

"I'm fine, Mom. Thanks for asking."

"Has your brother been by lately?" Charlotte asked as she headed toward the door.

"Will phoned this morning."

The immediate frown told Olivia that her mother wasn't pleased. She expected Will to visit at least three times a week, to commiserate and hold her hand.

"Mom," she protested. "Will's busy. He's working on getting the art gallery up and running, plus remodeling the living space."

"That's no excuse."

Olivia didn't bother to argue.

"You've seen him since Christmas though, right?"

"Of course." Actually, Will had come over on Christmas Day, looking a bit depressed. He'd gone to Shirley Bliss's home and—to his astonishment—she hadn't been there. Her brother had a massive ego and assumed that the world revolved around his schedule. It had never occurred to him that Shirley, one of his artists and a widowed mother of two, would be anywhere but at home, waiting, *longing,* for a visit from him. Olivia hoped her brother had learned from this.

"Don't forget I brought you my orange Bundt cake."

"I couldn't possibly forget." Although Jack would appreciate eating it more than Olivia. "You're trying to fatten me up, aren't you?"

Her mother didn't deny it. "I'll cook you a batch of my special lasagna next."

"Mom," Olivia said laughingly, "I won't fit into any of my clothes if this continues." Although she was far from having to worry about that. Her suits hung on her because she'd lost weight before Christmas, fighting off a serious infection. However, Olivia wanted her mother to know that while she valued everything Charlotte did for her, she was well on the road to recovery.

"Let me spoil you a bit longer," her mother said. "Please, honey?"

Olivia gave in with a smile. "All right, Mom."

Charlotte put on her coat and scooped up her purse and the empty basket. "I'm off to see Bess." One of her many friends. "You'll call if you need anything?" she asked. "Promise?"

"Of course," Olivia assured her.

Her mother grasped the doorknob. "And don't let Jack eat that cake all by himself, you hear?"

Olivia laughed again. "I'll do my best, Mom."

With a saucy wave, her mother was out the door. Olivia just hoped that when she hit eighty, she'd have as much energy, optimism and charm as her wonderful mother.

Four

There was someone pounding on Christie Levitt's front door as she stood over the bathroom sink, brushing her teeth. She rinsed her mouth and methodically set her toothbrush in the holder, then splashed cold water on her face. She had no idea who'd be at her door this early in the day.

"Hold your horses," she shouted and winced. Her head throbbed with what threatened to become a blinding headache.

Whoever was at the door was certainly persistent. On her way through the hallway to her bedroom, she did a quick mental review of the bills she'd paid. Yes, she specifically remembered that she'd mailed off checks to the electric and water companies.

Both utilities had been shut off before and in her opinion the companies were rather sneaky about it. No one had come to the door, at least not that she recalled.

Grabbing a housecoat, she slid her arms into the sleeves and belted the waist, doing her best to ignore the throbbing in her head.

"Who is it?" she demanded as she unbolted the lock. Her

head ached, her eyes stung. What she really needed was a cup of strong, hot coffee. The stronger the better, and it couldn't come any too soon. Waking with a mouth so dry it felt as though it was stuffed with cotton, she'd brushed her teeth first. Coffee was going to be her next step.

The moment she opened the apartment door, her sister pushed past her.

Christie groaned. She'd tried to avoid Teri. Her sister's persistent phone calls had gone unanswered. Christie had torn up the note Teri had slipped under her door without bothering to read it. No need; she knew what it said. She should've realized that Teri didn't know how to take a hint.

"What do you want?" Christie winced again at the pain that felt like a spear going through her head.

Teri, five months pregnant with triplets, glared at her indignantly. "You look like hell."

"Thanks." Christie walked into the kitchen and reached for the coffeepot. "Don't mince words or anything."

"I never have and I'm not about to start now." Teri followed her into the room, and without waiting for an invitation pulled out a chair and sat down. "Put some water on for tea if you would," she said. Her hands automatically went to rest on her protruding belly, and she raised her feet to the seat of the opposite chair, as if she intended to stay a while.

Great. Just great. Not only did Christie have a headache to contend with, she was stuck with Teri, too. In a minor act of rebellion, she started the coffee before filling a cup with water and slamming it into the microwave. She hit the timer button savagely.

"What are you doing here?" she ventured to ask,

although she could easily guess. This visit had to do with James Wilbur, Teri and Bobby's former chauffeur. Even mentally saying his name brought a flash of pain.

The scum.

The rat.

Christie had been *convinced* she was in love. Deeply, truly in love. Oh, she'd loved before, always unwisely as it turned out. She'd been married and divorced and had gone through a succession of men who all said they loved her…and fool that she was, Christie had believed them.

With James it'd been different; this time everything seemed right. But then he did what every man had done to her. He'd dumped her. He'd left her a cryptic message and taken off, and in the process broken her already wounded heart.

Well, no more. Never again.

Christie was finished with men.

Done.

She meant it this time. Loving someone, loving a man, simply hurt too much.

"Your car's parked outside the Pink Poodle," Teri announced, watching her closely as she moved about the kitchen.

"So?" Christie returned flippantly. Where she chose to leave her car was none of her sister's business. The microwave made a beeping noise but she ignored it.

"So," Teri echoed in the same sarcastic tone, "you've been drinking again."

"What about it? My friends are there." It wasn't any big deal if she chose to have a couple of beers with the guys after work. A few hours at the Poodle helped break the monotony and fend off loneliness. Going back to an empty apartment and spending the night in front of the tube wasn't much incentive to rush home.

"These guys are your friends? Yeah, right."

"Listen, if you're here to lecture me, then save your breath. I don't want to hear it."

Teri scowled. The way they were snapping at each other was reminiscent of the relationship they used to have. Over the past year that had improved, thanks in large part to James and to Bobby Polgar, Teri's chess-playing husband.

Teri broke eye contact, lowered her head and sighed. She sounded either hurt or offended, Christie wasn't sure which. But this reaction was so unlike her bossy forthright sister that Christie was immediately concerned.

"What's wrong?" Various possibilities raced through her head. A complication with the pregnancy, or trouble with Bobby, or maybe the problem, whatever it was, concerned their younger brother, Johnny. Or—

"It's the pregnancy," Teri blurted out. She closed her eyes. "I get light-headed from time to time. I'm fine. It's just that carrying three babies is taking its toll."

Christie felt a jolt of alarm. "Something's wrong with the babies?"

"No," Teri said, gesturing dismissively with her hand. "It's me."

"You're—"

"The doctor said my blood pressure would fluctuate and I'd have off days. Apparently this is one of those days and the kidlets are making sure I know they're there. But it's nothing to worry about."

Despite her sister's reassurances, Christie *was* worried. She shouldn't have ignored Teri's attempts to reach her. As a result, her sister had come in search of her. In every likelihood Teri had gone against doctor's orders by leaving the house, and all because Christie refused to pick up the phone.

The coffeemaker made a gurgling noise, signaling that the brewing was complete. Christie grabbed a mug, inspecting it to be sure it was clean before filling it to the brim. She pulled Teri's tea water out of the microwave and brought both to the table, along with an herbal tea bag, and sat across from her sister.

"All right, talk to me," Christie said and sipped her coffee, gasping as it burned her lips.

Teri slowly breathed in and out, her eyes closed. "I blame you for this."

"Me? What'd I do?" She did blame herself but wasn't prepared to admit it.

"All…all you think about is yourself." For a moment it sounded as if Teri was about to break into tears. Her voice quavered and her lower lip started to tremble.

Christie blinked. Teri was the strong, determined one in the family, and not usually given to emotional outbursts. Christie was the volatile sister—and this role reversal made her uncomfortable.

Whatever was bothering Teri, she couldn't seem to get the words out.

"What did I do?" Christie repeated.

Teri fumbled for a tissue and blew her nose with an inelegant honk before stuffing the tissue back into her purse. "You never thought about Bobby's feelings or mine."

"What do you mean?"

"We miss James, too. Bobby hardly knows what to do with himself. You're not the only one who's hurting!"

Her sister was right. Christie hadn't stopped to

consider what James's leaving had meant to Bobby and her sister. James had been Bobby's closest friend for many years. He was Bobby's confidant as well as his driver.

Recently an enterprising reporter had revealed that James was once a chess prodigy himself, and that he'd suffered an emotional collapse in his early teens and spent time in a mental institution. Afterward he'd disappeared from the chess world. When the news story broke, Bobby's friend had panicked and run.

The fact that James had deserted her and Bobby and Teri was cruel enough. And Christie knew she hadn't been much comfort to them because she was too devastated by what he'd done. She'd tried not to fall in love with him; again and again she'd rebuffed him, and still he'd pursued her.

James was unlike any man she'd ever known. He hadn't rushed her into bed, although she would've gone willingly if he'd asked. He didn't. Instead, he'd broken down her resistance, bit by bit, ever patient, undemanding and kind. No woman, no matter how emotionally strong, could resist such tender persuasion. Christie certainly couldn't.

Just before he disappeared, she'd laid out her past to him and she hadn't prettied it up, either. She'd told him everything, about the men she'd been with, the marriage that had crumbled under the weight of alcoholism and physical abuse. She'd left nothing out. If he was going to love her and be part of her life, she didn't want anything hidden in the shadows, to leap out at some unexpected time.

James had listened quietly, had held her and kissed her—and hadn't said a single word about his own history.

Christie had offered him her trust, something she'd

sworn she'd never give another man. She'd even started thinking about being married to James, having a baby with him.... What hurt so badly was that he hadn't loved her enough to share his past.

Well, that was that. Another painful lesson learned. James was out of her life now.

For good.

It didn't matter if he returned, and everyone seemed to assume that eventually he would. She was through.

"You didn't come for Christmas," Teri complained. Apparently it still rankled that Christie had missed the big family get-together. But as far as Christie was concerned, Christmas dinner with her ragtag family wasn't any real loss.

"I was volunteering, remember?" This was true, but she'd already decided not to show up at Teri and Bobby's place *before* she made that arrangement.

Teri looked over at her with big brown doe-eyes. "You were...volunteering?"

"Yeah. I told you. I served meals in Tacoma at the homeless shelter."

"Oh. Yeah."

"I delivered Christmas baskets to needy families, too, but that was before Christmas."

Teri shocked her when she suddenly began to laugh. "And I accused you of not paying attention to me. I'm almost as bad. I completely forgot you were doing that. Here I thought you were probably in some tavern, instead of with Bobby and me."

"No way." She hadn't wanted to talk about it, but at Christmas she'd still felt emotionally shaky. Being with Teri and Bobby was risky—there were too many memories associated with James at her sister's home. And it was hard to watch those two, with their romantic bliss and cozy domestic life. Her pain was too close to the surface. She was better now, stronger than she'd been in a long while.

"Then why haven't you answered my calls?"

Christie didn't have an explanation for that. All right, so maybe she wasn't as strong as she thought.

"You're drinking?"

"A few beers. Don't worry, I didn't get drunk." Although she'd downed enough alcohol to leave her with a killer headache. She figured the booze had affected her like this because she hadn't been drinking much lately.

"You were too drunk to drive."

Christie denied that. She wasn't stupid; she knew her limit.

Teri didn't seem to believe her. "Then why is your car at the Pink Poodle?"

"It wouldn't start." Christie didn't want to think about that piece of junk. Every day the engine fired to life was a day to be grateful for.

A few months ago, James had managed to jury-rig it into running again but there were too many things wrong with her sad excuse for a car.

"How'd you get home?"

"Someone gave me a ride."

Teri's gaze shot toward the bedroom.

"No one spent the night, if that's what you're wondering."

Teri had the good grace to look a little embarrassed. "But it wouldn't be the first time if someone did," she muttered.

Christie couldn't argue with that. When it came to men she was batting zero. As Teri had once said, Christie attracted losers the way an ice cream truck attracts children. Not that Teri should talk; she'd been fortunate enough to break the pattern of harmful and unfulfilling relationships when she met Bobby. Christie had been so sure that James was her Bobby.... He wasn't.

Teri drank some of her tea and sent Christie a smile. "I'm glad you weren't alone over Christmas."

"I am, too. It helped, you know?" Christie took a tentative sip of coffee.

"I know," Teri said.

"Instead of sitting home and feeling sorry for myself, I took the initiative and did something for someone else."

Teri didn't appear to be completely mollified. "You could've spent the day with Bobby and me. Johnny was there, and Mom came by. I wish you'd been there, too," she added plaintively.

In retrospect it probably wouldn't have hurt to make a token appearance. "How is Mom?" she asked, hoping to distract her sister.

"She's filed for divorce."

"Again?"

Christie had lost count of how many stepdads and "uncles" she'd accumulated through the years. "I don't understand why she marries these guys." She had to be on her fifth or sixth husband. Christie had stopped making an effort to remember their names; they never seemed to last long enough to bother. The fact was, she hadn't seen her mother in more than a year.

"I don't know why she marries them, either," Teri said. "At least she didn't get bombed this time. Maybe because what's-his-name wasn't there."

"Did Bobby put her purse by the front door again?"

Teri grinned at the memory. As Christie recalled, her

mother had vowed never to return. That vow, like every other one she'd made through the years, had turned out to be meaningless.

"I think Bobby was tempted to show Mom the door, but for my sake he restrained himself."

"He's a good man."

Her sister's eyes softened. "He is," she agreed.

"How's Johnny doing?" Their little brother held a special place in Christie's heart. Between them, the two sisters had practically raised him.

Christie was as proud as any mother when Johnny was accepted into the University of Washington. Having Bobby Polgar as a brother-in-law hadn't hurt. Teri had never said as much, but it didn't take a college degree to add two and two. Johnny never could have afforded the tuition and other expenses on his own, and there hadn't been any scholarships.

"He made the dean's list."

"I'm thrilled for him!" She'd have to call Johnny soon, congratulate him.

"Me, too." Teri sipped her tea. "I've been worried about you."

"I know." Christie's declarations of strength and independence were a lot of bravado. Spending Friday night at the Pink Poodle was testament to that. Waking up with a hangover wasn't the way she wanted to live the rest of her life. It wasn't the way she intended to live it, either.

"You know what I was thinking?" Christie said a bit sheepishly, half afraid Teri would laugh.

"No, tell me."

She gave a self-conscious shrug. "I handed out charity baskets with that group from the Methodist church at Christmas."

"Yes, you mentioned that."

"They were nice people."

Teri laughed. "Don't sound so surprised."

Actually, she was. Christie had expected those church people to make some comment about her lifestyle. Instead, everyone was friendly and welcoming. She hadn't been back, although she wasn't sure why.

"I'm going to go to church." Having said as much, Christie held her breath and waited for Teri's reaction.

"Why do you say it like that?" Teri asked in a puzzled voice.

"Like what?"

"Like you're standing up at an AA meeting and making a confession. Lots of people attend church, you know."

"What about you?"

"I go every now and then, and I always feel good afterward. I don't have anything against going to church and you shouldn't, either."

"I want to live a better life," Christie said, remembering how she'd felt when she was delivering the charity baskets. Instead of being so self-absorbed, so consumed by her own loss, she'd reached out to help others less fortunate.

"That's what I want, too," Teri echoed. "A better life than our mother's, a better life for my child…er, children." Teri grinned as she said it.

"Pastor Flemming wrote a note to thank me for volunteering," Christie said. The letter sat on the kitchen counter and she picked it up. When it first arrived, she'd been feeling depressed and had given it a cursory glance. The only thing she remembered was something about a backpack program sponsored by the church. She decided to find out what that was.

"Will you come to church with me on Sunday?" Christie asked.

Teri didn't even hesitate. "Of course."

"Thanks."

"I'd get up and hug you," Teri said, "but I'm too comfortable where I am."

Christie laughed and stretched out a hand to clasp her sister's.

Five

Sheriff Troy Davis closed the file concerning the break-in at Faith's home. Unfortunately, there'd been no progress, and he felt he should deliver the disappointing news in person. As he drove his patrol car toward Rosewood Lane, he reviewed the little he knew about the situation.

He'd spoken to his lead detective regarding the break and enter. Detective Hildebrand had assured Troy that his staff had done everything that could be done—the neighbors had been interviewed, and comparisons made with similar crimes in Cedar Cove and in nearby jurisdictions.

Instead of letting Hildebrand or his assistant call or visit Faith, he'd stepped in and volunteered to do it. She was, after all, his friend. Or at least, she had been. Mostly this visit was prompted by Troy's need to see how Faith was faring after the break-in.

When he'd parked in front of the house, he didn't leave the car immediately, mentally preparing himself for the meeting. He knew that seeing her would be hard. Faith had made it clear that she didn't want any further contact and he'd respected her wishes. This, however, was official business—even if it didn't have to be *his* business.

He marched up the steps leading to her front door, rang the bell and waited, hat in his hand.

She answered the door cautiously, and her eyes brightened when she saw him. That spark was quickly gone, however, replaced by a faraway look, flat and emotionless. In that moment, it demanded all his discipline not to pull her into his arms and beg for another chance. He needed Faith, loved her, wanted to marry her—and had destroyed any possibility of that happening.

"I have the report from the investigating officer," Troy said briskly, conveying that this was police business and not a social call.

"Oh, good." She unlocked the screen door and held it open for him to come inside.

Troy paused to examine the lock and was relieved to see that Faith had taken his advice and installed a dead bolt. Or rather, Grace and Cliff Harding, the owners, had arranged for it. Not surprisingly, Grace had been horrified by what she'd seen. This had been her home for decades—and Faith was her friend. Megan had told him that both Grace and Cliff had helped with the cleanup.

The house was tidy once again and back to normal. That couldn't have been an easy task. The aroma of baking reminded him that he'd worked through his lunch hour.

"I just took some bran muffins out of the oven. Would you like one?" Faith asked.

It'd been a long time since Troy had tasted anything home-baked. He wondered if she offered because she'd heard his stomach growl or if she'd noticed that he'd nearly swooned when he entered the house. Or maybe she was simply being polite. Whatever the reason, he wasn't about to turn her down. "That'd be great," he said, hoping he sounded casual.

"I have coffee on, too. Can I get you a cup?"

"Please." He followed her into the kitchen and watched as she poured the coffee and took a muffin out of the pan, setting it on a small plate. He waited until she was seated before he pulled out the chair across from her. It seemed to take her an inordinate amount of time to look at him. One quick glance in his direction, and then she lowered her eyes again.

"What did you find out?" she asked, folding her hands neatly in her lap.

Troy wished he had something positive to share with her. "Unfortunately, the news is…inconclusive."

"What do you mean? Your people were here for hours, dusting for fingerprints. They wouldn't let me straighten a thing until they'd finished. The deputy said they managed to lift a number of solid prints." Her eyes pleaded with him to explain this nightmare. Troy wished he could; he wanted to prove to Faith that he was her hero…and that she could trust him.

"You're right. The crime-scene technician was able to lift a number of fingerprints."

"But they were all mine?"

"No," he said. "Not all of them. But the clear ones weren't out of the ordinary. That's why we took the elimination prints." He shrugged. "We suspect the intruder wore rubber gloves."

She looked confused. "A professional, then."

"At this point, we can't say. My guess is this isn't the first home this person has broken into."

Her shoulders sagged. "I'd hoped—I was sure with so many prints…there'd be at least one that would identify whoever did this."

"We checked each and every fingerprint and they were all ones we could identify."

"Oh." She didn't disguise her disappointment.

"Have you made a list of what's missing for Detective Hildebrand?"

Faith nodded. "It doesn't make any sense."

"In what way?"

"The items taken. They're mostly things of sentimental value. Like you said earlier, this break-in seemed… personal."

"Give me an example."

She unfolded her hands and gestured helplessly. "They took a picture album I made when the grandchildren were born. You saw what they did to Carl's photograph. I had—oh, it's too silly to mention."

"No, it isn't."

Her lower lip trembled before she regained her composure. "A toy train… It was from Carl's boyhood. I had it sitting on the bedroom dresser. Scottie's son likes to play with it when they visit and—"

"That was stolen?"

Faith nodded again. "I never thought of it as a valuable antique, but perhaps it is."

"What about jewelry, cash?"

"I don't keep anything of real value lying around."

"That's smart." Thinking over what she'd told him, Troy peeled away the paper from his muffin. It was still warm enough to burn his fingers, and he left it to cool a moment while he doctored his coffee.

"I can't believe this happened to me!" Faith cried, then inhaled a deep, calming breath. When she spoke again, her voice shook slightly. "I just don't understand it."

He sympathized with her and knew how she felt—

angry, violated, afraid. "I want to assure you the department's doing everything within our power to find whoever is responsible," he told her.

"Why me?" she asked, her eyes wide and imploring.

Troy longed to reach across the table to take her hand. "I wish I could answer that, but as you said, none of this makes sense. I'd like to think it was a random act of violence, but that doesn't appear to be the case. Regardless of who did this and why, you were an easy target. From this point forward you won't be again."

"No, I won't." Faith straightened, tensing her shoulders as if to say she'd dare anyone to try breaking into her home again. Troy had encountered that determination of hers more than once and almost felt sorry for anyone who earned her wrath.

"Is there anything else you can tell me?" Troy asked. "You never know where a small piece of information can lead, no matter how insignificant it seems." He remembered a case years ago, when he was still a deputy. A break-in had occurred, and Troy had stopped to talk to some kids at a bus stop, asking if they'd seen anything unusual. A kid, who couldn't have been more than eight or nine, mentioned a white Jeep. The man who drove it wore a Mariners' baseball cap and had long, blond hair. The boy had claimed the man looked "mean."

A couple of days later, Troy had passed a white Jeep parked at a gas station. When the driver came out, he had on a Mariners' baseball cap, covering long, stringy blond hair. Suspecting this might be the same person, Troy ran the license plate number—and discovered that the Jeep had been reported stolen. He followed the man and arrested him without incident. It later turned out that this man was responsible for a series of break-ins all around

Cedar Cove. The best part of the story was that the majority of valuables had been recovered.

At his question, Faith hesitated. "I'm not sure this means anything," she said.

"Let me be the judge of that."

"Okay." A vulnerable look came over her. "I have a feeling that the person who broke into the house has been back."

Without revealing any outward sign of alarm, Troy asked, "What makes you say that?"

Faith stood and walked over to the kitchen sink and pointed out the window. "There was graffiti on the back of the garage."

"Show me," he said abruptly.

"I painted over it the next day…. The words were ugly and I didn't want my grandchildren to see them…. Or anyone else for that matter."

"Show me, anyway."

Faith grabbed a coat from the peg by the back door and led him outside. He shivered in the January cold as he followed Faith to the far side of the garage. He could see the fresh layer of white paint. "Although it might be embarrassing, tell me exactly what the message said."

Faith stared down at her feet and told him. She was right; they were ugly words. He wished she'd told him about this earlier, since it might have yielded evidence. Now, however, it was too late.

Troy frowned. "You think whoever was responsible for the break-in came back and did this?" It was definitely a reasonable assumption.

Faith nodded. "The other night…I woke up and heard noises. At first I was too terrified to move. I was afraid they were inside the house. It took me a few minutes to realize the sound came from the garage." She was obviously making an effort to control her voice, but despite that it started to tremble.

"You should've called 9-1-1," he said urgently.

"I know… I wish I had. Oh, Troy, I've been so scared."

Troy couldn't bear to see Faith upset. Instinctively he slipped his arms around her—and she willingly moved into his embrace. He felt her shudder and his hold tightened. He wanted to reassure her that he'd do whatever he could to prevent anything like this from happening again.

"You should've called 9-1-1," he repeated.

"But what if it was nothing? I thought my imagination might be running away with me."

"Then you saw the graffiti…."

"The next morning," she confirmed, "and I realized I'd been foolish not to call the authorities right away."

"You should have," he said. There was no telling what might've happened while she hemmed and hawed, afraid to risk a little embarrassment.

"Faith, listen to me." He cupped his hands around her face and raised her head so that their eyes met. "I would rather you had peace of mind. I don't want you lying awake at night, worrying that someone's on the property."

Tears welled in her eyes. "I'm not sleeping nights… I haven't slept more than two or three hours at a time since the break-in."

"Faith…"

"I know I was ridiculous. I won't ignore any noises again."

"Has this happened more than once?"

"No." She shook her head. "I don't know…I don't think so. I sleep so lightly now. I'm afraid someone will break in…. My emotions are all askew—just look at me.

I'm not a weak woman! I hate being vulnerable. I'm on the verge of tears, and all because I haven't been able to sleep. I'm afraid it's going to affect my ability to do my job. The worst thing—" she paused "—is the fear. Night comes and I'm terrified all over again."

Troy pressed his hand against her head, weaving his fingers into her thick dark hair. He was almost overwhelmed by the temptation to bury his face in the clean freshness of it. He'd missed her more than he'd dared admit, even to himself.

He wished he knew how to reassure her. But no matter how strong that desire, he refused to whisper platitudes, nor would he mislead her by making promises he couldn't keep.

Faith must have recognized that she'd said more than she'd intended. She eased out of his embrace and glanced self-consciously at the street. She folded her arms around her waist, as if she suddenly felt cold.

"Let's talk about this inside," Troy suggested, placing his arm around her again as they headed back to the house.

Once inside, Faith removed her coat and hung it by the door, first straightening the shoes and boots that stood there. Then she refreshed their coffees. Troy could tell that this busywork was an attempt to regain her composure.

For his part, he would've been content to spend the next ten years holding Faith, even if it meant standing in full view of the street on a bitter January day. With the woman he loved in his arms, physical comfort didn't matter. He'd hardly noticed the damp or cold—until she'd stepped out of his arms.

"Would you like another bran muffin?" Faith asked.

Before he could answer, she added, "I believe I got this recipe from my mother. If you like, I could pass it along to your daughter. I saw Megan the other day. Did she mention that?"

"Faith." Troy took off his damp coat and hung it over the back of a chair.

"She's a lovely girl, Troy."

"Faith," he said a bit more loudly this time.

She clutched the kitchen counter with both hands.

"I know how distressed you must be."

She spit out a laugh as though his statement had been an exaggeration. "I'm fine, really. Tired, but… Okay, I'll confess this break-in has me unnerved. But wouldn't anyone feel that way?"

"Of course they would. Now, promise me you won't hesitate to call 9-1-1 if you suspect someone's on the property."

"I…"

"Faith," he coaxed.

"I will," she finally said, "if I really think there's someone here."

Troy figured this half promise was about all he could wheedle out of her.

They stood just looking at each other for a moment, neither of them inclined to speak.

"Would you like me to stop by one evening?" he asked, hoping she'd agree to that, too. Maybe she'd let him come over occasionally and then, given time, he'd have the opportunity to regain her trust.

She considered his question, then slowly shook her head. "I appreciate your willingness to look in on me, but…but I don't think that's a good idea."

Personally Troy thought it was brilliant.

"Would it be all right if I phoned and checked on you in the morning?" Maybe he was pressing his luck, but he had to try.

"I suppose...but only this once."

"Only this once," he echoed. "I won't call again after tomorrow." The crack in her resolve to keep him out of her life was barely discernible but it was there.

Reaching for his coat and hat, Troy saw that he'd left a small portion of his bran muffin on the plate. He popped it in his mouth and gave Faith a lopsided grin. He swallowed, wishing he'd accepted a second one when she'd offered it. "I'll ask Megan to get the recipe from you," he said on his way to the door.

"I'll be happy to share it."

Troy lingered at the front door, but there was nothing else to say. Leaving Faith never seemed to get any easier.

Six

Will Jefferson knew he needed to play his cards carefully if he hoped to have a relationship with Shirley Bliss. Now that his divorce from Georgia was final, he was a free man. Of course, a wedding ring hadn't been much of a detriment in the past. He'd had a number of affairs, which wasn't something he took pride in. It was just…a fact. Georgia had repeatedly forgiven him, and he always *meant* to be faithful. His intentions were good—the best—but then he'd meet someone and the attraction would be there and, well, when it came to beautiful women, he was weak. That was all he could say about it. He didn't even attempt to defend himself, although, to be fair, it did take two to tango—and to do certain other things….

He experienced more than a twinge of guilt about cheating on his wife. Ex-wife. They should never have gotten married. The marriage hadn't worked for either of them. They were mismatched, and as time went on, there'd been less and less to hold them together. He hoped Georgia didn't resent him. But he'd begun a new life here in Cedar Cove, returning to his hometown, where he'd spent some of his happiest years. He wanted to become that person again, wanted to redeem himself, in his own eyes and those of his family and friends. Maybe Shirley Bliss would help him....

He'd met Shirley, a widow, when he'd purchased the art gallery. He'd felt an immediate attraction, but it was more than that. She was a widow, and therefore available, so perhaps that meant he'd moved beyond his compulsion to seduce women already involved with other men. Whatever the reason for his urge to stray—boredom, the thrill of conquest, the need to prove his own masculinity—he wanted to overcome it. Besides, he was genuinely interested in Shirley and impressed by her talent.

Will wandered over to his desk. The Harbor Street Art Gallery was doing well, better than he'd expected. That was due, in no small way, to Shirley. She'd given him some excellent suggestions, many of which he'd used. The idea for the new display cases had come from her. They'd cost more than he'd budgeted for, but they were worth it.

In appreciation for all her help, he'd made Shirley, who worked with fabrics, the featured artist for January and would be pleased to inform her that over the weekend he'd sold the largest piece she had on display. He had a check for her, and he thought she'd be as excited about this sale as he was.

When he picked up the phone, he did so with a sense of anticipation. Aside from his pleasure in her success and consequently his own, he felt challenged by her. And not merely as a potential lover. This was the perfect opportunity to get to know her better. She hadn't revealed any interest in him, however, which was puzzling. Not to brag, but he knew he looked good; at sixty he'd gained a stateliness that suited him. He was intelligent and had a natural charm, as so many other women—including Georgia—had told him. The possibility existed that Shirley was still in love with her dead husband. From what Will understood, it'd been a year or so since the accident that had claimed his life.

Will knew his own strengths and his weaknesses. He hadn't gotten this far without identifying his assets and using them. He didn't mind admitting that he was a man who generally got what he wanted; he'd also admit that this trait hadn't always been to his benefit. Georgia had called him a "serial philanderer," claiming he only wanted women he couldn't have—and when he got them he lost interest. He didn't deny it but he believed that Shirley would change all that.

He dialed her number and waited for her to answer. After four rings the answering machine came on. Then, just as he was about to leave a message, he heard someone pick up.

"Hello." Shirley sounded a little breathless.

"Hello," Will returned, smiling, glad they'd been able to connect.

"Who is this?" she demanded, irritation in her voice.

"It's Will. Will Jefferson from the Harbor Street Art Gallery," he told her. That she hadn't recognized his voice stung his ego. He'd hoped, despite her previous reticence, that she'd been thinking about him, too. Apparently that wasn't the case.

Her hesitation was just long enough to be noticeable. "I apologize if I snapped at you."

Will was more than willing to forgive her. "I'm guessing I phoned at a bad time."

"I usually try to work while Tanni's in school."

Tanni was Shirley's teenage daughter. He'd met her twice. The girl was dating a young man with an unusual first name. Shank? Shiver. Shaw…that was it. Shaw.

The kid had talent. So did Tanni, although she was the one who'd brought Shaw's work to Will's attention. Shaw's portraits, especially, had a lot of promise. He'd shown the kid's work to an old friend of his, Larry Knight, who was a successful and influential artist, and who happened to be in Seattle recently. Larry had confirmed Will's assessment. The way Will figured it, Shirley would be grateful for his help. And Will most definitely wanted to obtain Shirley's gratitude.

"I understand," he said smoothly. "I'll remember to call either early in the morning or closer to dinnertime."

"I'd appreciate that."

"Your exhibit's done well," he told her.

Silence.

Since she didn't seem inclined to continue the conversation, Will charged ahead. "I wanted to know if it would be convenient for me to stop by later this evening."

She hesitated again. "Is there a reason?'

The question put him slightly on edge; he'd expected a warmer welcome. He was disappointed that he needed an excuse, but then he'd already made more than one incorrect assumption with Shirley. "Yes, a very good reason," he said. "I have a check for you. The wildflower panel sold this weekend." The piece, a fabric collage, was a stunning work. Everyone who'd viewed it, including Will, had been enchanted.

Shirley squealed with delight. "It sold! It really sold?"

"Yes." Will had never heard her sound so uninhibited. "And the woman who bought it is interested in a couple of your other pieces, too."

"That's wonderful!"

"I thought you'd be pleased," he said. "I could drop off the check if you like." He didn't want her to think he was pressuring her.

"Ah...unfortunately I have plans this evening."

"I could visit tomorrow if that would be more convenient." He was trying not to come across as pushy; at the same time, he was curious to know what her plans might be.

"Well..." she said cautiously. "Maybe it would be best just to drop it in the mail."

Will's head was spinning. She didn't want to see him, or not at her house, anyway. That was a disappointment. "I have a better idea. Why don't you come to the gallery and pick it up?"

She leaped on the suggestion. "Sure...that would be great."

"When would be a good time?" he asked, implying that he was busy, too, and they should schedule this meeting.

"I suppose I could make it into town later this afternoon," she said.

They agreed on four-thirty and Will set the phone back in its cradle, smiling. He'd gone out of his way for her daughter's boyfriend at Shirley's request—or with her approval, at any rate. Shaw had talent, but talent was cheap. He was giving the teenager a leg up, and he wanted to make sure Shirley valued his effort and the fact that he'd called in a favor from a friend.

Now that their meeting was set, Will closed the gallery a half hour early, then took the time to comb his hair and change his shirt. Before returning to the main part of the gallery, he glanced at his reflection in the mirror.

Normally he would've been confident he looked good, but Shirley's reluctance made him feel somewhat insecure—not a familiar sensation.

While he waited for Shirley, he checked his watch every couple of minutes. He exhaled a sigh of relief when he saw her park in front of the gallery. She climbed out and started toward the entrance, paused, then turned back to her vehicle.

Will wasn't about to let her walk off. He hurried over to the front door and threw it open.

"Shirley," he called. "Come in."

She turned around. "The sign says the gallery's closed."

He laughed lightly. "It is for everyone but you."

"Oh…"

He opened the door wider and gestured her inside.

"Do you have the check?" she asked the moment she crossed the threshold. Then, as if she understood how rude she'd been, she added, "I, uh, know how busy you are and I don't want to detain you."

"It's in the office." When she didn't move, he repeated, "Come in."

After a short pause, she came all the way into the gallery.

Will closed the door and walked toward his small office, with her following. He handed her a white envelope, which held her check. "You know, I never heard if you received the wine-and-cheese basket I left on your doorstep during the holidays."

"Yes, I did…. I apologize. I should've written a thank-you note."

She did seem appropriately contrite. Will had paid a premium for that basket. This wasn't some run-of-the-mill wine-and-cheese ensemble, either. Everything had been imported from France.

"No problem. I just wanted to be sure you got it," he said nonchalantly.

"When did you bring it by?" she asked.

"Christmas Day," he said.

"Oh, I hope you weren't alone on Christmas Day."

He looked away. "I was, but it wasn't any big deal. I had a couple of invitations, but…I didn't feel well." He'd rather not admit he hadn't accepted those invitations—from Olivia and his niece, Justine—because he'd thought he could spend the day with Shirley. He'd made the mistake of assuming she'd be home and alone, the same way he'd been. He knew her kids would be there, but kids that age didn't enjoy hanging around with their mothers. As a result of his mistaken assumption, he'd ended up going to Olivia's for dinner and then watching *White Christmas* on TV in his apartment for what had to be the twentieth time.

"I apologize for not sending you that thank-you note," she told him again.

"It doesn't matter. I only wanted to make sure you found the gift." He brightened. "But…" he said in a teasing voice "…you could make it up to me." He'd keep it light, easy, relaxed.

"What do you mean?" she asked, frowning instantly. "How?"

"I know you're a widow."

She took a small step in retreat, as though the subject wasn't one she intended to discuss with him. That was fine; Will had no desire to draw her dead husband into the conversation. He just wanted to establish her availability—and his.

"As I mentioned earlier, I'm on my own, too. I thought we could get together one evening," he said, "or maybe we could meet one afternoon."

Shirley took another small step away from him. Now that she had her check, she seemed eager to leave.

"Nothing formal, you understand," Will clarified. "Lunch or coffee, that sort of thing."

She gave him a slight smile. "I'm not sure I'm ready to date."

"This wouldn't be a date," he said. "This would be a chat over coffee, a getting-to-know-you session, that's all. I'd love to hear more of your ideas for the gallery," he added, to remind her of the conversation they'd already had back in the fall. "I'm free now, if you are. I hear the Pot Belly Deli has an excellent selection of coffees and teas."

"You mean now? As in right now?"

"If it's convenient. We can walk down the hill. It's not far." At least she hadn't immediately turned him down—that was encouraging.

"Perhaps another time," she said after a long moment.

"Sure, whenever." He shrugged off her rejection.

"I'll call you," she said next, as if to suggest she'd prefer it if *he* didn't call *her.*

Okay, on to plan B. "I had some news regarding Shaw," he told her, hoping to give her extra incentive to accept his invitation.

"Really."

Her interest was piqued, he could see. That was good. He hated to resort to manipulation but she wasn't leaving him a lot of options. In the past, he'd rarely had to be so blatant.

"I had another talk with the friend who looked at Shaw's work." Will didn't offer any more information than that. Nor was he disposed to do so. If she wanted an update, she'd have to meet him for coffee.

With the check in her hand, she waited for an awkward

minute or two, and when the information regarding Shaw wasn't forthcoming, she made her excuses.

"I'll see you to the door," Will said, walking beside her.

"You don't need to do that."

He was tempted to extend the conversation, delay her parting. He could bring up any number of topics she'd find relevant or interesting. However, he said nothing.

"Thank you again," she murmured as she stepped into the darkening afternoon.

"You're welcome." Will closed the door and locked it behind her, knowing she'd hear the turn of the lock. That was intentional. He didn't want her to think he was begging or that he was desperate for her company. And yet, it was increasingly how he felt. She intrigued and attracted him and he felt intuitively that they could be good for each other. And, he had to acknowledge with a hint of shame, he wasn't immune to the thrill of the chase.

Briefly he wondered if something was holding Shirley back—some gossip she'd heard about him. He frowned. He didn't think Grace Harding had mentioned their Internet relationship. His sister wouldn't have, either. No, that couldn't be it.

What had happened with Grace was regrettable. Little did Will know then that within a few years he'd be returning to live in Cedar Cove. That whole situation, which had begun as a mild flirtation via the Internet, had become extremely unpleasant, and he was happy to put it behind him. He'd been genuinely fond of Grace, still was. Her husband was a nice guy—and not someone he wanted to cross. He was glad her marriage had worked out. Besides, he didn't believe in fouling his own nest, so to speak.

Will turned off the gallery showroom lights and went

upstairs to his small apartment. He'd made the transition from his previous apartment to the space above the gallery because he'd found someone to sublet the place he'd first rented. Mack, the son of P.I. Roy McAfee down the street, had recently joined the Cedar Cove fire department, so the timing was perfect.

His residence in the gallery still needed plenty of work, but it was adequate for now. Sighing, he decided to relax with a glass of wine. He had no idea how long he'd been sitting in front of the television when the phone rang, jolting him out of his stupor.

Caller ID informed him it was Shirley Bliss.

With a knowing smile, he muted the volume on the TV and reached for the receiver. "Hello, Shirley."

"Mr. Jefferson."

"Please call me Will."

"All right, Will… Is that invitation for coffee still open?"

"Sure." He tried not to reveal how pleased he was to hear from her.

"Great." She sounded anxious to see him now.

"When would you like to meet?" He set his wineglass on the side table and leaned back in his recliner.

"Could we make it this evening, like you suggested?"

"Perfect," he said. "It's a bit late now. Can I convince you to dine with me?"

"No." Her response was clipped. "Not tonight…. As I said, I have a previous engagement."

"Oh, yes, I'd forgotten that. Coffee it is, then."

"Could we meet at Mocha Mama's?"

"Of course." He didn't particularly care where they went. He hoped to put her at ease, and if everything went as he wished, this "previous engagement" would disappear as the evening progressed.

"Shall we say in fifteen minutes?" Shirley asked.

"I can manage that." Will lowered his feet from the ottoman.

"Would it be okay if I brought my daughter along?"

That definitely wasn't part of his game plan. "Why… sure."

"Shaw's at work. When I mentioned to Tanni that you had some information for Shaw, she called him and he'd like to join us, too."

"But if he's working…"

"He is," Shirley elaborated. "At Mocha Mama's. We'll see you in fifteen minutes," she said cheerfully.

"Okay," he responded. "I'll be there." But she'd already hung up.

Seven

Rachel Peyton lightly sprayed Grace Harding's hair and turned the stylist's chair around so she could see the full effect in the mirror. Grace held up the small hand mirror, then shook her head and watched as her hair swung forward.

She'd told Rachel she'd been looking for a new style, something short, sassy and easy to care for. "I like it," Grace said, smiling.

It was always a relief to have a customer confirm her own feelings. "This is shorter than I've ever seen you wear your hair." Initially she'd had her doubts that such a breezy style would suit Grace, the town's head librarian, but she'd been wrong.

"Seeing that Olivia has short hair now, it seems only fitting that I do, too. We've always been best friends." Grace laughed. "Actually, she's completely bald. I love her, but I'm not willing to go that far."

"Her hair will grow back," Rachel said, "but it might be a different color or texture." Olivia had come in earlier that week and had what remained of her hair shaved off. She'd started her regimen of chemotherapy, and after the second session her hair had fallen out in clumps. Rachel had cut it quite short before the chemo, so the change wasn't as great as it might have been.

"The way I see it," Grace continued, "Olivia and I can let our hair grow back together—unless I like this style so much I don't want to change."

Rachel unsnapped the cape and removed it.

"I heard you and Bruce Peyton got married," Grace said as she stood. "Right around Christmas, wasn't it?"

"Yes. We were crazy to have our wedding at that time of year but we didn't want to wait."

"What about a honeymoon?"

"We haven't been able to plan it yet. We'll take one later, probably around Valentine's Day." Which was when their wedding was originally scheduled to take place. "It's just that with Bruce's work schedule, Jolene's schedule and mine, it's hard to find a time that fits everyone."

Grace's smile was warm. "Cliff and I ran into that problem, too. In the end we simply eloped, although I wouldn't recommend it." She shook her head. "Unfortunately we upset a lot of people, but afterward we had a huge party and everything worked out."

"Apparently we've done the same thing," Rachel told her. The girls at the shop had felt hurt about being excluded. Everything had been so rushed. In retrospect, perhaps they should've waited until February, after all. But circumstances had prohibited that, since Rachel had given up her rental house, which had a new tenant. Bruce had been eager to marry her, and she'd felt the same way. They'd gone ahead despite her reservations, but even now Rachel wondered if they'd made the right decision.

"These things tend to take care of themselves," Grace said. "Cliff and I are happy and I can see you are, too, if the new-bride glow is anything to go by."

"We are."

"That's wonderful." Grace reached for her purse and paid for her haircut at the front counter. She also made another appointment for early March, about six weeks away.

With a small broom, Rachel swept up the brown curls that circled the styling chair. It wasn't an exaggeration to say she was happy. She was, gleefully so, but she also felt sexually frustrated. Bruce did, too, and it was fast putting a strain on their relationship.

What Rachel hadn't expected, or Bruce, either, was Jolene's reaction to their marriage. Jolene, at thirteen, felt threatened by the upheaval in her life.

Bruce's daughter had been Rachel's special friend for years. They'd started meeting after Stephanie Peyton's tragic death in a car accident. Jolene had only been five at the time. She'd badly needed a woman in her life and had latched on to Rachel when she'd given the little girl a haircut.

Rachel's own mother had died when she was young and she'd been raised by an unmarried aunt. Because she understood what it was like to be a motherless child, Rachel had voluntarily stepped in. The two of them had quickly bonded.

Jolene had often played the role of matchmaker between Rachel and Bruce. But obviously she'd never realized what would happen once Bruce and Rachel fell in love....

Rachel's marriage to Jolene's father had changed the dynamic within the family. Jolene was too immature and vulnerable to accept that. She feared being excluded or losing her place in Bruce's life. The girl had been demanding and unreasonable ever since the wedding.

Rachel and Bruce rarely had a moment alone. Making love had become a challenge. Jolene had always been a light sleeper and the slightest noise woke her. Her timing was impeccable; three times in the past week alone, Jolene had inadvertently interrupted their prologue to lovemaking. Or *was* it inadvertent? At any rate when she went back to bed, Bruce was either asleep or so irritated that the opportunity had been ruined.

"Your next appointment just called and canceled," Joan, who handled the reception desk, told her.

"Wasn't that the color job?"

Joan checked the schedule. "Yup."

That was two free hours. Two whole unexpected hours. Rachel's heart raced as she glanced at her watch. "I don't have any other appointments this afternoon, right?"

Joan checked again. "Not that I can see."

An idea was taking shape. "Terrific. Thanks." She grabbed her purse, pulled out her cell phone and punched speed dial to connect with Bruce.

He answered on the second ring. "Bruce speaking."

"What are you doing?" she asked excitedly.

"Working, what do you think?" Bruce ran a small independent computer-support business, with a couple of employees.

"Can you meet me at the house?"

"I suppose… Any special reason you want me home?"

Rachel giggled, and no doubt sounded like a schoolgirl. "Oh, yes, there's a *very* special reason. My last appointment canceled and Jolene's got basketball tryouts after school."

Bruce caught on right away. "You mean we would be *alone?*"

"That's what I figured." She giggled again.

"Give me ten minutes."

"You got it." Rachel closed the phone and held it against her heart, grinning wildly. She saw Joan watching her, eyebrows raised.

"I take it you don't want me to schedule anything for the rest of the day?"

"Please." Rachel hurried into the back room where she threw on her coat. She was a woman with a mission.

She got home first and tore into the bedroom, where she closed the drapes, then pulled off her clothes and hopped into the shower. Her best friend, Teri Polgar, had bought her a sheer negligee as a wedding gift, which Rachel had yet to wear. She was finally going to initiate it.

The front door opened and Bruce dashed inside. "Rachel?"

"In here," she called back, hoping she sounded sultry and sexy. She climbed onto the bed and lay on her side, facing him, the provocative black negligee revealing far more than it concealed. Her chin was propped on one hand.

Bruce came into the room and stopped dead in his tracks.

"Looking for someone?" Rachel purred.

He swallowed visibly. It was a moment before he was able to move or speak. "I need a shower," he croaked.

Rachel rolled onto her back. "Hurry."

"Oh, I'll try." He started throwing off his clothes as he trotted toward the bathroom. His shirt fell onto the carpet next to the bed. It was a testament to the quality of the garment that the buttons hadn't been ripped off in his haste. His shoes were next; one was kicked under the bed and the other bounced against the wall and into the bathroom.

"We have all afternoon, you realize," she said. "Shall I pour us a glass of champagne?"

The shower door opened. "Champagne?"

"Another gift from Teri and Bobby."

"Sure..." His gaze was riveted on her. "You are so beautiful."

"That's how you make me feel," she whispered.

While Bruce showered, Rachel went into the kitchen. Although it was an odd contrast with the negligee, she wore her old terry-cloth robe, not wanting to risk being seen through the windows. She opened the refrigerator and sorted through the milk and yogurt and eggs to the farthest reaches of the bottom shelf, where she'd stored the champagne. Moët et Chandon, something she'd never expected to taste.

By the time she heard Bruce, the flutes were out and ready. She'd lit several scented candles, too. The mood was set except for the music. She found an appropriate CD and put it on.

A minute or two later, Bruce met her in the kitchen. He was barefoot and naked with a towel around his waist. His dark hair fell in wet tendrils, dripping moisture onto his neck and shoulders. As far as Rachel was concerned, he'd never looked sexier.

Rachel turned to greet him with a shy smile. She held the champagne bottle in her hand and removed the wire top. "Someone once told me that the correct way to open champagne is to twist the bottle and not the cork. When properly opened, it should sound like a contented woman."

Bruce pretended to leer. "I'm more than eager to hear the sound of a contented woman."

"The champagne or me?" she asked.

He grinned. "Both."

Rachel attempted to follow the opening directions for champagne, and the cork popped much more loudly than she'd expected.

"You can be as noisy as you want, too," her husband joked, taking the bottle out of her hands. He filled both flutes and gave her one. Clutching his own, he leaned forward and pressed his mouth to hers. Their lips clung as the kiss deepened. Although only their mouths touched, an overwhelming physical response rippled through her.

Bruce groaned and put down his champagne. "Maybe we could drink this later?" he asked, hardly sounding like himself.

"What do you have in mind?" she asked as he took the flute from her and set it on the kitchen counter.

"Don't you think it's a bit warm in here?"

"Hmm. I know what you mean."

"You have too many clothes on."

Rachel smiled. "You could be right." She glanced out the kitchen window, saw no one, then peeled off her robe.

Bruce led her down the narrow hallway to the master bedroom, then lifted her into his arms.

"Bruce, I'm too heavy," she protested but not too strenuously.

"Well…it's not far from here to the bed." He shoved the door with his foot, closing it partway.

Looping her arms around his neck, Rachel nibbled at his earlobe and felt his body shiver with excitement. She was excited, too. The freedom to make love without fear of waking or disturbing Jolene was heaven.

Bruce reverently placed her on the bed, his eyes glowing with love and wonder. "These past few weeks…"

"I know, I know." Reaching for her husband, she urged him down so that he was sprawled across her. They kissed until Rachel was breathless with desire. "Oh, Bruce," she sighed. "I want you so much."

No sooner had the words left her lips than the front door opened and closed.

Bruce froze.

Rachel did, too.

"What's Jolene doing home?" Bruce whispered fiercely. "She's supposed to be at basketball tryouts!"

"Rachel?" Jolene called out. "Are you home? Dad?"

"I'll be out in a minute," Rachel called back as Bruce scrambled off her. He'd just managed to grab the towel and cover himself when his daughter appeared in the doorway.

A look of sheer horror came over her. She scrunched up her face and cried, "Gross!"

"Jolene." Rachel hurriedly hid her negligee with a pillow. "What are you doing here?"

"I live here, remember?" She knotted both hands into fists at her sides.

Rachel could feel her cheeks burning with embarrassment.

"If you'd kindly give us a few minutes of privacy," Bruce said from between clenched teeth. Keeping his hand clamped on the towel around his waist, he walked to the bedroom door and closed it completely.

"I knew this would happen," Jolene cried from the other side. "It's like I don't even live here anymore. All you think about is…*that.*"

Apparently *that* was a synonym for sex.

The girl marched down the hallway to her room and slammed the door. The sound reverberated through the house.

"Jolene, that's not true." The kid had no idea of the restraint she and Bruce had employed since they'd been married.

"Leave her be," Bruce said with a disgusted sigh. "This is getting ridiculous."

"I know." Rachel was disappointed, too. She stepped up behind him and slipped her arms around his waist. "She needs time to adjust."

"She's had time."

"It's been less than a month."

"I thought she *wanted* us to marry," Bruce argued.

"She did. Only she's afraid of what it's going to do to her relationship with you."

"Nothing's changed," Bruce muttered. He broke away long enough to jerk on his pants.

"But, Bruce, it has. Don't you see?"

"Frankly, no." Every movement conveyed his frustration and anger. "We're married, and I want to make love to my wife. It isn't right for us to be sneaking around because we're afraid Jolene might know what we're doing. She *should* know. That's what married couples do."

"Listen, Bruce, I'm as frustrated as you are, but we need to be sensitive to Jolene's feelings. We should never have rushed into this."

Bruce whirled around, his face contorted. "So now you regret marrying me?"

"No!" she insisted. "I love you and Jolene more than I could ever express. What I wish is that we'd given Jolene time to get used to the fact that I was going to be moving into the house." Rachel didn't want her husband to think for even an instant that she didn't want to be married. "For seven years it was just the two of you and I was conveniently tucked away for whenever Jolene wanted to visit or chat. Now I'm here 24/7, and she feels threatened."

Bruce sat on the edge of the bed and rubbed his face. "This is torture."

Rachel sat next to him and leaned her shoulder against his. "It is for me, too. But remember, there's always tonight."

"What I want," Bruce said, "is to be able to make love and not worry about the bed creaking."

It wasn't funny but Rachel couldn't help laughing. "We'll find a way."

"I just hope it's soon." Bruce left the bedroom, and a few minutes later Rachel heard the front door close. He must have gone back to the shop.

Wondering how best to approach her stepdaughter, Rachel changed out of the negligee and into her clothes. She gently tapped on Jolene's bedroom door.

"Jolene?"

No response.

"Let's talk about this."

"Go away."

"I thought you had basketball tryouts after school," she said.

"That's on Monday."

"The notice said it was today."

"Well, it isn't. Tryouts got canceled because the coach is sick."

"Oh."

"Go away."

"Not until we talk."

"I don't want to talk."

Rachel stood by her stepdaughter's bedroom door for a long time and tried to cajole Jolene into coming out so they could discuss this.

After a while Jolene stopped answering her.

Rachel turned the handle, figuring that if Jolene wouldn't come to her, she'd go to Jolene.

Only the bedroom door was locked.

Eight

Troy was still in the parking lot outside city hall when Mayor Benson came charging toward him. He'd just returned from a speaking engagement at the local Rotary, but other than that, it hadn't been a good day. Two of his deputies had phoned in sick. The flu bug had hit his department hard, and he was stretched to the limit. His conversation with the Seattle reporter, Kathleen Sadler, hadn't improved his mood, either. The woman was demanding responses to questions he simply couldn't answer. Judging by the angry look on the mayor's face, Troy's day was about to get even worse.

"What can I do for you, Louie?" Troy said.

"I just got off the phone with Kathleen Sadler."

Troy wanted to close his eyes and groan. When he hadn't supplied the information she was after, the reporter had obviously called Louie. No wonder the mayor was in such a state.

"Kathleen Sadler," Mayor Benson repeated. "I thought you were going to take care of it. I already told you how important it is that we keep this story out of the public eye."

"I did speak to her," Troy said. "She refused to accept

what I told her. She kept saying there has to be more to the story."

"That's exactly what I was afraid of." Louie clenched and unclenched his fists.

"If you wanted to avoid her, you should've forwarded the call to me." Troy didn't understand why Louie felt obligated to talk to the woman, especially since she seemed to be making a pest of herself. If there *was* a story behind those remains, the facts would come out eventually. But at this point, there was nothing either of them could tell her.

"I did suggest she contact you," Louie said, "only it turns out you were at the Rotary meeting and, fool that I am, I took the call."

In Troy's opinion, that was the mayor's problem. "I'll talk to her again, if you want."

"I do. Apparently she's coming to Cedar Cove on Wednesday and wants to interview the teenagers who discovered the body."

"That is *not* going to happen." Troy would do everything within his power to make sure of it. Philip Wilson, better known as Shaw, was of legal age but his name hadn't been released to the press. Tanni Bliss, the other teenager, was still in high school. He'd contact their parents and give them a heads-up about this reporter. Both kids had been pretty shaken, as Troy recalled—Tanni more so than Philip.

"Good," Louie said and gave a satisfied nod of his head. "You deal with this."

"I will."

"Do it fast. I gather she's bringing a photographer to take a picture of the cave. She's writing a feature story on this, and with our tourism initiatives, the timing couldn't be worse. You've got to convince her there's nothing to report."

Troy shrugged. "Why do you suppose she's so interested?"

"How would I know?" Louie flared. "Like I said earlier, this is bad timing. Jack's doing a feature on tourism for the *Chronicle* that we hope will get picked up across the state, and this woman's article is bound to overshadow his. Cedar Cove could do without the negative press." He shook his head. "That's not the half of it, either. The council just put together a request for state funds to enhance tourism in our area." He looked up at the heavens. "Why is all of this happening *now?*"

Troy didn't have an answer for him. "I'll do my best to make it go away."

Louie seemed slightly mollified. "I'd appreciate that." He handed Troy a slip of paper. "In case you need it, here's that reporter's phone number. You try and reason with her."

Troy sighed. The thing he'd noticed about reporters was that the more fuss he made, the keener their interest. Any bit of information he fed them was never enough; they demanded more. Then they'd dig around until they found what they wanted—or a reasonable facsimile thereof. Over the years, Troy had learned that the best policy was to say nothing, or at least nothing of substance. He was polite and cordial, but his lips were sealed.

After the mayor left, Troy hurried to his office. He'd just sat down at his desk when his cell phone chirped. He rarely received personal calls. A quick check told him it was his daughter.

"Hello, sweetheart," he said.

"Hi, Daddy. I wanted to tell you I saw Faith."

Hearing Faith's name produced an instant flash of anticipation, immediately crowded out by regret.

"She gave me something for you."

Troy sat up straighter. "She did?" He hated the hopefulness that elevated his voice.

"It's a recipe for bran muffins."

"Oh." His hopes quickly deflated.

"You didn't tell me you'd been over to her house."

"It was a routine call. I stopped by to follow up after the break-in."

"I think it's terrible that someone would do that to Faith."

Troy agreed.

"Have you seen much of her lately?" his daughter inquired. She sounded as if she'd been taking classes from a trained investigator.

"Just that once since the break-in."

"I see," Megan said. "Faith looked good, didn't she?"

In Troy's opinion, Faith always looked good. "Yes, she did," he murmured.

"She said you really enjoyed the muffins and suggested I bake them for you."

As he recalled, he hadn't had anything to eat that particular morning and had skipped lunch. The fact was, he would've eaten sawdust if Faith had served it.

"I thought I'd bake these for you and bring them over this evening."

"Wonderful, thank you." A reminder of Faith was the last thing he needed.

"Can I drop them off after dinner? I mean, you'll be home, won't you?"

"Where else would I be?"

This was obviously an exploratory question to see if he'd be with Faith.

"Craig wanted to run a couple of errands tonight and I figured I'd go with him, then we'll stop at your place. Should I call first?"

"No need. I'll be home."

"Okay." She seemed disappointed. "I'll see you around seven. We won't stay long."

"You're welcome anytime, Megan, you know that."

"I know," she said.

They chatted for a few more minutes before Troy closed his cell and slipped it back inside its case. His daughter sounded better than she had since Sandy's death. Troy was well aware that she missed her mother, but Megan had come to terms with her grief, the same way he had.

Before he went home, Troy left a message for Kathleen Sadler at the Seattle paper. For the second time, he asked that she direct all future calls to him. She probably felt Louie Benson was an easier target, but Troy planned to put a stop to that. He'd prefer the mayor not question him in the parking lot again.

On his drive home, Troy decided to swing past Rosewood Lane. He didn't expect to see Faith, although he hoped he would. It'd been more than a week since they'd talked.

As it happened, he saw her struggling with a heavy bag of groceries, dragging them from the backseat of her car. She glanced up just as he drove slowly past. Since she'd already seen his vehicle, Troy pulled over to the curb and parked.

"Let me help you with that," he said, moving toward her.

"I'm fine." But even as she said it, she surrendered the two heavy bags.

Troy trailed her up the back steps and into the kitchen, where he set the groceries on the counter.

Faith stood against the stove, hands braced behind her. "Thank you."

"You're welcome." How polite and stilted they sounded, like strangers brushing past each other on the street.

"I don't want you to think I make a habit of driving by your home, Faith," he explained. "I've asked Deputy Walker to make a couple of detours this way during the course of his shift."

"Thank you," she said again. She lowered her gaze as if she found something on the floor of infinite interest.

"How are you sleeping?" he asked, reluctant to leave.

She didn't answer right away. "Better," she finally said.

"Any more unexplained noises?"

She didn't respond.

"Faith, if there's a problem I want to hear about it. You aren't the kind of woman who imagines things."

She shrugged. "It was probably nothing."

"So you *have* heard something?"

"Last night…"

When she didn't finish, Troy prompted her. "What about last night?"

"I…I thought I heard someone in the side yard. I got up and turned on the porch light and—"

"Don't tell me you decided to investigate on your own!"

"Oh, honestly, Troy, I'm not stupid. I didn't wait for a storm, light a candle and then go walking on the cliff's edge like some gothic heroine, if that's what you're suggesting. I did phone 9-1-1, but while I waited for a patrol car I turned on the house lights and made a bunch of noise, as if I was ten people instead of just me."

A smile tilted his lips. "Exactly how did you do that?"

"Well," she said, grinning, too. "I banged a few pots, put the television on and started talking loudly to my imaginary son, who happens to be a professional wrestler."

Troy laughed out loud.

"When the officer arrived, whoever was outside—if there *was* anyone outside—had long since left."

Troy supposed that was why he hadn't heard about this. He didn't want to downplay its seriousness, nor did he want to alarm her. "Next time let the officer do his job and don't distract the intruder. We want to catch whoever's doing this, Faith."

It took her a long time to respond. "Yes… It's just that…well, it's hard to wait around and do nothing. I don't want this…this intruder to get the idea that I'm a willing victim."

"If you want to do something while you're waiting for a police response, phone me." Although he made the suggestion sound offhanded, he meant it. He needed to know she was safe.

Faith shook her head. "I won't do that."

"It's an option, Faith. I'll come, no questions asked."

She sighed. "I know you would." She glanced toward the back door as if to signal that it was time to go.

He knew he should take the hint, but Troy couldn't make himself do it. "I got a call from Megan this afternoon," he said.

"Oh, yes, I expected she'd contact you." The phone rang and she immediately reached for it, no doubt relieved by the interruption. "Hello," she said. "Hello?"

Troy remembered when he used to call Faith and how his heart would race each time she answered. She'd always sounded so pleased to hear from him….

After a moment, Faith hung up. "A wrong number, I guess."

"Have you gotten many of those lately?" he asked, his suspicions rising.

She exhaled slowly. "Now that you mention it, I seem to be getting more than usual."

Troy frowned. "What did call display tell you?"

"It said 'private caller.' That's what it said before, too."

"Hmm…"

"I have an unlisted number," she was quick to inform him.

"That isn't much help, Faith."

"Why not?"

"Anyone who really wants your information can get it. Having it unlisted doesn't make the number inaccessible."

"Oh, dear."

"People who have a bit of computer savvy can find whatever they want." Having said that, Troy walked over to the phone and punched in the callback code. Nothing. "You don't have automatic callback?"

"No," she admitted. "I didn't think it was necessary when I got my phone service."

"Order it, and the next time someone calls and hangs up, get the phone number."

She wrinkled her forehead. "You think it would be a good idea for me to return the call?"

"No! Give the phone number to me and I'll take care of it." When he saw the worry in her eyes, Troy wondered if he'd frightened her. "Will you do that?"

The stubborn look was back.

"If not for your own peace of mind, then for mine."

"All right, if you insist," she said with a resigned shrug.

"I do."

Once again she glanced at the door.

Troy started in that direction. "Have a good evening, Faith," he said, touching the brim of his hat in farewell.

"You, too."

She followed him to the front door and watched him walk away. Troy felt her eyes on his back and wondered if she had as many regrets as he did. He wondered if she missed him half as much as he missed her.

By the time he got back to his house on Pacific Boulevard, it was pitch-dark. Troy let himself in and, without thinking, picked up the television remote control. He didn't actually watch many programs. Mostly he appreciated the noise.

The local Seattle news flashed across the screen as Troy hung up his coat. He was about to close the closet door when he saw a reporter with a microphone in a setting that was far too familiar.

Troy stared. It was the area outside the cave where the skeletal remains had been discovered.

"This is Jean Everson with a story that's more suited to Halloween than January," the young woman said, her voice low and intense. "I'm here in Cedar Cove to report that the unidentified remains of a young man have been found in this cave directly behind me. A youth. No one in Cedar Cove is talking. No one appears to know who this young man might be. The autopsy report indicates that he was sealed inside this cave for approximately thirty years. However, local law enforcement has apparently made no progress in resolving this tragic case."

All Troy could hope was that Louie Benson hadn't seen this news item. The woman's voice droned on in the distance, and she finally ended with something about "...this sleepy town, where dark secrets might be buried along with those unidentified remains. This is Channel 7 Eyewitness News. Jean Everson reporting from Cedar Cove, Washington."

After a day like the one he'd had, this wasn't what Troy wanted to see on his TV.

No more than a minute later his phone rang. He didn't need to check caller ID to figure out who it was. Louie Benson wanted to talk to him for the second time that day.

Nine

All week, Mack McAfee had been looking forward to seeing Mary Jo Wyse and her infant daughter. He'd delivered the baby on Christmas Eve at the Hardings' ranch. Appropriately enough, Mary Jo had named her Noelle.

It had been Mack's first delivery, the only time he'd ever witnessed, let alone participated in, a birth. Being with Mary Jo, being the very first person to hold Noelle, had been one of the most emotional experiences of his life. Later on Christmas Day, when he'd gone to visit his parents, he hadn't been able to stop talking about it. He'd never felt anything like this before—this exhilaration, this sense of joy, of *significance.* Everything else he'd ever done paled in comparison. He'd been overwhelmed by the power of that moment.

Mack was a firefighter with EMT training. He'd worked at a number of jobs and trades through the years, but being part of the Cedar Cove fire department suited him best. He felt it was where he belonged, the kind of work he was meant to do.

He turned down the radio as he crossed the Narrows Bridge in Tacoma on the drive to Seattle. His thoughts were hectic and disorganized; he needed to settle down before seeing Mary Jo again. Noelle was two days shy of being a month old. A lot could have changed since his visit a couple of weeks earlier.

When they'd last spoken, Mary Jo had sounded pleased to hear from him, but she had bad news. The insurance company where she'd worked had downsized and she'd been given a severance package. The future felt uncertain and he could tell she was trying hard to be optimistic. Wanting to encourage her, Mack had phoned twice since his previous visit, and their conversations, although short, had gone well. Still, he wished there was some way he could help her. Frankly he couldn't think of anything. She wouldn't accept financial assistance from him; she didn't even like taking it from her brothers.

He knew she'd rather not live with them but there really weren't many options, especially now that she was unemployed. She tried to minimize her growing frustration, but Mack sensed how she felt.

Having lived in the Seattle area for most of his life, he had no problem navigating the route to Mary Jo's address. As he'd already discovered, it was a nice house in a pleasant neighborhood. He knew she'd been raised in this very home, the youngest of four children. Her brothers considered themselves her guardians and had done so ever since their parents had died in an automobile accident.

Holding the huge teddy bear he'd bought, Mack walked up the pathway that led to the house. He stared at the front door for a long moment, his heart pounding, before he pressed the bell.

Mary Jo answered almost right away. She carried Noelle, supporting the baby against her shoulder. The baby cried, a steady, plaintive whimpering, her tiny head wobbling.

"Hi," he said.

"Hi," she returned, smiling up at him.

Mary Jo looked…dreadful. No other word for it. She was dressed and her hair was brushed, but her makeup didn't disguise her paleness or the circles that darkened her eyes. Those tired eyes did light up when she saw him, though.

She moved aside so Mack could step into the house, which he noted was tidy. A white bassinet was set up in the living room close to the sofa, and there was a stack of disposable diapers on the coffee table.

"I'm so sorry," she said. "I planned to have Noelle bathed and ready to receive company…but she had a bad morning." She patted Noelle's back. "And consequently, so have I."

"No need to apologize," Mack told her.

Mary Jo made a halfhearted effort to stifle a yawn. "Noelle kept me up most of the night. I thought she'd be tired this morning, but no such luck. Whenever I put her down, she starts to cry all over again."

"Is she sick?"

She shook her head. "I talked to the nurse and she said it's a classic case of colic. It generally hits at about three weeks." She sighed. "All Noelle does is fuss and cry. I don't think I slept more than an hour all night."

"You should've phoned. We could have rescheduled." He would've been disappointed but could easily have stopped by some other time.

"I probably should have," she agreed, "only I'd been looking forward to showing you how much Noelle's changed since you saw her."

On his initial visit Noelle had been sleeping peacefully, wearing a tiny pink knit hat. She'd slept the entire time, so he hadn't had the opportunity to do more than gaze at her admiringly.

Mack set down the teddy bear and saw that Noelle had already acquired a dozen or so stuffed animals.

"My brothers spoil her terribly," Mary Jo said, pointing to the heap of plush lions and puppies and bears. "Especially Linc. He's the oldest, and really should have a family of his own by now. His problem is that he takes his responsibilities—or what he sees as his responsibilities—too seriously. I think that's what caused his breakup with… Oh, you don't want to hear all this." She nodded toward the sofa. "Please make yourself at home."

Noelle squirmed in Mary Jo's arms.

Mack took a seat, feeling awkward, since she was still standing. Mary Jo paced and patted the baby's back, but Noelle sent up a wail that startled him with its intensity.

"Do you want me to take her?" he asked.

"It won't do any good."

Mary Jo looked as if she was about to fall asleep standing up.

"Let me try."

She sighed. "All right. Thank you. I'll put on a pot of coffee. I need caffeine if I'm going to function for the rest of the day." She placed Noelle in his arms.

Mack hadn't spent much time—virtually none, in fact—around babies, so this was a new experience. Noelle continued to yell and thrash her arms and legs. He stared down at her. Her small face was red and fierce with anger as she lay on his lap. Not knowing how to calm her, Mack offered his finger, which she instantly grasped. Then he rested his large hand on her tummy and began to hum a tune he remembered his mother singing to him. He didn't recall the words, but the melody had stayed in his mind.

Noelle blinked up at him and suddenly went still. Then her eyes opened wide. Although it was highly unlikely, it seemed to Mack that the baby recognized him.

Mary Jo poked her head into the room. "What did you *do?*" she asked. "How did you convince her to quiet down?"

"I...hummed," he replied, a bit embarrassed. "As soon as she heard my voice, she stopped crying. I think she remembers me." If her hold on his finger was any indication, Noelle was happy to see him. The feeling was mutual.

Mary Jo watched the two of them. "You certainly have the touch," she said. "And I'm grateful."

When he glanced down, he saw that Noelle had closed her eyes and drifted off to sleep. The poor kid was probably as exhausted as her mother. "I've often heard I have this mesmerizing effect on women," he joked.

Mary Jo smiled and Mack smiled back. He felt bad about the way David Rhodes had lied to her and mistreated her. The man wasn't just scum, he was an idiot to walk away from someone as wonderful as Mary Jo.

A few minutes later, she brought in a tray holding two filled coffee cups, along with a small pitcher of cream and a sugar bowl. She placed it on the table in front of the sofa, then took Noelle from his lap and tucked her inside the bassinet.

While she covered the infant with a knitted blanket, he added cream to his coffee.

"This is the first time she's slept since about five," Mary Jo whispered, obviously afraid of waking the baby.

"I can't believe how much she's grown in just a month."

Mary Jo's gaze rested on her sleeping daughter. "I

know… What *I* can't believe is how demanding motherhood is."

"Your brothers don't help?"

She sat down on the other end of the sofa and reached for her coffee with a soft laugh. "You're joking, right? All three of my brothers are scared to death of Noelle," she said as she spooned in sugar and stirred. "I don't think Linc's held her more than once and he looked terrified the entire time."

"What about Mel and Ned?"

Her smile grew. "If Noelle even burps, they come running for me. As for changing diapers, there's no way."

Mack could understand their fear. Noelle was so small, so fragile, so helpless. It was all too easy to imagine dropping her….

The conversation fell off, and Mack broached the subject that had been on his mind. "Have you heard from David Rhodes?"

Mary Jo stiffened noticeably. "No, and I'm glad of it."

Mack was disgusted with the other man for abdicating responsibility for his child, and he couldn't resist commenting. "He *is* Noelle's father."

Mary Jo shook her head as if anything to do with David Rhodes distressed her. "I'd rather not discuss him," she said tersely.

"Of course." He supposed it wasn't polite to bring up such an unpleasant subject.

"I'm embarrassed by how gullible I was," she went on, "and how willingly I accepted his lies."

Mack just nodded. Mary Jo was the one who'd said she preferred not to talk about Noelle's father, but once she'd started she couldn't seem to stop.

"He fed me all this garbage about loving me and

wanting our baby. He claimed to be thrilled that I was pregnant, and he said that once he had his finances straightened out, we'd get married."

She became more agitated as she spoke. Mack wanted to assure her that it wasn't necessary to tell him all this. But she was in mid-rant, and he couldn't get a word in.

"Then, of course, I didn't hear from him for weeks on end. I even put off taking the birthing classes because when we did speak he told me how much he wanted to be with me when the baby was born. Yeah, right. And then—" she paused and took in a shuddering breath "—then he told me he'd be in Cedar Cove for Christmas with his family, which, as we both know, was another big, fat lie."

She scowled. "His father and stepmother were on this cruise, and when I arrived in town there was no one, and I had to depend on the kindness of strangers. You'd think by this time I'd be smart enough to question anything he said. But did I? Oh, no, I swallowed *that* lie like all the rest."

As if she could no longer sit still, she vaulted to her feet. "After Noelle was born, Ben let David know he had a daughter. You might expect him to contact me, but not so." She started pacing, her arms tightly crossed. "Not that I *wanted* to hear from him, mind you. I might be a slow learner but once I figure something out, I don't forget." She wagged her finger at Mack. "I never want to see or talk to David Rhodes again as long as I live. I mean that."

"Well, I—"

"I refuse to accept a penny from Ben Rhodes, either. He offered, you know. His son's a real problem to him. Ben didn't say that outright but I could tell. I thanked him—it was a lovely, gracious thing to do—but Noelle isn't his responsibility. She's David's. I don't expect him *ever* to do the right thing, though. Neither does Ben. Otherwise he wouldn't have offered." Another quick breath. "I did let him set up a trust fund for Noelle, but that's all."

Mack waited a moment before he attempted to speak. When her tirade was apparently over, he ventured a comment. "In my opinion, Noelle's better off without David in her life."

"I agree with you! Not that I have any worries there. He doesn't want anything to do with her—or with me. Which is just as well. But one thing's for sure."

"What's that?"

She nodded once, in a slow, stately movement. "I won't be so easily fooled again. Men aren't to be trusted, especially the good-looking, sweet-talking kind. Like David—you could frost a cake with his words!"

"Your brothers—"

"Don't get me started on *them,*" she broke in. "Linc's a stubborn know-it-all, and as for Mel and Ned, they're oblivious. A woman who got involved with one of my brothers would need her head examined." She paused long enough to breathe. "Don't get me wrong, I love my brothers. They've been wonderful about Noelle, but they're clueless."

"Well, I—"

"Oh, I shouldn't have said that," Mary Jo blurted out. "It's just that they're at the garage all day and aren't exposed to females in the workplace. Except for women who bring their cars in, of course. And *they're* always impressed." She rolled her eyes.

"I was impressed with Linc, too, when I met him." Mack felt he had to tell her this. He and Linc had talked for a good thirty minutes after the aid car had taken Mary Jo and Noelle to the hospital. At the time, Mack had been excited, and so had Linc. He was an uncle now and thrilled with the idea.

"Of course you'd side with my brothers," Mary Jo muttered. "You're a man."

"Well, I—"

"No, I'm finished with men. Done. Forever. You know what they say, once burned and all that. Well, I've got third-degree burns and there is no way in this lifetime that I will ever trust a man again."

Mack didn't like the sound of this. "What exactly does that mean?" he asked.

The look she shot him said it all. "You don't want to know."

"Actually, I do."

"No, you don't, because you'd feel obliged to defend the male gender and it would only end with us agreeing to disagree. You can't tell me anything Linc hasn't already said."

"Like what?"

Crossing her arms again, she sighed loudly. "That all men aren't like David."

"They aren't."

"I realize that. My dad was a wonderful husband and father, and there are still a few decent men left in this world. Cliff Harding, for example."

He noticed *he* hadn't been mentioned but decided not to take it personally. "If you believe that," he said, "then why are you finished with men?"

"Because," she said, leaning forward, "I know there are good guys. That's not the problem. The problem is being able to tell who's good and who's a jerk. Unfortunately, my jerk detector is clearly out of whack."

"I think you're being too hard on yourself."

"Nope. Because you know something? David wasn't the first."

Mack's eyes narrowed.

"I mean…I never went as far…got as involved with a man the way I did with David. But before I met him, there was a guy at work who completely charmed me. Not until later did I discover he was married. We never really went out or anything—I just had lunch with him or a drink after work. Nothing more than that. But I had no idea he was lying, too. Lying by omission, anyway." She glanced at Mack over her shoulder as she paced. "Other women seem to have that filter, you know, the instinct that tunes them in to a man's motives. I don't, so I can't trust myself with men. Another relationship isn't worth the risk."

Setting down his coffee cup, Mack mulled over her words. "So I guess that's it."

"That's it. I have my daughter, and from now on it'll be just the two of us. As soon as I find another job, I'm going to get an apartment and move there and live on my own, free of my brothers and free of men entirely."

Mary Jo looked over at him as if daring him to comment.

"This wouldn't be a good time to ask you out on a date, then, would it?"

Her head reared back in surprise and she smiled. "Are you sure you mean that?"

Mack grinned up at her. "As a matter of fact, I do."

Ten

Grace Harding was working in her small office at the library when Sally Overland, a recent hire, knocked politely at her half-open door. Grace wondered how she'd be able to concentrate on the endless stack of paperwork if she was constantly interrupted. The morning was already gone, and she'd hardly made a dent.

"Come in," she called. None of her other assistants would've waited for permission.

Sally stuck her head in the door. "There's someone by the name of Olivia who's here to see you. She said she's a friend."

Grace leaped to her feet, nearly upending her chair. "Olivia's here?"

Sally, who was young and somewhat lacking in confidence, widened her eyes. "Yes. I hope I did the right thing. I told her you were busy, but she said you wouldn't mind."

"Of course I don't mind."

Sally stepped aside and Olivia entered the office wearing her long black wool coat and a bright red knit cap.

Grace walked around her desk and gave her closest friend a careful hug. Olivia was pale, but then she had been for months. Pale and thin…and now bald.

"What are you doing here?" Grace demanded.

"What do you mean?" Olivia asked in the same tone of voice. "I brought back a library book and wanted to see if you'd had lunch yet."

"No. Do you feel good enough to be out and about?"

"Yes. I wouldn't be here otherwise," Olivia stated with perfect logic. "Where would you like to go?"

"You choose," Grace said. She knew Olivia didn't have much of an appetite and whatever appealed to her was fine with Grace.

Olivia shrugged. "Anyplace will do. What sounds good is a cup of tea."

"That's all?"

"Maybe some soup."

"Pot Belly Deli?"

"Great."

Olivia smiled, and Grace grabbed her coat, scarf and purse. Together they headed toward the main library door. Grace quickly told Sally where she'd be.

Although the deli was less than three blocks away, Grace insisted on driving. She didn't want Olivia to risk catching a chill while her immune system was compromised because of the cancer treatments. Nor did she want her to get tired out from the walk.

Just before Christmas, Olivia had been hospitalized with a massive infection. A shiver of fear skittered down Grace's spine at the memory of how close they'd come to losing her. No, she wasn't taking any chances.

"You're treating me as if I'm made of porcelain," Olivia complained, but not too strenuously, Grace noted.

"Don't waste your breath arguing."

"You always were bossy," Olivia said as she slid into the passenger seat.

"Uh-huh." Grace wasn't about to let her friend have the last word.

Thankfully, she found a parking spot directly in front of the deli. It was late enough that the noon crowd had left, so they had their pick of tables.

As soon as they were seated, Grace smiled at the young waitress. "What's your soup for today?"

"Cream of broccoli," the girl, who didn't look more than eighteen, told her.

"We'll both have that," Grace said.

"With tea," Olivia added. "Earl Grey, please."

The girl made a notation on the pad and disappeared. Once she was out of earshot, Olivia leaned forward. "Mom's got the best broccoli soup recipe. I think she had it here first and then went home and created her own version. My mother should have a cooking show, don't you think?"

Grace laughed. "Can't you picture it? Chef Charlotte making muffins and chatting up celebrity guests." She removed her scarf and unfastened her coat, then folded it over the back of her chair. "She'd be terrific. And she can make *anything* taste wonderful."

Olivia nodded, smiling. "She believes in cooking with quality ingredients—and love."

"I've only seen your mother in passing since the cruise. She had a good time?"

"She did. Ben, too, although they were hit with the news about David's baby the minute they got home, which upset them both."

"That's too bad," Grace said, her voice grim. She

blamed David, maybe not for the pregnancy, since both partners had played a role in that, but he'd clearly lied to the poor girl about his intentions. And his behavior afterward had been appalling—his refusal to acknowledge the baby or accept his responsibilities as a father.

"I think this is the final straw as far as Ben is concerned," Olivia said, smoothing her napkin across her lap. "Apparently he's only spoken to David once since they got home from the cruise. He told Mom that if David phones again, he doesn't want to talk to him."

"I can understand why Ben's so upset."

"So can I," Olivia said. "He's taking this hard. Ben's such an honorable man that his son's behavior—deceiving and deluding a sweet girl like Mary Jo—makes it all the more painful." She shook her head. "I didn't stop by to discuss David, though. The subject depresses me."

"Me, too."

"Did I tell you what Mom's been doing lately?"

"You mean other than visiting you?" Grace joked. It was common knowledge that Charlotte made a habit of checking up on Olivia every few days.

"She's been collecting all her favorite recipes for Justine's tearoom. Which means she's writing some of them down for the very first time."

Grace had driven past the construction site that morning and was astonished by the progress that had been made in the past month. "The building's really coming along, isn't it?"

"When my daughter wants something, she tends to get it."

"She's another Charlotte in the making."

"That and more," Olivia said. "She's starting a brand-new business, balancing that with looking after her family and getting ready for the baby…."

"How's she feeling?"

"Very well, she says. She's just begun to show. I hope she has a girl this time." Olivia hesitated as if she'd suddenly realized what she'd said. "Of course we'd welcome another grandson with equal enthusiasm."

"Of course you would."

"How are your girls?" Olivia asked.

"Maryellen and Kelly are doing great."

The door opened at that moment and in walked Sheriff Troy Davis. He touched the brim of his hat when he saw them, a habitual gesture of his, then stepped up to the counter and ordered coffee to go.

As Grace was filling Olivia in on the latest news about her grandchildren, Troy came to their table, clutching his take-out mug.

"Nice to see you both," he said. He frowned at the wool cap Olivia wore, then quickly glanced away.

Grace could see that Olivia was trying to squelch a smile. "Hey, Sheriff, don't be so worried. I'll live."

"Glad to hear it. So, what are you two doing here at—" he looked pointedly at his watch "—the middle of the afternoon?"

"I'm on leave," Olivia said, although she knew he was well aware of that.

"I'm having a late lunch," Grace added.

He motioned toward the front window. "Is that your vehicle in the disabled parking space?"

"Ah…my car?"

"I guess you didn't see the sign."

"Oh, dear. Did you give me a ticket?" Usually she was more observant than this.

"No, but I'd advise you to move it before one of my deputies does."

Grace scooped up her purse, grateful for the warning. "I'll be right back."

"Take your time," Troy said. He seemed to be watching her as she left.

Grace saw that as soon as she was out the door, Troy slid into her seat. Not until she reached her vehicle did she realize the disabled space was one down from where she'd parked. She was perfectly legal exactly where she was.

It wasn't like Troy to make that kind of mistake, and she started back toward the deli. Then it dawned on her that Troy had purposely sent her on a wild-goose chase because he wanted time alone with Olivia. Assuming that was the case, she'd accommodate him.

Grace slid inside the car and circled the block twice, then located another slot close by. She figured that would give Troy ample opportunity to divulge whatever he had on his mind. Naturally she intended to drill Olivia the instant they were alone.

When she returned to the deli, their soup and tea had been served, together with a basket of sourdough bread. When Troy saw her, he stood and made his farewells.

The moment the door closed behind him, Grace said, "I wasn't parked in a disabled space."

"I know."

"Troy just wanted to get rid of me."

Olivia's spoon hovered over her soup. "I know that, too. He asked me to apologize."

Grace waited for an explanation that didn't seem to be forthcoming. She couldn't understand why her friend was suddenly so tight-lipped. "Aren't you going to tell me why he found it necessary to speak to you alone?"

"I haven't decided," Olivia answered with an exaggerated sigh.

"Olivia! Don't hold out on me now."

"All right, all right," Olivia said, doing her best to hide a smile. "He wanted some advice."

"About what?" Grace narrowed her eyes. "I didn't realize you and Troy were such bosom buddies."

"We aren't. He just knows me better because of my years on the bench."

"He knows me, too! Good grief, we all went through twelve years of school together. What could he possibly say to you that he couldn't say to me?" She felt a bit hurt that Troy had sought out Olivia and not her.

"Okay, if you *must* know," Olivia said, "he wanted to ask me about Faith Beckwith."

Grace shook her head. "Faith's our tenant, remember? If he needed to find anything out, he could've asked me."

"Well, he told me the two of them had a thing going, and—"

"That's not news! Although they don't seem to be dating now. I wonder what happened…." She let the rest fade, hoping Olivia would fill in the blanks.

"Unfortunately Troy didn't have time to go into detail," Olivia said. She looked at Grace with mock disdain. "It might have taken you a *bit* longer to find a parking spot, you know."

Grace had no intention of responding. She wanted facts—now. "Okay, so they had a 'thing' going and then what?"

"He didn't really say other than that he broke it off, regretted it and, when he wanted to get back together, Faith wasn't interested."

"That's understandable."

"Maybe, but we both know Troy isn't fickle. Faith should give him a bit of leeway, don't you think?"

Grace considered that. "Depends." She didn't want to get caught up in a debate about the right or wrong of his decision, not when there was obviously more to the story. "So what else?" she pressed.

"Like I said, he didn't have time to give me any details." She raised her eyebrows, which Grace ignored.

"And now Troy's upset because he loves Faith and wants her back." How like a man!

Olivia took Troy's side. "She broke his heart."

Grace pretended to be sympathetic, but in her opinion he got what he deserved. "Poor Troy," she said in a perfunctory tone.

"That wasn't exactly what he wanted to talk me about, though."

Oh! This was getting interesting. "He didn't want advice about Faith?"

"Well, sort of. Something else happened that's got him in a real state."

When Olivia didn't immediately continue, Grace snapped, "For heaven's sake, don't stop there! What happened?"

"Last night, on his way home, Troy saw Faith having dinner with another man."

Grace picked up her spoon, then put it down again. This was far more intriguing than cream of broccoli soup. "What do you mean, he saw her with someone else? What did he do, drive his patrol car through a restaurant door?"

"Of course not. He was hungry and felt like some Chinese food, so he ordered takeout from Wok 'n' Roll. He walked inside to pick up his order—and who should he see?"

"Faith," Grace answered.

"Yes, Faith, and she was with…a man. She had her back to him but Troy knew it was her and she seemed to be having the time of her life."

Grace had another question. "So, who was he?" she asked, lowering her voice. "This man she was with."

Olivia acted as if Grace hadn't even spoken. "Poor Troy was devastated. He said it was all he could do not to march up to the table and tell…this other man to stay away from Faith."

"Not a smart idea."

"I said the same thing."

"So what did he do?" Grace asked.

"Nothing much. He paid for his dinner, left and then seethed for the rest of the night. Judging by his expression, I'd say it's still bothering him."

"Did Faith see him?" Grace wanted to know.

"He thinks she might have."

"In that case, they probably both feel bad. Because Faith would know he was upset, and she isn't the kind of woman who enjoys hurting someone else."

"That's true."

"Okay, so tell me who Faith's hot date was."

Olivia paused, and Grace's heart sank. "He's married, isn't he? That's why you don't want to tell me."

"No, that's not it. In fact, once I say his name it won't surprise you at all."

So Olivia was going to make her guess. That wasn't fair—and then it came to her. Shocked, she pressed both hands against the table and half stood. "No way?"

Olivia knew immediately that Grace had figured it out. Slowly, with her eyes closed, she nodded.

"Your brother, Will Jefferson, is dating Faith?"

Olivia exhaled sharply. "So it seems."

"Well…he's divorced and she's a widow. So I guess there's nothing really wrong with it."

"But the last I heard," Olivia said, "he was interested in Shirley Bliss."

Grace tore a piece of bread. "I know Will's your brother and you love him, but I also know a basic fact about him. He's not a one-woman man."

Olivia sighed. "I certainly can't deny it, at least going by previous experience."

"Are you going to say anything to Faith?" Grace asked.

Olivia shook her head.

"Then I won't, either."

Eleven

This was so embarrassing. Unfortunately, Christie didn't have any alternative. She needed a vehicle; otherwise, she wouldn't be able to get to work except by walking or biking. A bicycle might be okay once spring arrived, and she could probably buy one secondhand, but that didn't help her now. So far, winter had set all kinds of records for cold and snowfall. Slogging through slush and fierce wind left much to be desired.

The sad reality was that after many temporary fixes, her car was dead. There was no possibility of reviving it. The junkyard had offered her a flat hundred bucks and she took it. That hundred dollars, however, wasn't going to provide reliable transportation. Her only recourse was to ask for a loan—and the only person she could approach was her sister, Teri.

With a knot in her stomach, Christie made the call. Teri answered so quickly, she must've been sitting next to the phone.

"Can you talk?" she asked, trying to keep any hint of anxiety out of her voice.

"Sure. What's up?"

"I'd rather do this face-to-face," Christie told her. She felt like weeping, which was an anomaly on its own. She didn't easily give in to emotion. Oh, she'd cried her share of tears, but generally it took a crisis like having her bank account emptied by some low-life scum she'd been convinced she could reform. She'd wept buckets over that, and her divorce, too. What upset her this time was the fact that it wasn't a man but a stupid car.

"Come on by," Teri said. "I'd love the company."

"That's…the problem. I don't have a car."

"What happened?"

Christie didn't want to go into all of that now. "Has Bobby hired a new driver?"

"Not yet. Bobby's positive James will return. I—"

"Please don't talk about James," she interrupted stiffly. Even his name was enough to make her stomach tense.

"Okay, if that's the way you want it."

"I do."

"Take a taxi to the house and I'll pay for it."

Although Christie appreciated the offer, she refused to do that. "I'll take the bus."

"Christie, don't be silly."

"It's no problem. Buses run regularly this time of day."

Still Teri hesitated. "I'd come and get you myself but the doctor doesn't want me driving."

Christie wasn't surprised. Teri was due in May, although with triplets she'd probably deliver early. "When did he say you couldn't drive?"

"At my last visit. Doc wants to play it safe. Okay, I know it's for a good reason, but I have to tell you I'm going *crazy* sitting around the house. I could definitely use a distraction."

"I'll be there as soon as I can."

"Grab a taxi," Teri insisted again.

"I'll think about it." Actually, Christie already had and she'd dismissed the idea. She was coming to Teri for a loan as it was and she didn't want her sister having to open her wallet for cab fare before they'd even begun the conversation. And no way was she spending fifteen hard-won dollars herself if she didn't have to.

There was nothing wrong with the bus. She would normally have considered it for transportation to her job, but she worked the early shift at Wal-Mart and the bus schedule was extremely limited at that time of the morning.

The queasiness in her stomach hadn't lessened as she made the long trek down Teri and Bobby's driveway. Walking to the house, she automatically glanced at the garage and the apartment above it, where James had once lived. She chastised herself for looking.

James was out of her life, out of all their lives. Bobby might be deluding himself that his driver and best friend would return. Best friend, now that was a joke. Some friend James had been!

When she finally reached the door and rang the bell, her nose had lost feeling. Her winter jacket was little protection against the wind, which seemed to slice straight through her. She kept her hands clenched in her pockets for warmth.

"You're frozen!" Teri shrieked when she saw her. "I *told* you to take a cab."

Rather than start an argument, Christie conceded. "Yeah, I should have."

"Come in, come in." Teri pulled her into the house and helped her off with her coat and gloves.

Mutely Christie followed her sister into the kitchen and gladly accepted a mug of hot herbal tea. The first sip burned all the way down her throat, but Christie didn't care. The taste and aroma of the tea revived her.

Slipping onto a stool at the breakfast bar, she braced her elbows there, clutching the mug with both hands, as she considered the best approach to asking her sister for the loan. This was even more difficult than she'd expected. It made her feel like such a failure when she was working so hard to get her life on track. Her credit had been ruined by yet another deadbeat she'd thought she could transform. There'd been a transformation, all right—a negative one. The guy had become an even bigger jerk, and he'd ripped her off, to boot. Why was it lessons like this had to be so painful, with consequences that lingered for years?

Teri seemed to be waiting for her to say something.

"I took your advice," she said conversationally.

Teri set her mug on the counter and clambered onto the stool directly across from her. "What advice was that?"

"Remember when you said I should make some positive changes in my life? You were right. I've signed up for two courses at the community college in Bremerton."

"Really?" Teri seemed impressed.

Actually, Christie was impressed with herself. "I never figured I'd be hanging around a college campus at my age."

"You're not old."

Christie laughed. "I am compared to most of those kids." Shaking her head, she sighed. "Were we ever that young?"

"We were born old," Teri said with a sad look. "The education we got wasn't in history or literature, it was in the ways of the world."

That was true. Having grown up with an alcoholic mother and a series of stepdads and "uncles," Christie knew they'd both been robbed of a normal childhood.

"So tell me—" Teri changed the subject "—what are you taking?"

Christie's heart raced with excitement as she said the word. "Photography."

Teri's eyes widened. "Why photography? I didn't know you had any interest in that."

"I didn't until recently." She might as well let it all out. "I went in to the agent to pay my car insurance premium—while I still had a car—and he was on the phone." It'd been one of those rare instances, Christie realized later, when an opportunity had presented itself at precisely the right moment. "He was bemoaning the fact that there isn't anyone locally to document household inventory for home insurance purposes."

"So…"

"So when he got off the phone, I asked him what would be involved in learning to do this, and he told me. On his advice, I registered for Basic Photography and Elementary Business. He said if I was willing to follow through, he had two assignments coming up that he could give me. Plus, he'd pass the word along to other agents in town."

"That's great!"

Christie shrugged. "I started the class last week and there's a lot more to taking a picture than you'd think. This isn't just point and shoot. I have to learn about lighting and lenses and all kinds of stuff."

"But you'll get there."

Teri's confidence in her was reassuring. Christie sipped her tea again, then decided she couldn't delay this any longer. With a deep breath, she looked up at her sister.

"Do you know why I'm here?"

Teri didn't answer; instead, she reached for her own

tea. Her dark hair was pulled away from her face and secured at the nape of her neck and she wore no makeup at all. Under ordinary circumstances she wouldn't consider herself dressed without styling her hair and applying lip gloss. That was the bare minimum.

"Do you really want to play guessing games?" her sister asked.

"No." Christie straightened and met her eyes. "I need a loan."

There, it was out, although the words had nearly stuck in her throat.

"How much?"

"I need reliable transportation."

"You mean a new car?"

"Yes. Well, no. A used car."

"Have you found one?"

"Not yet..."

"Will five thousand be enough?" Teri asked.

Christie nearly swallowed her tongue. "No."

"Ten?"

"No, no, I meant five thousand would be far too much." Christie fully intended to pay back every penny, with interest. If her credit rating hadn't been ruined, she would've applied for a bank loan. But that was out of the question now. Reestablishing her credit was taking far longer than she'd thought it would.

"Three thousand?"

"I was thinking more along the lines of one thousand," Christie said. She should be able to repay that amount within a reasonable period of time.

"That's not enough! You'd only be getting yourself another junker. We'll begin with five thousand," Teri insisted.

"Teri...I can't."

"You can and you will, and that's the end of it."

Undecided, Christie bit her lip. "You'll want to talk this over with Bobby."

Teri sipped her tea. "I already did. He only had one stipulation."

Maybe Christie should've been surprised that her sister had known the purpose of her visit, but she wasn't. "Which is?"

"That you let someone help you."

"In what way?"

"Finding the right car."

"Okay." She didn't want to admit how inadequate she felt when it came to purchasing a vehicle. Generally she looked at the interior. The cleanliness and appearance of the car indicated how well the previous owner had cared for the engine—at least, that was her theory. Perhaps not a very accurate basis for judgment, but Christie knew next to nothing about anything mechanical.

"Who?"

"Bobby has a friend who'd be willing to do the research."

"What's his name?"

"It's a guy in the business. Let Bobby handle it, okay?"

"Okay." Christie had no objection to that; in fact, she was grateful. "Fine by me. If this guy doesn't mind, have him pick it out and buy it. I don't need to be there," she told her sister. Besides, between her job at Wal-Mart and her photography and business classes, she didn't have spare time to be running around checking out used cars.

Then, because she was afraid she hadn't adequately expressed her gratitude, Christie added, "Thank you." Her voice trembled.

"I *want* to help," Teri said. "You're my sister."

"I'm so glad I have a sister." For far too long they'd done their best to ignore each other.

"I'll sign loan documents." Christie had a stipulation of her own. She wasn't a charity case and wanted Teri to understand she wouldn't accept this money as a gift. This was a loan and an opportunity to prove herself. "I'm going to pay that money back, plus interest."

"Whatever you want." Teri sounded as if repayment was of little concern to her.

"It's more than what I want, Teri," Christie said. "It's the right thing to do."

Teri smiled down at her tea.

"What's so funny?" Christie asked.

"My little sister's finally grown up."

It would've been easy to take offense at that comment, with its implication that Christie was—or had been—immature. However, her sister's willingness to fork over the money precluded that. And, in all honesty, Christie couldn't completely disagree.

Bobby walked into the room just then. His eyes went instantly to his wife. He didn't seem to notice that Christie was there, too.

"Hello, Bobby," she said, loudly enough to catch his attention.

He inclined his head slightly in acknowledgment. "Did you tell her?" he asked, directing the question to Teri.

Bobby Polgar was a man of few words, but Christie could never doubt that he loved her sister. From a very young age Bobby's world had revolved around chess; it had been his whole life until he met Teri. According to her, the defining moment in their relationship had come the day Bobby confessed that his whole existence was about *thinking*. Chess required strategy, deliberation and the ability to forecast consequences, and he'd transferred those cerebral skills into every aspect of his life. But Teri made him *feel.*

Christie realized that James had just the opposite effect on her. For most of her adult life, her decisions had been driven by emotion. But he'd made her think. He'd made her reconsider the way she was living—from one day to the next with no greater ambition than getting to the end of the week and going to the Poodle for a beer. Because of him she had goals and purpose. His defection had made her even more determined. James had hurt her, and hurt her terribly, but this time, for the first time, she was using the pain inflicted by a man to learn and to grow.

Christie dismissed the thought. James was no longer part of her life.

Teri caught her eye. "He phoned."

Playing dumb was her only option. "I don't know who you're talking about."

"James," Bobby said excitedly.

Christie stopped herself from asking where James was living now and how he was doing. No doubt he'd escaped to someplace far from Washington. It didn't matter. Nothing that happened to James Wilbur or Gardner, or whatever he called himself now, concerned her.

"Oh." That was all she was capable of saying.

"Don't you want to know what he said?" Teri asked.

"No." She shook her head.

Teri huffed out a sigh. "That's not true. You're dying to hear the details, but you're too stubborn to admit it."

Shaking her head more adamantly, Christie denied that. "Nope."

"He's sorry," Bobby said. He stood behind Teri, his hands on her shoulders.

No man would ever look at her the way Bobby Polgar regarded her sister, Christie realized. She wasn't jealous; she ached to be in a relationship as caring and real as the one Teri had with her husband. *Well, get over it,* she mused. *Because it's not going to happen.* Nor would the children she'd always dreamed of having…

"Who's sorry?" she asked, continuing the pretense.

"James." Teri rolled her eyes. "You're pretty transparent, little sister, so drop the act."

"It's not an act." Christie slid off the stool. "Anyway, I should get home." She had a long walk to the bus stop and didn't want to waste time on idle conversation with her sister. Especially if James Wilbur was going to be the topic.

"All right," Teri said in that superior way of hers. "Whatever you say." She made her skepticism abundantly clear.

"Fine." She hungered for information about James but refused to ask, refused to let Teri or Bobby say one word about him. She wasn't giving James an opportunity to creep back into her thoughts or her life.

Teri insisted on calling a taxi and tucking a twenty into Christie's pocket. Although she made a fuss, Christie was thankful. Before she left the house, she hugged both Teri and Bobby, and Teri promised to call as soon as she heard about the car.

True to her word, Teri phoned less than twenty-four hours later. Bobby's friend had located an older vehicle in relatively good condition for under five thousand dollars. The gas mileage was low; it even had a CD player and automatic locks.

"Perfect!" Christie said, so happy she could barely hold still. "What color is it?"

"What color?" Teri repeated. "White."

Christie couldn't squelch her disappointment. "I was hoping for blue."

"You can have it repainted later if it bothers you that much."

"It won't—I'm just being silly. I'm so grateful to have a car." And if it was as reliable as her sister seemed to think and had such nice extras, she wasn't about to complain.

"Shall I have it delivered to your apartment?"

"Please," Christie said. "Thank you, Teri," she said, "thank you, thank you. I promise I'll pay you back—with interest."

"Okay. It'll get there soon."

Fifteen minutes later, the knock on her door told her that her new car had arrived.

When she saw James Wilbur standing on the other side of the torn screen, she followed her instinctive reaction, and that was to slam the door. A torrent of emotion overwhelmed her as she leaned against the wall. Her knees gave out, and she started to slide downward.

There was another knock, this one louder and more insistent. She had to answer, Christie thought reluctantly. Any kind of reaction would encourage him and that wasn't Christie's intention.

Collecting herself, she straightened and opened the door again. She had to admit James looked good, although she made every effort to stare right past him.

"I apologize," she said. "The door, uh, got away from me."

He smiled at her explanation as though it amused him. Well, fine, he could be as amused as he liked. But not at her expense.

She was furious with Teri and Bobby. They'd tried to

pull a fast one on her—and they'd succeeded. Christie supposed she should have figured it out. Teri's vague talk of a friend "in the business," the sudden mention of a phone call from James… Why hadn't she asked more questions? Teri would be hearing a few angry words about this.

No, she decided. She'd put her anger aside and overlook their trick in gratitude for all their help—although she wouldn't forgive them a second time.

"I brought your car," he said and held up the keys.

"Thank you," she said, keeping her voice emotionless. Indifferent. But her awareness of him had never been sharper than it was just then. Despite that, or perhaps because of it, she'd rather keel over dead than give James Wilbur any indication of her feelings.

"Can I show it to you?" James asked. His eyes burned into hers, sending silent messages—that he needed to talk to her, be with her.

"That won't be necessary, but thank you for offering." She opened the screen door far enough to pluck the keys from his hand. Then, with a polite smile, she quietly closed the door.

To be on the safe side, she turned the dead bolt—unsure whether this was an attempt to keep him out or her in.

Twelve

Footsteps. Faith Beckwith heard them outside her bedroom window. Whoever was there made no effort at stealth. Someone was about to break into the house and didn't care if she knew.

Paralyzed with fear, Faith stopped breathing. The clock radio said 2:14. At first she'd assumed the movements, which couldn't be more than a few feet from her window, were just her imagination. But now there was no question—someone was there, crunching through the hardened snow in the backyard. Whoever it was might even be looking inside. Although she was buried under blankets and the blinds were closed, Faith felt the trespasser's stare, felt his presence as clearly as if he was standing over her bed.

Her breath came again in gasps as her mind raced frantically. Rolling carefully onto her side, she reached for the bedside phone and drew it under the sheets with her. Then, hidden under the covers, she used the lighted dial to punch out 9-1-1. Whispering, she told the operator that someone was outside her bedroom window.

The operator assured her a deputy was on his way.

Without thinking, Faith disconnected the line. Oh, dear, that was foolish. Then she understood what her heart had been telling her from the first—it wasn't a 9-1-1 operator she wanted reassurance from, it was Troy Davis.

Troy had said she should call but she couldn't. Not in the middle of the night and, really, what could he do?

He'd been on her mind ever since the evening he'd come into the Wok 'n' Roll when she was dining there with Will Jefferson, a friend from her high-school days. He'd been two years ahead of her and a real heartthrob.

Naturally, Troy pretended he hadn't seen her with Will. She'd done exactly the same thing and acted as though he was invisible. If anything, she'd gone out of her way to prove she could enjoy another man's company. It'd seemed like a good idea at the time; now, in retrospect, she wasn't so sure. She couldn't resist letting him think she had an active social life.

Will Jefferson, while charming and as good-looking as ever, didn't interest Faith. For that matter, he wasn't interested in her, either. He happened to be eating alone when she came in, and Will had invited her to share his table. They'd spent an hour catching up and exchanging news of mutual friends, laughing frequently at various reminiscences. They'd had a friendly visit—and that was it. Faith hadn't heard from Will since and didn't expect to, which suited her fine.

The footsteps outside her window seemed to be receding. Faith exhaled and then, acting purely on impulse, grabbed the phone again. She hesitated; she had plenty of time to change her mind, plenty of time to be ruled by reason rather than emotion.

Troy answered on the second ring. "Davis here." He sounded awake. Alert.

"Th-there's someone outside my bedroom window," she said, struggling to speak coherently.

"Faith?"

"I—I shouldn't have called."

"Hang up and call 9-1-1." Each word was spoken clearly and distinctly.

"I already did. You suggested I phone you, too—it was silly. I shouldn't have. I'm sorry."

"Don't hang up," he commanded.

"I'm fine.... Your deputy will be here any minute. I'm sorry to bother you, Troy." She disconnected. With her fingers trembling violently, she felt more than a little embarrassed to have given in to her impulse. Her weakness.

Faith could hear a car pull up and hurried out of bed. She threw on a housecoat, then waited by the door until the sheriff's vehicle came into view. Turning on the porch light, she stepped onto the porch.

"There—at the back of the house, near the bedroom on the south side," she called out, pointing in that direction.

Wrapping the housecoat more securely about her, she returned to the house. As she waited, she paced the living room. When she heard a loud knock at her front door, she rushed to answer it—and found Troy Davis standing there, looking grim and hard-faced.

"Are you hurt?" he demanded.

He sounded angry, as he had every right to be. What an irrational, irresponsible thing she'd done in calling him.

"I'm...shaken up," she told him, hoping that would be enough to explain why she'd behaved so illogically.

"Wait here," he said and left her.

Faith lowered herself into her favorite rocker. She sat

there for long moments, unmoving, not knowing what to think or why someone had targeted her.

That was obviously the case. She'd done her best to ignore the fact, pretend this couldn't be happening. Now, whoever this person was, he'd come back, bolder and even more aggressive. After the initial break-in, he—or she—had spray painted her garage. Now—

"There's clear evidence of someone outside your bedroom window," Troy said sternly as he came through the front door. "Deputy Walker saw footprints in the snow." His tone was almost…accusatory.

Faith looked up at him and blinked, bewildered.

Troy's nod was curt and professional as he prepared to leave.

But Faith sensed his hesitation.

"Did you lock the dead bolts before you went to bed?" he asked.

She confirmed that she had. "I also purchased a pair of old work boots from Goodwill and set them on the porch. I bought the largest size I could find—fourteen. Then I added a huge dog dish and a bone, so it would look as if I have a dog." She figured that since she was pretending she had a dog, she might as well make him big. Her son and daughter had found her antics amusing. Troy apparently didn't.

"Did you get a *real* security system?" he snapped.

That she hadn't done. This was a rental house and she had a six-month lease. She hoped to buy a home within the next few months. It seemed a waste of time and money to invest in a security system when she didn't intend to live here much longer. And she didn't feel an alarm system was the landlord's responsibility.

"No," she admitted.

"Then I recommend you do so."

Faith nodded.

Troy turned to leave again.

Frightened, she didn't want to be alone, but she didn't know how to stop him. "Why are you so angry?" she cried out.

Troy's back was to her. He held himself stiff, and then she saw his shoulders deflate as he faced her. He didn't seem to have an answer.

"It was wrong of me to call you. I apologize, I really do." She didn't remind him that he'd been the one to make that suggestion. It had stayed there, in her mind, like a thorn caught on a piece of fabric. In her weakened state she'd done what she'd wanted to all along and now regretted it.

Still Troy didn't speak, didn't move or give even a hint that he'd heard her.

"I realize I shouldn't have…."

He accepted her answer with a curt nod. "You've made it plain you don't want me in your life."

Heat rose in her cheeks, embarrassing her even more. "Yes, I know. I—"

"Then why, when you felt you were in danger, did you reach out to me?"

He was obviously determined to make this difficult. She told him the truth, since she couldn't come up with any other explanation. "I feel safe with you."

He glared across the room at her.

It felt awkward to be sitting while he loomed over her, even if he was on the other side of the room. Faith stood abruptly. She hated to let him see how upset she was by this latest disturbance.

"I need some coffee," she said, knowing there was no point in going back to bed now. "Would you like some, Troy?" she asked, refusing to allow his anger to affect her.

"No."

It didn't sound as if he meant that, so she proceeded into the kitchen, immeasurably pleased when he came, too, a few paces behind her.

"I have the names of a couple of companies who install security systems," he said. "I'll have Megan pass them on to you."

Faith continued to prepare the coffee. "I'd appreciate that. Thank you, Troy."

He seemed on the verge of leaving again. She resisted the urge to stop him, although she didn't want to be alone. No, it was more than that. She wanted Troy with her. She needed him.

"I saw the TV report about the cave and the skeleton on that Seattle station," she said conversationally. "I hear everyone in the area's talking about it. I hope all this media attention hasn't caused your office any problems." The reporter had started all kinds of speculation, and as a result Kitsap County seemed to be alive with rumors, some of them pretty ridiculous.

Troy didn't answer, but he didn't walk away, either.

She glanced over at him, waiting for a response.

"Mayor Benson isn't happy about it," he finally said. "Neither am I."

"It puts a lot of pressure on you and your staff, doesn't it?" She brought a mug to the kitchen table and set it down while the coffee filtered into the pot. "Is that the reason you're so cranky?"

Again he didn't answer.

"Or does it have to do with Will Jefferson?"

Troy's jaw tightened, but he didn't speak.

"You *did* see us, didn't you?" she said.

Once more he declined to respond, but she went on as if he had.

"I thought so."

Troy remained stoic. "I didn't know the two of you were seeing each other," he said tersely.

"As it happens, we aren't." She went on to explain that she'd run into Will at the restaurant. If her explanation satisfied him, he didn't say. He seemed determined to keep her out of his life. Well, that was what she'd wanted, wasn't it? What she'd asked for.

The coffee gurgled behind her, and the slow dripping sound came to an end.

"It's none of my business who you have dinner with."

"True, but I felt you should know."

He nodded as though acknowledging the information. That was encouraging.

"Are you sure I can't talk you into having coffee with me? It's almost four, and there probably isn't enough time to go back to sleep."

He hovered uncertainly in the kitchen doorway.

"Why is that such a difficult decision?" Faith asked, half joking.

"I should go."

It was hard to hide her disappointment. "I understand." Thankful for an excuse to turn away, she filled her mug and added cream. When she turned back, she discovered that Troy had taken a few steps into the kitchen.

"Before I do, I want you to tell me again what happened tonight. Start with the fact that someone was at your bedroom window."

She sipped her coffee, letting the warmth seep through her. "Yes. I heard the footsteps."

"You heard noise out by the garage on another occasion."

"Yes, there was that spray-painting incident."

"Has there been anything since?" he asked. "Before tonight?"

"Not that I'm aware of."

"Well, you *should* be aware," he said in a brusque voice.

Faith exhaled slowly, unaccustomed to dealing with Troy when he was angry. This was a side of him she wasn't familiar with. Troy Davis had never revealed a temper in her presence, not in the past and not recently. Until tonight.

His mouth tightened.

"I…I probably should keep closer tabs on the garage and the house, too," she said.

"Yes, you should."

"You're making me feel foolish."

Troy ignored the comment. "Have the interior security system installed, and ask Grace and Cliff to place a motion light above the garage."

"I'll do that at the first opportunity."

"Don't put it off," Troy warned.

"I won't. I promise."

He nodded, but didn't meet her eyes.

"Good night, Troy," she said softly.

For a long moment he didn't say anything. "I appreciate knowing you're not involved with Will Jefferson."

"Why's that?" she asked.

Troy looked down at the floor. "He's not a good match for you, Faith."

"So who do you think *is* a good match for me?" she pressed.

This time Troy Davis didn't hesitate. His eyes met hers. "We both know the answer to that."

She leaned forward expectantly.

"It's me, Faith. It's always been me."

Thirteen

Will Jefferson glanced at his watch. It was Saturday night, and he'd made reservations at D.D.'s on the Cove. The restaurant was one of the nicest in town and he intended to impress Shirley Bliss.

They'd seen each other twice now. Once for coffee at Mocha Mama's, when she'd brought her daughter. The meeting hadn't gone badly. With Tanni there, Shirley had been relaxed and easygoing. Shaw and Tanni had bantered back and forth, and they'd all laughed. He'd enjoyed it, somewhat to his surprise, and he could tell that Shirley had, too.

Their second date wasn't technically a date, either. They'd met by accident late one Sunday afternoon outside the mall. Will had been at loose ends and apparently she had, too. He'd invited her to the movies. The day was dreary and cold, and it'd been an offhand suggestion. He'd been delighted—and astonished—when she agreed.

He ate popcorn. She didn't. As the credits started to roll he offered to take her to dinner. He was eager to discuss the movie, which was a complicated drama about the meaning of identity, real and fake. However, as soon as they left the theater, Shirley seemed to find it essential to get home. He let her go but spent the next few days wondering how to proceed with her. It might have worked out better if Tanni had been with her that night, too. One thing was apparent—at least to him. Shirley was frightened to death of falling in love again. Will hoped he'd be the man to allay her fears.

If he wanted a relationship with Shirley, he'd need to be patient, gentle, persistent. Her nervousness around him had puzzled him at first—but it meant she was aware of him. That gratified Will because he was certainly aware of her. She might be just the woman to tame his restless spirit….

After their movie date, Will had bided his time. Seven restless days later, he'd risked phoning her. He had a good excuse—another of her pieces had sold.

Again he offered to deliver the check, and again she'd refused. But she'd come to the gallery the next day. She seemed distracted and a bit troubled, and he suggested it might help to talk about her problems. He'd felt her hesitation, but in the end she'd agreed to meet him at D.D.'s for dinner on Saturday night. Will had been walking on air ever since.

The waitress brought him a glass of his favorite New Zealand sauvignon blanc. He thanked her with a smile. She was pretty enough. Young, too; no more than thirty-five, with nice legs.

He savored the wine while he waited. He'd arrived early and was already on his second glass when Shirley entered the restaurant. Standing, he greeted her. Always a gentleman, he helped remove her coat, then lightly brushed his lips against her cheek.

He recognized his mistake immediately. He'd moved

too quickly for her, presumed too much. He needed to remember that.

"Sorry I'm late," Shirley said, a little breathless, as she slid into the booth opposite him.

Caught up in his thoughts, Will had lost track of the time. A quick check showed that she'd kept him waiting twelve minutes.

"I'm afraid Tanni and I had an argument," Shirley said, fumbling with her linen napkin as she placed it on her lap. Her face was flushed and he wondered if it was due to the dissension with her daughter or the cold.

Never having had children, Will wasn't sure he should comment. "The teen years can be difficult," he ventured, although he had little or no experience with that age group.

"She's seeing too much of Shaw," Shirley said.

Will motioned to the waitress to take Shirley's drink order. He was pleased when she accepted his suggestion to try the New Zealand wine. "Bring us a bottle," he told the waitress.

Shirley hurried to stop him. "Oh, no, that's far too much! I'm sure I won't drink more than a glass."

"This is one of my favorites. What you don't want, I'll have."

Shirley glanced at the parking lot.

He grinned. "Don't worry, I walked. It's only a few blocks from the gallery."

"Yes. Walking…that's a good idea."

The waitress returned with a bottle, which Will examined. "My ex-wife and I visited the Marlborough region of New Zealand a few years ago and discovered their exquisite wines." He hoped to put Shirley at ease and distract her from the difficulties she'd experienced earlier with her daughter. As he recalled, Tanni was sixteen or seventeen. She'd probably be out of the house soon, attending college in Seattle or elsewhere.

Shirley took her first sip and he could see that she liked the wine. Settling back in the booth, he studied her.

"Tanni and I seem to be at odds more and more," she murmured, her eyes darting around the room.

Obviously this situation was weighing on her and she seemed incapable of setting it aside.

"I wasn't sure I should still meet you for dinner," she said. "I would've canceled if I'd been able to get in touch with you."

Thankfully he must've already left the gallery and she didn't have his cell number.

"This argument with Tanni is about Shaw, you said." If talking helped her, then he was willing to listen.

Shirley gripped the stem of her wineglass and stared into the distance. "They're constantly together. It's...dangerous. Tanni's at a vulnerable point in her life—she was close to her father and she misses him desperately. She and Shaw are too serious, and now that they discovered those remains, it seems everyone wants to question them. I don't know how the press got hold of their names—probably from other kids at school," Shirley said. "The sheriff asked Shaw and Tanni not to say anything but Tanni's been tricked into talking to reporters more than once."

Will sent her a look of sympathy. He'd heard about those skeletal remains; it'd been in the news for weeks. Every time there was the tiniest bit of information, it was blown out of all proportion, and interest was revived. One of the Seattle television stations appeared to be leading the way.

"You'd think, with economic problems, political scandals and natural disasters, there'd be more important things for them to report on," he said.

"But that's exactly why this story is so interesting to people—it's a distraction. An escape. And it's local."

"Yeah, I guess so. And everyone loves a mystery."

"Those reporters have made life for Shaw just as difficult," she went on, "catching him at Mocha Mama's, hounding him for more details. The poor kid doesn't know what to say or do. It's a mess."

Will was finished with this topic—he didn't have anything else to add—but she seemed preoccupied and unsettled. The more she mentioned the incident, the more agitated she became. "The sheriff's doing what he can, but for heaven's sake, those bones have been there for years and years!"

Will nodded; that was true enough.

"All this negative attention has drawn Tanni and Shaw closer together. I think they both need breathing room. A break from each other."

"It couldn't hurt," Will agreed. After a moment, he said, "Shaw's a talented artist. Especially of portraits."

"Tanni is, too," she was quick to remind him.

"Definitely, although she doesn't want her work displayed."

"I don't understand it. Ever since we lost...my husband, Tanni insists her work is for her alone. I'd hoped that once Shaw's portraits were displayed in the gallery, she'd be willing to place a couple of her pieces there, too."

Will had also hoped for that. Not because he felt her work would sell easily. It wouldn't. Her paintings and drawings were dark, moody and didn't really appeal to him. But he believed in presenting a range of work. And if he were to display Tanni's art, he'd have more of an opportunity to talk to Shirley. Maybe not the most commendable of motives, but he couldn't deny it.

"When I saw Tanni before Christmas," he said, "I talked to her about putting her art in the gallery."

"You did?" Shirley's gaze shot to him.

"Yes. She's as good as Shaw, and she's more versatile."

"She wasn't interested, right?"

"Right." He supposed that eventually she'd agree, but he hadn't pressured her. The girl seemed to champion her boyfriend, wanting to give him the edge. She'd soon learn what a mistake *that* was, he thought cynically.

"I appreciate what you've already done for Shaw."

He shrugged. Again, his motives had been far from pure. Yes, Shaw was talented, but Will knew very well that he might not have taken the kid's work to Larry Knight if not for his connection to Shirley.

"I might be able to help you," he said, reaching for his wine.

That immediately got Shirley's interest. "How?"

"The friend I mentioned."

"Yes?"

"It's Larry Knight."

Shirley pressed her hand to her heart. "*The* Larry Knight?"

"Yes. He's from San Diego, but the two of us worked together on a charity function some time ago in Atlanta. We've kept in touch through the years." Actually, Georgia, his ex, had done a lot of the work, heading up the volunteer committee. But she'd never been comfortable in the limelight, unlike Will, who enjoyed being the center of attention. So she'd asked him to handle the public functions.

"You mean to say *Larry Knight*—one of the best-known artists in the country—is the one who looked at Shaw's work?"

"Yes."

"Oh, my goodness…"

"I'm thinking I might ask another favor of Larry," he said. Picking up his menu, he read through it, giving Shirley a chance to consider his words.

"What kind of favor?" Her voice was guarded.

Will glanced over the top of his menu. "As you know, Larry has a…certain amount of influence with art schools around the country."

"Yes…I imagine he would," she said breathlessly.

Will was determined not to offer; he wanted Shirley to ask, wanted her to understand that she was in his debt. He'd had plenty of experience at cajoling and persuading women. Interesting how those skills, for lack of a better word, kicked in so automatically.

"You…said he was impressed with Shaw's work?" she began.

"Larry had quite a bit to say about Shaw." Will set his menu aside. "I believe I'll have the fried oysters. This says they're from the Shelton area."

She nodded absently.

"Have you decided?" he asked.

"Decided?" Her eyes met his; a moment later, she appeared to realize he was referring to her dinner order. "Oh, sorry, I haven't looked." She scanned the list. "Their crab Louie's always been one of my favorites."

"You should try something different."

Her brow creased in a frown. "Why?"

"Be…cause," he said, dragging out the word, "if you're anything like me, you tend to order the same dishes from the same restaurants. Before you know it, you're in a rut."

The lines on her forehead gradually relaxed. "You're

right. That's exactly what I do. I order chili rellenos when I'm eating Mexican and the chicken hot-sauce noodles when I order Chinese."

"Consistency is comforting," he said, "but every once in a while it's good to venture out, try something new. Take a risk." He hoped she understood that he was talking about more than food—that he was referring to their relationship, too.

He guessed she'd been with one man her entire adult life and the thought of being with another intimidated her. Will hoped his advice would expand her view of more than just meal choices.

Shirley picked up the menu again and studied it carefully.

"I recommend the fried oysters," he told her. "I had them for the first time a few weeks ago. See?" he said with a grin. "I tried something new and I liked it."

She shook her head. "I already know I don't like oysters."

Not easily discouraged, Will asked, "When's the last time you ate them?"

"I don't remember."

"Then do it."

She shook her head again. "I could order the seafood sampler—it includes oysters and shrimp and cod."

"Excellent."

"But all that fried food..." She frowned.

Will listened to her go through practically the entire menu, discussing each selection in detail and dismissing one after the other. The waitress returned three times before Shirley was finally ready to order.

She looked at Will and grinned sheepishly. "I'll have the—"

"Oysters," he said, cutting her off. "The lady will try the oysters."

"Actually, I won't," Shirley said. "I'd like the crab Louie." She threw Will an apologetic glance. "I'd rather stick to something familiar."

He wondered if there was a message to him in these words—a response to his message. "I'll give you one of my oysters and you can try it." That seemed a fair compromise.

"Okay."

The waitress left and Shirley had a little more of her wine. "You were telling me about Larry Knight."

"Ah, yes." He rested his back against the polished wood bench and lifted his glass. "Like I was saying, Larry has a lot of sway with art schools around the country."

Shirley soaked in every word. "Do you think he might open doors for Shaw? I mean, I don't know what Shaw's financial situation is. I seem to remember Tanni telling me his father disapproves of Shaw's dream of being an artist. He's an attorney and wants Shaw to attend law school. He'd probably need a scholarship."

That was understood; one look at Shaw was enough to convince Will that the kid didn't have a dime to his name. "I figured he would."

"Would you be willing to do that for Shaw? To ask Larry?"

But Will knew she also welcomed the prospect of Shaw's departure, for her daughter's sake.

"Only if *you* believe Shaw's talent is sufficient," he said.

"Oh, I do," she said earnestly.

Will set his glass on the table, holding on to the stem, gently swirling the wine. "I'm sure Larry gets these sorts of requests all the time."

"I'm sure he does. I didn't mean to imply that he should

recommend Shaw unless his talent warrants such an advantage."

He nodded. "I've already had him look at Shaw's work, so Larry's familiar with what the boy can do."

"Then you'll ask?"

He nodded again, slowly. "I'll call Larry on Monday morning, then let you know what he has to say."

Shirley's face lit up with a huge smile. "I can't tell you how grateful I am."

He couldn't resist the thought that maybe, when the time came, she could *show* him. No, that was the old Will talking, he reminded himself. The new Will wanted something more genuine with this woman. Something lasting.

Their meal was splendid and, true to her word, Shirley sampled one of his oysters.

"Well?" he asked, confident that she'd order them the next time they dined at D.D.'s. "What did you think?"

She smiled across the table at him. "It was better than I remembered. But then, it's hard to find fault with anything deep-fried." With a wry grimace, she added, "That's why I usually stay away from that kind of food."

Will chuckled. "Me, too. But I allow myself extravagances on special occasions." He wanted her to understand that being with her *was* one of those occasions.

"All in all, though..."

"Yes?" he said, eager to hear her verdict.

"I'll stick with the crab Louie."

Fourteen

"Cut off a little more on the sides," thirteen-year-old Jolene instructed Rachel, examining her reflection in the bathroom mirror.

Rachel had set her up in the small hallway bathroom for a haircut. Some of their best conversations came while she was busy with Jolene's hair.

Over the years, Rachel had developed a theory about why that was the case. When she was working on a customer's hair, Rachel was in that person's space—by invitation. This proximity created a sense of intimacy that made clients feel comfortable enough to share some of the most private details of their lives. She figured that was also why so much gossip got started—or at least spread—at hair salons.

"It looks really cute," Rachel said.

Jolene turned her head from side to side. "You think so?" she asked, her voice uncertain.

"I do." Rachel plugged in the electric razor. "Lean forward and tuck your chin down."

"Do you think Dad will like my hair this short?"

"Absolutely," Rachel assured her, although she wasn't

sure. Jolene bowed her head, and Rachel clipped the hair at the base of the girl's neck.

When she'd finished, Jolene raised her head and their eyes met in the bathroom mirror. Slowly Jolene exhaled. "I'm not mad at you and my dad anymore."

"Good." It'd been an uncomfortable week or so after Jolene had caught the two of them in bed in the middle of the afternoon. Rachel could laugh about it now.

Not Bruce.

He'd been in such a state—of embarrassment, frustration and anger—that it'd taken him days to put the incident behind him.

Meanwhile, Jolene had given them both the silent treatment for nearly a week.

"I'm glad you're my stepmother," she said.

"I'm glad I am, too." Rachel held the girl's gaze in the mirror. "I like being your stepmother."

Jolene pointedly broke eye contact. "If I tell you something, do you promise not to be mad?"

Rachel wasn't about to make that kind of promise. "I'll try not to be. Okay?"

"Okay." With an exaggerated sigh, the girl repeated, "I'm glad you're my stepmother," then added, "but I really wish you and my dad weren't married."

The words stung and Rachel couldn't respond for a moment. "I love you and your father very much, Jolene. It's important for me to be part of your family."

"I know. Dad needs you...and I do, too. I feel selfish and mean for...for complaining."

"Then we should talk about it." Rachel needed to put aside her own emotions and listen carefully to what Jolene was saying. "Tell me why you feel this way."

Rachel sat on the edge of the bathtub, hands braced

on either side, ankles crossed, hoping that if she looked relaxed, she'd encourage Jolene to confide in her.

"But…I don't want you to get mad at me."

Rachel shook her head and reached out to give the girl's shoulder a gentle squeeze.

Jolene kept her head lowered. "Before you and Dad got married, I was afraid that if…if you moved into the house, Dad wouldn't have time for me anymore."

"Do you think that's happened?"

"No," she said after a moment. "Not exactly."

That was good, because Rachel knew Bruce had put a lot of effort into spending extra time with his daughter. He did more than drop her off at basketball practice these days. Twice now he'd stayed and watched, just so Jolene would know he was interested. Naturally, when the actual games started, Bruce and Rachel would attend them together.

"What do you mean, not exactly?" she asked, unwilling to leave the smallest detail unexplored.

"It isn't just Dad," Jolene whispered.

"I'm not sure what you mean."

"You were always my…special friend. I could talk to you about anything."

"That hasn't changed." At least, not to Rachel it hadn't.

"Yes, it has," Jolene insisted.

"Okay," Rachel said. "Tell me how."

"Well…" The girl seemed at a loss. Then she blurted out, "I'm just going to say it, all right?"

"Of course."

"I see how my dad looks at you."

"With love?" she asked, hoping that was the answer.

Jolene shook her head. "He wants to get you into bed so you can do…*that.*"

"Make love," she elaborated. This was what she'd expected…and feared. It was probably best to have the conversation, bring it out in the open once and for all. "Married couples make love, Jolene. It's a normal and healthy part of marriage."

"Dad wants to do it all the time." Jolene sounded mortified. "He doesn't think I notice, but I do. And that's not all. You're my friend and now I have to share you with my dad and I don't want to and…and I have to share my dad with you." This came out on one long breath. Jolene's eyes met hers in the mirror again. "Am I making any sense?"

"Yes, you are," Rachel told her. "You're making a lot of sense."

"Things are…different. Just like I was afraid they'd be."

Rachel couldn't argue with her. But perhaps she could explain it to Jolene in a way she'd find more reassuring. "That happens when a couple's first married," she said.

"You mean it'll stop?" the girl asked hopefully.

Rachel did her best to hide a smile. "Not…completely."

"Oh."

"Does that answer your questions?"

Jolene looked at her fearfully. "Are you pregnant?" she asked, as if this would be truly dreadful, the most dreadful thing she could imagine.

"No."

The girl's shoulders relaxed. "Good."

Rachel felt it was critical to address Jolene's concerns about her marriage to Bruce before they even thought about adding to the family.

"I know you were afraid that once your father and I were married, we'd be so involved with each other you'd feel excluded."

Jolene's gaze held hers.

"We've tried very hard to make sure that hasn't happened."

Jolene shrugged, raising one shoulder. "Yeah, but I wish…you know."

Unfortunately, Rachel did. This was becoming more than a minor problem, not only for Jolene but for her and Bruce, too. Being discovered that one afternoon had had a devastating effect on their love life. They'd barely touched since.

If, as Jolene claimed, Bruce looked at her longingly, there was a very good reason. They were both experiencing sexual frustration.

That evening Rachel had dinner ready by the time Bruce walked into the house. "How are my girls?" he asked, pausing to kiss Rachel on the cheek.

"Hey, Dad," Jolene said. "What do you think?" She waltzed into the living room and twirled around so her father could see her new haircut. "Rachel said you wouldn't mind if I got it cut real short. You like it, don't you?"

"Ah…"

Rachel cast him a pleading glance.

"It takes some getting used to."

"But you like it?"

He grinned and managed to nod enthusiastically.

Overjoyed, Jolene rushed to his side and threw her arms around him.

"Would you set the table, please?" Rachel asked her. She followed Bruce down the hallway and into the bedroom. He usually showered as soon as he got home from work.

The moment their door closed, Bruce pulled her into his arms and kissed her hungrily.

Rachel eased her mouth from his. "We need to talk."

"Now?"

"No, later, after Jolene's asleep."

"I have other plans for then."

Rachel dropped eager kisses along his neck. "I do, too, but we need to talk first."

When he started to protest, she kissed him again. "I'll make it worth your while," she said seductively.

Sliding his hands up and down her arms, Bruce's eyes melted into hers. "I'm holding you to that."

Quietly she slid out the door and hurried back to the kitchen.

Jolene frowned at her and set the water glasses on the table with a lot of unnecessary noise.

Rachel was willing to be patient and understanding, but she couldn't allow a thirteen-year-old to dictate the terms of her marriage.

"I love your father, Jolene," she said, looking directly into the girl's eyes, "and if I want to talk to him alone for a few minutes that shouldn't upset you."

Jolene nodded contritely. "I know."

"Okay, then."

The evening passed, with everyone involved in various tasks—laundry, homework, bill paying—and other than Bruce making exaggerated yawning noises and darting glances at the master bedroom, everything went smoothly.

"Isn't it your bedtime?" he asked Jolene when the clock chimed nine-thirty. He and Rachel were watching TV by then.

She closed her textbook and kissed them both on the cheek. "Night."

"I'm going to watch the news," Rachel announced.

She wanted Jolene to understand that they weren't going to jump into bed the minute she was out of sight.

"I guess I will, too," Bruce muttered.

Jolene walked past Rachel and rolled her eyes. The kid wasn't fooled.

When their daughter's bedroom door shut, Bruce shifted closer to Rachel. "Okay, talk to me."

Rachel had been waiting for this moment all evening. "Jolene and I had a good discussion today while I cut her hair. She talked about you and me and her place in this family." Rachel wouldn't tell him *everything* Jolene had shared.

"You're my wife!"

"Yes, but—"

Bruce grimaced, unwilling to listen. "You know, I'm getting sick of this. I've done my best to be sensitive to Jolene's feelings. I've spent more time with her in the past two months than at any—"

"Yes, it's just that—"

"The frustration is killing me, Rachel. I want to make love to my wife. I'm sick and tired of tiptoeing around my daughter and her insecurities. The longer we kowtow to her, the more complicated and difficult this becomes."

"But, Bruce—"

Again he cut her off. "What we need is time away, just the two of us."

"No," she countered swiftly. She couldn't disagree more. "That'll make every insecurity Jolene already has that much worse. She's feeling excluded as it is. Sharing me, sharing you… If we abandon her for even a week-end, it'll feel like a betrayal."

Bruce stared at her for several seconds before throwing his head back, eyes closed. "I don't believe this."

"We haven't been married very long. Give Jolene a chance. The two of us made progress today."

Bruce exhaled and finally nodded.

The ten o'clock news came on, and they cuddled together on the sofa. They held hands, and every now and then he'd lean forward to kiss the side of her face. Rachel's eyes drifted shut as a river of awareness flowed through her.

"Do you think she's asleep yet?" Bruce whispered after the last news segment.

"I certainly hope so."

"Not as much as I do..."

Turning out the lights as they went, Bruce led Rachel down the hallway to their bedroom. He didn't bother with the light. Rachel heard him slip out of his clothes. She did, as well.

They got into bed, and Bruce reached for her. Rachel moved into his arms. They kissed passionately, caressing each other, until she was weak with longing.

"So far, so good," Bruce whispered.

"So far very good," she whispered back and the kissing continued.

The bed creaked, and it seemed to reverberate through the room. They both froze.

There was a long hesitation, in which they held themselves suspended, afraid to move or even breathe.

Then they heard Jolene's bedroom door open.

The sound of the door was followed by the patter of feet going down the hallway to the bathroom.

"What if she comes in here?" Rachel whispered.

"She wouldn't dare," Bruce muttered fiercely.

Rachel ran her hands tenderly down her husband's back. "Do we risk it? Remember what happened last time."

Groaning, Bruce rolled away from her. Without a word, he marched into the master bathroom and a moment later she heard the shower.

Rachel didn't need him to tell her he'd turned on the cold water.

Fifteen

"Dad, you've got to *do* something," Megan wailed.

Troy Davis had just walked into his house when the kitchen phone rang. He picked up, not surprised to hear his daughter's voice; she'd left a message at the office but he'd forgotten to call her back. Troy's day had been interesting and he was eager for an opportunity to analyze what he'd learned that afternoon. The coroner's office had finally sent him the complete report on the remains discovered in the cave, and the information had given him pause, to say the least. He needed an opportunity to digest what had been revealed and decide how to proceed. His one hope was that media interest had died down sufficiently to let this latest development pass without attention.

"Dad, are you listening to me?" Megan asked impatiently.

"What is it you want me to do something about?" Troy asked, just so she'd know he'd heard her the first time.

"You didn't return my call," she said.

"I was in a meeting."

"I know, that's what Cody said, but I asked him to explain that this was important."

Troy's assistant had mentioned the phone call and that Megan had sounded upset. "I'm sorry, sweetheart, I had every intention of phoning you back, but time got away from me." He didn't want Megan to feel he didn't consider her calls important; however, since she'd gotten pregnant, his daughter seemed to be in a perpetual state of crisis. "Tell me what's wrong," he said, setting the mail on the kitchen counter. The microwave clock told him it was ten to seven, which explained why his stomach was growling. He hadn't even had a chance to remove his coat. A light rain had begun and tapped against the kitchen window.

"It's about Faith," Megan began.

Troy stiffened. "What's happened now? Has there been another disturbance?" He'd been worried about the prowler and wondered if she'd taken his advice and installed an alarm. He hoped she'd asked Grace and Cliff about a motion sensor light, too. He'd recently checked with his deputies about the neighborhood; according to Deputy Weaver, things had been quiet on Rosewood Lane. If anyone was pestering Faith, she hadn't reported it, nor had she contacted Troy.

"Nothing's happened at the house that I know of—not that Faith's said, anyway."

"Then what's the problem?"

Megan sighed and he was afraid she might break into tears, an occurrence that had become commonplace in the past few months. It'd been the same with Sandy, Troy recalled. His wife's emotions had been volatile during her pregnancy.

"Faith's *moving,*" Megan said, her voice low.

Frankly, Troy didn't blame her. In fact, he approved.

"Well?" Megan demanded.

"Well, what? Actually, I think it's a good idea."

"You can't mean that," Megan said with a gasp. "What's the matter with you? You can't let Faith move away! You just can't."

Clearly Troy was missing something. "Okay, let's go over this again. Start from the beginning."

"Okay," Megan said impatiently. "I met her for lunch. We do that every so often, you know."

Troy did, and was grateful for any information his daughter could provide regarding Faith.

"She's helping me with the blanket I'm knitting for the baby. I'm practically finished and it's really nice."

Troy smiled, excited all over again at the prospect of becoming a grandfather. He knew one thing for sure—his grandchild was going to be a very spoiled baby.

"She almost didn't tell me. In fact, I had the distinct feeling Faith wasn't going to mention it."

"She realized you'd eventually pass it on to me."

"Probably," Megan agreed. "At any rate, just as we were leaving and Faith was putting on her coat, she said she'd decided to move. She said that coming back to Cedar Cove had been a mistake. Her home in Seattle sold so quickly, she hadn't thought everything through. Now she thinks it might be better if she left the area entirely."

Shock rippled through Troy.

"Aren't you going to say anything?" Megan asked.

Troy couldn't speak for a moment. Faith wasn't moving from one house to another; she'd be moving to another town. Troy knew why. She wanted to get away from him.

"I...see," he finally managed.

"You aren't going to *let* her leave, are you?" Megan

asked, sounding like a little girl who wasn't happy with the answer she'd been given.

"There's nothing I can do to stop her."

"Dad!"

The shock was still fresh and he hadn't absorbed this new information. So Faith was leaving town. He wanted to protest, demand she reconsider, but he had no right to ask. All he could do was stand back and keep his opinions to himself.

"I'm not seeing Faith anymore," he reminded Megan.

"But you love her."

Troy didn't deny it. He did love Faith. Her plan to leave Cedar Cove cut him to the quick, but he couldn't think of a single thing he could do to change her mind.

"How do Scott and his family feel about this?" Troy asked. One reason Faith had moved to town was to be closer to her son and grandchildren.

"I asked her that," Megan told him. "And she pointed out that her daughter, Jay Lynn, lives in north Seattle. Jay Lynn said that after all the problems Faith's had in Cedar Cove, she should consider leaving."

He doubted Jay Lynn was referring only to the prowler. He felt she was insinuating that the disappointment he'd brought into Faith's life was a problem, too—a good reason to leave. Troy couldn't blame her family. They were concerned about their mother's physical and emotional welfare.

"Daddy, you have to do *something,*" Megan said again.

Troy leaned against the kitchen counter. "I'll do whatever I can." Although he had no idea what that would be…

"I like Faith so much."

"I know." He liked Faith, too—more than liked her—and he wished he could persuade her to stay in Cedar Cove.

"Thank you, Daddy. You'll find a way. I'm sure you will."

A couple of minutes later, the conversation ended with Megan inviting him to dinner the following weekend, and Troy replaced the receiver.

The day just seemed to get more complicated. Needing a distraction, he walked into the living room and switched on the evening news, wondering if the Seattle TV stations had gotten wind of the coroner's report. Thankfully there was nothing.

After half an hour or so, he decided it was time to eat. Searching through the cupboards, he found a can of chili. Opening it, he dumped the contents into a bowl, which he set in the microwave. While his meal warmed, he sorted through the mail, his thoughts still on Faith.

"No!" He said the word aloud. Megan was right; he had to talk to Faith, convince her that leaving Cedar Cove would be wrong. He didn't know if he'd be able to talk her out of this—or if he even had the right to try. The thing was, he couldn't idly stand by because Faith meant too much to him. She *belonged* here.

He reached for the phone just as his chili was done. Ignoring it, he punched out her number. The phone rang four times before the answering machine informed him that no one was home. Rather than leave a message, he hung up.

More depressed than ever, Troy paced the kitchen, gulping down spoonfuls of chili as he considered his options.

Perhaps it was just as well that he hadn't spoken to Faith, he told himself. If she felt she had to escape Cedar Cove, then maybe he should simply let her go.

That conviction stayed with him for five whole days—until late Wednesday afternoon. On his drive home, Troy saw Faith's car in the Safeway parking lot. He needed bread, anyway, he reasoned, and pulled into a space as far from hers as he could find. He didn't want Faith to assume he was seeking her out—although, in truth, he was.

The weather, overcast and gloomy, matched his mood. Ever since Megan's phone call, his appetite had vanished and he wasn't sleeping well. Although he longed to talk to Faith, he realized he couldn't ask her to remain in Cedar Cove, and yet…he had to. If she left, he'd always regret it.

After their last meeting, he'd felt hopeful that at some point they'd be able to put their differences behind them. He didn't know anymore. Although he'd developed good instincts about people and situations in his years of police work, he couldn't read Faith or understand her feelings.

Two weeks ago, when she'd called him about the intruder outside her bedroom window, reconciliation had actually seemed possible. He'd been depressed after seeing her with Will Jefferson, but that night he'd let her know how much he loved and needed her. He hadn't used those precise words but he couldn't have made his feelings any more obvious.

The way he figured it, the next move was hers. He hadn't pressured her, assuming his patience would eventually be rewarded. Apparently he'd been wrong.

By the time Troy had walked across the Safeway parking lot and grabbed a cart, his coat was damp. Once inside, he did a wide sweep of the perimeter, hurrying past the deli, the fresh fruits and vegetables and then the frozen-food section. Finally he spotted Faith halfway down one of the center aisles. She appeared to be reading the back of a box of pasta.

Attempting to look casual, he entered that aisle and

slowed down as he drew close. Faith glanced up and her eyes widened when she saw him.

"Hello, Troy."

He inclined his head in acknowledgment and maneuvered his empty cart next to hers. He wished he'd had the foresight to toss in a few items to give her the impression that he'd been in the store a while.

"Faith," he murmured.

They stared at each other a long moment, and Troy decided to wait her out, let her speak first. Silence was a common investigative technique; most people felt uncomfortable with a gap in the conversation and rushed to fill it. They often revealed more than they intended.

"How are you?" she asked awkwardly after half a minute of silence.

When he was speaking to a suspect, Troy generally answered a question with one of his own. He did that now. "Did you have that security system installed like I suggested?"

"I did and it was worth every penny," she told him. "It's given me peace of mind."

He reached for a bag of spaghetti noodles and dropped it into his cart, as if that was the sole reason he'd come grocery shopping. Her reaction to his next question would tell him everything he needed to know.

"When's moving day?"

She blanched. "Oh, so Megan told you."

"Wasn't that what you wanted?"

Frowning, she looked down at her cart as though she'd forgotten something on her list and couldn't remember what it might be.

"Wasn't it?" he repeated, unwilling to let her sidestep the question.

Her shoulders sagged. "I suppose I did," she mumbled.

"You couldn't have phoned me yourself?"

"I...I..." She shifted her weight and stared down at the floor; he could tell his questions unsettled her. "Every time I see you lately, you're angry." She looked up and met his gaze.

"I'm not angry," he said. "You're welcome to live wherever you wish. If you want to move away from Cedar Cove, then be my guest." He snapped his mouth shut before he could say another word.

Faith's head flew back. Her eyes narrowed and he could see the anger welling up inside her. Biting her lip, she placed both hands on her cart and began to walk away.

He started after her, shoving his cart ahead of him. "Faith! Hold on a minute."

She disregarded him, rounding the corner with long strides. He was catching up, feeling like a participant in a stock-car race, when he heard a familiar voice behind him.

"Sheriff Davis!"

Troy reluctantly came to a halt, and glanced over his shoulder to find Louie Benson wheeling his grocery cart toward him. *Not now,* Troy thought. But he was trapped. Much as he wanted to hurry after Faith, he dared not ignore the mayor.

"I'm glad I caught you," Louie said.

Troy offered him a weak smile. "What can I do for you?"

"I read the coroner's final report but haven't had a chance to discuss the details with you. I assume you've read it?"

"I did," Troy replied crisply, trying to defer this. He

wanted to apologize to Faith, make amends if it wasn't already too late.

The mayor hesitated. "Did you see the statement that, judging by the skull, the young man had Down syndrome?"

"I did."

"This opens up an entirely new front in your investigation, doesn't it?"

"I—"

"I just hope the media doesn't pick up on it," he murmured.

"So do I," Troy said. He was off duty and wanted out of this conversation. "If you'll excuse me, there's someone I need to talk to."

"Of course. Sorry if I interrupted you."

"It's okay," Troy said, rushing down the aisle, abandoning his cart. If he was lucky, he might still be able to catch up with Faith and apologize.

Luck was with him, and he saw her at the checkout stand. He waited outside until she'd finished paying for her groceries.

As soon as she stepped through the doors into the gloomy afternoon, he approached her. "I'd like to apologize, Faith."

"What for?" she asked, moving past him.

Troy had seen that expression before and knew it wasn't a good sign.

"I came at you like…like an angry bear."

"Not at all," she countered, walking purposefully toward the parking lot.

Troy followed her.

"You were right," she said. "I was foolish to mention my plans to Megan. It was the coward's way out and I was immediately sorry I'd done it." Her pace clipped, she headed for her vehicle.

"You *wanted* me to know." She'd admitted to using Megan to inform him of her plans. He couldn't help feeling encouraged by that.

Perhaps Faith had done this, spoken to Megan, because she secretly—or not so secretly—hoped he'd talk her out of it. Maybe this was her way of telling him she'd prefer not to leave, that she wanted him back in her life. Instead, Troy had gone on the attack. He felt like kicking himself for being so insensitive.

"Like I said, it was wrong of me to tell Megan, knowing she'd pass the word along," Faith said stiffly. "You see, I didn't want to phone you directly, because I was trying to avoid unnecessary contact. The less we see of each other, the better. I'm sure you agree."

Troy's jaw tightened.

Faith opened the car door and shoved her shopping bags inside.

Not giving him a chance to respond, she climbed into the front seat and slammed the door shut. The engine roared to life and she pulled out of her parking space before Troy could say another word.

Well, that was that.

His prospects with Faith couldn't look any worse.

Sixteen

With property values lower than he'd ever seen them, Mack McAfee figured there was no better time to purchase a house. He'd been looking on and off for an investment ever since he'd moved to Cedar Cove. When the real estate agent had shown him the duplex on Evergreen Place, he'd made his decision.

A few years earlier, Mack had bought a home in north Seattle that was badly in need of repair. He'd managed to get it cheap and spent most weekends putting on a new roof, replacing the kitchen countertops, installing new carpeting and doing whatever else was needed to update the house. He'd put a lot of effort into the improvements, most of which he'd done himself. Over the years he'd picked up various skills doing odd jobs. When he'd finished the house, right down to the landscaping, he'd planned to move in, but someone had driven past one afternoon, stopped and made him an offer on the spot. A healthy six-figure profit had been sitting in the bank ever since, collecting interest.

The duplex was the perfect house to invest that money

in. It was an older place, one story, with two doors on either side of a shared walkway. The building was in decent shape, but there was room for improvement. With a substantial down payment, he could live in one half and rent out the other. He put in an offer, which was accepted the next day. He'd just signed the papers and was driving home when his cell phone jingled, indicating that he had a text message.

He waited until he'd pulled into the apartment parking lot before checking his cell. When he saw Mary Jo's name on call display, he reacted immediately, his heart speeding up with excitement. They communicated quite a bit, usually by texting. She sent him regular updates on baby Noelle, often including photographs. He was careful not to overdo it with Mary Jo, since she was still emotionally fragile after her experience with David Rhodes. He'd been tempted to send her flowers for Valentine's Day, but felt that was too much, too soon. Mack was willing to bide his time. He knew he wanted to pursue a relationship with Mary Jo; meanwhile, he enjoyed their "conversations" and occasional visits.

Today it wasn't a picture of Noelle that she'd sent. Instead, it was a request. Can U meet me this afternoon?

He typed his response, eager to see her and the baby. Tell me when & where. Fortuitously this was one of his days off. He pushed the send button and sat in his truck, awaiting her response. It wasn't long in coming.

I'll take Bremerton ferry. Gets in 2:30.

I'll pick U up. He punched out the letters as fast as his fingers could type.

It was now quarter after one. Mack bolted down a sandwich, then showered and changed his clothes. He'd started cleaning the apartment but caught sight of the time and rushed out the door.

When the Bremerton ferry slid into the dock, Mack was standing outside the terminal. The walk-on passengers disembarked first, and he saw Mary Jo with the baby almost right away. She smiled and waved, and he returned the gesture.

Noelle was bundled up in an infant carrier that doubled as a car seat. Only her knit cap was showing, above a yellow blanket. Mack hurried to meet Mary Jo and took the heavy carrier from her hands.

He moved the blanket aside, smiling down at the baby. Noelle stared up at him and gurgled a greeting—at least, he chose to interpret the sound as one of recognition and greeting. A smile broke out across his face. He was sure that what he felt for this baby was love, pure and simple. He'd read about the bonding phenomenon and wondered if he'd been susceptible to it, since he'd brought her into the world. Maybe she'd imprinted herself on his heart when she was born.

And Mary Jo… He found himself thinking about her far more than he should. Over the years he'd gone out with plenty of women, but no one had captivated him the way she had. He realized she wasn't ready to enter into a new relationship, but he wanted her to understand that he was nothing like Noelle's father.

"I'm so glad you could meet me," Mary Jo said as they reached his truck.

"I am, too," he murmured. He tucked the baby carrier in the back and buckled it in place, then helped Mary Jo climb into the passenger seat and got in himself.

Once they were inside with the heater blasting warm air, he waited for Mary Jo to tell him why she'd found it necessary to escape in the middle of the week. "So, are you here for any particular reason?" he asked, which was probably more direct than he should've been.

"Nothing really," she said. "I needed to get away for a while. I hope I didn't interfere with your plans. I remember you telling me you had Tuesdays off this month. Was I being presumptuous?"

"Not at all." He wanted her to know her company was always welcome.

"It's just that...well, an afternoon out sounded like a good idea."

"Your brothers?" Mack asked. Linc, Mel and Ned were often a topic of conversation between them.

Mary Jo fastened her seat belt and, without glancing in his direction, nodded.

"I thought so."

"I hope you don't mind. I haven't been back to Cedar Cove since the night Noelle was born and..." She let the rest fade. A moment later she resumed the conversation. "I've kept in touch with Grace and Cliff. They're the nicest people."

Mack shared her opinion. He was beginning to make friends in Cedar Cove, and the Hardings were people he wanted to know better. "I was surprised—but definitely pleased—to get your message," he told her truthfully.

Her smile was shy. "I'm glad. I like texting you," she said. "It's as if I'm talking to a good friend."

"I feel the same way." Generally she initiated their conversations, which was fine with him. He knew he had to let Mary Jo set the pace.

"Anyplace you'd like to go?" he asked.

"Would it be all right if we stopped at the library and visited Grace?"

"Of course." Grace had opened her home and her heart to Mary Jo on Christmas Eve; it was only natural that she'd want to see the woman who'd been so kind. "Off to the library we go."

The drive around the cove took about thirty minutes, and Mack used that time to draw Mary Jo out regarding her three brothers. She didn't say much other than that they were suffocating her with their concern. Mack was properly sympathetic but careful not to seem too critical. The baby slept the entire way. According to Mary Jo, Noelle seemed to be suffering less with colic these days. The doctor had said it could last as long as three months but rarely beyond that.

When they entered Cedar Cove, Mack pulled up in front of the library and helped Mary Jo and Noelle out. Then he went in search of a parking spot in the adjacent lot. By the time he returned, he found Mary Jo at the checkout desk chatting with Grace, the head librarian. Grace smiled at him.

"I called Olivia," she said, "and told her Mary Jo was coming in for a visit. She asked to join us."

"Great." He tried to sound enthusiastic, but he was slightly jealous that these ladies would have Mary Jo and Noelle to themselves when he'd been looking forward to being alone with them.

"I arranged for tea and cookies in the break room," Grace added. "I hope you'll stay."

Now he was expected to be part of a tea party. If the crew at the fire station heard about this, there'd be no end to the razzing. The whole situation was just too…feminine. "Why don't the three of you visit while I run a few errands," he suggested.

Mary Jo's eyes begged him to reconsider. "Please stay."

"Well…okay. Unless I'm intruding."

"You wouldn't be," Grace told him.

Mary Jo touched his arm, mutely imploring, and Mack didn't see how he could decline. Without further protest, he joined Grace and Noelle in the back room.

As Mary Jo unbundled Noelle, Olivia Griffin arrived. She wore a knit cap over a head scarf, but it was easy to see that she was bald underneath. Still, despite the cancer, despite the treatments she was undergoing, the judge exuded vitality. He'd met her Christmas Eve, the night of the birth, and he'd always heard good things about her. His parents only had praise for Olivia, as a friend and as a judge; he could certainly understand why. This was one impressive woman.

Grace and Olivia paid plenty of attention to Noelle. The baby laughed and cooed, and Mack experienced a sense of fatherly pride he had no right to feel. Noelle gripped his finger, apparently determined not to let go.

"I asked Mack to pick me up at the Bremerton ferry this afternoon," Mary Jo explained as Grace poured tea all around. "I had to get away for a few hours. The boys are driving me crazy."

"Her brothers," Mack said, leaning forward.

He left his tea and unfastened Noelle from her carrier, adeptly scooping her up as if he'd done exactly this dozens of times. While the women chatted, he walked around the room, gently stroking Noelle's back. Her head wobbled a little; then she rested it against his shoulder and promptly fell asleep. Every once in a while, he met Mary Jo's eyes and they smiled at each other.

"So, what's going on with your brothers?" Grace asked, holding out a plate of oatmeal cookies.

Olivia shook her head, while Mary Jo accepted one.

She sighed. "Oh…they all seem to know what's best for me and the baby. Before I met David, I was saving money to get a place of my own. I had quite a bit set aside. Then I found out I was pregnant. After that, with all the stuff I needed for the baby, I didn't have any choice but to stay with my brothers."

"You're feeling the need to move out?"

Mary Jo nodded. "Oh, yes. They mean well and I appreciate everything they've done for me, but…it's time. Noelle's almost two months old and I need to think about getting a job again."

"It's too bad you can't return to the place you worked before," Grace said.

"Why not?" Olivia asked. "They can't fire you for having a baby!"

"The insurance company had to downsize, and my position disappeared right after the first of the year. I got a severance package, but that won't last forever. I have to find a way to support Noelle and me and still be a good mother."

Although he wasn't part of the conversation, Mack interjected his opinion. "You could always move to this side of Puget Sound." He'd probably come across as too eager but he couldn't contain his enthusiasm.

"You could," Olivia agreed.

Grace nodded and brushed her hands free of cookie crumbs.

Mary Jo glanced from one to the other. "I'd like that, I really would, but as I said I'd need a job and a place to live, and it all seems impossible at the moment."

"I saw my brother last week," Olivia said. "And he mentioned that he's looking for part-time help."

Mary Jo's eyes brightened and then just as quickly

dimmed. "I'd need more hours if I was going to pay for child care and our living costs. Babies are expensive."

Olivia seemed undaunted. "Will said the position would expand as the gallery picked up more business. Do you have accounting and office skills?"

"I do," Mary Jo told them. "In fact, I worked in the accounting department at the insurance company."

"Wonderful!" Olivia clapped her hands delightedly.

"But there's day care and rent…and who's to say your brother would find me a suitable employee?"

"I'm sure he will," Olivia said.

"As for day care—" Grace jumped into the conversation "—my younger daughter told me just this morning that she's looking for a means of adding to their family income. Kelly's a stay-at-home mom with a baby of her own. Taking care of Noelle would be perfect for her."

"And I know of a place to live," Mack said. "A duplex that's about to become available. The rent's extremely reasonable." He hadn't consciously thought of this before, but maybe the idea had been there all along….

Everything was obviously moving much too fast for Mary Jo. "I'll have to think about this."

"That would be wise," Olivia said as Grace nodded. "This is a big step."

"But a necessary one," Mary Jo murmured. Glancing up at Mack, who still held Noelle in his arms, she said, "And there's someone other than me to consider now. A move will affect Noelle, too."

"In a good way," Mack said.

"I hope so." Mary Jo spoke hesitantly. "I've made so many wrong decisions in my life that if I do move to Cedar Cove, I'll have to work everything out beforehand. Just to be sure…"

The women talked for another ten or fifteen minutes and then Mack noticed that Olivia seemed to tire. Grace noticed it, too, and got up to carry the tea things to the staff kitchen while Mary Jo bundled up Noelle. Mack had reluctantly handed over the sleeping infant, hoping he'd have the chance to hold her again.

When they left the library, Mack drove them to his apartment. It was small, but the view of the cove was unbeatable. While he hurried about straightening up the place—he wished he'd done that earlier—Mary Jo stood in the living room, gazing thoughtfully out at the water with the navy ships gleaming in the distance.

"Do you want to tell me what's really going on with your brothers?" he asked.

Abruptly she turned to face him. "They want me to go after David," she said.

Mack frowned. "Go after him?"

"For child support. I understand what they're saying, and they have a point. On the surface, anyway. David has a responsibility to support Noelle. She *is* his child and a blood test will prove it."

An automatic objection formed, but he managed to quell it. Biologically—and in no other way—David was Noelle's father. The man was nothing more than a sperm donor.

"The thing is, I don't want David in my life," Mary Jo said emphatically, "and I certainly don't want him to have access to Noelle."

"Based on everything I've heard, I think you're right."

Her expression softened. "I'm so grateful you agree with me. Linc's adamant that David pay support. I've told my brother that David has constant money problems, but Linc still believes he should pay. How's he going to do *that?*"

"In other words, there's no getting blood out of a turnip."

Mary Jo glanced down. "I wouldn't care if he had all the money in the world. I still wouldn't want my daughter anywhere near him."

Again Mack agreed.

"Ben Rhodes has generously set up a trust fund for Noelle, like he did for David's other daughter. He also offered to help me financially, knowing his son either couldn't or wouldn't."

"Yeah, I remember. Are you sure you should turn him down?"

"Yes," Mary Jo was quick to tell him. "I wouldn't feel good about it."

Mack understood—and shared—her point of view.

"I really like this town," Mary Jo said next in a transparent effort to change the subject. "From the moment I stepped off the ferry on Christmas Eve, I felt at peace here, almost as if…as if I belonged. I suspect that when I asked to visit this afternoon, I was secretly hoping to find a way for Noelle and me to live here."

"I'd be happy if you did."

Their eyes held and Mack felt the tension building between them. Under other circumstances he might have kissed her but he was afraid of frightening her off.

Mack was a patient man, though. He knew what he wanted, and every minute he spent with Mary Jo and Noelle made him more aware of what that was.

Seventeen

Charlotte Rhodes worried about Ben as she poured his first coffee of the day while he retrieved the morning paper from the porch.

Ben just hadn't been himself since returning from the cruise. Even her special homemade coconut cake didn't interest him, and that was *highly* unusual.

When they'd come home from the Caribbean, she'd assumed his malady was physical. In the weeks since, she'd realized that what ailed him was emotional. Her husband was depressed.

"The Seniors' Potluck is this afternoon," she reminded him as she carried in his coffee. Harry, her cat, had curled up on Ben's lap and made himself comfortable. Harry hadn't initially accepted Ben, but once he had, the cat had become her husband's constant companion.

"Would you mind if I skipped it this time?" Ben mumbled from behind the paper.

Charlotte started to protest, then stopped herself. "Aren't you feeling well?" she asked, sitting on the ottoman by his chair. She rested her hand on his knee and gazed up at him, wanting so desperately to help.

Ben lowered the paper and looked at her briefly, then stared into the distance. "I'm fine," he said with a half-hearted smile. "I'd just prefer to stay home this afternoon."

"All right, dear, if that's what you want."

"I do." He reached out his hand to squeeze hers. "Thanks for understanding."

After lingering for a moment, Charlotte returned to the bedroom, where she dressed and got ready for her day. She'd never, ever thought Ben would purposely avoid the Seniors' Potluck. It was the social highlight of their month, when they saw their dearest friends. Half the widows in town were in love with Ben, and Charlotte knew why. He wasn't only handsome, charming and witty, he was a man of integrity. He'd truly blessed her life.

All their friends were bound to ask about him and she wasn't sure what to say. Well, she'd think of something. Poor Ben. She had to assume his depression stemmed, at least in part, from his son David's appalling behavior. She wished she knew how to help him through this, yet she felt at a loss. Offering comfort and reassurance was all she could do.

As soon as she'd finished dressing, Charlotte went back to the kitchen to prepare her contribution for that day's potluck. As in most family homes, the kitchen was the center of activity. Not only did she do her cooking and baking there, but her best thinking took place while standing in front of the sink, washing dishes. Most serious discussions with her children had taken place here, as well.

What to bring to the potluck? Her broccoli lasagna had been a huge hit in January, and she'd received numerous requests for the recipe. In fact, these meals generally turned into a recipe exchange. Some of her favorite ones came from the potlucks, and from wakes, too. The recipe for the best casserole she'd ever tasted had come from the wake for her husband Clyde's dearest friend, Sam. Every time she served it, she thought of him. Of *both* of them.

"Ben," she said, stepping out of the kitchen as she tied her apron around her waist. "Should I bring the stuffed peppers or my chicken potpie?"

He didn't respond right away, as if he was considering the decision. "The potpie."

"Good. I was leaning toward that myself."

He nodded.

"I'll make three, so there'll be plenty for you, and I'll take one over to Olivia and Jack this afternoon."

"Great idea." He set aside the paper to pet Harry, who slept contentedly in his lap.

Charlotte returned to the kitchen and got out the flour and lard. None of those store-bought piecrusts for her! She had the time and a recipe she'd inherited from her mother, one that couldn't be matched.

"Come and chat with me," she called out to Ben as she kneaded the flour and lard. The dough was soft and supple; her mother had always warned her not to knead it too long, but the timing had become a matter of instinct. Charlotte sighed. Her mother, God rest her soul, had been a wonderful cook.

Some of the recipes she'd been collecting for Justine and her new restaurant were from Charlotte's mother. Admittedly, there were a few that were a bit challenging to translate for a modern kitchen—and a cook who couldn't spend all day preparing them!

"What's so amusing?" Ben asked as he slid into a kitchen chair.

"Oh, I was just thinking about my mother and her recipe for dumplings."

"Oh?"

"For years she told me it was a secret family recipe. Some secret. Flour and water were the two main ingredients."

"That's it?"

"Oh, there are a couple of other things, but no big deal. The real secret was in cooking them for a good long while. That's what she used to say—a good long while. I decided that was too vague and imprecise for Justine, so I left the recipe out."

"Have you given them to her yet?"

"No, but the collection's nearly ready." Many of the original recipes had been lost over the years—or never written down—and Charlotte had to reconstruct them from memory. The project had helped fill the dreary winter days. With Ben so depressed lately, she'd stayed close to home.

"I feel guilty using grilled chicken from the deli in this potpie," Charlotte confessed. She'd picked up two of them the day before, since they came in handy and never went to waste.

Ben dismissed her concern. "No one will know."

"I will, but it's nearly as tasty and it does save me time."

Ben got up and poured himself a second cup of coffee. "I heard from David yesterday afternoon."

Charlotte's hands momentarily stilled. The call must have come while she was out getting groceries. She waited for him to elaborate, and when he didn't she felt compelled to remain silent. Ben would tell her as soon as he was ready.

"He wanted another loan."

That was hardly a shock. The only time his youngest son called was when he needed financial assistance. David was a user and had no skills when it came to money management. No ethics, either—he'd lie about anything to anyone, including that young girl who'd just had his baby. And his father.

"What did you say to him?" Charlotte asked.

"I told him no."

"And he got angry with you." This was a pattern. Ben had held firm to his stipulation. He refused to lend his son any more money until David paid back the loans he'd already made. Over the course of their marriage, Ben had received a few checks from David, but they'd all bounced due to insufficient funds.

Nothing had upset her husband more, however, than discovering that his son had fathered a child and then abandoned the mother—and this was after his divorce. Naturally David denied that he was responsible for Mary Jo's pregnancy, but given his history and given the girl's sincerity, that denial was just another lie.

"We had an argument," Ben murmured, obviously distraught.

Charlotte dumped the pie dough on a floured board. "I have a son who's disappointed me, too," she said, wanting to reassure him that many parents faced such trials. She rarely referred to Will as a disappointment, but the fact that he'd been repeatedly unfaithful to his wife had distressed Charlotte deeply. Like any mother, she wanted to believe the best of her child. Sadly, she recognized that was no longer possible with the man Will had become.

Ben shook his head. "Will's transgressions are bad enough, but they don't come close to David's."

"I suppose so..." At least Will hadn't tried to steal from her or, she was positive, anyone else. And he'd been a good brother to Olivia during her illness.

"I keep wondering what I could've done to set David straight when he was young," Ben said.

"You can't blame yourself," Charlotte countered quickly, "any more than I can blame myself for Will's... weaknesses."

Ben seemed to agree with her. "Intellectually I know you're right, but that doesn't wipe out the regrets."

Charlotte identified with his sorrow. When she'd learned how Will had taken advantage of Grace Sherman, how he'd lied and misled her, she'd been horrified. Acknowledging character flaws in one's child was a dull ache in a parent's heart.

"Besides, Will's straightened out his life," Ben said. "It sure looks like it, anyway."

Charlotte fervently hoped that was the case, but she couldn't be positive. He'd never shown her that deceitful side of himself. Outwardly he was the perfect son but she couldn't ignore the less-than-salutary aspects of his behavior.

"I talked to him recently," she said, "and the gallery seems to be doing well. It's good to see him excited about what's happening there."

"I heard he's seeing Shirley Bliss."

Charlotte had heard that bit of local gossip, too. The artist had immediately caught her son's eye. She hoped this relationship was right for them.

Ben wandered back to the living room and his paper, and Charlotte continued her cooking. After she'd placed the bottom crusts in three different casserole dishes, she made the gravy and added the cut-up chicken and sautéed vegetables. When she'd finished, she poured the mixture into the piecrusts, arranged the strips of lattice on top and set all three dishes in the oven.

She threw a load of laundry in the washer, then joined Ben in the living room. He was doing the crossword puzzle and she sat across from him and picked up her knitting. For forty-five minutes they worked quietly while the pies baked, lost in their own thoughts.

Just before eleven-thirty, Charlotte removed the hot dishes from the oven, put on her coat and retrieved her purse. This was the first potluck she and Ben hadn't attended as a couple since they were married.

Ben carried the warm chicken pie to the car and kissed her before she left. "Have a good time."

She kissed him back. "I'll be home as soon as I can."

"No need to rush. Harry and I will hold the fort."

Despite his encouragement to linger and visit with their friends, Charlotte returned to the house two hours later, her head buzzing.

Ben met her at the door and took the empty casserole dish from her hands. "Did you enjoy yourself?"

"Oh, yes, I always do. Everyone asked after you and I said you were a bit under the weather." Thankfully, she'd managed to sidestep other questions. A number of their friends had pressed her for details, certain Ben must be suffering from a nasty virus currently going around. She'd reassured everyone that Ben was fine, and physically he was. Emotionally, that was another story.

He brought the empty dish to the kitchen sink and looked at her, frowning slightly. "What's wrong?" he asked.

"Nothing's *wrong,* but I do have some interesting news."

"Sit down and tell me."

Charlotte pulled out a kitchen chair. "Sheriff Davis stopped by to speak to the group," she said.

Ben reached for the notice mailed once a month to seniors who belonged to the center. Charlotte had propped it on the kitchen table. He quickly scanned the details. "It says here that Grace was supposed to be the guest speaker."

"Oh, she was, and she did a fabulous job." Although Charlotte volunteered at the library, it never ceased to astonish her how many books she hadn't noticed. "Grace was kind enough to bring in a box of bestsellers and she gave a short synopsis of each. Oh, Ben, they all sound like such good stories. I made a list of several I knew we'd both enjoy."

"When did Sheriff Davis speak?"

"After Grace. He came by unexpectedly and asked to address the group." Troy visited once or twice a year but generally as a scheduled speaker. Charlotte had always been fond of him and appreciated his tips for seniors.

"What did he have to say? Another warning about not giving out personal information over the phone?"

"Not this time. He asked for our help."

"How so?"

Charlotte drew her chair closer to the table. "You remember reading about the remains in the cave outside town, don't you?"

"Of course. It was a little before Christmas. And there've been a few press and TV stories since."

"Yes, and now there's additional information. According to the coroner's report, the remains are those of a young man who had Down syndrome. The sheriff asked if any of us remembered a family with a Down syndrome boy."

"Was someone able to help him?" Ben asked.

Charlotte shook her head. "There was plenty of discussion, and Bess had a vague recollection of a woman with such a child. I do, too, but for the life of me I can't remember who she was."

"I'm sure you will in time."

One of the most annoying effects of aging was this forgetfulness, these infernal memory gaps. The name was there, right on the edge of her consciousness, but it remained just out of reach. This was going to bother her until she came up with it.

"You'll probably think of it in the middle of the night," Ben said.

His confidence in her was reassuring.

"After Troy left, Bess and I talked about who it might be. We threw around a few names but none of them felt right. It seems to me the woman was a relative of someone who once lived here—a cousin, aunt or some such. Why can't I remember?" She tapped the side of her head with her index finger.

Ben sat back in his chair. "Tell me what you *do* remember and maybe that'll jog your mind."

"I know I met the boy once."

"Just once?"

"Yes, his aunt had him, I believe.... At least, that's what I seem to recall. She complained to me that his mother kept him inside most of the time. The mother, whose name has completely escaped me, was terribly protective of him, sheltering him from just about everyone. She was something of a recluse herself, I believe."

"When was this?"

Charlotte shook her head. It'd been so many years now…. "I can't say for sure, three or four decades ago. Maybe more. His aunt or whoever it was had taken him to the waterfront park. He was enthralled with it. She said it was probably the first time he'd ever set foot in a park."

"What were they doing?"

"Even now I can see that boy on the merry-go-round. He was laughing, so happy to be outside in the sunshine."

Her memory was slowly coming back. Talking about it was helping, just as Ben had suggested.

"Go on," he urged.

Charlotte closed her eyes. "His aunt seemed delighted by everything he did." She smiled at the memory, although she couldn't picture the woman clearly. Oh, why couldn't she remember her name? "The mother loved that child. The aunt, too. If anything happened to him, I'd stake my life on the fact that neither of them had anything to do with it."

"But there's nothing to say this is the same child."

"I know." Charlotte nodded. Nevertheless, she suspected it *was* the same boy. Frowning, she stood.

"Let your mind rest," Ben said. "The name will eventually come to you."

He was right, only it was difficult advice to take. She knew this family or had known them at one time, and she kept worrying away at it.

"Didn't you tell me you wanted to bring Olivia one of the pies?"

"Oh, dear, I'd nearly forgotten."

"Would you like company?" Ben surprised her by asking.

The spark was back in his eyes, and that encouraged her. "I'd love it."

"I've decided I can't let my son's weakness disrupt my life. All I can do is make an effort to be the best grandfather I can." Ben's gaze met hers and he took her hand. "Shall we go, my dear?"

He was going to be all right; she was sure of it.

Eighteen

It was almost the end of his workday—if a cop's day ever ended. Megan had asked him to stop by the house before he went home, and Troy had agreed. She hadn't said why, but she'd let him know it was terribly important. Seeing that the last time he'd ignored her request he'd been sucker punched by the news about Faith, he thought he should make at least a token appearance.

The phone rang just as he was leaving the office. He considered not answering but, with a sigh, reached across his desk and grabbed the receiver.

"Sheriff Davis."

The call was from Kathleen Sadler, the Seattle reporter who'd been on a mission to embarrass Cedar Cove. She wanted the latest update on the skeletal remains.

Polite but firm, Troy gave her a stock answer, made his excuses and disconnected. He'd addressed the seniors' group earlier that week to request help and information, and that had brought his most promising lead to date. He'd acted on impulse, dashing into their monthly gathering. Sometimes crimes were solved in unexpected ways.

Because of the phone call, he was a few minutes later than he'd told Megan. Even before he got to the front door, she'd flung it open; it was as if she'd been looking out the window, waiting for him.

"I thought you weren't going to come," she cried.

"I said I'd be here." He didn't understand why it was so all-fired important that he show up on a Thursday evening. She must've rushed home from work herself.

"I know, it's just that..." She hesitated. "Never mind. Come in. I baked your favorite oatmeal cookies."

After the day he'd had, Troy was grateful for an excuse to relax. Sitting heavily in a kitchen chair, he muttered, "What's the occasion?"

"Think of it as a late Valentine's Day gift."

This year's Valentine's Day had been a disaster. He'd bought a large box of expensive chocolates for Faith. He'd never expected to pay that much for *candy.* He'd bought a bouquet of red roses, too. They should've been gold plated for what they cost. As it turned out, he might as well have flushed all that cash down the toilet. The day before he'd intended to drop them off, he learned that Faith was leaving town.

So much for romancing her with flowers and candy! The roses were wilting in a vase on the mantel and he'd stuck the chocolates in the fridge. If she wanted to go back to Seattle—or wherever—he wasn't going to stop her. Not that he had the power to do so, anyway. The woman had a mind of her own, and he could see that it was already made up.

"Do you want coffee or tea with your cookies?" Megan asked, standing attentively beside his chair.

"Coffee." Anything was better than the stale brew at the station. The stuff was often as black as tar and just as thick.

His daughter brought him a plate holding four cookies and a mug of coffee with a touch of half-and-half, which was exactly the way he liked it. "I assume you want something?" Treats like this generally came at a price.

"Daddy!" Megan put her hands on her hips, her expression one of shock. "How can you even suggest such a thing? We hardly ever have time to talk anymore, just you and me."

"Okay, what shall we talk about?" He crossed his legs and leaned back. He was certain this little rendezvous was leading *somewhere.*

Before his daughter could respond, the doorbell rang. A look he could only describe as panicked flashed across Megan's face.

"Are you expecting anyone?" he asked.

She shrugged and glanced away. "Not really."

Megan hurried to the front door and in that instant everything became clear to Troy. This hadn't been a random invitation. His daughter had decided to do some matchmaking.

Troy stood, pushing aside the cookies and his coffee, and entered the living room. "Hello, Faith."

Her face fell when she saw him. She was obviously as surprised as he was—perhaps more so.

"Megan asked me to stop by so she could show me the baby blanket she finished knitting." Faith's tone implied that she wasn't a party to this arrangement.

Troy didn't need anyone to tell him the entire setup was Megan's doing.

"I'll get the blanket," Megan said cheerfully, acting oblivious to the tension between Faith and Troy. "Why don't you two talk while I...find my knitting."

As soon as Megan left the living room, the silence

seemed louder than any words they might have said. Troy wondered which of them would speak first. He'd decided it wasn't going to be him.

Apparently Faith had made the same decision. They both stood there examining the carpet, each pretending to ignore the other.

Okay, fine, he'd take the initiative. "I apologize for this," he said curtly. "I had no idea Megan was setting us up."

"I didn't, either," Faith told him.

It was pleasant not to be snapping at each other. Only months ago, they used to talk for hours on end. They'd laughed together and shared memories and dreams.

Troy exhaled a sigh. "Listen, about the other night—"

"Last week in the grocery store—" Faith started speaking at the same time.

They both stopped and stared at each other.

"Ladies before gentlemen," Troy said and gestured toward her.

"You spoke first." She motioned back at him.

Troy hardly knew where to begin. He made a couple of awkward attempts. "When I saw you..." He paused. "I never should've said the things I..."

Faith smiled and her expression softened. "Are you actually apologizing, Troy Davis?"

He chuckled and conceded with a nod. "I am."

"Do the words always get stuck in your throat?"

"With you they seem to."

"That's a sad commentary, isn't it?"

He had to agree.

Her shoulders relaxed. "I admit no one has the power to unsettle me as much as you do."

They continued to stand in their respective areas, Faith near the front door, Troy on the other side of the room.

"Is that good or bad?" he asked.

She took a moment to consider. "A bit of both, I guess."

With that, it seemed they'd said everything there was to be said. The strained silence returned. When Troy could no longer stand not knowing, he asked, "Are you still planning to move?"

Faith broke eye contact. "I don't know…. I think it might be for the best."

"Because of me?"

She smiled at that. "Why is it men always assume they're the sole reason for a woman's decisions?"

"I don't know. Why?"

"You ask that as if I'm going to give you a punch line." She shook her head in amusement. "I guess the answer is that men tend to be self-centered."

He didn't argue with her. "You're probably right."

Troy thought he saw Megan poke her head around the corner, but she didn't return with her "found" knitting.

His pride felt like a lump in his throat. Somehow he managed to speak around it. "Don't leave, Faith." If she moved away, he knew he'd regret that he hadn't asked her to stay. He'd regret that he hadn't tried to stop her.

To his utter astonishment, her eyes filled with tears. He had no idea what he could've said to cause such a reaction. Every time he opened his mouth he upset her. That was the last thing he wanted. Feeling completely helpless, he covered the distance between them and wrapped his arms around her.

At first she resisted and then, gradually, he felt her resolve weaken as she leaned against him. Troy held her enclosed in his embrace.

Megan cleared her throat as she entered the room.

They broke apart like guilty teenagers.

"Here's the blanket," his daughter announced in an unnecessarily loud voice.

"Oh, let me see," Faith said with more enthusiasm than warranted. Almost eagerly she walked away from Troy and toward Megan.

Troy could see that Faith's skin was flushed with embarrassment. While she examined Megan's knitting, Troy's mind whirled with hope and excitement, and his spirits felt lighter than they'd been in weeks.

In his heart of hearts, he was convinced Faith loved him as much as he loved her. This being apart was ridiculous. He knew what he wanted, and that was to have Faith in his life. They were meant to be together. He felt sure that, given time, she'd admit it, too.

"Oh, Megan, you've done a splendid job."

His daughter fairly beamed at Faith's praise. "Did you notice the mistake I made here?" she asked, pointing to what must've been a small flaw in the blanket.

"No, and no one else will, either."

"I do, but I have to look for it. Remember what you told me when I first started knitting?"

Faith frowned and gave a slight shrug.

"You said," Megan reminded her, "that if it bothered me I should rip it out and repair the mistake, but if it was something small and barely noticeable I should simply forget it."

"Remember there are three stitches in knitting. Knit, purl—"

"—and rip," Megan completed for her. "That isn't technically a stitch, but it's certainly part of *my* knitting process."

"It's part of everyone's process," Faith said, and they both laughed.

Faith made a couple of other complimentary remarks about the blanket while Troy waited patiently.

"I should be going," he said pointedly when Megan brought out the new yarn she'd purchased. It was obvious that she and Faith had become good friends and shared an easy camaraderie.

Faith turned and her gaze immediately found his. "I should go, too. Oh, look at the time," she said. "Craig will be home soon, won't he? You two will want to have dinner."

"Okay," Megan said. Troy supposed she figured her work was done.

Troy held the door for Faith and was about to follow her when Megan placed her hand on his arm, stopping him. "You're not upset with me, are you?"

Troy looked over at Faith and saw that she stood next to her car, waiting for him.

"Not in the least."

"Someone had to do something, and I could see you were too stubborn."

"Me? Stubborn?" Troy protested. "What about Faith? *She's* the stubborn one."

"Maybe so, but I doubt it." Megan rose up on the tips of her toes and kissed his cheek. "Don't let her get away, Dad."

"I won't," he promised.

"Good." She gave him a gentle shove. "Now what are you doing standing here? Go talk to Faith."

"That's exactly what I plan to do." He bounded down the steps and met Faith in the driveway.

The words he'd planned to say were trapped in his throat.

"Would you like to stop by the house for a little while?" Faith asked when he reached her.

By some miracle he managed to nod.

"Shall we say in fifteen minutes?"

"Ten?" he suggested instead.

Faith laughed. "Five?"

"Why don't I just follow you home?"

She nodded.

Troy started toward his own car. "I'll see you there."

"Troy?" Faith stopped him, sounding uncertain.

"Yes?" He turned to face her again.

She paused. "I want to settle these…these differences between us."

"I do, too."

"It's just that… Oh, I don't know…"

"Faith," he said softly, walking back to stand in front of her. "Let's not make any decisions yet. Let's talk honestly and openly, and if we both decide a relationship is wrong, we'll lay it to rest once and for all. Does that seem fair to you?"

She looked up at him, her eyes vulnerable, exposing what was in her heart. "It does," she whispered.

He touched her cheek, then hurried to his car.

On the short drive, Troy felt almost drunk. Drunk on love and hope…. For no real reason he burst into laughter.

They were finally going to resolve this situation between them.

It wasn't until Troy made the turn onto Rosewood Lane that he saw the twirling lights of two patrol cars. Both were parked outside Faith's house.

Troy was out of his vehicle before Faith had even pulled into her driveway.

"What's going on here?" he asked Deputy Weaver, who met him halfway up the walk.

"The alarm company phoned in a breach."

Faith hurried toward him, eyes wide and frightened. "Troy, what's happened?"

"It appears someone broke into the house." In an effort to calm her, he slipped his arm around her shoulders. "The alarm company alerted my office."

"A 9-1-1 call came in from a neighbor, as well," Deputy Weaver added.

Faith covered her mouth with both hands. "Is this *ever* going to stop?" she cried. "What do these people want from me?"

Unfortunately, Troy didn't have any answers.

After conferring with his deputies, he entered the house with Faith. The destruction was minor—a broken window, a lamp on the floor and a toppled vase. Still, it was bad enough. Faith gasped and he put out a hand to steady her.

Troy stayed while his deputies finished their report. After they'd left and the house was quiet again, he turned to her.

"I'll help you straighten up."

"No," she said and shook her head. "I can't deal with this now. I'm going to spend the night with Scott and his family."

Troy could understand how upset she must be. He'd give just about anything to solve this and to find out why Faith, of all people, was being targeted.

"It seems to me," she said, her voice quavering, "that while you'd like me to remain in Cedar Cove, someone else wants me to leave."

Nineteen

It was the first Tuesday of March and Christie had driven her almost-new car over to Teri's. She tried to visit every few days, especially now that Teri hardly ever left the house anymore.

Christie carried the teapot into the family room, where Teri sat with her swollen feet propped up. "You look wonderful," she told her sister. Despite everything—Teri's obvious discomfort and the inconvenience of enforced bed rest—it was true.

"I feel like a blimp." Teri rested her hands on her protruding abdomen. "I've got three and a half months to go and by the time I'm ready, they'll have to get a forklift to move me."

Christie laughed. Triplets! Something like this would only happen to Teri. Triplets—and without fertility drugs, too.

"You'll probably deliver early."

"Thank goodness," Teri said wryly.

"You feel okay, though. Right?" Christie placed the tray with the teapot and two cups on the coffee table and sat on the sofa.

"I feel like Sigourney Weaver in that movie. You know, where she gives birth to an alien. You wouldn't believe what it's like to have three little soccer players kicking away at my ribs and—"

"Oh, Teri."

"Wipe that smirk off your face."

Christie couldn't stop smiling. "You're going to have so much fun with your babies."

Her sister shrugged. "Yeah, maybe."

"I plan to have fun with them myself. I'm going to love being an aunt." She knew she'd probably never be a mother, so Teri's babies would have to be hers, too.

Teri and Bobby were both elated, and Christie had never seen a husband more attentive and caring than Bobby. He'd brought Teri real happiness; she'd told Christie that when she'd imagined she was happy in the past, those feelings didn't even compare to what she felt now.

For a while, Christie believed she'd found that same kind of happiness with James Wilbur, but as was so often the case, she'd been wrong. He was like every other man she'd ever cared about—only it'd taken him a bit longer to reveal his true nature.

As if her sister had been reading her thoughts, Teri glanced speculatively at Christie. "James—"

"Don't even start," Christie warned. Teri seemed convinced that Christie could be as fortunate, as contented, as she was; Christie knew better. She poured the herbal tea, and handed Teri a cup.

Her sister gratefully accepted it. "You can't ignore James forever."

"Who says I can't?" She crossed one leg over the other and swung her foot to hide her nervousness.

Teri's eyes grew sad. "You love him and you know it. I had no idea you could be so stubborn."

"Sure you did," Christie returned, remembering their youth. Her sister was more familiar with her character flaws than anyone. "You want to defend James and that's your choice, but I've made my decision."

"James loves you!"

"Sure he does. That's why he walked out on me."

"He panicked," Teri said, defending him. "It had nothing to do with you."

"Uh-huh." That just proved her point; when he was in trouble, when he'd needed help, it hadn't occurred to him to confide in her—the woman he supposedly loved.

But Christie didn't want to argue with her sister. They'd done enough of that through the years. "Would you mind if we didn't discuss James?" she asked instead.

One look told her how disappointed Teri was.

"Let me tell you about my classes," Christie said. To her own surprise she liked her courses. The photography was an interesting challenge, and she'd mastered the basics. She'd been working with a camera provided by the school but planned to buy her own. She'd met Jon Bowman, Grace Sherman's son-in-law, once or twice; maybe he'd be willing to recommend a digital camera. And since she was starting her own business, she knew she needed some accounting skills. To her delight, she'd discovered that she thoroughly enjoyed the classes and had no problem with the homework.

Even as a kid Christie had always had a head for math. She never had difficulty remembering phone numbers after hearing them only once or twice. Her skill with figures was one of the reasons she'd made cashier at Wal-Mart. Balancing her bank account had never been a problem, either—especially since her balance generally hovered around zero.

"You sent back his Valentine gift." She paused. "The flowers were gorgeous—I know because he ended up giving them to me."

Christie forcefully expelled her breath. "Are you back to James again?"

Teri's gaze pleaded with hers. "Explain it to me."

"Explain what?"

"Why you're so unforgiving. Why can't you accept the fact that once the news story broke, James felt he had no option but to run. Surely you can put yourself in his position."

"No," she snapped. "I can't."

"I don't believe that," Teri said. "Poor James, he—"

"He walked out on you and Bobby, and he walked out on me, just like every other man I've ever loved."

"Christie, you've got to know James isn't like anyone else. He's *James*. His childhood was hell. His parents drove him to mental collapse, to the point that he ended up in a psych ward. Once it was obvious that he couldn't play chess anymore, they turned their backs on him—their own son! If it wasn't for Bobby, I don't know what would've happened to him."

"He doesn't seem all that grateful to Bobby—or at least that's how it looks from where I'm sitting," Christie said. "When Bobby needed him, James left."

"You mean when *you* needed him, James left."

"Yes," she flared. "I thought James was different. I thought I could trust him. What an idiot I was."

"He came back because of you," Teri said quietly.

"Too bad. I'm not interested."

Teri pretended not to hear. "James realized it didn't

matter what kind of ugly sensationalism that reporter put out there. He decided to stop hiding."

She paused as though she expected Christie to appreciate how hard it'd been for James to confront his past. Okay, Christie could understand his fears; still, that didn't justify the way he'd abandoned her.

"Can't you imagine what it must have been like for him?" Teri asked rhetorically. "He's stayed in the shadows all these years and then to be thrust into the limelight without his knowledge or consent. It was his worst nightmare. Instinct took over, and he ran. Who's to say what either of us would've done in the same situation? But once his head cleared, he came back, and the first person he asked to see was you."

Christie's resolve remained unchanged. "I learned something important about myself through all of this," she said. "I don't need a man." It'd been a liberating insight. After each breakup, she'd instantly gone in search of a new relationship, afraid to be alone. Afraid that on her own she hadn't been *enough.* All those associations had been with a certain type—drunks, drug addicts, assorted losers. Men she felt she could rescue with sufficient love, sympathy and understanding. Not to mention money…

In the dark, lonely hours after James's defection, Christie had arrived at some conclusions. First, she *was* good enough—and no man would ever make her feel whole or complete. That had to come from within herself. Second, she had an excessive need to be needed. She recognized that about herself now and wasn't about to fall back into the same patterns.

While she enjoyed her job, she wanted more. With her photography and business classes, Christie was going to establish a career. Initially, she'd take photographic assignments on her off-hours, while she still had the protection of a steady paycheck. No matter how long it took, she wasn't about to let a man, any man, ruin her chances or stand in her way.

"I know you're feeling hurt," Teri said, "but I wish you'd give James another chance."

Unwilling to bend, Christie shook her head.

Once she succeeded in steering the conversation away from James, she enjoyed the visit with her sister. Although Teri was positive and uncomplaining—other than in humorous asides—Christie knew this pregnancy had taken a toll on her. Teri was an active, social person, and she found being confined to the house extremely difficult.

Even though Christie preferred to avoid any possible contact with James, Teri needed her. She promised she'd stop by again in a day or two.

Bobby walked her to the front door, which was unusual. She figured he wanted to tell her something out of earshot of his wife. He glanced furtively at the family room, where Teri was still sitting.

"She's doing well," Christie said reassuringly.

"All three are boys," Bobby announced without preamble.

"You know already?"

Bobby nodded. "I saw the picture. Teri wouldn't look but I did."

"Three sons," Christie repeated, smiling widely.

"Teri wants a girl," he said with a frown.

"Trust me, my sister won't be disappointed," Christie told him.

"She'll want to get pregnant again—until she has her girl. I'm just not sure she should."

Christie knew he was concerned about Teri's health and the physical demands of this pregnancy. But she also knew the power Teri had over him.

"What you mean is that if my sister wants something and you can make it happen, you will. Right?"

Bobby lowered his eyes.

Christie had to struggle not to laugh. He adored Teri so much, he could refuse her nothing. Oh, to have a man who loved her that intensely. Christie hoped Teri knew how lucky she was.

"Trust me," she said again. "Once these babies are born, the last thing Teri will think about is getting pregnant again."

Alarm crossed his face. "She'll still…you know…" The rest of his words fell away as though he assumed she'd grasp his meaning.

Christie did. Only Bobby would ask something like this. "Oh, I imagine she'll be as warm and loving as always, probably even more so."

Bobby's shoulders sagged with relief.

Leaning forward, Christie kissed his cheek, then walked out the front door.

When she got to her car and opened the driver's side, she gasped. There, on the seat, lay a single, perfectly shaped, long-stemmed red rose.

Anger rushed through her. She snatched up the rose and marched across the driveway to the garage. James used to live in the apartment above; presumably—obviously—he was back. Christie charged up the steps, breathless when she reached the landing.

Pounding on the door with her fist, she suddenly realized what she'd done but didn't have time to retreat. James was there, standing in the doorway. Seeing her, he smiled, his eyes warm…and loving.

Everything she'd intended to say disappeared. Confronting him had been a mistake. A big one.

The urge to cry nearly overwhelmed her, but thankfully that passed quickly, replaced with a fresh surge of anger. This rose nonsense was a trick he'd played on her before. Every time Teri had sent him to pick her up or drive her home, there'd been a rose on her seat. In the beginning, Christie had thought the flowers were put there by her sister. Not until much later did she learn they were from James.

"Christie?" His voice was soft, almost a whisper.

She continued to stare at him but suspected she only looked foolish. Hurling the rose at his feet, she whirled around and stormed back down the stairs, practically stumbling in her haste.

James followed at a more sedate pace.

She ran ahead, intent on climbing into her car and speeding away. However, when she went to open the door, she discovered she must have inadvertently locked it. Furious when the door refused to open, she staggered clumsily backward, straight into James's chest. He caught her by the shoulders.

She broke away from him, shouting, "Don't touch me!"

"Actually," he said, as calm as she was annoyed, "I think about touching you quite a bit."

"Well, don't." Shaking the hair out of her face, she fumbled with her car keys and in her frustration dropped them on the pavement.

"Allow me," James said politely and bent down to retrieve them.

"Don't *ever* bring me another rose. Understand?"

He handed back her keys. "I do understand. Unfortunately I can't guarantee that I'll stop."

"Well, force yourself." Turning away from him, she inserted the key in the lock.

"I love you." His words were gentle. Sincere.

"I don't care!"

This was not supposed to be happening! Her plan was to react to him with cool indifference; instead, he'd flustered her so badly that she was on the verge of weeping, intelligible speech beyond her. Gulping for air, choking, she couldn't manage a single word.

To Christie's horror, tears rained down her cheeks. Then, all at once, the lump in her throat eased and she could breathe again. And speak again.

"I *don't* love you." She pronounced each syllable emphatically.

"Liar."

She was embarrassed that he could so easily see through her facade. "I admit I did love you at one time, but not anymore," she said.

"I don't believe that."

"Believe what you want." Unwilling to become involved in a useless verbal exchange, she slipped inside her car and slammed the door. Blinded by tears, she started the engine and backed up without looking behind her. If James was stupid enough not to get out of her way, then it was his own fault if she ran over him.

Once she got home, it took her a full hour to stop shaking. She paced and chewed her fingernails, a habit she detested. Then she turned on the television and sat down to watch for about thirty seconds before she was on her feet again.

Sleep was impossible that night.

She was still working the early shift so she could attend her afternoon business class. The sky was dark when she walked out to the apartment parking lot the next morning. Her breath made small clouds in the chilly air, and she rubbed her bare hands together to chase away the cold.

She opened the car door—and when the interior light flashed on she saw another beautiful, long-stemmed red rose.

Christie closed her eyes in frustration. Then she grabbed the flower, threw it on the ground and stomped all over it.

Twenty

Grace had been planning this surprise for Olivia for almost two weeks. As soon as she'd mentioned it to Peggy Beldon, Peggy had called Corrie McAfee. Soon Faith was part of the scheme, too. Within a few days Charlotte had spread the word to a number of Olivia's friends, and Grace had more volunteers than she could use. Olivia was loved by everyone who knew her.

All they needed was a day without drizzle. In the Pacific Northwest the month of March was notoriously—in a word—wet. Friday morning, however, Grace woke to clear skies and sunshine. After weeks of continual misty rain, this was a welcome change.

The television weatherman predicted sunshine for the rest of the day, with cloudy skies and rain to follow overnight. Grace figured a few hours of sunshine was enough to accomplish what she had in mind.

Reaching for the kitchen phone, she was about to punch in Peggy's number when Cliff wandered into the kitchen and poured himself a mug of coffee. He'd already been in the barn to feed his horses. He never slept past seven; his horses' schedule didn't permit it.

"Morning, sweetheart," Cliff said. He took a gulp of coffee, then set his mug down and slipped up behind her to nuzzle her neck.

"Cliff," she chastised, laughing. "I have to call Peggy." She breathed in deeply. He smelled of fresh hay and leather, and the combination struck her as immensely virile. These were the scents she associated with her husband.

"You weren't complaining last night," he reminded her as she made her call.

He had a point. "But I wasn't on the phone then."

"Good morning, Thyme and Tide," Peggy said with her usual friendliness. She had a gift for making people feel appreciated, even over the phone.

"Meet me at Olivia's at eleven," Grace said, trying to ignore her husband's roaming hands. "Can you…can you let Corrie know?"

"Sure thing," Peggy told her. "I'll meet you at Ace Hardware in an hour."

"Great." That was all Grace could manage with Cliff nibbling on her neck. She sighed with relief as she hung up the phone, then twisted around in her husband's embrace. "You're asking for trouble, Cliff Harding."

"Uh-huh." He kissed her soundly on the lips.

Grace loved his playfulness and responded in full measure.

After a few minutes, Cliff released her but his eyes were still closed. "You make me mighty glad I'm a married man."

"Good. Now hold that thought until I get home later this afternoon."

"Will do."

Grace opened the refrigerator and took out a small container of yogurt. That, together with coffee, would constitute her breakfast.

"What's up with you and Peggy?" he asked. He got the peanut-butter jar and dropped two slices of whole-wheat bread into the toaster.

"It's for Olivia, remember?"

When he seemed uncertain, she explained. "A few of us are getting together and planting flowers in Olivia's yard. It's sort of a get-well-soon bouquet on a larger scale."

"Yeah, I remember now. But isn't it a bit early to be planting flowers?" he asked.

"Some varieties do well in this weather, and when April comes they'll be in full bloom."

His toast popped up and Cliff set both pieces on the counter, slathering them with a thick coating of peanut butter.

Grace opened the cupboard and pointedly handed him a plate.

He accepted it with a lopsided grin. "If you insist."

"I do."

Leaning against the counter, Cliff took a bite of his breakfast while Grace retrieved a spoon from the cutlery drawer and sat at the table. Years ago, she'd read a diet book that said never to eat standing up. She'd followed that advice ever since.

"Back to Olivia," Cliff continued. "She's getting through this cancer ordeal, isn't she?"

"I think so, but it's really too soon to tell. I thought this would lift her spirits. She's gone through a rough patch, and I figured she could use a bit of cheering up." According to Jack, the second and third sessions of chemo had been harder on her than the first.

"Peggy and Corrie wanted to help," Grace went on, "and then Faith joined in. Charlotte's going to bring us all lunch."

Cliff pulled out a chair and sat down across from her. "You're a good friend, Grace."

Grace dismissed his praise with a shake of her head. "Olivia's my best friend. This is the very least I can do for her."

"I'd be happy to help, too," Cliff offered.

She smiled gratefully at his willingness to pitch in. "Thanks, honey, but I think we have it covered."

"Okay, but let me know if there's anything you need."

"I will," she promised, finishing her yogurt. She deposited the container in the garbage and started to leave when Cliff stopped her.

"I don't suppose you let Jack in on this plan of yours?" he asked.

"Oh." Actually, she hadn't.

He grinned. "Go on. I'll take care of that for you."

"Thanks."

By nine-thirty, Grace and her accomplices met at the local Ace Hardware next to the craft store. Peggy arrived in her pickup, with Corrie sitting in the front seat beside her. Faith had come in her own vehicle and Charlotte was waiting in the parking lot, along with Ben.

When Grace parked next to her friend's truck, Peggy climbed down and hugged her. "Bob built four flower boxes for Olivia's front porch."

"What a sweetheart," Grace said delightedly.

"Roy wanted to contribute, too," Corrie said. "So he painted them. They're white, and they really look nice—I know Olivia's going to be pleased."

"Wonderful!"

"Charlotte has so much food in the backseat, she could feed an entire navy fleet," Ben told her.

"How can you say that, Ben Rhodes?" Charlotte muttered. "I just hope I brought enough. After all that physical labor, these girls are going to be hungry."

Walking into the store, they each grabbed a cart. After they'd chosen their supplies and selected a variety of seedlings, they loaded everything into Peggy's truck. Then they set off en masse.

The caravan got to Olivia's home on Lighthouse Road just before ten-thirty. Jack met them on the front porch. "Hi, everyone!"

"I take it Cliff got hold of you?" Grace asked, hurrying up the walkway to meet him.

"This is a terrific idea."

"Does Olivia know?"

"Not yet," Jack said. "I thought I'd let you tell her."

Grace ran up the porch steps. "How's she doing today?"

Jack hesitated. "She had a rough night."

Grace suspected Olivia had gone through a lot of those recently. When they'd spoken on the phone yesterday, Olivia had sounded tired. The last chemo had weakened her, left her exhausted.

"Anything I can do?" Grace asked.

Jack's gaze held hers. "I think you're already doing it."

Grace walked past Jack and into the house. "Olivia," she called out, her voice echoing through the living room. "Where are you?"

"Back here." She heard Olivia's thin, weak voice from down the hallway.

Grace found her in the back bedroom, where Olivia had set up a sewing machine. She'd decided to make a quilt for her oldest granddaughter; she'd been working on it for weeks, doing a little each day until she was too tired to continue. The project had given her purpose and helped take her mind off what she was enduring.

She sat at the sewing machine, pale and slumped. Grace struggled to hide her reaction. Olivia's bald head glistened in the light and around her shoulders she wore a prayer shawl knit by one of the ladies from church.

"Did you tell me you were coming by?" Olivia asked in puzzlement, as if she must have forgotten. "For heaven's sake, why are you dressed like that?" She gestured at Grace's torn jeans and faded Mariners sweatshirt.

"Come outside and see for yourself."

"See what?"

"I'd rather show than tell," Grace persisted.

Olivia got slowly to her feet, correcting her balance as she did, then trailed Grace into the front room. The door was wide open.

"What's going on out here?" Olivia asked.

"Come and see." Grace ushered her out. On the front lawn, pitchforks and shovels in hand, stood Peggy, Corrie and Faith. They'd emptied the truck bed; boxes of annuals and perennials lay spread about the lawn.

"What's everyone doing with all those flowers?" Olivia asked.

"You mean you can't guess?"

Olivia looked at Grace for an explanation. "No."

"We're here to spruce up your yard and bring a bit of spring," Grace said.

Olivia blinked rapidly, but couldn't fend off the tears that filled her eyes.

"Coming through!" Jack said, carrying a huge box from the trunk of Charlotte and Ben's car, Ben on his heels with an equally large carton. Both were packed with containers and covered bowls.

"Your mother provided lunch."

Olivia seemed to have trouble speaking. "Oh...oh, my goodness," she finally murmured. "Whose idea was this?"

"Who do you think?" Jack said, joining them on the porch. He slid one arm around Olivia's thin shoulders and drew her close.

"Grace. Oh, Grace." Olivia reached for her hand and squeezed tightly.

"Now, go back inside where it's warm," Grace said urgently. "We've got things to do out here. We'll call you when we're done so you can inspect our work."

Olivia dashed away tears and nodded.

As soon as she was safely back in the house, Grace and company began their task. With everyone pitching in, it took only an hour to get the flower beds weeded and planted.

Peggy, an experienced gardener, turned the soil and added mulch before Corrie inserted the tender plants into the rich-looking earth.

With Jack's assistance, Grace and Faith set the flower boxes on the ledge around the front porch and arranged ivy and pansies in each.

Charlotte and Ben were inside, getting everything ready for lunch.

Just as they broke off before going in to eat, Sheriff Davis's patrol car turned the corner and stopped directly across the street. He got out, strolling toward them. "I received word of a disturbance on Lighthouse Road," he said in mock-serious tones.

Everyone laughed, but although he'd addressed the whole group, his eyes sought out Faith. Grace glanced over at her companion, whose face was flushed with what Grace assumed was pleasure.

The last she'd heard, they'd ended their relationship.

Judging by Faith's heightened color and the intense look in Troy's eyes, there'd been some kind of reconciliation. However, neither seemed prepared to speak.

Grace thought it was time to intervene. "Hello, Sheriff," she said, pulling off her gloves. "What can we do for you?"

"I came by to see if there was any way I could help. I, uh, heard about what you're doing and I'd like to be part of it."

"We've got everything under control, but thanks for the offer."

"We were about to stop for lunch," Jack said. "Care to join us?"

Troy hung back. "Are you sure there's enough?" he asked uncertainly.

"Charlotte did the cooking," Jack told him. "So, trust me, there's *more* than enough."

"In that case, thanks. I'd like to."

"Good," Grace said with genuine happiness—a feeling visibly shared by Faith. She wondered what had happened to change things between those two.

They took turns washing up. By the time they were all finished, Charlotte invited them into the dining room to eat. Grace smiled at her yellow apron with its sunflower-shaped bib.

"We're serving buffet style," she announced, waving her arms expansively.

"I can't believe you'd do this," Olivia said, standing next to her mother. "All of you."

"We wanted you to know how much we care," Peggy said, plate in hand as she circled the table. "Wow, look at this fabulous food." There were three different kinds of salads, deviled eggs and freshly baked bread with ham, turkey and cheese slices for sandwiches. Charlotte had also included canned goods from her garden—sweet pickles, dill pickles, pickled beets, plus jams, jellies, peaches and pears.

"Oh, my goodness, I nearly forgot," Grace said. She hurried to the door. "I left something in the car. Be right back."

Grace returned two minutes later, carrying a pie box. "Goldie sent this over from the Pancake Palace."

Olivia's face broke into a delighted smile. "Coconut cream?"

"What else?"

They served themselves and sat in a circle around the room, balancing their plates on their laps.

"I feel like the luckiest woman alive," Olivia said, once more sounding close to tears.

"We love you and want to see you well again," Corrie told her.

"And back in the courthouse where you belong," Sheriff Davis added.

He'd taken the chair beside Faith's.

Grace was startled by a sudden knock at the door; before Jack could get up to open it, in walked Cliff, Bob Beldon and Roy McAfee.

"I hoped we'd timed it so we'd be here for lunch," Cliff said.

"Help yourselves, boys," Charlotte said. She stood and got them each a plate and a napkin, while Jack and Ben brought out three chairs from the kitchen. The new arrivals filled their plates and joined the circle.

"I don't know how I'll ever be able to thank everyone," Olivia said.

"We don't need any thanks," Grace told her. "We

wanted to do this. In fact, it's been in the planning stages for weeks—I actually had to turn people down. So many of your friends wanted to contribute. You are loved, Olivia, and this is just our attempt to let you know that."

"Well, I'd say you've done a more than adequate job…."

Olivia looked around the room, her gaze resting on each one in turn. She wiped the tears from her cheeks and smiled tremulously at Grace. "I'll have a piece of that coconut cream pie now."

Twenty-One

"I got a job!" Mary Jo's excited voice burst over Mack's cell phone.

He turned away from the other men in the break room at the fire station and concentrated on his phone. He hadn't expected a call from Mary Jo and it jolted him, since they almost always communicated by texting. "That's great." He mentally reviewed their past messages and he couldn't recall her mentioning another job interview.

"I probably shouldn't have phoned you at work, but I'm so thrilled I can hardly sit still. A job changes everything."

He assumed the job was in Seattle, and his heart sank. The interview with Will Jefferson hadn't led to employment; the owner of the Harbor Street Art Gallery had only been able to offer a part-time position. Will couldn't tell her when the job would become full-time—"eventually" was the most he could promise—so Mary Jo felt she had to pass. Mack didn't blame her, although he'd been disappointed.

Meeting Will Jefferson had given her confidence, and she'd decided to start applying elsewhere, presumably in Seattle; she hadn't referred to any particular places.

"Tell me about your job," he said, trying to hide his own lack of enthusiasm. Ever since he'd talked to Mary Jo about moving, he'd created the ideal scenario in his mind. He pictured Mary Jo and Noelle living next door to him and imagined the three of them spending time together. A *lot* of time…

"I'll be working in an attorney's office," Mary Jo was saying, "which I thought would be perfect, because, well…you know?"

This seemed to indicate that she'd have a built-in resource should David Rhodes try to interfere with her and Noelle.

"The money isn't as much as I could make in Seattle, but the cost of living in Cedar Cove is quite a bit less, right?"

It was 4:00 p.m., and the shift change was taking place as they spoke. Mack waved to his friends, cell phone to his ear, and started out of the station house. "Wait!" Not until he was close to his car did it hit him. "Are you saying you have a job *here*—in town? In Cedar Cove?"

"Yes." She sounded surprised by his question, as if he should know. "I'll be working for Allan Harris."

"Where are you now?"

"Mocha Mama's," she told him. "I'm celebrating with a latte."

"I'll be there in ten minutes." Five, if he could manage it.

Mack snapped his phone shut and trotted the last few steps to his car. He'd had plans but they could wait; seeing Mary Jo was more important. His next shift at the fire station wasn't until Friday, which gave him two full days to finish painting both units. Once that was accomplished, he'd be all set to rent out the other half of the duplex. He'd already moved in, but for the moment was more or less living in chaos.

He knew exactly who he wanted as a tenant. Mary Jo would need a place to live—and what better place than right next door to him? He'd mentioned it once but in a vague way, not identifying himself as the owner. He didn't feel completely comfortable with the deception, but wasn't sure how she'd react if she knew. Mary Jo was cautious and uncertain about men, all men. Given her history, Mack could understand it. He'd like to meet David Rhodes in a back alley someday, but that wasn't likely to happen; for one thing, the guy was obviously avoiding Cedar Cove.

Mack drove down the hill to Mocha Mama's and parked nearby. As he hurried inside, through yet another light rain, he saw Mary Jo sitting by the window, sipping her latte. She smiled when he walked in.

"Hi," he said, brushing the moisture from his coat and hair.

"Hi!" she returned, grinning widely, her happiness unmistakable—an uncomplicated joy he hadn't seen since the night Noelle was born.

He suddenly realized Noelle was nowhere in sight. "Where's the baby?"

"A friend of mine is watching her this afternoon. This is the first time I've been away from Noelle, and I feel like part of me is missing. Jenna said I have to stop phoning, because whenever I do I wake the baby."

Mack glanced over his shoulder. "I'll get an espresso and join you in a minute."

The young man he recognized as Shaw was behind the counter. They exchanged greetings, then Shaw brewed Mack his double shot. Back at Mary Jo's table, Mack sat across from her, draping his coat on the empty chair beside him.

"So," he said, leaning toward her. "Tell me how you came to hear about the job with the attorney."

"Kelly Jordan told me Mr. Harris was looking for an assistant and—"

"Sorry, who's Kelly Jordan?"

"Grace Harding's daughter. Don't you remember, Grace was the one who suggested Kelly as a possible day-care provider? It was the day we met at the library." She smiled. "Kelly's little girl, Emma Grace, is starting to walk now."

"Oh, yeah." He had a dim memory of the conversation; he'd been too occupied with Noelle to pay much attention. "So you found someone to do day care before you had a job? That was smart."

"Well, yes. I had to be okay with whoever was going to be taking care of Noelle before I could even think about employment."

He nodded.

"Men just don't consider things like that," she went on. "I know Linc didn't, but then my big brother can be pretty dense."

"Oh, yes, your big brother. How's Linc doing these days?" Mary Jo's brother was overprotective to the point of obtrusiveness, and she resented his domineering attitude. Mack sympathized with her, but he also understood Linc's point of view.

Mary Jo stirred her latte. "As you might've guessed, Linc's not very happy with me at the moment."

"Why not?" But of course he *had* guessed.... With a job in Cedar Cove, she'd presumably be moving away from her brother's house—and his control.

"He doesn't think it's a good idea for me to leave Seattle," she said wryly. "According to him, family should stick together."

"I believe that, too," Mack told her, "but it doesn't mean everyone has to live in the same house."

She sighed. "Linc doesn't understand why I feel he's suffocating me. He seems to assume that the minute I'm out of his sight, some terrible fate will befall me."

Mack didn't bother to remind Mary Jo that she'd met David Rhodes while living with her three brothers. He wondered where Linc had been *then.* He suspected she hadn't told her brothers about David until she was already pregnant.

"Anyway, I don't want to talk about Linc," Mary Jo said. "Not when there's so much else to discuss."

"Fine with me." Mack struck a relaxed pose, leaning back in the chair and stretching out his legs.

"Did I tell you the attorney is Allan Harris?"

"You did." He frowned as he tried to remember where he'd heard the name. "Of course! His assistant's the one who was arrested just before Christmas."

"What?" Mary Jo's hand flew to her throat. "Mr. Harris didn't say anything about that."

"He wouldn't. His legal assistant stole jewelry from one of Harris's clients. Apparently, Geoff—that was his name, Geoff Duncan—tried to frame Pastor Flemming for the theft."

"Oh!" Mary Jo looked thoughtful. "That explains a lot."

"In what way?" he asked.

"I almost didn't apply for the job because I don't have any paralegal background. But Mr. Harris said he wanted to hire someone who was willing to do on-the-job training. I think this is how he plans to keep a close eye on his employee. I'm just grateful he's willing to give me a chance. He said he'd interviewed quite a few candidates and felt I'd work out the best." There was a sparkle of excitement in her eyes. "I interrupted your story," she said. "Sorry."

Mesmerized as he was by her, Mack couldn't recall what he'd been talking about.

"Mr. Harris's assistant," Mary Jo said.

"Oh, yeah. Geoff Duncan. Fortunately, Sheriff Davis saw through his ploy. According to my dad, Allan Harris was pretty shocked. He didn't have a clue Geoff would do anything like this. The crime was bad enough. Implicating an innocent man makes it that much worse."

"But why would his assistant do something so stupid? He was bound to get caught sooner or later, don't you think?"

Mack shrugged. "I can't say for sure. The gossip is that he was trying to impress his fiancée."

"How would stealing stuff impress her?"

"Well, Lori Bellamy's from a wealthy family. The Bellamys own quite a bit of property on the Kitsap Peninsula. Geoff must've got in a credit crunch and didn't want to tell Lori he couldn't afford the things she wanted and then panicked. I guess he wanted to act as if he had the same kind of money she did. Maybe he was afraid that if he couldn't keep her in the lifestyle she was used to, she'd leave him. I heard that he pawned the jewelry for cash—and now he's behind bars." Mack had discussed the case with his older sister, Gloria, who worked for the sheriff's office. He'd only learned of Gloria's existence a few years ago and had been making an effort to develop a relationship with her. Since he and Gloria both lived in town now, they managed to have dinner or drinks at least once a month. Despite that, he still felt a reserve in her. A hesitation that was difficult to explain. He hadn't said anything to his parents but couldn't help wondering if they'd noticed it, too.

"So when do you start work?" he asked Mary Jo.

"Monday."

That gave her less than a week to get all her arrangements in order. "Not a lot of time," he murmured.

She nodded. "The next thing I need to do is find somewhere to live."

Mack wondered if she remembered the suggestion he'd made that February afternoon at the library, and suspected she didn't.

"I can always commute from Seattle with Noelle if I have to," she was saying, "but that would make for a very long day."

Mary Jo had just handed him the perfect intro. His one fear was that if she knew he owned the duplex she might be leery of renting from him. A landlord-tenant relationship could complicate things.

He decided to gauge the situation with a comment. "I, uh, might have mentioned it, but I recently moved into a duplex and the second half is empty."

"Really?"

He forged ahead. "The rent's reasonable, too."

"How…reasonable?"

He named a figure that was about half the going rate, which was what he speculated she'd be able to afford.

"*How* much?" Mary Jo sat up straight. "There must be something wrong with the place."

"Not really. Oh, it could use a bit of paint and cleaning, but basically that's about it." Then, pressing his luck, he added, "The owner's a nice guy. He's currently…out of town, but you can meet him later if you like. I'm acting as his manager." That was an inspired idea, he thought, and not a lie. He *was* the manager. And this conveniently "out-of-town" owner would appear sometime in the future. Mack had no intention of misleading her for long; his objective was to get her moved to Cedar Cove. Once she'd made the transition he'd find a good opportunity to tell her about the "owner." In the meantime, he'd have her write the rent checks to his accountant, Zachary Cox.

Nibbling on her lower lip, Mary Jo mulled this over. "Would it be a problem…you know, having me and Noelle next door?"

"A problem?" he repeated. "Not for me. What about you?"

She shook her head. "I think it'd be great. But I wouldn't want to be a bother."

"I can't see that happening." In fact, he had to work at not showing how thrilled he'd be to have Mary Jo and Noelle as his next-door neighbors.

Mary Jo continued to look speculative as if her instincts were telling her this wasn't a wise decision.

"Would you like to see the duplex?" he asked, hoping to distract her.

"Oh…sure."

"I was painting before my shift at the fire station, so it's pretty messy."

"Why were you painting?" she asked. "Isn't that the landlord's responsibility?"

"Normally it would be," Mack said, trying to sound nonchalant. "I offered to do it in exchange for a reduction in rent. He, uh, wants first and last months' upfront."

"I have that in savings, so I'm not concerned."

They finished their drinks and Mack drove Mary Jo past the Senior Center to 1022 Evergreen Place.

Mary Jo's eyes darted up and down the street. "This is a nice neighborhood," she said appreciatively.

Mack had thought so, too, which was one reason he'd made an offer. This was a good place to raise a family.

"Now I *really* don't understand why the rent's so low," Mary Jo said, frowning.

"Like you said earlier," he rushed to explain, "the cost of living is less on this side of Puget Sound."

"I had no idea it would be this much less."

Mack was beginning to think he might have overdone it. "You can always check out other rentals."

"I could," she agreed, "but I like this one."

Mack relaxed. "I understand there's an eligible bachelor in close proximity, too." The instant the words were out of his mouth, Mack regretted them. Mary Jo was emotionally fragile, and he didn't want to frighten her off by appearing to pursue anything but friendship. He ignored the reproach that nagged at him—that he was being manipulative.

In any case, his joke didn't elicit a response. Instead, Mary Jo stared out the window. After a moment, she said, "I'm not going to be dating anyone for a long while."

It was a veiled warning, a signal. He considered offering reassurances, but that would have led to more lies, or half-truths, anyway. So he asked, "Would you like to take a look inside?"

"Please."

He wanted to give her an opportunity to get to know him—and trust him. Living side by side as neighbors and friends was the way to do that. Her brothers weren't going to appreciate his efforts, but that was their problem.

Mack helped her down from the truck. "I have the key," he told her. "You'd be in Unit B." He opened the door and gestured her inside. A sheet lay across the living room floor with a bucket of paint, a roller and brushes resting next to it. The fresh, clean smell of recently painted walls greeted them. On his mother's advice, he'd chosen a pale, buttery yellow, which worked with the small rooms yet had a subtle warmth.

"I only have a few pieces of furniture," Mary Jo said as she moved from one room to the next. The kitchen was compact but adequate. The two bedrooms were across the hall from each other.

"There's one bath?"

Mack nodded. "And a laundry room."

"I don't have a washer and dryer."

"They come with the place."

Or they would by the time she moved in.

"I have my bedroom set, of course, and there's the crib for Noelle and her changing table." She paused as if calculating what else she could bring. "I have a rocking chair, too, but that's it in the way of living room furniture."

"What about a television?"

Mary Jo shook her head. "I had an old TV in my room, but it's not worth taking."

"I've got an extra one you can use."

Again Mack saw her hesitate.

"Thanks for the offer, but I'd rather not do that."

"I could sell it to you cheap," he said impulsively.

This appeared to interest her. "How cheap?"

"Cheap." He came up with a price he felt she could probably afford. "Fifty bucks."

Mary Jo laughed. "Sold."

"Great! I've been wanting to get rid of that piece of junk."

"Mack!"

He held up both hands. "Just kidding."

"Good thing you are, buddy."

With the easy banter between them, Mack relaxed. "Would you like me to contact the owner and tell him he's got his second renter?"

Mary Jo smiled over at him. "Okay, it's a deal."

"And listen, don't worry about me pestering you." He wanted to make sure Mary Jo understood that.

"I'm more worried about pestering *you.*"

On the contrary, he figured that having Mary Jo and Noelle this close might be the best thing to happen to him in a long, long time.

Twenty-Two

When Troy finished shaving on Friday morning, he did something he didn't usually do—he splashed on a citrus-scented aftershave, hoping the scent would last long enough for Faith to notice later that evening.

If anyone in the office caught a whiff, he might be teased, but any teasing would be worth the possible return. After several short phone conversations, Faith had finally agreed to have dinner with him and Troy could hardly wait. They had a lot to discuss, but the item at the very top of his list was this purported move. He didn't want her walking out of his life again, so he had to let her know how he felt in no uncertain terms.

Troy was encouraged. He'd come away from each brief conversation with a hopeful feeling. He sensed that she might be willing to start again. Troy assumed that this evening, over dinner, they'd decide once and for all whether to pick up where they'd left off.

He arrived at the office, his mood still optimistic. It wasn't long before reality struck its first blow.

Troy hadn't been at his desk more than ten minutes when he received a visit from his most recently hired deputy, Gloria Ashton. Gloria was the daughter of private detective Roy McAfee and his wife, although they'd met her only four years ago. Apparently, Roy and Corrie had broken up for a while in college, not knowing Corrie was pregnant. She'd relinquished the baby for adoption.

Years later, Gloria, now an adult, had sought them out. Troy was astonished by how similar father and daughter were, in personality and in interests. They'd both gone into law enforcement, although Roy had retired from the Seattle police.

"Morning, Sheriff." Gloria entered his office, hands clasped in front of her.

"Sit down," he said, gesturing toward one of the visitor chairs.

"If you don't mind, I'd rather stand."

"Whatever you prefer." She seemed uncomfortable and he wondered why.

Her shoulders were squared, her back straight and her eyes just managed to avoid his. "I thought I should give you a heads-up about an arrest I made last night."

"All right." It was obvious that this hadn't been a routine matter. "Tell me about it."

Again she avoided eye contact. "I saw a car with a burned-out headlight. When I turned around and followed the vehicle, the driver made an effort to evade me."

"You pulled the car over?"

"I did." She paused. "I quickly assessed that the driver was intoxicated. I asked him to get out of his car and step away from it, which he did without hesitation. After performing the routine checks, I gave him a Breathalyzer test and it showed an alcohol level exceeding .08. I immediately placed him under arrest."

So far, this was nothing out of the ordinary and didn't

warrant Troy's attention. "Is there a reason you've come to tell me this personally?" he asked.

"Yes." She nodded curtly.

At that moment it was easy to see that Gloria was Roy McAfee's daughter. The set of her jaw, the unyielding line of her mouth, was all Roy.

"The driver was Mayor Louie Benson."

Troy felt like groaning out loud. Well, so be it. The law was the law. "I see."

"He lawyered up right away," Gloria went on to tell him.

Troy wouldn't have expected any less. "His brother Otto's an attorney. I imagine Louie has him on speed dial."

She nodded again. "His attorney met us at the jail."

This was awkward, but he'd handled awkward situations before. "I appreciate the advance warning."

Her gaze found his and he read the doubt in her eyes. "I wanted you to know…."

"Did Mayor Benson point out that he was an elected official or did you recognize him?"

"Both," she said. "I knew who he was as soon as he stepped out of the car and then he told me. The thing is—" She hesitated and then looked away. "He was belligerent when I first pulled him over."

"I…see." Troy had known Benson for years on a casual basis, although they'd never been close friends. The mayor had been kind when Sandy died and insisted Troy take all the time he needed. To the best of his knowledge, Troy couldn't remember seeing him with a drink in his hand, not even at the social functions they'd both attended. This behavior seemed completely out of character.

Gloria appeared to be waiting for Troy to comment. "I came to discuss this with you because I wanted to be sure I'd done the right thing, taking Benson into custody."

"You did." Awkward situation or not, Gloria wasn't to blame because a local politician hadn't had the good sense to know when enough was enough. Sometimes people in the public eye felt they'd been awarded some form of entitlement that placed their actions above the law.

"Mayor Benson asked me to cut him some slack." Gloria clasped and unclasped her hands. "I checked his driving record, and it's clean. He doesn't have so much as a parking violation."

Troy nodded. Still, that didn't give him a clear picture. It could mean that in the past Mayor Benson had been granted a free ride or some deputy had conveniently looked the other way.

Gloria stared down at the floor. "He said if I issued him a DUI, he'd see to it that I was fired from my job."

"In other words, he threatened you." Troy had to believe Louie didn't know what he was saying. He could charge the mayor with a further offense, but he didn't want to do that, as much for Gloria's sake as Louie's.

Gloria frowned slightly as though she'd never intended to admit this. "I…think he was too drunk to remember everything he said. The thing is, Sheriff, I enjoy working in Cedar Cove and I'd hate this incident to tarnish my career in law enforcement—or worse, end it."

That wasn't going to happen. Not on Troy's watch, anyway. "You have nothing to worry about, Ashton. You did your job. If there's any political flack over this, I'll deal with it."

He felt, more than saw, his deputy relax.

"I thought later that I should've contacted you at the time of the arrest."

"Don't second-guess yourself. You made the right

decision." Although in retrospect, Troy wished she had called him. It wouldn't have made any difference to the outcome, however. Benson would've ended up in jail regardless. But it might have eased Gloria's mind. Instead, she'd spent a restless night, worrying about Troy's reaction to the news.

"Like I said, you did your job." He glanced at his watch. "Aren't you off duty?"

"I am."

"Then why are you still here?"

Her mouth twitched with a half smile.

"Again, I appreciate that you brought this to my attention. I'll handle it from this point forward."

"Thank you." The relief in her voice was evident.

When Gloria had left his office, Troy decided he'd better talk to the mayor immediately; otherwise, this whole affair could blow up in his face. Briefly he wondered if Louie was a secret drinker. In any case, Troy was not the kind of lawman who'd bow to influence or intimidation.

But the reasons for the mayor's behavior, whatever they might be, were irrelevant. Louie was in the wrong, no question about it.

When he called the jail, he discovered that Mayor Benson had been released on his own recognizance.

Their confrontation wasn't going to be pleasant. Lately he seemed to be at odds with the mayor over a number of issues. This certainly wouldn't improve their relationship.

Troy found Benson in his office at city hall. The mayor glanced up when Troy was announced, then glanced away. He looked dreadful—pale and disheveled with bloodshot eyes. From his appearance, Troy suspected Benson hadn't had much sleep.

"Your department seems to enjoy embarrassing me," Louie said, taking the defensive even before Troy had opened his mouth.

"I'd say you're doing a mighty fine job of that all by yourself," he countered.

Louie got up to close his office door. When he turned to face Troy, his mouth was set in a grim line. "I'd like this matter to disappear. I trust you can make that happen."

Nope, he couldn't. "Unfortunately, the outcome is out of my control."

It was as if the other man hadn't heard him. "Your deputy's overzealous. She targeted me because of my position as mayor."

"That's simply not true. Ashton is a good officer. She—"

"I was only fractionally over the legal limit, Sheriff. The officer refused to listen to reason. Do you have any idea how humiliating it is to be put in handcuffs and escorted to jail?"

"You broke the law."

"By a *fraction* of a point," he said, tapping his desk.

"You're the one who decided you were sober enough to drive. Don't cast blame other than where it belongs." After a meaningful pause, he added, "If you want to make a fuss, perhaps I should mention that not only did you break the law, you threatened one of my officers."

The mayor ignored Troy's comment as he paced, his steps agitated and angry. He seemed to be weighing his options. Finally he sighed, shaking his head. "Okay, whatever. You're right—I shouldn't have gotten behind the wheel. I accept full responsibility. Still, once word of this gets out, it could ruin me."

"Possibly." Troy wasn't going to downplay the situation.

"But that isn't your problem, is it?" The question was tossed at him flippantly.

"How you cope with the political fallout is up to you."

The mayor walked back to his desk and braced his hands against the edge. "I've never done anything like this before. I…I don't drink and drive."

"I'm glad to hear it."

Benson was quiet for a moment, then looked up at Troy. "Do you have any suggestions on how to deal with this?"

Troy didn't wait for an invitation; he sat down and met the other man's eyes without flinching. "I believe honesty really is the best policy. Admit that you made a mistake and that you'll take responsibility for your actions."

Slowly the mayor sank into his leather chair. "That's harder than you think," he muttered.

"It would be helpful for the public to know how easily something like this can happen." Troy frequently dealt with similar cases. A couple of after-work beers or glasses of wine in quick succession, and then people would drive home, unaware of how much the alcohol had affected them. Mayor Benson wasn't alone.

Apparently he didn't like Troy's advice. Frowning, he said, "So now you want me to turn this into a public service announcement."

Troy didn't feel that was worthy of a response. "However you approach it with your constituents is up to you," he said dispassionately.

Louie's face seemed to pale even more. "You're right…it's just that…" He left the rest unsaid. Sighing again, he hung his head. "I guess the best way to deal with this fiasco is to face it head-on. I'll contact Jack Griffin at the paper and give him the story before he prints it on his own."

"Smart idea." Jack, the *Chronicle*'s editor, was a good person for the mayor to talk to, for more than the obvious reason. Jack was a recovering alcoholic with quite a few years of sobriety. If the mayor had a drinking problem, there was no one better than Jack Griffin to confide in.

The two men parted amicably enough. The arrest was acutely embarrassing for Louie and at the same time it might be the wake-up call he needed. What happened now was entirely up to Louie Benson.

After that bumpy start to the day, Troy was hoping his afternoon would run smoothly. Unfortunately, that wasn't to be.

Faith's call came in at close to one o'clock. Troy couldn't disguise his pleasure in hearing from her. "Faith! This is a nice surprise."

"I apologize," she said and hardly sounded like herself, "but I'm going to have to cancel our dinner date."

Troy's spirits did an automatic nosedive. "Oh?" He did his best to seem nonchalant, as though this was a minor disappointment. It wasn't.

"Someone slashed my tires last night."

"*What?*" Troy gritted his teeth as anger surged through him. "Did you report it?"

"What good will that do?" she cried. "I've reported the vandalism before and nothing seems to help."

Troy was too agitated to discuss this over the phone. "I'm on my way over to your place."

"Troy—"

"Ten minutes." He hung up, grabbed his hat and coat and was out the door. Although this wasn't technically an emergency, he turned on his lights but not the siren.

He wished he could determine why Faith had been targeted—and how to stop it. But whatever it took, he was determined to put an end to this.

When Faith opened the door, she looked pale and drawn, with dark shadows beneath her eyes. He wanted to pull her into his arms and comfort her but reminded himself that he was there as a professional, not as her friend—or would-be lover.

"Tell me what happened," he said in his most authoritative voice.

Faith led him to her living room and slumped down on the couch. "I was supposed to go to work this morning, but when I went out to the car, I saw that…that my tires were slashed."

"All four?"

She nodded.

This was no small expense.

"I called the clinic and told them I couldn't come in today. Then I contacted the auto service. They had to tow my car to the tire place…. I won't have it back until tomorrow."

"I'm sorry, Faith." As the town's sheriff, Troy felt responsible. "Did the neighbors see anything?"

Faith shook her head. "I already asked. It must've happened after midnight, which is when the McCormicks next door went to bed. No one saw or heard a thing."

Troy closed his eyes in frustration.

"I was so upset, I phoned my daughter, and Jay Lynn insisted I spend the weekend with her. Frankly, Troy, I need to get away. I'm at the end of my rope. Someone doesn't want me here and after today…after this morning, all I can say is I don't want to be here, either."

"You don't mean it," he said.

"I do. I made a huge mistake the day I moved to Cedar Cove."

His hand tightened on his hat brim, crushing the felt. "It was exactly the opposite for me. It was one of the best days of my life."

"Apparently you have a short memory," she chided, then smiled weakly in his direction. "I was shocked when the Seattle house sold so quickly—but even more shocked when you said we shouldn't see each other anymore."

If Troy could take back those words, if he could unsay them, he would. Breaking off the relationship with Faith had been one of the biggest blunders of his adult life, and he'd paid for it every day since.

"Listen," Faith said, "I don't mean to rehash old arguments. I'm tired and upset and a weekend away will do me good."

Troy agreed, although he would've liked it a whole lot better if she'd decided to visit her son instead of Jay Lynn. Scott, at least, lived in town.

"Is there anything I can do?" Troy asked.

She gazed up at him, her bruised-looking eyes meeting his. "There's nothing anyone can do. The best thing for me is to leave town."

"No!" he objected loudly.

"For the weekend," she amended. "What happens after that can wait. Now isn't a good time for either of us to make a decision about…whether we have a future together."

Troy disagreed with her. He wanted Faith with him. He wanted to marry her. But first he had to convince her that they *did* have a future together. A future in Cedar Cove.

Twenty-Three

Linc Wyse was not in favor of this idea of Mary Jo's. If his sister wanted to move out of the house, fine; she was free to do so whenever she wished. That said, in his opinion the timing didn't make any sense.

As a young mother, Mary Jo needed to be home with her baby. It went without saying that she resented his attitude—but then that was par for the course. He knew that by today's standards it was perfectly normal for a mother to return to work three months after giving birth. Their own mother had been a stay-at-home mom and he had strong feelings on the subject. Okay, maybe that wasn't a popular stance and it certainly wasn't one his sister shared. When he became a husband and father—he instantly dismissed that thought. Marriage wasn't likely to happen for someone like him, not with his old-fashioned views. That saddened him but he might as well accept reality.

He'd found it more difficult than he would've believed to watch Mary Jo pack up and move across Puget Sound. Despite that, he rather liked Cedar Cove. He'd driven all around the area on Christmas Eve, searching for Mary Jo, and—for the most part—he'd had a good impression of it. His recent visits had confirmed that. It was a nice little town, welcoming and friendly. The only drawback was the distance. In the past week alone, he'd made four trips to the Kitsap Peninsula to see his sister and the baby. To check up on both of them.

According to Mary Jo, not a single one of those trips had been necessary. But Linc wouldn't sleep at night if he hadn't personally seen to his sister's and niece's well-being. He'd always taken family responsibility seriously.

It only seemed right that he visit Noelle on her very first St. Patrick's Day. Their family background—like that of so many Americans—was motley, with English, French and German that he knew of. He was sure there must be some Irish in there, too. Just in case, he'd bought her a plush leprechaun doll. But he had an even better excuse for this visit; he'd located a new sofa and chair in a closeout deal. He'd wanted to bring them himself, which saved delivery fees. The truth was, he looked forward to surprising his sister.

Mary Jo had him pegged as some sort of ogre and that just wasn't true. He hoped this peace offering would help.

When he parked in front of the duplex, he saw Mack McAfee on a ladder, cleaning out the gutters. Linc hadn't quite made up his mind about McAfee. Mack had been with Mary Jo during the most critical time of her life. Still, having him live right next door was a little too convenient. Linc wasn't sure he approved.

He'd made the mistake of voicing his concerns, and Mary Jo had nearly bitten his head off. He'd kept his trap shut ever since. Apparently, when it came to McAfee, his sister didn't care for Linc's advice. Fine. He'd keep his opinions to himself—and keep an eye on McAfee.

"Hey, Linc," Mack called out. He climbed down from the ladder and thrust out his hand, which Linc willingly shook.

"I don't suppose my sister's home?" Linc already knew the answer. He asked because he wanted to know how closely the firefighter kept tabs on his little sister. This was one of those catch-22 situations. He wanted Mack to watch over her. At the same time, he wanted to be sure the guy wasn't paying her more attention than warranted.

It was a thin line, and Linc planned on being around often enough to see that Mack didn't cross it.

"Mary Jo's home."

"Good."

"I see you brought her some furniture."

Well, at least he was observant, Linc thought a little sarcastically.

"I think she'll be pleased with the sofa," Mack was saying.

Linc hoped so. Hard to tell with Mary Jo. Or with any woman, he realized. He simply didn't understand women or know how to communicate with them. Over the years he'd had a number of relationships, all of which had come to an abrupt end. The way he figured it, the fault must lie with him. Mary Jo had often told him he was too domineering, too bullheaded and a chauvinist to boot. He'd honestly tried to change, tried to be more sensitive, but that hadn't worked, either. As far as he could tell, he was destined to remain unmarried. Until Noelle, the fact that he'd never have kids hadn't bothered him.

It did now.

He loved his niece more than he ever could have foreseen. With Mary Jo and Noelle living in Cedar Cove, the house was strangely quiet and empty. Mel and Ned led busy lives; they were often out. They didn't have the problems Linc did with women. They were both in relationships and he assumed they'd be married soon.

When Linc wasn't at the house, he was at work. He ran the car repair shop his father had opened nearly fifty years earlier. Because he was the oldest, he considered it his duty to hold the family business, as well as the family, together. Ever since their parents' deaths, he'd done his utmost to manage the shop, keep the peace and make sure everyone was okay.

"How's Mary Jo doing?" Linc asked.

"Why don't you ask me directly?" she said. She stood in the doorway of her half of the duplex, arms crossed. "It's not like I'm living in China, you know."

"Right." For fear he might say or do something else to upset her, Linc shoved his hands into his pockets.

"Since you asked, I'm doing very well, thank you."

"And Noelle?"

"The same."

Linc cleared his throat and turned to Mack; the return stare told him he was on his own.

Gesturing to his truck, Linc said, "I brought you a housewarming gift."

"Another one?"

"Ah…it seemed you could use more than one."

Mary Jo smiled. "That was nice of you."

Linc felt the tension ease from his shoulders and the back of his neck.

He handed over the stuffed leprechaun, which was added to Noelle's growing pile of toys. Then, with Mack's assistance, he hauled the sofa and chair into Mary Jo's living room. She indicated where she wanted them, then changed her mind not once but twice. He wasn't annoyed, and neither was Mack.

Noelle had been asleep but woke shortly after Mary Jo was satisfied with the arrangement of the furniture. Sitting down on the new chair, Linc held his niece, who smelled deliciously of baby powder and shampoo, and kissed her forehead. She yawned and arched her back, raising her elbows as she did. Babies fascinated him. At first, when Mary Jo had brought Noelle home, he'd been terrified of hurting her—dropping her or squeezing too tight. Gradually he'd become more relaxed around the infant. It helped that she'd outgrown the colic. As it was now, he could hold this little one for hours and be content.

"Do you want to feed her?" Mary Jo asked Linc, after seeing Mack to the door.

"I thought…you know, breasts…" The words seemed to stumble all over themselves and he knew he was blushing furiously.

"Since I work now, I'm using a breast pump."

Some subjects were best not discussed between sister and brother. Breast pumps fell into that category. "I…think maybe you should feed her." He knew he sounded gruff but couldn't help it.

Noelle smiled up at him and he smiled back. He dared not look at his sister as he muttered, "Are you seeing a lot of that neighbor of yours?"

There was a short hesitation. "What makes you ask?"

Linc shrugged, grateful she hadn't taken offense. "It's just that he seems to be around every time I stop by."

"He lives next door. What do you expect?"

Her reply held an edge that warned him against pursuing this line of questioning further. Difficult though it was, Linc didn't ask anything else. If his sister did become involved with her neighbor, maybe it wouldn't be so bad. As long as Mack understood that Linc wouldn't allow another man to take advantage of her.

He was well aware that Mary Jo would never talk to him again if he asked McAfee what his intentions were. Still, Linc wanted to know.

Mary Jo offered him dinner but he declined. He'd stayed too long already. It was time to hit the road.

After thanking him for the living room set, Mary Jo walked Linc to his truck. "Drive carefully, okay?"

"I will," he promised.

"You know, don't you, that it's not necessary to check up on me every day?"

He shrugged in response.

"Or even every other day."

He grinned.

"You don't need to hold the family together anymore, Linc. We're all adults. And we're all capable of making our own decisions, learning from our own mistakes. You're sweet to want to protect me, but it really isn't necessary."

Then, to his utter amazement, Mary Jo rose up on tiptoe, placed her hands on either side of his face and kissed his cheek.

As he drove away, Linc considered what she'd said. The truth was, he realized his sister was right. Mel and Ned didn't like him looking over their shoulders, either, any more than Mary Jo did.

Rather than take the ferry home, Linc decided to drive across the Narrows Bridge. He hadn't driven more than a mile down the freeway when he saw a car parked on the side of the road. The vehicle's taillights flashed, indicating some kind of mechanical problem. A woman stood helplessly outside, obviously waiting for someone to stop.

Cars zoomed past. Linc didn't want to stop. He'd had a long day, it was now dark, and he was tired. Besides, he had a ninety-minute drive ahead of him. As he neared the woman in distress, Linc knew that he couldn't in good conscience drive by.

Parking his truck, he climbed down and walked toward the woman. She was delicate-looking, blond, petite. Smaller even than Mary Jo, who stood five-three.

"What's the problem?" he asked.

The woman stared up at him as if he'd stepped out of a *Friday the 13th* movie. Her eyes widened in what appeared to be genuine panic.

Linc supposed he could be intimidating, although what she expected him to do to her on the freeway with cars barreling past, he couldn't imagine.

"My name's Linc Wyse and I'm a mechanic," he explained, hoping an introduction would put her at ease.

"It…just stopped running. I was on my way to Gig Harbor and out of the blue, my car just stopped. I was fortunate to get it off the road before it went completely dead."

"Did you call Triple A?" he asked.

"Ah, no… Well, yes, I did and learned that my membership had expired. I—I've gone through a bit of emotional turmoil lately and it must've slipped through the cracks." She seemed ready to break into tears. "You don't want to hear any of this. Sorry."

She was right about that. He wasn't interested in her personal problems. "Did the car choke before it quit running?"

She shook her head. "I tried to look under the hood, but I couldn't figure out how to open it."

Typical. Most women barely had a clue about the fundamentals of operating a vehicle.

He must have given some indication of his thoughts because she added, "I'm not stupid, you know."

Linc knew better than to respond to *that* comment. He leaned in and released the hood lever, then walked around to the front of the vehicle. He raised the hood and quickly checked all the easy fixes.

The woman stood next to him and studied the engine. "That's not quite true," she said.

"I beg your pardon? What isn't?"

"The thing I said about being stupid." She gazed past him to the traffic streaming by. "You've been very kind, and I'm grateful."

Praise disconcerted him, so he ignored her remark. "I don't see anything wrong with your engine."

"I can't believe this is happening now, on top of everything else."

"Everything else?" Linc wondered if he was going to regret asking.

"My fiancé. Geoff. Ex-fiancé, I should say. He's a thief." She bit down hard on her lower lip. "I broke off the engagement, and my family's upset—not because I canceled the wedding but because I didn't have the sense to know that the man I loved is completely unsuitable as a husband and a failure as a human being." She expelled a deep sigh. "I apologize. None of this has to do with my car. Frankly I have no idea what I would've done if you hadn't stopped. Calling my father wasn't an option."

This was the first time Linc had taken a good look at her...and he saw that she was even lovelier than he'd realized.

"You think you know someone and you think you love

him and then you learn the truth and it's just so...so heart-wrenching to discover that the person you loved isn't the person you thought he was."

Linc started to move away from the vehicle. "When's the last time you gassed up?"

Her brow furrowed. "You think I might be out of gas?"

"Let me get in and see." The woman seemed incapable of clear thought. Linc slid into the driver's seat and turned the key. Sure enough, the needle pointed to empty.

Apparently she was going through some sort of emotional breakdown. Lucky him that he'd stumbled onto her path. This was what he got for playing the Good Samaritan. No good deed goes unpunished, and all that.

The woman slipped into the passenger seat next to him and shut the door. She began to tremble with what he assumed was the effort not to weep. "I'm so sorry. You're being kind and I'm being hysterical. How stupid of me not to know I'd run out of gas." She closed her eyes and lowered her head.

"It happens to the best of us," Linc said in what he hoped was a comforting tone.

She turned to him with her nose red and her eyes swimming with tears. "Do you ever feel that nothing you do is right?" she asked him.

Despite the fact that he felt as if he'd stepped into the middle of a soap opera, Linc nodded.

"Me, too."

This was becoming awkward. "I have a gas can in the back of my truck," he said, eager now to be on his way. "I'll drive to a gas station—pick up a couple of gallons. That should be enough to get you wherever you're going."

"You're leaving me here?"

"Uh… Do you want to come with me?"

"Could I?"

Linc's mind darted in ten different directions at once. He couldn't believe he'd offered, any more than he could believe she'd asked.

To avoid wearing down her battery, he turned off the ignition and passed her the car keys.

"My name is Lori Bellamy," she said and held out her hand.

He shook it, almost shocked by the softness of her skin against his calloused fingers. "Linc Wyse."

"Hi, Linc."

"Hi." The awkwardness returned, the same unease he experienced whenever he was around women, especially petite ones. Small women like Lori made him feel clumsy and…too big. Linc moved carefully and spoke quietly, not wanting to overwhelm or frighten her.

He got out of her car, hurried to his truck and cleared off the passenger seat.

Once she'd clambered inside—with his assistance—she snapped the seat belt into place and smiled over at him. "Are you always this kind?"

"I have a sister," he said. "If her car had broken down I'd want someone like me to stop and help."

He started the engine and merged with the traffic. They sat in silence as he drove, but it wasn't uncomfortable anymore, nor did he feel the need to make conversation. After a couple of minutes, she murmured, "You're very easy to talk to."

"Me?" he asked, startled.

She nodded. "You listened patiently even though I was saying the most ridiculous things."

"Like what?"

She grimaced. "About Geoff. You stopped to help with my car—not to hear about the shambles my life's in."

"Sometimes it's good to talk to a stranger." Linc didn't know that for a fact, but it made sense.

"Well, I certainly didn't mean to blurt out the most humiliating details of my life." She gave a short, embarrassed laugh. "My car running out of gas just seems to confirm that my life's in a downward spiral." She shrugged despondently. "I guess Geoff proved that I don't have very good judgment about men."

Linc grinned. "Then we're equal. Because when it comes to male-female relationships I'm at a complete loss." Feeling emboldened, deciding to take a chance, he took his eyes from the road long enough to look in her direction. "Would you like to have dinner with me?"

"Tonight?"

"Ah…sure." Actually, any night would be fine with him. It wasn't as if he had a calendar crammed with social events. "Tonight would work," he said in an offhand way.

"Okay, but only if you let me treat, seeing all the trouble you've gone to on my behalf."

He hesitated, afraid he was about to ruin the most promising encounter to come along in the past few years. "Sorry, I can't do that. It's not how my daddy raised me," he added, trying to inject a bit of humor. He paused to gauge her reaction. "Call me old-fashioned, call me a male chauvinist, call me whatever you want, but I intend to pay for our dinner. I asked *you* out, remember?"

"Old-fashioned," she repeated. "I prefer *old-fashioned.* Isn't the term *male chauvinist* kind of dated, anyway?"

"You mean it's old-fashioned?" he said, and they both laughed.

Linc found a gas station and asked the attendant for

directions to the nearest restaurant. It was a mom-and-pop burger joint. They ordered hamburgers and french fries and sodas and talked nonstop for two hours. Lori told him about Geoff, and he told her about his sister moving to Cedar Cove. Then he described his shop and how he'd changed the name to Three Wyse Men when he and his brothers took over. She explained that she worked in a boutique near the mall and had recently moved to Cedar Cove.

They might've stayed longer if he hadn't noticed obvious signs that the place was closing. Linc hated to see the evening end. Unlike most women, Lori made him feel relaxed and comfortable. Their conversation interested him. Apparently neither of them was skilled at small talk, and when he mentioned that, she'd said, "So what? We'll talk about big things, then." And they had.

Everything changed once they were in the truck again and he was taking her back to retrieve her car. The silence seemed strained when it hadn't been before. Linc didn't understand why and wondered what he might've said to upset her. He decided to find out, but didn't know how to broach the subject, how to ask what was bothering her.

"Linc?" She put her hand on his arm. "Do you mind if we just sit here for a moment?" He'd parked on the roadside, a few yards from her car.

"No…I mean—no, of course I don't mind."

She turned and stared at him with the biggest, darkest brown eyes he'd ever seen. "You have trouble with relationships, right?"

He nodded.

"I do, too. But I feel different with you."

He nodded again, unsure how to explain his feelings in words.

"You're a good person. You stopped to help me when everyone else drove past." She gestured at her car. "No one cared except you."

He wanted to brush aside her gratitude, but she seemed so intent that he didn't speak for fear of destroying the mood.

"You care about your family, too, and you've kept your dad's business going. I admire that." She closed her eyes, then opened them. "I'm sick of it all."

"Sick of what?" he asked, puzzled by the abrupt leap.

"Dating."

"Does that mean you won't go out with me again?" He couldn't keep the disappointment from his voice.

"No…listen, don't say anything yet, but I'd like to suggest something so far out in left field you'll probably jump out of your truck and head for the hills."

"What?"

She chewed on her lip, then shook her head. "No, it's too crazy. Never mind."

Linc couldn't imagine what she was about to suggest and wished she'd blurt it out, damn the consequences.

"I'm an old-fashioned kind of woman." She paused. "Just like you're an old-fashioned kind of guy."

Linc agreed; he liked that about her.

"You seem to have problems with relationships and it's the same way with me."

Again, he agreed.

"You're as sick of the whole dating game as I am, right?"

"Right."

Lori drew in a deep breath. "You want to skip all that?"

"I…beg your pardon?" He was missing some step in her logic.

She kept her gaze fixed squarely on something ahead,

although he couldn't tell what. "Would you be interested in skipping all the stuff that leads up to…marriage?"

The silence seemed to echo. "Lori," he said cautiously. "I might be wrong about this, and if I am, if I'm being presumptuous, forgive me." He swallowed. "Are you asking me to marry you?"

She cleared her throat. "I know this is probably the most bizarre, impulsive thing you've ever heard, but I have to ask."

"You're serious?"

"Yes," she said solemnly. "We both want to get married, right?"

That was true. Linc could feel his pulse speed up.

Lori continued. "You've been burned. I've been burned. Let's do away with all the nonsense. Let's just go for broke and do it. Would you be willing?"

"I never expected a woman to propose to me, but seeing that you have…"

"Did I completely throw you?" she asked.

She had, although Linc wouldn't admit it. "Do you want an answer now?"

"Please."

He took a quick breath. "Okay. I'm willing to give it a try if you are."

Lori's smile lit up her whole face as she grabbed his arm. "I can't believe we're doing this! It's crazy!"

"I guess it is."

She rested her head against his shoulder and expelled her breath, as if some great weight had been lifted from her.

"Then we're getting married," he said.

"We're getting married," she repeated.

"Soon?" he asked.

"Soon."

Twenty-Four

Ben was feeling—and acting—more like his old self lately, which greatly relieved Charlotte. She knew he'd spoken with David twice in the past few weeks. While the first call had disturbed him, he'd been less agitated after the second one. In the days that followed, his mood had lightened considerably.

Ben hadn't shared any of that conversation with her but Charlotte knew he'd contacted Roy McAfee shortly afterward. At first Charlotte was disappointed that Ben hadn't confided in her. Since then, she'd worked it out in her mind. Thoughtful man that he was, Ben didn't want to involve her in this latest mess with his son.

"Ben," she called, fussing with her hat in front of the mirror. She so seldom wore a hat these days, but this was a celebration and nothing said that better than a nice hat. In their last conversation, Olivia had told her she'd decided on a hat, too—for different reasons, obviously—but this was also why Charlotte was wearing hers. To make sure her daughter didn't feel self-conscious. Olivia had a lovely wig, but found it hot and uncomfortable, so her family and friends urged her to go without.

"Are you ready to leave?" she asked Ben.

"The grand opening's not for almost an hour," he called back.

Charlotte secured the fedora with a fancy pin that had belonged to her mother. "Ben, darling, I don't want to be late."

"Charlotte," he said, joining her in their bedroom. "It'll only take five minutes to get to the tearoom."

"But there might be a crowd."

Ben hugged her around the waist. "Very well, my dear, if it'll reassure you, we can leave now."

"Thank you, sweetheart."

After months of construction, her granddaughter's Victorian Tea Room was about to open. The pink building with the lavender trim was the talk of the town, and that wasn't surprising. There'd never been a place in Cedar Cove like it.

In preparation for her granddaughter's venture, Charlotte had collected her most cherished recipes. Ben had helped her type them. Then, with no small amount of fanfare, they'd delivered the binder to Justine. Charlotte was delighted to see that a number of her recipes had been included in the tearoom menu.

Charlotte sprayed on some cologne—Evening in Paris, her lifelong favorite. Just as she'd finished, she heard the doorbell. What terrible timing!

When she walked into the living room, she saw Roy McAfee, coat still on, briefcase in hand, talking to Ben.

"Roy, how nice to see you," she said politely.

She waited for Ben to announce that they were leaving for the tearoom. Family and close friends were gathering there before it opened for a blessing ceremony. Pastor Flemming would invoke God's blessings on this enterprise, and Charlotte didn't want to miss a second of it. But instead of deferring Roy's visit, her husband invited him to take a seat.

"We won't be long," Ben said, apparently guessing her thoughts.

"Would you like me to make coffee?" she asked the two men.

"No, thanks," Roy said. "I just need to give Ben a report."

It was clear that Ben had hired Roy to check up on something and that something undoubtedly concerned David.

Ben gestured to the empty space on the sofa. "Join us, please."

Charlotte sat down beside him. He reached for her hand, holding it tight. She could feel how tense he was, how weary of dealing with David and his problems, and gave his fingers a reassuring squeeze.

"As you're probably aware," Roy said, seated across from them, "Ben asked me to look into David's story."

Ben turned to Charlotte and said, "When David and I last spoke, he'd told Mary Jo he wanted a paternity test. She was against it, but because I asked her to comply, she did. Test results prove that Noelle is his daughter. There can be no doubt of that now."

"Is David going to step up and accept responsibility?"

"He *said* he is," Ben answered. "He came to me and explained that he'd left his job with the insurance company and is now working for a bank. He told me he's trying to make positive changes in his life and asked for my help."

"Financial help?" Charlotte asked.

"No, and that encouraged me. I felt for the first time in years that perhaps my son had learned his lesson and was willing to become the man I've always believed he could be."

Charlotte's gaze flew to Roy, unsure why Ben had involved him.

"The thing is, I've been led down the garden path with David before," Ben continued. "It's difficult for me to judge his sincerity because, as his father, I naturally lean toward trusting him. But rather than blindly accept his word this time, I asked Roy to check out David's story."

Roy bent down to open his briefcase. "I have a full written report for you here," the investigator told them, getting up to pass Ben a file folder.

"Because we're a little tight for time," Ben said, "would you be kind enough to summarize it for us?"

"Of course."

Charlotte noticed the way Roy's back stiffened—as though he dreaded what he was about to tell them. "When David said he'd left his job, he was telling the truth, although the termination wasn't his choice. The company fired him with cause. Apparently there's been a sexual harassment charge filed against him. He didn't receive a severance package."

Charlotte wasn't surprised David had been let go from his job.

"But he has this new position, correct?" The question came from Ben.

"No, I'm afraid that's another fabrication," Roy said. "He's been unemployed for three months."

Knowing how close to the edge David was financially, Charlotte felt she had to ask, "How is he living, then?"

Roy looked to Ben as if to ask the older man's permission to respond. Ben gave a slight nod.

"David's moved in with a…friend."

"Male or female?" Ben inquired, frowning.

"Female."

Charlotte sensed his disappointment in his son—his even greater disappointment, she amended.

"In other words," Ben said, betraying none of the emotion Charlotte had recognized in him, "my son is letting a woman support him."

Roy nodded. "That appears to be the case."

"What about all this talk of being a father to Noelle, supporting her financially and bringing her into his life?" Charlotte looked at Ben.

"I can only guess he's saying all the things I want to hear in an effort to convince me of his sincerity."

"There's something else you might find significant," Roy said after a short hesitation.

"Yes?" Ben returned his attention to the investigator.

"David is currently living in Seattle."

"Seattle?" Ben repeated. "How long has he been this close?"

"According to what I've learned, it's been a couple of months."

Ben's son had been a ferry ride away and hadn't bothered to notify his family. More telling was the fact that he hadn't even attempted to see his daughter, who until recently had lived in Seattle, as well. This was a blow, and Charlotte knew that Ben had taken it hard.

"I see," Ben said after a moment. He'd made an obvious effort—a painful effort—to absorb the shock of this latest revelation.

"I wish I had better news," Roy was saying.

Ben shook his head. "Don't worry. I'd rather deal with the truth now than uncover it later."

Charlotte placed her free hand over Ben's. She felt like weeping on his behalf. In only a few minutes, her husband looked as though he'd aged several years.

"Is there anything else I should know?" Ben asked.

Roy shrugged. "As I mentioned earlier, everything's in the report. That'll give you a clearer picture of your son's life."

"You mean there's more?" Ben cried. "If so, just tell me straight out."

Roy sent Charlotte a questioning glance. "Ben needs the truth," she said softly.

"Is it drugs?" her husband asked.

"No. It seems that David has a gambling problem."

Ben closed his eyes briefly. "I feared as much. What about alcohol?"

Roy winced. "I'm sorry to deliver so much bad news, especially on an important day like this."

"Day?" Ben asked.

"When the Victorian Tea Room is opening its doors."

"Oh, yes," he said, his voice waning. "It…slipped my mind. Charlotte and I were about to leave when you dropped by."

Ben sounded as if he were in a trance. He stood in the middle of the room, staring at nothing, as Charlotte walked Roy to the door.

"I'm sorry, Charlotte. Is there anything I can do?" Roy whispered.

"No, but thank you for asking."

Lingering in the doorway, Charlotte watched Roy walk down the steps and across the street to his car. All the while, she tried to figure out how she could help her husband deal with yet another devastating blow from his youngest son.

When she turned around, Charlotte was surprised to find Ben standing behind her. His eyes met hers and he smiled.

"Do you want to stay home?" she asked.

Ben shook his head. "My son is on a path to self-destruction. As much as I hate to see him wreck his life, there's nothing I can do to stop him." He exhaled slowly and held out his arm. "I can't allow David to drag me down and I can't live his life for him. I'd hoped he was making better choices, but that doesn't seem to be the case."

"You're sure you're up to this?" she asked.

His returning smile was gentle. "I'm not about to let David ruin this perfectly wonderful day. We're meeting the others at the tearoom for Pastor Flemming's blessing. Then you and I are going to be among Justine's very first customers." He looked at his watch. "We should be right on time."

Twenty-Five

Shirley Bliss sat in her workroom, which her children often referred to as the Dungeon. She'd been doing some preparatory work for her newest piece, and she'd lost track of the hours. Shadows crept across the daylight basement walls, telling her it was now late afternoon. Tanni would be home from school soon.

She hoped.

It was hard to read her. Anytime Shirley dared question Tanni regarding her whereabouts, her daughter grew argumentative and defensive. After a while Shirley had stopped asking. As best she could, she monitored Tanni's comings and goings, and she tried to remain aware of her friends. At the moment, that was mostly Shaw.

One of the problems between Shirley and her daughter was that Tanni blamed her for the motorcycle accident that had claimed her father's life. It might not be logical, but in Tanni's adolescent view of the world Shirley was responsible. She'd been the one who'd finally capitulated and agreed that Jim could commute into Seattle on his Harley.

Tanni was convinced that if Shirley had held her

ground, her father would still be alive. That question would be forever unanswered.

Sighing, Shirley made her way up the stairs and realized she'd skipped lunch. That often happened when she started work on a new project. She'd spent the day selecting different fabrics and designing a quilt using suede, cotton prints, silk, linen and yarn, as well as ribbons and cords. When the creative mood overtook her, food didn't enter her mind. In fact, it wasn't unusual for her to work without a break. Her best pieces were created during long stretches of time that went far into the night. Jim and the children were accustomed to her strange schedule. Now there was only Tanni at home. Jim was gone and Nick away at college.

For Shirley, her art was a refuge and an escape. It had been for Tanni, too, although her daughter kept her drawings to herself these days. That was probably a good thing, because Shirley had been worried by the unrelenting anger and bitterness in Tanni's sketches. She'd become introspective, shunned most of her friends and refused to talk to Shirley, to a counselor, their pastor, anybody.

Things had changed when she started seeing Shaw, although the transition had been gradual. Despite her concerns, Shirley was grateful that in Shaw, Tanni had found someone to share her feelings with. Like her daughter, he was an artist. Unlike Tanni, Shaw had never had formal training.

No doubt about it, he was talented. Shirley had gone out of her way to help him get the schooling he'd need if he was going to make a living as an artist. She'd be the first to admit that her motives weren't exactly unsullied.

Shirley was worried that the two teenagers, both

burdened with a multitude of problems, were too close and would become sexually active. She was afraid Tanni might end up pregnant or, at the very least, broken-hearted, devastated by another great loss. The fact that Tanni and Shaw had discovered the skeleton in the cave outside town had only strengthened the bond between them. They'd become nearly inseparable ever since, and Shirley knew the dangers of that, knew where it could lead. She wanted to protect her daughter from the painful consequences of too intimate a relationship too young.

In an effort to smooth the way for Shaw, Shirley had agreed to go out with Will Jefferson. Fortunately she rather liked Will and he was definitely attractive, but she remained wary. More to the point, Will was friends with Larry Knight, an artist she greatly admired. At Shirley's urging, Will had approached him in an effort to get Shaw a scholarship to a reputable art school.

She'd tried to hide her relief when Shaw was accepted into the San Francisco Art Institute. He was scheduled to fly out there in two days; he'd be working for a friend of Larry Knight's before the summer term started in May. Although they hadn't discussed Shaw's leaving, Shirley realized her daughter felt torn. This was a great opportunity and she was happy for Shaw; at the same time she was worried about what it would do to their relationship.

The front door opened and Tanni came inside. She dropped her backpack on the carpet and kicked off her shoes. Without a glance in Shirley's direction, she headed for her bedroom. A few seconds later, the sound of the bedroom door slamming shut echoed down the hallway.

Shirley wanted to chastise her daughter—for her rudeness, for disregarding Shirley's frequent requests that she take her backpack to her room, for being inconsiderate of anyone's feelings but her own. She might as well be howling at the moon for all the response she'd get.

And the truth was, Shirley didn't dare instigate a confrontation right now. She was too afraid Tanni would react by doing something impulsive, something foolish.... She opened the cupboard and chose a can of chicken noodle soup. Anything frozen or canned was quick and easy. Shirley didn't have the patience to cook.

Once the soup came out of the microwave, she sat down at the kitchen table. She'd eaten her first mouthful when her daughter walked in. Tanni looked around, saw her mother and then just as quickly turned around and left.

That was typical.

"How was school?" Shirley called after her.

"Fine."

"You hungry?"

"No. I'm going to my room."

"Okay." Tanni's terse rejection wasn't unexpected. Still, Shirley had to try.

After she'd finished her soup, she set the bowl in the sink and turned on the evening news and picked up her needles and yarn. She'd started knitting lately, nothing creative or complicated. Everything she knit, mostly squares and scarves, was for charity. Knitting freed her mind. At the end of the day, the comforting, repetitive action relaxed her and allowed her to reflect on the events of her life.

To her astonishment, about fifteen minutes into the newscast, Tanni walked into the family room and sat in the chair next to hers. Shirley opened her mouth to utter a welcoming comment, but at the last second decided against it. If she spoke, Tanni might leave. No, it was best to let her daughter do the talking.

"He's going to meet other girls, you know," Tanni finally said.

Shirley didn't need Tanni to explain who she meant. "Yes, he probably will. Are you afraid of that?"

Tanni shrugged, which said she *was* afraid. She knew she risked losing their relationship once Shaw left for art school.

"Do you want him to stay in Cedar Cove?"

Tanni looked at Shirley and a half smile formed, as though the question had amused her. "No!"

"But you don't want him to leave either, right?"

"Mom, think about it! Shaw's the only real friend I have. I'm going to miss him."

"Yes, you will." Maybe, just maybe, that would force Tanni to find other friends—the friends she'd had before the accident, the friends she'd abandoned.

"He says he loves me."

"And you love him." Shirley wasn't about to discount the intensity of their feelings. The problem was, they were both so young and didn't have the life experience to handle such a powerful emotion.

"I love Shaw more than *anything*—more than my life."

A shiver of fear ran through Shirley, which she worked hard to disguise. It took her a moment to realize that Tanni's words had simply been a way to communicate the depth of her feelings for Shaw.

"He says he'll e-mail or phone me every day."

"I'm sure he will."

"I know, but I wonder how long it'll last."

So did Shirley, although it would've been foolish to admit that. "He'll be back for visits."

"Not often enough," Tanni complained. "Everything's going to change and I don't want it to."

Tanni sounded like she had as a little girl, needing her mother's comfort.

"Would you like a hug?" Shirley chanced asking.

Her daughter glared as though the offer had offended her.

"A hug wouldn't hurt," Shirley added.

Tanni shrugged. "I suppose so."

Shirley put down her knitting, then stood and walked over to her daughter. She couldn't remember the last time Tanni had permitted her to show any affection. An involuntary sighed escaped as she slid her arms around her daughter.

To her shock and delight, Tanni hugged her back.

"You're going to do just fine," Shirley said. "And so is Shaw."

Tanni leaned her head against her mother's shoulder. "I hope he does."

"I know you do."

"But I'm afraid," Tanni whispered. "What if he's so successful he doesn't want anything to do with me?"

Shirley wasn't sure how to reassure Tanni. She couldn't promise that wouldn't happen and some part of her actually hoped it would.

Tanni broke away and straightened.

Shirley returned to her knitting; Tanni stayed in the room. After a couple of minutes, Tanni said, "The school passed around a notice from Grace Harding, the woman who runs the library."

"A notice for what?"

"The library's looking for volunteers to work with kids and dogs," Tanni told her.

"Dogs in the library?"

"That's what it said. Ms. Harding is bringing in dogs from the animal shelter and letting children with reading problems read to them. A lot of kids at school say it's silly, but I think it's a great idea."

"Why would the library need volunteers? Don't they already have quite a few?"

"I'm not sure, but this is something I'd like to do."

"Okay. It sounds interesting."

"There's a meeting next week and I want to go."

"I'll be curious to hear more about it."

"I'll let you know." Tanni started to leave. Halfway across the room, she stopped and glanced over her shoulder. Then, in a casual tone, she said, "Thanks for listening, Mom."

Tears welled up in Shirley's eyes. "You're welcome," she whispered.

A year after losing her husband, it almost felt as if she had her daughter back.

Twenty-Six

Saturday evening, after spending eight hours on her feet at the cash register, Christie was tired. Bone-deep tired. For months, day after day, it'd been nothing but work and school. She couldn't even remember her last visit to the Pink Poodle.

They'd had exams that week and Christie decided she deserved a small reward. She'd done all her assignments, studied hard and become proficient with both a camera and a calculator. One beer wouldn't hurt, and it would be good to reconnect with her friends.

She pulled into a parking space, and out of the corner of her eye saw a limo at the back of the lot.

No. It couldn't be. James? Had he come looking for her? Was he waiting there on the off chance she'd show up?

Well, it wouldn't be the first time he'd dropped by the Pink Poodle, but it would be the last! Climbing out of her car, she slammed the door and marched toward the parked limo.

Rapping hard against the dark windows, she didn't immediately realize the vehicle was empty.

She rubbed her knuckles. If James wasn't in the limo,

that probably meant he was in the bar. That was fine with her. She'd flirt with her friends and ignore him, a prospect that filled her with renewed energy.

Walking into the tavern, Christie first spotted Kyle, a divorced plumber. Several other guys were there, too, mostly sitting at tables. A few of them were playing pool.

"Hey, look who's here." Kyle lifted his beer mug in salute.

"Christie!" Bill slid off his stool to give her a hug.

Larry, who worked the bar, automatically got her a draft.

It didn't take her long to find James. He sat alone in a corner of the room. That wasn't a beer he had, nor did it resemble a mixed drink. From the looks of it, he was sipping a soda.

"Where've you been?" Kyle asked when Christie slipped onto the bar stool next to her old friend.

"Oh, around."

"I heard you been taking college classes," Larry commented, setting the frothy mug in front of her.

"Yeah, I decided it was time to get serious about a career."

If James had noticed her, he didn't give any sign.

Bill sidled up next to her.

"What's with the guy in back?" she asked, pointing at James.

"We call him the Professor," Larry said and his voice fell to a whisper.

"Does he come here often?"

Kyle shrugged. "Once or twice a week."

"Been comin' by every so often for the past couple months. Never says a word. All this time and none of us even know who he is."

"He's James Wilbur," she said automatically. She

hadn't meant to acknowledge him. Her problem, one of many, was her inability to keep her mouth shut.

"You know him?"

Rather than lie, she took her first sip of beer while she tried to come up with a reasonable response. "Not really. I thought I knew him at one time, but I was wrong." She wasn't sure how much sense that made—at least to them.

"Hey, just a minute." Kyle glanced from Christie to Bill, and then to Larry. He held up one finger. "I remember him."

"You do?" The question came from Bill.

"He's the guy who hung out in the parking lot before Christmas."

Larry nodded in recognition. "The guy in the limo!"

"Is it out there now?" Kyle asked. He and Bill hurried to the door. "Yup," Kyle told them a moment later. "Sure is."

"Looks like he finally worked up the courage to step over the threshold," Christie said, playing along.

All three men laughed, causing a few of the other patrons to turn in their direction.

"You might want to say hello," Larry said.

Christie shook her head. "Why would I do that?"

"You said you knew him. He's been pretty morose, sitting there nursing his Diet Coke."

Diet Coke. The man was as skinny as a rail and he drank Diet Coke? For some reason she couldn't explain, the thought made her furious.

"Sure, Christie, go say hello." That was Kyle, throwing in his two cents' worth.

"I'll bet he's been waiting for you all this time," Bill said in a teasing voice.

"Oh, puleese."

All three grinned.

"Hey, he looks like he could use a friend."

Talking to James hadn't been part of her plan, but when the guys urged her to go over, she found the suggestion irresistible. At this point she didn't have a clue what she intended to say. It'd probably end up being something stupid. But even knowing that wasn't enough to stop her.

James didn't look up as she approached, which sort of ruined things. She didn't wait for an invitation to pull out a chair and join him.

"What are you doing here?" she demanded.

He answered by lifting his Diet Coke and taking a sip.

"What's the matter, have you forgotten how to talk?"

"No."

James had always been a man of few words, but never fewer than now.

"The guys said you've been coming around for a while. Any reason?"

"You."

She rolled her eyes. She hated one-word responses. "Would you care to elaborate?"

"No."

"Fine. If that's the way you want it." She sat sideways in the chair, crossed her legs and made idle circles with her foot. It felt good to sit after spending so many hours on her feet.

James ignored her and she ignored him. After a few minutes, she could see this wasn't going anywhere, so she started to stand. His hand shot across the table, stopping her.

"What?" she snapped, shaking herself free. If he wanted to limit his responses to one word, she'd do that, too.

"Stay."

"Why?" She wondered how long this could continue. Not long, she decided. "Stay? You treat me like I'm your pet dog."

"*Please* stay."

Two words. Well, that was an improvement. Slight, but an improvement nonetheless.

Silence stretched between them. James was the one to break it. "I came because I felt close to you here."

"I hope you know I didn't stay away because of you."

"I realize that. You've been taking business and photography classes. Teri told me."

Her sister the traitor.

James looked directly at her then. "Is it so hard to forgive me?" he asked quietly.

Rather than explain, she simply nodded.

His mouth tightened. "I'm sorry for you."

Christie raised one hand to her chest. "For *me?*"

James shook his head sadly. "Haven't you figured out yet that no man will ever love you as much as I do?"

"Right," she muttered sarcastically. "Trust me on this, Mr. Chauffeur, plenty of men have claimed undying love, just like you did, and then walked out. You're no different and you proved it."

"If you'd be willing to let me have a second chance, I'll prove otherwise."

"Sorry, I've handed out all the second chances I plan to give." She sounded definite and sure of herself, but she could feel her resolve weakening.

He hesitated, then shrugged in resignation. "That's a shame."

"Oh, yeah, I'm going to regret this, right? Well, I'm way past regret, James Wilbur or whatever your real name is. Way, way past that. I've already suffered all my regrets—the day you ran off."

He nodded and stood.

She flinched involuntarily when he reached out to run his finger down her cheek. His touch was light, a caress. "We would've had beautiful babies." With that he walked away.

She wanted to shout after him that it was a B-movie line—but she was paralyzed, her breath locked in her lungs. When she'd managed to exhale, she vaulted out of her chair and ran outside. James was halfway across the parking lot.

"Wait just one minute!"

Silently he turned to face her.

Christie stabbed her finger into his chest. "That was low and completely underhanded and…and cruel. And you know it!"

Because, clichéd line or not, he'd struck her weakest point—her desire for a baby. He knew this about her because she'd been honest with him, confided all her hopes and failures and dreams. It was the one thing he could've said that was guaranteed to send her running after him. If Christie hadn't been so angry, she would've broken into sobs. Her longing for a child had been shoved aside for so many years that whenever it surfaced the ache became unbearable.

James studied her and in the dim light of the streetlamp she saw the tenderness in his eyes. Although she tried to resist, he slipped his arms around her and pulled her against him.

When she finally surrendered, leaning into his strength,

James whispered in her ear, "Oh, Christie, Christie, how long until you see I'm not like those other men?"

She so badly wanted to believe him, yet knew she couldn't. Too many times before, she'd been duped. She couldn't risk it again.

Still, when he lowered his mouth to hers, she offered no resistance. Sliding her arms around his neck, she yielded to his kiss. His lips were warm and moist as he half lifted her from the pavement. His gentleness made her knees weak and her heart race.

When he released her, she was surprised she was still upright.

"I'll be waiting for you," he said. "I'll be here when you're ready. I'm not going anywhere, Christie."

She wanted to argue but couldn't.

He touched her cheek again, then left her standing alone in the Pink Poodle parking lot.

Twenty-Seven

If he didn't know that Faith's tires had been slashed two weeks ago and that her home had been vandalized in January, Troy wouldn't have guessed that anything untoward had happened at 204 Rosewood Lane. But the harassment had been intermittent from the moment she'd moved in. Troy was at a loss to explain why Faith had been singled out. She wasn't the kind of person who made enemies; anyone who met Faith was immediately drawn to her. He hated the fact that neither he nor his deputies had been able to determine who was responsible.

He stood in front of the house, recalling the morning he'd come to talk to Grace Sherman.

Dan had disappeared and at that point no one knew the tragic truth—that his lifelong depression over an incident in Vietnam had driven him to suicide. Troy had vivid memories of that visit and the one a year later, when he'd come to bring Grace the news that Dan's body had been found.

Sandy had been alive when Dan Sherman went missing. Troy had told her about the case. She'd lost much of her ability to communicate verbally by then, but her expressive eyes had revealed her sympathy for Grace.

Troy sighed. He was surprised by how often he thought of Sandy. He wished he could talk to her now. She'd always been a good listener and while it might seem odd that he'd want to discuss his feelings for another woman with her, he sensed that if Sandy had known Faith, they would've been friends.

Catching him off guard, the front door opened and Faith stepped onto the porch, standing in the afternoon drizzle. Spring had officially begun a week ago, and as the old saying went, March showers brought April flowers. Or was it April showers that brought May flowers? In either case, it was still a winter sky, bleak and gray, although the days were noticeably longer.

"Troy," Faith called, her arms crossed protectively over her chest, "what are you doing here?"

Grinning, Troy walked up the pathway to the house. "Just checking to make sure you're safe and sound."

"I have a feeling you check on me quite a bit."

Troy didn't deny it. It'd become habit to drive by at least once a day and sometimes more often, although he didn't want Faith to know *how* often. "I keep turning up like a bad penny, right?"

Faith smiled, and her lovely face seemed even lovelier. "Do you feel like a cup of decaf coffee?"

One thing he wouldn't do, and that was refuse to spend time with Faith. He loved her. He knew she loved him, too. For the most part they'd worked out their differences but the situation between them remained tentative. Although they'd known each other practically their entire lives, the setbacks of the past year had nearly destroyed any promise of a lasting relationship.

He followed Faith into the house and saw that she'd been knitting. The television was on the twenty-four-hour news channel, and the aroma of cooking wafted toward him. Whatever it was smelled delicious.

He took a seat and Faith brought him a mug. "There's something on your mind," she said matter-of-factly. "But I know that whatever it is doesn't have anything to do with me."

She was right on both counts, and her ability to read him so easily reminded him of Sandy. Despite his lawman's poker face, Sandy could always tell when he was disturbed by a case, and now it seemed Faith shared that trait.

She sat across from him. "Can you talk about it?" she asked.

He shook his head. This was information he couldn't share. A visit from Charlotte Rhodes earlier that afternoon had most likely given him the solution to one of his most difficult outstanding cases. Even now, Troy wasn't sure how to handle the situation, especially since it involved someone he knew well.

"I wish I could…but I can't."

"It doesn't matter," Faith said in that soothing way of hers.

He held his coffee with both hands, letting the heat chase away the chill of late afternoon. "How'd you know something was on my mind?" he asked curiously.

Faith picked up her knitting and gazed into the flickering light of the fireplace. "I'm not sure."

Troy stared into his coffee. "That's not true, Faith."

She laughed. "How do *you* know?"

"Touché." It would be so easy to sit with Faith for the rest of the evening. Who was he kidding? He'd like nothing better than to be with her for the rest of his *life*. A contentment that had escaped him all afternoon settled over him.

"Okay, I'll explain," she said, her fingers nimbly working the yarn. "You have a 'tell.'"

"A 'tell'?"

"Yes," she said, brightening. "I've been watching that poker show on TV. I don't know how I got started, but now I'm hooked."

"And a 'tell' is?" He knew very well what it meant, but he wanted to hear her definition of it—and, even more, what she felt his "tell" was.

Faith's response was enthusiastic. "You've noticed that a lot of poker players wear dark glasses? The reason, according to the commentators, is that other players can read their eyes and know if they're bluffing or not. I saw one player who shuffled his chips every time he was dealt a good hand. I could tell he had decent cards by his body language."

"In other words, you can read me the same way you read that poker player?"

"Yes," she answered smugly.

Troy was enjoying this. "Would it be divulging too much to ask what my 'tell' is?"

She smiled again and stopped knitting for a moment. Leaning forward slightly, she said, "You squint."

"I most certainly do not," Troy said.

"Oh, but, Troy, you do. Your eyes narrow and you frown. It's like you're trying to read tiny, tiny print."

As if to prove the opposite, he widened his eyes, which made Faith laugh outright.

"When did you first see this 'tell' of mine?"

"Christmas."

The only real interaction he could remember was at the Christmas tree farm, where Megan and Craig had dragged him for their annual outing. Faith had been with her son and her grandchildren, and they'd met there.

"Can you be more precise?"

She lowered her eyes as though her knitting suddenly demanded her full attention. "The night I ran into you at the tree farm," she said.

So he was right. "Ah, yes."

"I knew the instant I saw you that you didn't want to be there."

That much was true. The only reason he'd gone was for Megan's sake. The choosing and chopping down of the Christmas tree had long been a family tradition, and although he'd tried to beg off, his daughter had insisted.

"You were furious with me, as I recall."

"Yes, I was," she said.

"But you aren't anymore, right?"

Faith shook her index finger at him. "You aren't going to distract me. We were talking about your 'tell,' remember?"

He gestured toward her. "By all means, continue."

"As I was saying," she said, her mouth quivering with a smile. "You squint. You squinted that night when you saw me."

"And you pretended you hadn't noticed me."

"Not as successfully as I'd hoped," she said, amusement still evident on her face.

He grinned, too. "I guess this means I should never play poker," he said lightly.

"Not with me, you shouldn't," she told him, as her fingers moved quickly, looping the yarn onto the needles.

Troy had never asked her what she was knitting. He thought of the socks she'd made him; he still wore them but never without a pang of nostalgia—and remorse.

He reluctantly set his coffee aside. "Nothing's been going on around here, has it?"

Faith looked away. "Nothing of significance."

"Faith…"

Sighing heavily, she stared down at her knitting. "Someone, probably a kid trying to make trouble, overturned my garbage can. No harm done."

Troy rubbed his face. "I wish I knew why you've been targeted for this vandalism."

"I wish I did, too."

"If only we—"

"I've done everything you've suggested," she broke in, a bit defensively. "Scott was over last week and set up motion detector lights over the garage. Don't worry, Troy, nothing's happened since my tires got slashed."

"Good." He stood and glanced at the door. "You'll call if anything else comes up?"

"I will," she promised.

"I mean it, Faith."

She walked him to the door and wrapped her arms around him. Troy held her close, loath to release her. He wanted to kiss her, but needed a sign, an indication that she wanted his kiss. It came a few seconds later when she turned her lips to his. Their mouths met softly—sweet and comforting. They'd known passion, but this gentleness was different and in some ways better, although he wouldn't have thought that possible.

When he ended the kiss, he pressed his chin against her hair and breathed in her perfume, wondering when he'd see her again. Or would he have to find another convenient excuse to visit?

Ten minutes later Troy pulled into his own driveway. He couldn't remember a single detail of the ride between

Faith's house on Rosewood Lane and his own place at 92 Pacific Boulevard. His conversation with Charlotte Rhodes that afternoon weighed heavily on his mind. He needed time to consider the information she'd given him, to think it through.

As Troy stepped out of his car, he realized there was a second vehicle parked outside his house. The doors opened and two men emerged. Because it was dark and the porch light dim, Troy couldn't immediately identify them. Then he recognized one as the mayor; the other was his brother, the attorney.

"Louie," Troy said, extending his hand to the mayor. "Otto."

"I want you to know," Otto said gruffly, "as my brother's attorney, I advised him against this, but he insisted."

Troy nodded. "Would you like to go down to the station?" he asked the mayor.

"No."

Louie was pale, and sweat had broken out on his forehead.

"I want to talk to you," Louie said. "Privately."

Troy hesitated. "We've known each other a long time. If you're asking me to—"

"My brother hasn't admitted to any wrongdoing."

"Otto," Louie barked. "Just let me tell him. If he needs to arrest me, then so be it. I'm not asking for any personal favors." He looked directly at Troy. "I'd prefer to talk here, if that's all right. If you want me to repeat what I tell you over at the station, then I will."

"Agreed." Troy showed them into the chilly house, switched on the lights and turned up the heat, then gestured for the two men to sit down.

Louie perched on the edge of the sofa; Otto sat next to him, his back straight, his expression guarded.

"I'm not sure where to start," the mayor said, glancing up at Troy. His hands dangled between his parted knees.

"You saw Charlotte Rhodes stop by my office earlier this afternoon, didn't you?"

"No," Louie said starkly. "She came to see me afterward and suggested I speak to you." He gave a long sigh. "I figured it was either come to you and tell my story or wait for you to seek me out. I'd rather clear this up once and for all. I don't want it hanging over my head anymore."

"My brother can't be held responsible—"

Louie raised a hand to silence his brother. "I'll do the talking. I appreciate that you're here, Otto, but I'm going to do it my own way."

"I—"

Again Louie silenced his brother, this time with a look.

Troy settled back and waited.

"I married my first wife while I was in college," Louie said.

Troy didn't know the mayor had been married more than once. Donna had been Louie's wife for as long as he could recall.

"My marriage to Beverly wasn't good," Louie told him. "My wife had…medical problems."

"What my brother's trying to say," Otto cut in, "is that Beverly had *emotional* problems. Or, more accurately, psychiatric ones."

"She was agoraphobic," Louie said as if his brother hadn't spoken. "In the beginning, everything seemed fine. Beverly was shy and she didn't like being around a lot of people but that didn't bother me. After we were married I realized this tendency of hers was more than simple aversion. To be fair, we had a few good months together." Louie paused, sighing, before he went on. "I was about to graduate from college and we decided it was time to start our family."

"That's when the trouble began," Otto said. "And—"

Louie cast his brother another quelling look and Otto didn't complete the sentence.

"As I was saying," Louie continued, "Beverly got pregnant easily enough but miscarried in the third month. Losing the pregnancy devastated her."

Troy remembered how hard Sandy's miscarriage had been on both of them, and more recently, how painful the loss of Megan's baby had been. He nodded sympathetically.

"Afterward she withdrew completely. I couldn't get her to leave the house."

Otto leaned forward and added, "Louie did everything he could for her—to no avail. He couldn't persuade her to see a psychiatrist, and the problem got worse and worse."

"By then Beverly and I had no relationship to speak of. Some days she didn't get out of bed." Louie rubbed his palms together as if to warm his hands. "It didn't help that her younger sister—who wasn't married—got pregnant. The father was some sailor she met during Seafair in Seattle. Here today and gone tomorrow. Apparently Amber didn't bother to ask his name. She didn't want the baby, but Beverly did. She told her we'd raise the child. I was willing to adopt Amber's child," Louie said, "hoping that a baby would give me back the woman I married."

"Did you legally adopt the baby?"

"No," he said, sighing once more. "That meant Beverly would have to leave the house—go to court, for one thing—and she refused to do that."

Troy nodded, indicating that his friend should go on.

"When the child was born with Down syndrome, it made no difference to Beverly. She mothered him, gave him all her love and attention."

"But nothing changed," Otto said. "Beverly was still a recluse."

"Her only joy was her sister's son," Louie said. "She doted on him, loved and pampered him and then—"

Troy interrupted with a question. "You stayed in the marriage?"

Louie looked away, then finally shook his head. "Eventually we divorced."

"My brother did everything he could to save the marriage," Otto insisted.

Louie raised his hand. "None of that's important now. Beverly didn't seem to care that we were no longer married. Timmy was her entire world."

Sensing there was more to this story, Troy turned to Otto, who—strangely—remained quiet.

"A few years after the divorce, I met Donna," Louie said, lowering his voice. "I was living in Seattle then. We got engaged. She knew I was divorced but I didn't mention Timmy."

"Louie kept in touch with Beverly and Timmy and saw to their needs."

"I brought her groceries once a week, made sure her bills were paid and checked up on her," Louie elaborated. "Otherwise, I don't know what would've become of them. Although we were divorced I still felt some responsibility for her and Timmy. I was often tempted to call Child Protective Services but they would, most likely, have taken Timmy away, which would've destroyed Beverly completely. I guess he was a kid who slipped through the cracks. No one from any official agency knew about him—and I didn't tell them."

"What happened to Beverly?" Troy asked.

"I'm getting to that. When Timmy was in his early teens, I noticed that she'd started to lose weight. Soon I realized it was something physical. She became gaunt and spent practically all her time in bed. I begged her to see a doctor but no matter how much I pleaded she refused."

Otto did speak up then. "Louie phoned to ask for my help. I had a good friend who was a medical student. He went to the house to examine her—over her protests—and diagnosed her with cancer. Stomach cancer."

"It became apparent that unless she got immediate medical treatment she'd die, and frankly I think that's what she wanted. Life had become too painful for her."

Louie's expression was tormented. "I did *everything* I could to convince her to seek medical help. For Timmy's sake, I pleaded with her to go to a hospital."

Troy gave a slight nod. He believed Louie. He knew nothing about any of this because he'd been in the service at that time.

"She kept refusing," Otto inserted. "I was with him on more than one occasion and what he's saying is the truth. The thought of leaving the security of her house was more than she could bear. It was a sad, difficult situation." He shook his head. "Eventually, when she was too weak to resist, we had her taken to Seattle by ambulance. She didn't last much longer."

"What about the boy?" Troy asked.

"I stopped by to visit a couple of weeks before that—

and Timmy was gone." He leaned forward, bracing his elbows on his knees.

"Did Beverly tell you where he was?"

Louie nodded. "She said her sister had come and taken him away." He swallowed visibly. "Beverly knew she was dying and couldn't look after him anymore."

"You checked this out?"

"No. I…I know I should have. I can't tell you how many sleepless nights I've spent wondering. Beverly said Amber had promised to take the boy to an aunt of theirs who lived near Cedar Cove. This aunt, whom I never met, apparently used to visit once in a while."

Troy let that information settle before he asked, "Did you ever hear from Amber again?"

"Never."

Otto said, "She died a year after Beverly in an automobile accident."

"I didn't find out about it until several years later," Louie clarified. "By then, Donna and I were married and we'd moved back to Cedar Cove and started our family."

"So you believe the body in the cave is Timmy," Troy said.

Louie stared down at the floor. "I strongly suspect it is. The…skeleton was wearing the baseball cap I gave him. He loved that thing and wore it constantly."

"We'd need dental records to confirm his identity," Troy said. He paused. "I assume there *are* dental records?"

"Yes," Louie told him. "He'd been to the dentist two or three times. He broke a tooth when he was eight, and I took him to Dr. Hudson myself."

"Fine. I'll get the chart from Hudson and send it to the pathologist."

"It's Timmy," Louie insisted. "You can compare dental records if you want, but in my heart of hearts, I know it's Timmy."

This brought up something else. "Charlotte Jefferson knew about Timmy. She met the aunt—Amber and Beverly's aunt—in the park."

Closing his eyes, Louie nodded.

"So you believe the aunt is responsible for Timmy's death?" Troy asked.

"I don't know what to believe," Louie said, his voice ragged. "If I were to speculate, I'd guess Amber did take the boy to live with her mother's sister. But you have to remember that Timmy had only been away from Beverly for the briefest periods of time. He couldn't possibly have understood what had happened and why he had to leave the only home he'd ever known."

"My assumption is that he ran away," Otto said. "Somehow he found the cave and hid out there...."

"Wouldn't his aunt have looked for him or reported him missing? Is she still alive?" Troy asked urgently.

Louie shook his head. "I learned a few years later that she died of a sudden heart attack about two weeks after Beverly. I figured the boy had gone to a group home or something. I...I suppose that's what I *wanted* to believe."

"Timmy died due to a tragic series of events." Otto stood. "My brother hasn't done anything culpable."

"Maybe not, but I should've made sure Timmy was okay, that he was settled and happy. The truth is, I was young and selfish and relieved not to be responsible for the boy anymore. I feel wretched now to realize my self-centeredness might have contributed to his death. The night I was arrested for drunk driving was the night I could no longer deny what I'd suspected from the beginning—it was Timmy in that cave."

Troy knew that no one would be harder on the mayor than he'd been on himself.

"If you feel you need to press charges, then do so," Louie said brokenly.

"On what grounds?" Otto demanded.

"Neglect," Louie whispered. "Amber wasn't to be trusted and I knew it. I was far too willing to let her take Timmy to this aunt of hers and then, when I discovered the aunt was dead…I didn't look for him or try to find out where he was."

"We'd prefer to keep Louie's name out of the press," Otto said. "By the time Timmy died, he'd been divorced from Beverly for a number of years."

"I don't see how mentioning Louie is relevant to the case. You had no legal obligation toward Timmy."

"Perhaps not a legal obligation but a moral one. I should never have been so willing to slough him off."

Troy agreed that morally Louie had been in the wrong even if legally he wasn't. But in his view, the mayor had suffered enough.

"Once I get confirmation from the pathologist," he said, "I'll write up a short press release, merely indicating that the remains have been identified. What was Timmy's last name?" he asked as the thought suddenly occurred to him. "Was it Benson?"

"No, Amber gave him her name—Beverly's maiden name—which was Gilbert."

"Fine. I'll identify the body as that of Timothy Gilbert."

"You won't mention Louie?" Otto asked. "We can count on that?"

Troy nodded. "I can't see that dragging his name into this matter would serve any useful purpose."

Louie hung his head and whispered, "Thank you."

"You've been a good husband and father during the years since," Troy said thoughtfully. "You've served your community well. I suggest we leave things as they are."

"I'd like to bury Timmy," Louie said. "It's the least I can do."

"I'll see that the remains are released to you."

"I think Beverly would want him buried with her."

Troy agreed.

Twenty-Eight

Mack knew something was wrong the moment he arrived home from his shift at the fire station. Mary Jo threw open her front door, as if she'd been waiting for him. She stood there, looking small and frightened.

Not bothering to go to his own place, Mack walked toward her. She was chewing frantically on her lower lip.

"What happened?" he asked.

She seemed to have trouble speaking, and he noticed how close to tears she was.

"Is Noelle sick?"

The three-month-old had come down with a cold earlier in the week, but it didn't appear to be serious.

"I…I saw David."

Mack stiffened instantly. *"When?"*

"Here…a few minutes ago. I'd just got home with Noelle." It was now about five-thirty, so David had known to come after Mary Jo had left the office and picked up Noelle. Mack supposed Mary Jo's address wouldn't be too difficult for someone like David to find. Access to a computer was probably all he needed.

Taking her by the elbow, Mack led Mary Jo inside and

sat on the sofa with her. Clasping her hand, he held it between his own. He felt her tremble as she gathered her composure.

She breathed in deeply before she spoke. "He wants Noelle."

Mack bit off an angry retort. "He's living in a dream world if he thinks any court in the land will take this baby away from you."

"He said he has an attorney…."

"And you believe him?" Mack had never met David but he'd heard enough about him to realize the other man wasn't to be trusted. Apparently he expected to use his infant daughter as leverage for his own purposes. Whatever his specific objective, Mack was sure it had everything to do with cold, hard cash.

"I…I don't know," she said, scraping her hair off her forehead.

"This is the first time you've seen him since before Noelle's birth, isn't it?"

Mary Jo nodded.

"Do you still have feelings for him?" She'd said she didn't but he had to ask. Had to know. David was Noelle's father, and at one time Mary Jo had loved him. Mack struggled to hide the anger he felt at the thought of David threatening Mary Jo.

"I don't." Her response was loud and immediate. "I can't believe I *ever* cared for him. How could I have been so blind and…and so gullible?"

Mack couldn't answer that, although he didn't want Mary Jo to change in any way. He'd fallen in love with her and he loved Noelle, too. David Rhodes had a hell of a fight on his hands if he thought he could walk away with

Mary Jo's baby—with the baby Mack considered *his* more than David's.

"Why do you think he has this sudden interest in Noelle?" Mack asked. All he could figure was that David saw some financial advantage in claiming Noelle.

"I have no idea why he came," Mary Jo cried. "I haven't heard from him in all this time and then out of the blue he shows up demanding his parental rights. It doesn't make sense."

"What about Ben?" Mack asked. "Has David been in touch with his father?"

Mary Jo nodded slowly. "Apparently he went to his father a little while ago. I don't know if he asked for money or not, but he has in the past. Ben assured me he wouldn't give his son any child support money because there's no guarantee David would use it for Noelle."

Mack frowned. "Is it possible that David assumes his father will give him money if Ben knows Noelle is living with him?"

"I'm not sure." Panic edged her voice. "Maybe."

"He didn't seriously think you'd just hand Noelle over to him, did he?"

"I don't know," she said again.

"Did he say he was coming back?"

"He said he was and that, when he did, he was bringing the authorities."

Mack nearly laughed out loud. "That's a bold-faced lie." He clenched his fists, wishing he'd been home when David had come to the house. Rhodes might be able to intimidate Mary Jo, but not Mack. He would gladly have taken him on.

"I don't care if he comes back or not, I can't risk losing Noelle."

"What are you going to do?"

Mary Jo's eyes brimmed with tears. "I'm moving back home. He's never been there, and after everything I've said about my brothers, I doubt he'd show his face."

Mack wanted to argue. He'd gotten accustomed to having Mary Jo and Noelle so close, accustomed to sharing special moments with them. Everything had been going so well. He'd thought Mary Jo had begun to return his love, but obviously she wasn't ready....

"Is moving away what you really want?" he finally asked. If he voiced his objections too strenuously, she'd guess the strength of his feelings, and that might scare her off. He sensed she still wasn't ready for a new relationship, other than being friends.

"No!" She buried her face in her hands. "It's the last thing I want, but my daughter's future is at stake. Her well-being takes precedence over my personal desires."

"Can your brothers do anything I can't do?" he asked, hoping she'd listen to reason.

"No...I don't suppose they could. But there are three of them and only one of you."

Mack couldn't argue with her logic. As much as he would've liked to spend every minute of every day standing guard over her and Noelle, that would be impossible.

"I left a message with Linc and asked him to contact me as soon as he could."

"I see." Mack's heart sank.

"Leaving Cedar Cove *isn't* what I want," Mary Jo insisted again. "But I'm afraid, Mack."

The way her voice shook told him how upset she was. He offered reassurances but he wasn't sure he'd convinced her. "David's bluffing," he said. "This is just another scheme of his."

"I *want* to believe that." She gazed up at him, tears glittering on her lashes. "But I can't be a hundred percent certain and neither can you."

"I could beat him up for you," Mack said, half-humorously.

Mary Jo punched his arm playfully.

"Have you discussed any of this with Allan Harris?"

"My legal situation is complicated, he says, because I've acknowledged David as the father and the DNA test confirmed it. Plus, he has parental rights and he claims he wants to exercise them. So..." She took a deep breath. "Allan tells me we'd be in for a protracted court battle."

Mack nodded grimly. This was what he'd feared.

"Noelle's going to miss you so much," Mary Jo said tearfully.

"And what about her mother?" Mack needed to know she'd miss him, too.

Looking away, Mary Jo gave a slight shrug. "I didn't think I could..." Her voice trailed off.

"Didn't think you could what?"

Avoiding his glance, she whispered, "I didn't think I could ever trust a man again, but I trust you."

Although Mack was grateful for that much, he wanted more. He wanted her love. Before he could formulate an appropriate response, the phone rang and a panicky feeling trapped the breath in his lungs.

Mary Jo stood up to answer, but Mack stopped her, catching her hand. "Let me get it."

"Why?" she asked with a frown.

"It might be David."

"Oh..." She seemed to collapse onto the sofa.

Mack marched across the room and grabbed the receiver. "Wyse residence," he said in his most official voice.

"What are you doing at my sister's place?" Linc demanded rudely. At least he wasn't David.

Mack answered that question with one of his own. "How quickly can you get here?"

"Why? What's happened?"

"We need to talk. The three of us." Mack wasn't interested in relaying the details over the phone.

"Give me two hours."

"Okay."

Noelle was wailing in the background; Mary Jo leaped to her feet and hurried into the baby's room. Mack followed, standing in the doorway. He watched as she took the infant from her crib, then efficiently changed her diaper. Noelle turned her head and gazed at Mack while her mother dressed her. She cooed contentedly and waved her arms.

"Who was on the phone?" Mary Jo asked. "My brother?"

"Yeah, it was Linc. He'll be here in a couple of hours. Probably around eight."

Mack grinned at the baby, utterly enchanted by her. He couldn't stand the thought of not having her and Mary Jo in his life anymore. Yes, he could visit them in Seattle, but it wouldn't be the same.

"Why don't I take you to an early dinner," Mack suggested. "You could use a distraction for an hour or so."

Reluctantly she shook her head. "I couldn't eat. Thanks, anyway." She lifted Noelle into her arms and walked toward him. "You go ahead, if you want." But even as she spoke, she reached for his hand.

He was deeply gratified to know she didn't mean what she'd said. She wanted him with her.

"I'm not leaving you." He meant more than she realized he was saying.

"Thank you." Mary Jo sounded both relieved and embarrassed.

"I'll stay here with you and we'll wait for Linc."

Mary Jo sent him a grateful look. "Thank you," she repeated.

He held out his arms for Noelle, and Mary Jo handed him the baby who settled instantly in his embrace. He smiled down at her, tickling her chin with his index finger. Outwardly he remained calm, but he was thinking furiously, wondering exactly what he should say to Mary Jo—and how he should say it.

"I should start packing," she said.

Mack raised one hand, stopping her. "Don't."

"But—"

"I have an idea that might work."

She blinked. "What kind of idea?"

"An idea that'll let you stay in Cedar Cove."

Her expression grew hopeful. "What?"

Mack gathered his resolve. "You could marry me."

The color seemed to drain from her face, and for a few seconds he was afraid she might faint.

"What do you think?" he asked, terrified that she'd reject him outright. His heart felt as if it had shot into his throat and lodged there.

"You don't mean that."

"I do."

Mary Jo leaned against the wall. "That won't solve anything," she said.

Mack disagreed. "The next time David comes around, he'll be dealing with me, your husband. He'll be speaking to both of us. Trust me, if he does try this trick again, it'll be the *last* time."

"You don't have to marry me to—"

"It would give me the authority to tell him to stay away from my family."

"But—"

"I'll legally adopt Noelle." He watched as her eyes flared with what he assumed was happiness. Then almost immediately her face fell.

"David won't let you adopt Noelle, especially if he's planning to use her to manipulate his father for funds."

Mack shook his head. "He'll surrender his rights if we pressure him for child support. We could probably prove without too much trouble that he's an unfit father." Mack suspected that as soon as David Rhodes realized he wouldn't be able to use his daughter as leverage against Mary Jo and his father, he'd be willing to sign over all parental rights.

Mary Jo seemed to consider his proposal. "It's…very nice of you to offer."

She was going to reject him. Mack held himself rigid, bracing for her next words.

She must have sensed his disappointment because she quickly added, "I need time to think about this."

Mack checked his watch. "You have an hour and twenty-five minutes." He didn't mean to make this sound like an ultimatum, but there was a practical reason for the time limit.

She obviously understood what it was. "Before Linc arrives?"

Mack nodded. "I'd like to explain all this to him, so he's comfortable with me as his brother-in-law."

"And if I say no?"

Mack expelled his breath. He didn't want to contemplate that possibility. He'd deal with it if he had to and would volunteer his protection and friendship regardless, but…

"I'm hoping you will agree to marry me," he said.

She turned away from him and her shoulders rose, then fell. "First my brothers and now you! Why do all of you feel you know what's best for me and Noelle?"

Mack closed his eyes and recognized that he'd gone about this wrong, but he wasn't sure how to rectify his blunder. "You're right," he said in a low voice. "I *don't* know what's best for you. The problem is, I don't think I could bear to live without you and Noelle."

She turned back to look at him, her face tense. She met his gaze, her eyes dark and speculative. Finally she nodded. She'd reached a decision. "Okay. But I want to wait six months and...and this is important. I won't sleep with you."

"Ever?" he gasped.

"Not while we're engaged."

"But you'll stay in Cedar Cove?"

She nodded again.

That lightened his mood. Still, there was this six-month engagement she was insisting on. "Why wait that long?" he asked.

"It'll give both of us enough time to decide if a marriage will work. At the end of six months, we can reevaluate. If there's no physical contact between us, it would be easier for either one of us to break off the engagement and walk away."

Mack's mouth went dry. He didn't know how to respond.

"Take it or leave it."

"Ah..."

"Should I assume our arrangement's off or do we wait six months?"

"Okay, okay, if that's how you want it."

Mary Jo relaxed and held out her hand for him to shake. "Then we agree?"

"I guess."

"Becoming engaged is serious, Mack. 'I guess' is not a sufficient answer."

He swallowed tightly. It was either accept her terms or risk losing her and Noelle. The baby gurgled and smiled up at him. "Okay, we'll do this your way," he muttered and they shook hands.

"So we're engaged," Mary Jo said.

Engaged. To the woman he loved. But it seemed more like a business deal—and not a very advantageous one, either.

Twenty-Nine

"Are you sure you want to go through with this?" Linc felt obliged to ask. He and Lori Bellamy stood in front of the Kitsap County Courthouse nearly three weeks after their initial meeting. Their hands were tightly clasped. Linc wore his best suit. Fact was, he only had the one suit—and he might be wearing it a second time this year at Mary Jo's wedding. Her engagement to Mack McAfee wasn't a *complete* surprise, and it did give him a certain measure of reassurance.

Lori was so beautiful in her pink dress it was an effort not to stare. She responded with a delicate nod. "I'm ready if you are."

"Did you tell your parents?"

"No." Her eyes connected with his. "Did you tell your brothers? And your sister?"

Linc shook his head. He didn't feel it was necessary for his brothers to know just yet.

"You have the license?"

Linc patted his suit pocket. "Right here."

"We'll need witnesses."

Linc had forgotten all about that. "Someone from the judge's office can stand up for us."

Lori swallowed hard and looked away. "I didn't tell anyone because I knew if I did, everyone would try to talk me out of it." She blushed slightly, her right hand clutching the small bouquet he'd bought her. "I want to marry you."

"Me, too." Linc wanted a wife, an "old-fashioned" woman who shared his values and wanted to make their family her career, at least while their children were young. Although he didn't know Lori well, what he did know suited him just fine. They'd had a number of intense conversations, mostly on the phone.

"If anyone knew I'd agreed to marry a man I'd seen a total of four times, they'd think I was mentally unbalanced." She looked up at him. "Can I ask you something before we go inside?"

"Of course."

"Linc…" She turned away from him.

"Yes?"

"Do you love me?"

Linc had been afraid she might ask this, and he wished he knew what she wanted to hear, what she expected him to say. As tempting as it was to lie, he didn't feel that would be a good start to their marriage.

"No," he said, then immediately qualified his answer. "I don't love you yet, but I like you more every time we talk."

"We talk a lot, don't we?"

Every day, which pleased him. They needed to lay the groundwork for their relationship, set everything in place and work out any disagreements before they said their vows. As a result of their lengthy conversations, he'd made concessions and so had she. He felt that marrying this woman was the right decision, despite their short acquaintance.

"I put in an offer on a commercial property off Harbor Street—the one we talked about."

Lori suddenly averted her eyes. "My father owns that piece of land. I didn't know until recently."

That shouldn't complicate the situation as far as Linc could see. "I offered a fair price," he said.

As soon as they were married, Linc intended to move to Cedar Cove and set up his own car repair business. He'd move in with Lori until they found a place of their own. Lori said she wouldn't be comfortable in Seattle; she preferred to live in a small town. She worked at a dress shop in nearby Silverdale and would continue to do so until they had their first child. Linc believed he could make a success of his new business. He planned to become a silent partner in Three Wyse Men, the family repair shop, leaving its day-to-day operation to Mel and Ned.

"I'm not changing my mind about our marriage," Lori assured him again.

"Me, neither." Linc squeezed her hand. Together they walked up the steps to the courthouse.

The ceremony itself was shockingly brief. It hardly seemed legal that they could be practically strangers one minute and married the next.

Linc hadn't expected the emotion that overcame him when the judge pronounced them husband and wife. In that instant, he experienced a rush of tenderness for Lori that nearly brought tears to his eyes. He was baffled by it, and a little embarrassed, too.

He realized with astonishment that if he hadn't stopped to help her that night, none of this would be happening. It would've been an ordinary Friday afternoon.

Lori didn't say anything, either, and he wondered if

she'd felt the emotions he had. If so, she didn't mention it. In fact, neither of them had anything to say until they were seated in Linc's truck.

Lori smiled at him. "Hello, husband," she murmured.

Linc returned her smile. "Hello, wife."

Wife. What a powerful word that was. A word that said companion, friend, partner…lover.

As he started the engine, he asked, "Is there anyplace you'd like to go first?" It was a few minutes before five.

"Maybe we should have an early dinner."

"Sure." Linc hid his disappointment. He'd hoped she'd suggest they go straight to her place. He'd brought his suitcase and wanted to unpack, settle in before… He'd been looking forward to sleeping with Lori. So far, their physical relationship consisted of a few less-than-chaste kisses. Her response to their tentative lovemaking had led him to believe they'd definitely be sexually compatible.

"I'd like to introduce you to my sister before we do that," Linc said, trying to take his mind off their wedding night.

"You mean now or…after?"

"Now."

"Okay." Lori slid a bit closer and placed her hand on his arm.

Linc enjoyed having her touch him even in the most casual way. When she'd asked if he loved her, before the wedding, he'd been as honest as he knew how to be in his response. Now he asked himself if the tenderness he felt, this joyful expectation, could be love. He hoped so. He wanted to love Lori. He was excited about having children with her. She'd be a good mother and he intended to be a good father.

The courthouse wasn't far from his sister's duplex. When he parked there, he saw Mack working outside, pruning some forsythia bushes. Mack was the kind of guy who always found something to do. If he wasn't painting or doing repairs, he was puttering in his garage or gardening.

Mack and Linc had talked the previous week regarding Mack's relationship with Mary Jo. Linc felt his sister had made a smart choice when she agreed to marry him. He'd come to like Mack and believed the other man would not only look after Noelle, he'd do what he could to keep David Rhodes from using his daughter to manipulate Ben.

Mack met him as Linc opened the passenger door and helped Lori out. His soon-to-be brother-in-law sent him a questioning glance.

"Mack McAfee, this is my wife, Lori."

Mack's mouth fell open. "Your *wife?*"

Lori moved closer to Linc's side.

"When did this happen?"

"About ten minutes ago."

"Does Mary Jo know about this?"

"Not yet. We stopped by to tell her."

Mack stared at them both.

The door to Mary Jo's half of the duplex opened and when she saw Linc in his suit—with Lori beside him—she frowned. She looked at Mack for an explanation.

"Your brother's got news," Mack said, standing back, his fingers in the pockets of his jeans.

Mary Jo returned her attention to Linc, who placed his arm around his wife. "Mary Jo," he said formally, "I'd like you to meet your new sister-in-law, Lori Bellamy."

"Lori Wyse," she corrected.

Mary Jo's mouth sagged open, much the way Mack's had. "You're *married?* The two of you?"

Linc grinned sheepishly and nodded.

"You didn't say a word about this to me!"

"To anyone." Linc wanted her to understand that she hadn't been excluded. "The boys don't know yet."

Shaking her head, Mary Jo turned to face Lori. "You really married my brother?"

Lori nodded. "I love him."

"You do?" Linc echoed. When Lori had asked him if he loved *her,* it'd never occurred to him that she might be that sure about her own feelings, especially this soon.

"She must love you," Mary Jo said. "Well, come on in. Your name is Lori?"

"Yes." Lori broke away from his side and followed Mary Jo into the house.

Linc remained outside with Mack. He inclined his head toward the door. "Mary Jo's not upset, is she?"

Mack lifted his hand in a gesture that suggested Linc's guess was as good as his. "I'd say we're both more surprised than anything. You could've said something, you know."

"I could have," Linc agreed, "but I didn't."

Mack laughed. "If you'd been willing to wait, we might have had a double wedding."

"We didn't want to wait." Linc kicked at the grass with the tip of his shoe, then figured he might as well disclose the other changes he planned to make. "I'm moving to Cedar Cove."

Mack's nod didn't reveal anything one way or the other.

"Lori," he suddenly said. "Lori Bellamy. She's the ex-fiancée of that guy who used to work for Allen Harris—"

"Yes," Linc interrupted sharply. "But that's in the past."

Mark nodded again. "What are your plans now?"

"I'll be moving in with Lori right away and making the commute to Seattle until Mel and Ned feel okay about running things on their own." Privately, Linc had set a time limit of two months.

"What then?"

"I'm starting an offshoot of the business here."

"What about Lori?"

"She'll continue working until she gets pregnant." Linc intended to do his part to make sure that happened as quickly as possible. "After the baby's born, she wants to stay home."

"Mary Jo wants to keep her job," Mack said.

That didn't surprise Linc. He just hoped Mack understood what he was letting himself in for when he married her. He'd never known a woman more obstinate than his little sister.

The two men went into the house and Lori smiled at Linc. "I invited Mary Jo and Mack to join us for our wedding dinner."

Linc forced a smile in response. "What about the baby?"

"My mother would welcome the opportunity to babysit Noelle," Mack said.

"Do you want me to phone her?" Mary Jo asked.

"Sure, go ahead."

Not five minutes later, the whole dinner party was arranged. Reservations were made at a place called D.D.'s on the Cove, after which they all drove over to the McAfees' house to drop off Noelle. At Mack's suggestion, Linc and Lori waited in the truck; then they headed to the restaurant for their six-thirty reservation.

Linc would've preferred dinner with just Lori. However, he'd acceded to her wishes. Mack ordered champagne, which went straight to Linc's head. Come to think of it, he hadn't eaten since early that morning. When the food arrived, he was the first to finish his meal.

The others didn't seem to be in any hurry. He yawned several times as a broad hint that they should wind things up, but no one noticed his impatience. When they were finally ready to go, Lori announced, "I need you to drive me back to Mary Jo's place."

Linc sat with his key in the ignition and turned to look at her. "You do?" He couldn't hide his disappointment. "Why?" He wondered if Lori was making excuses to delay their wedding night.

"She has something for me," Lori explained, gently patting his knee. "It won't take long, I promise."

Reluctantly he followed Mack and his sister back to the McAfees' house to get Noelle, which meant another ten-minute delay.

"What's this thing my sister has for you?" Linc demanded as they waited in the car. "Can't you get it some other time?"

Lori gave an exaggerated sigh. "Are you *sure* you want to know?"

"Yes," he insisted.

"Okay… It's a special nightgown for our wedding night. It's from France and it's black silk. I…should've planned for this—only, well, I didn't and now I'm sorry."

"And where exactly did my sister get this?" Frankly Linc didn't like the idea of Mary Jo passing off some secondhand nightgown to Lori.

"She said a friend gave it to her when it seemed she was going to marry Noelle's father."

"Oh."

"You don't mind, do you?"

He couldn't very well broadcast his intention of removing this fancy French nightgown ten seconds after she put it on, so he answered with a halfhearted shrug. "I don't mind if it's important to you."

"Everything about tonight is important to me."

"Me, too," Linc admitted.

After Noelle had been loaded into Mack's car, Linc drove to the duplex on Evergreen Place. Lori hopped out of the truck, ran inside with Mary Jo and was back in less than five minutes.

By the time she returned she was grinning from ear to ear.

"What's so funny?"

"Your sister. I like her. We're going to be good friends."

Wonderful, just wonderful. "You got that nightgown?"

"Got it." She balanced the box on her lap. "Mary Jo wanted me to tell you it's her wedding gift to you and me."

"Great."

Following Lori's instructions, he drove to her apartment building and parked in the lot. He came around to help her out, then reached into the back for his suitcase. They walked toward the building arm in arm.

He'd never been to her apartment so he hadn't realized how delicate and feminine it was, although he probably should've expected it. There were floral prints on the walls and the white sofa was decorated with a variety of pink pillows in varying sizes and fabrics. The kitchen was one that would make Martha Stewart proud. That was fine by Linc. He was thoroughly tired of his brothers' cooking, not to mention his own.

"Should I put this in the bedroom?" he asked, grabbing his suitcase. The idea was to steer Lori in that direction as quickly as possible.

"Sure."

Linc was in and out of the room in two seconds flat. "The bed's got a canopy!"

"Yes, I know."

As far as he was concerned, this should've been revealed long before their wedding night. "I can't sleep under a canopy." Call him silly or macho or anything you wanted; it was something he just couldn't tolerate.

Lori said nothing. After a moment she gestured helplessly. "I only have the one bedroom."

"Okay, fine, we'll sleep on the sofa tonight."

She studied him as if he'd lost his mind. Maybe he had. One thing was certain: he wasn't sleeping in pink sheets with a froufrou canopy over his head. It would make him feel like...like he'd charged into the private domain of some princess.

Without commenting Lori disappeared inside the bedroom and quietly closed the door. Linc didn't follow. Sitting down on the sofa, he picked up a magazine and started to flip through the pages.

He didn't notice how many minutes passed before she came back, and when she did, the issue of *Home and Garden* slipped from his fingers and fell to the carpet.

Lori posed in the bedroom doorway, wearing a little piece of black silk. A little piece of nothing. Something seemed to be stuck in his throat as he tried not to stare. It didn't work. He couldn't look anywhere but at her.

"My sofa doesn't turn into a bed, Linc," she told him. "If we sleep there, we'll both be uncomfortable."

Sofa? What sofa?

"I'll make sure the canopy comes down in the morning, okay?"

He nodded several times and still had trouble swallowing.

Lori held out her hand and Linc stood and walked toward her. She smiled up at him, her eyes filled with love.

Bending down, he slid his arms around her and half lifted her from the floor before lowering his mouth to hers. She threw her arms around his neck and returned his kiss with a soft, welcoming moan.

Oh, yes, it was a good thing they were married.

Then he picked her up in his arms and carried her over the threshold of her bedroom, old-fashioned to the last.

Thirty

The phone woke Christie out of a deep sleep. Only after several rings did she realize the irritating sound wasn't part of some dream. Blindly, she fumbled for the receiver.

"Hello," she said groggily.

"It's time." She didn't recognize the voice.

Christie sat up and shook the hair out of her face. "Time? Time for what? Who is this?"

"Bobby."

Instantly Christie was wide awake, her heart clamoring. "Are you telling me Teri's in labor?"

"Yes." Her brother-in-law sounded odd, nothing like his normal self.

"Where are you?" Christie asked.

"At the birthing center in Silverdale." His answer was clipped and, most alarming of all, fearful.

"It's early, isn't it?" Teri hadn't quite reached thirty-four weeks; thirty-six would have been more favorable. A couple of days before, Christie had been to visit her. Teri had, in her own words, looked as big as a house and felt about as uncomfortable as a migraine. Her ankles had swollen and she complained bitterly about the no-salt diet her obstetrician had put her on. Despite her discomfort, it'd been a good visit. The subject of James hadn't come up even once. That helped.

"Yes, too early…Teri's afraid," Bobby continued. "She's afraid she's going to lose the babies."

"I'm on my way." Christie wasn't sure what she could do; all she knew was that she had to be with Teri and Bobby. Her sister needed her and Bobby did, too.

"Thank you." The relief in his voice was palpable.

Christie nearly leaped out of bed and threw on yesterday's clothes. She didn't bother with makeup and took only long enough to run a brush through her hair.

Teri was having the babies.

A surge of emotion blasted through her, and she felt like a rocket launched into space. A few minutes earlier she'd been dead to the world. Now she flew around the room, getting ready and, strangest of all, fighting back tears.

Christie wasn't a weeper. Oh, she lowered her guard on occasion, but it wasn't something she made a habit of doing. If she was going to let herself cry every time she experienced emotional distress, she should buy stock in a tissue company.

Ten minutes after Bobby's phone call, Christie slammed out the door. She suspected the only reason she didn't get a speeding ticket on the thirty-five-minute drive to Silverdale was the time—2:15 a.m. She took up two parking spaces when she screeched into the lot, then jumped out of the car as if it'd burst into flames.

When she exploded into the foyer at the birthing center she found James Wilbur pacing the area, waiting for her.

Christie stopped cold. In her rush to get to Teri, she'd forgotten about James. Of course he'd be at the hospital. He would've driven Teri and Bobby there.

"I have your badge information filled out for you," he said. "They'll need to check your identification."

"A badge?" Her mouth felt dry as she struggled to hide her reaction to seeing him again. It'd been weeks since they'd last spoken. She'd only recently begun to win the battle of keeping thoughts of him at bay.

"Before you're allowed in the birthing area," he said in dispassionate tones, "you have to be cleared. As soon as you show your identification, you can have the badge. Without it you won't be admitted."

"Oh." She reached for her purse, took out her driver's license and was issued the badge.

Once it was in her hand, James said, "I'll take you."

"Thank you." All of a sudden she sounded the way Bobby had on the phone—anxious, uncertain, afraid.

James nodded toward the receptionist, who buzzed them through the double doors. He led Christie down the hallway to a waiting area outside the labor rooms.

"Where's Bobby?"

"He's with Teri."

"Oh." Of course. So apparently she'd been delegated to sit and wait for news with James. That wouldn't be so bad, except it meant she'd have to be in the same small space with him.

He stared at her for a moment, then broke eye contact. "I'll let Bobby know you're here."

"Good. Thanks." Christie sat down on the sofa, sliding to the edge of the cushion, and nervously rubbed her hands.

James returned with Bobby. Her brother-in-law looked terrible. Christie had never seen anyone with less color. Bobby seemed about to collapse.

She got up and walked over to hug him. "Everything's

going to be fine," she said, although she had no assurance of that.

"Teri's in *pain.*"

"I know."

"But she wouldn't let the doctors give her anything…."

Christie couldn't keep from smiling. Knowing her stubborn sister, Teri was probably swearing a blue streak.

Bobby continued, his hands clenched at his sides. "The doctors don't want anyone in the room but me."

"I'll be right outside," Christie promised. "Just keep me updated, okay?"

Bobby nodded.

"Does Teri want me to call our mother?"

Bobby shook his head. "After, maybe, but not now."

Christie was in full accord with that decision, although she felt she had to make the offer. Teri hadn't seen or talked to their mother since Christmas. Neither had Christie, and in her opinion, it was just as well that Ruth had stayed out of the picture.

"Okay," Christie told him. "Give Teri my love and tell her I'm in the waiting area if she needs anything."

Bobby nodded again.

"Give her my love, too," James added.

Bobby hugged Christie, waved at James and returned to the labor room. When he opened the door, Christie heard her sister swearing.

James grinned at her—and, despite herself, Christie smiled back.

They sat in the small waiting room across from each other. In an effort to avoid conversation, Christie picked up a magazine. It sported a Christmas tree on the cover. After flipping idly through the pages, she set it aside and looked at her watch. It was just after three.

When she took a chance and glanced up, she found James studying her. He turned away but not before she caught him.

"What?" she demanded irritably.

"Nothing."

"Just tell me." If James had something to say, he might as well spit it out, otherwise they'd both be on edge.

"You don't want to hear it."

"You don't know me as well as you think you do. I wouldn't have asked if I wasn't interested."

He shrugged. "Fine. You asked, so I'll tell you." His eyes met hers. "I was just thinking how much I love you, how much I wish it was you in that labor room, having our baby." He looked down at his hands. "I was kicking myself for being such a fool and not realizing what I had with you and how much I regret ruining everything."

James was right about one thing—she didn't want to hear it. Men had said almost identical words to her before and she'd wanted to believe them. Then, each time, she'd finally recognized that it had all been a spiel, an attempt to get what they wanted—which was exactly what she'd given them. Christie was determined not to fall victim to her own weakness again.

"I don't believe you," she muttered.

His shoulders sank and he looked away. When he spoke again, his voice was sad. "I know."

After that, neither spoke for what felt like hours. James stood and walked out of the waiting room. Christie felt strangely bereft without his presence. She was afraid he wouldn't return but about ten minutes later he strolled back, carrying two cups of steaming coffee. He handed her one of them, and she thanked him.

Then Bobby appeared, looking even worse than before. "They say the labor's not progressing."

It didn't seem possible that he could be any paler and yet he was.

"They decided to do a caesarean," he said next. "They've already taken Teri into surgery.... I can't go with her. The doctor said they're afraid I'll be in the way."

"They won't let you stay with Teri?" The situation must be serious.

"I can wait outside the operating room—but I wanted to let you know what's happening."

"Thank you," Christie whispered. For the first time she was truly afraid for her sister.

Bobby left and she slowly sank back into her chair. James took the one beside her. Again they didn't speak, but after several minutes he reached for her hand.

Christie knew she should pull away, but she craved the comfort of his touch. As they locked their fingers together, heat seemed to radiate up her arm...and through her entire body.

"Teri and the babies will be fine," Christie whispered. "My sister's a trouper."

Apparently James had nothing to add and after a moment she leaned her head against his shoulder. Then his arm slipped all the way around her....

After another thirty or forty minutes, Bobby raced back into the waiting room, flapping his arms like a bird about to take flight. "Three boys!" he cried. "Perfect, small...but alive. They're being put in a preemie machine.... Teri's fine."

"Names?" Christie managed to ask as she leaped to her feet. Her sight had blurred with tears.

"Names, names... Oh, yes, names. Robbie, for me,

Jimmy for James and Christopher for Christie." Grinning, he hurried back to rejoin his wife and three sons.

Instinctively Christie turned to James. At the same time he turned toward her and then, without even knowing who moved first, they were in each other's arms, clinging hard.

"I knew everything would be all right," Christie said with a sob. The truth was, she *hadn't* known and had been frantic with worry.

"A little boy named after me," James whispered into her hair. It seemed almost more than he could take in.

"And me." Christie felt the same way. She'd never dreamed her sister would do something like this. Teri was close to their brother, Johnny, and Christie had assumed that if she was going to name any of the triplets after a family member, it would be him.

"And Bobby, too," James said.

Bobby was elated. He wasn't one to openly display his feelings, but he did now. The love and joy in his face was enough to reduce Christie to another embarrassing rush of tears. She wiped them from her cheeks, using both hands, as James continued to hold her.

"A boy named Jimmy." His voice was awed.

They still clung to each other and neither seemed willing to let go first. Christie rested her head against James's chest. She heard the strong, even beat of his heart. James had come back—to Teri and Bobby, to *her.* He wasn't like the other men in her life.

Just when Christie was about to speak, they were interrupted.

"Christie?"

James released her and Christie turned to see Rachel Peyton, Teri's friend from the salon.

"Did Teri have the babies?" Rachel asked eagerly.

Christie broke into a wide grin. "Three boys. Bobby came to tell us a few minutes ago."

"Are they…?"

"Small but perfect," Christie said. "I don't know the exact weights. Bobby was too excited to give us any more details."

"They're early."

"How'd you find out Teri was in labor?" she asked, curious to learn who had contacted Rachel.

"I phoned her," James said. "Teri asked me to."

As if her legs were no longer able to support her, Rachel staggered to a chair and sat down.

Christie crouched beside her. "Are you okay?"

Rachel pressed her hand to her heart. "I…I thought I was going to pass out."

Teri's friend looked ill. When she closed her eyes, Christie glanced at James, who nodded, obviously aware of what she meant. He left and came back a few minutes later with a nurse.

"I'm fine, I'm fine," Rachel insisted, although she seemed anything but fine.

The nurse escorted her into an examining room, and once again James and Christie were alone.

"I feel like I've worked an eight-hour shift," Christie said, suddenly exhausted.

"I do, too." His smile held her gaze.

"I…I should probably go home and make a few phone calls." But Christie didn't want to leave.

James put his arm around her waist. "Don't go."

Indecision kept her silent.

"Not yet," he cajoled. "Stay a bit longer."

"I would like to see the babies," she murmured. That was true, but it wasn't the only reason she felt inclined to linger.

"Little Jimmy."

"Little Christopher," Christie said, grinning wildly.

James brought her even closer to his side.

They walked down the corridor like that, and after a long sigh, Christie looked up at James. "If you ever leave me again, I'll…I don't know what I'll do, but I guarantee you it won't be pleasant. Furthermore—"

"I won't ever leave you again," James broke in.

"I'm serious, James. I can't take the pain."

He faced her and set his hands squarely on her shoulders. His eyes grew dark and grave. "I'm serious, too."

"I'm going to finish my schooling."

"I'll do everything I can to help you achieve your dreams, Christie. A man does that for the woman he loves."

She'd been prepared for an argument. He didn't offer one. Her gaze steadily held his. "I want babies of my own."

"Babies of *our* own. And I'm all for it."

"Don't be so agreeable," she snapped. "It confuses me and I—"

He silenced her with a kiss, right there in the hospital hallway. Christie's arms slid up his chest and looped around his neck as she returned his kiss.

"Three?" he asked in a husky voice when they drew apart.

Christie nestled into his embrace. "Not if they all arrive at once." On second thought, she mused, that might not be so bad.

James rubbed his hand down the length of her back. "We'll have beautiful babies."

She remembered his remark about beautiful babies the day he'd come to the tavern. It was why she'd run after him… "Yes, we will," she murmured.

He kissed the tip of he nose. "But they won't play chess."

"They can if they want to," she countered.

"Okay," he agreed, "if they want to play, they can."

The nurse who'd led Rachel away returned. "I've called your friend's husband," she said.

"Is everything okay?" Christie asked anxiously.

"No, it isn't," Rachel said, a few steps behind the other woman. She seemed about to burst into tears.

"What's wrong?" Christie hurried after her into the waiting room.

Rachel sat down and buried her face in her hands. "This can't be true. It just can't."

"What can't?"

Teri's friend dropped her hands and glanced up. "I'm pregnant," she wailed.

"But that's wonderful news," Christie said. "Isn't it?"

"It should be," Rachel said. "I should be happy, but…we'd decided not to have a baby right away and then there's Jolene. She isn't ready to deal with this. We promised we'd give her time to get used to us being married first. We *promised.* I should've gone on the pill, but I didn't." Looking from Christie to James, she shook her head. "This is what happens. I told Bruce we were playing Russian roulette, but he was so sure we were safe…."

"So what you're saying is—"

"Sex!" Rachel exclaimed. "This is what happens when you have the most wonderful sex…in the middle of the afternoon. We've been meeting at noon—oh, you wouldn't understand."

James tightened his grip on Christie and whispered, "Is it noon yet?"

Despite herself, despite her worry about Rachel, Christie smiled.

A moment later, Rachel smiled, too….

Thirty-One

"What do you mean you're engaged?" Linnette McAfee shouted over the phone.

Mack knew this would shock his sister—just like it would shock his parents once he told them. The engagement felt… He searched for the right word. *Strange,* he decided. Yes, strange. And awkward, too.

In the short time since they'd become engaged, things had changed between Mack and Mary Jo, and not for the better. Instead of drawing the two of them together, it seemed to have driven them apart.

Ever since that night two weeks ago, Mary Jo had gone out of her way to avoid him. Mack didn't understand it. He'd accepted her stipulation. Nonetheless she seemed to believe that Mack would treat her as badly as Rhodes had. That told Mack she didn't really know him or trust him, although she claimed she did.

Another equally unpleasant possibility was that she didn't actually care for him and was just using him as protection against David Rhodes. He was perfectly willing to play that role and had said as much. But pride—and his own feelings for her—demanded that Mary Jo marry him for reasons other than fear.

"I hadn't even heard that you were dating anyone," Linnette said, breaking into his thoughts.

"It's Mary Jo Wyse and—"

"Isn't she the woman who had the baby on Christmas Eve?"

"Yes. I delivered Noelle and we've been—"

His sister cut him off a second time. "Tell me again why you haven't said anything to Mom and Dad?"

"It's complicated."

"Uncomplicate it for me."

"Well, for one thing, David Rhodes, Noelle's birth father, is threatening to go for custody."

"He wouldn't dare."

"He won't now that I'm in the picture, that's for sure."

"Just a minute," Linnette said in that irritating big-sister way. "You don't need to marry her to keep David Rhodes out of her life. Obviously, there's more to this story than meets the eye."

Maybe informing Linnette that he was engaged hadn't been such a good idea, after all.

"You love her, don't you?"

"Yes…"

"But you aren't a hundred percent convinced she returns your feelings?"

Apparently his sister possessed some form of psychic ability because she'd immediately homed in on the one subject Mack wanted to avoid.

"Uh…"

"You're afraid she's using you to keep Noelle's father at bay?"

When he didn't answer, she continued. "Mack…do you love her that much?"

Mack sat on a kitchen stool with his cell pressed tightly against his ear. He closed his eyes and whispered, "Yeah, I love her that much." It would be a whole lot easier if he didn't.

"Oh, Mack, you've got it bad."

One thing Mack didn't want was his sister's sympathy. He regretted even telling her what was going on between him and Mary Jo. And yet…he felt at such a loss to explain this new tension between them. He'd hoped Linnette might offer him some insight. Some explanation.

Since their engagement, Mary Jo had barely looked at him. It used to be that she'd often invite him to dinner on the nights he wasn't at the station. In the past two weeks he hadn't been to her place even once.

That wasn't all. Before they became engaged, they'd played UNO and other card games. They'd talked every day. They'd laughed together. From the moment they'd discussed marriage, she'd treated him as if he had some communicable disease.

"Okay, little brother, if you honestly feel that way, then why—"

"Can I say something?" he asked.

"No," Linnette said. "Answer my question first."

"All right. If you must know, Mary Jo agreed to marry me but she insisted on a six-month engagement."

"Six months? Well, that's not so bad."

"She also insisted there be no…physical contact between us."

"What?"

Mack was not repeating that information. "You heard

me." Just saying the words out loud convinced him Mary Jo didn't care the way he did. He was a means to an end. He would protect her and Noelle so Rhodes couldn't threaten her. And the worst of it was...he'd suggested it himself.

"Nothing...physical for six months?"

"Mary Jo felt that would give us time to get to know each other—or so she said," he grumbled. That excuse seemed lame in light of the recent awkwardness between them.

"So you aren't...you know—"

He groaned. "I don't ask you about your love life, do I?"

"No, but maybe you should."

Mack let her comment slide.

"Remember," his sister said, "Mary Jo has some real trust issues. I can't blame her for that."

"You haven't even met her," Mack reminded Linnette. But what she'd said was true. Mary Jo did have trust issues; she'd admitted it and the reasons were obvious. That, however, didn't explain the change in her attitude since she'd agreed to marry him.

"For someone who's about to become a husband and father, you don't sound very happy."

"I'm not. The fact is, I'm not sure why I told you. No one else knows except Mary Jo's brother."

"You told me because I'm your big sister and you want advice—only you won't come right out and ask for it."

"Am I that transparent?"

"Afraid so."

He sighed. All of this would be easier if he didn't have such strong feelings for Mary Jo.

"Does she know your real name is Jerome?"

"She knows." He'd insisted on being called Mack from the time he was in grade school. He'd been named for his paternal grandfather, and while Mack had loved his grandpa Jerry, he wasn't fond of the name.

"Why don't you want to tell Mom and Dad?" Linnette asked. "They'd be thrilled."

Tentative as the situation between him and Mary Jo was, Mack didn't feel he could involve his parents. He slouched against the kitchen counter and rested his elbows there. "I have my reasons."

"When do you plan to tell them?"

"I haven't figured that out yet."

"Mack, if Mom finds out from someone else, she'll be devastated."

"I know." Although that wasn't likely to happen.

"So will Dad."

Mack knew that, too. In hindsight, he wished he'd already mentioned the engagement to his parents.

"Okay, I understand why you want to keep it a secret," Linnette surprised him by saying.

"You do?"

"Of course. You want to wait until you're certain she wants to go through with the wedding. The way things stand right now, you're feeling hesitant—"

"It's not me who's hesitant. It's Mary Jo."

"Are you sure about that?"

No question. "Very sure."

After a moment, Linnette asked, "Can I trust you with a secret, too?"

"Of course." His sister, however, had never really kept secrets. She'd always been the model student and the good daughter, whereas Mack and his father often fought. It worried him that keeping his engagement from his parents threatened the truce he'd established with his father. He'd risked a great deal for Mary Jo and his biggest fear was that it was all for nothing.

When Linnette wasn't immediately forthcoming, Mack said, "So what's your big secret?"

His sister's voice dropped so low he couldn't hear.

"Say that again," he said.

"Okay, fine, I will. I'm married."

"You're *what?*"

"Married."

"When?"

"December twenty-ninth. On the drive back from Cedar Cove to North Dakota after Christmas, Pete and I took a detour to Las Vegas. Neither of us had ever been before and it was sheer craziness.

"At first, we couldn't find even one hotel room, let alone two, and when we finally managed to locate a room—there was just the one. That's when Pete said he didn't care what the advertisements said—what happens in Vegas doesn't necessarily stay there, so we got a wedding license and got married the same day."

"You married Pete?" His sister barely knew the farmer, although it was obvious he'd fallen for her, and fallen hard. Anyone with eyes in his head couldn't possibly miss *that.* Linnette had been more circumspect, especially around their parents, but she must've felt the same way. "You married him because you could only find one hotel room?"

"Yes."

"Linnette, that's insane!"

"Now just a minute, little brother. If that's not calling the kettle black, I don't know what is."

She had him there. Mack wanted to argue and tell her

she hadn't known Pete nearly long enough. He wanted to say she had better sense than this. Besides, less than a year ago she'd been crazy in love with Cal Washburn.

"You've been married a lot longer than Mary Jo and I have been engaged. Why keep it a secret?"

"Well…" Linnette exhaled slowly. "I figured Mom and Dad would be disappointed that I hadn't gone for the big wedding, so Pete and I decided there was no reason to say anything right away. I promised Mom I'd be home this summer, and I thought we could have a second wedding there."

"Why not tell them now? They like Pete. It isn't like they're going to be upset about *who* you married."

"I know," Linnette agreed. "But I was afraid they'd think I married Pete on the rebound. I didn't. I genuinely love him and, living so far away, it's not hard to keep it a secret."

"So that's what you plan to do? Say nothing and just go ahead with a second wedding?"

Linnette sighed deeply. "I haven't got that part worked out yet. Getting married on the spur of the moment isn't as simple as it seems."

Mack could sympathize.

"We've been married for almost four months, and Pete keeps asking when I'm going to tell my family. It was so easy to delay it and now…now it's been so long. Mack, I'm not sure what to do."

Mack didn't have any advice to give her, considering that he'd phoned her with his own troubles, looking for help. "I don't know, either."

"You're not upset with us, are you?"

"Of course not! I couldn't be happier for you both."

"Thanks, Mack."

"I'd suggest you tell Mom and Dad soon, though."

"I will..."

They spoke for another ten minutes, and his sister updated him on the medical clinic in the small town where she lived. She told him Pete had moved out of the farmhouse and into Buffalo Valley to be with her. Linnette seemed content, happy with her marriage, her work and her life, and that pleased Mack. In the past few years, she'd changed from an insecure, dissatisfied woman to someone who'd become confident in herself and her choices.

After the conversation with his sister, Mack went outside, determined to work on his garden. He chose the south side of the house for exposure to the afternoon sun. He started digging, shoveling up lawn and dirt to create new flower beds.

The area would need a load of topsoil and plenty of fertilizer. Mack had big plans for this garden. Although the mid-April weather was still cool, he soon broke out in a sweat. Pausing to take off his shirt, he worked steadily until Mary Jo parked in their shared driveway.

Mack checked his watch and saw that it was after five. The afternoon, his last afternoon off this week, had sped by. His next shift started at eight tomorrow morning and would last until Saturday. He liked the extended periods of time off this job gave him.

After removing Noelle from her car seat, Mary Jo walked directly past him as she had every day that week. To his surprise she stopped abruptly and stared at him. Mack waited for her to say something. She didn't, so he continued digging as tenaciously as if he were inches from a vein of gold.

"Hi," Mary Jo said shyly.

Mack raised his head and leaned against the shovel, trying to suggest that he'd only just noticed her. "Oh, hi. I didn't see you there."

She seemed to be studying him closely. "Something wrong?" he asked. Maybe he had on two different shoes. He generally didn't care that much about what he wore.

Mary Jo looked away. "No, sorry, I didn't mean to stare."

"Have I got mud smeared on my face?"

"No." Her neck had gone a warm shade of pink.

"Tell me."

She appeared even more uneasy. "You look…good. All muscular and tan."

Hey, that was promising. "I do?"

"I've never seen you without a shirt before."

"I am a firefighter, you know. There's a reason we're the preferred candidates for those hunk calendars." He resisted the urge to pump his arm muscles in order to impress her with his prowess—or, more likely, make her laugh.

Mary Jo smiled at his comment. "Would you like some iced tea?" she asked.

This was definite progress. "I'd love it."

"Okay if I leave Noelle here? I'll be right back."

Mack gazed down at the sleeping infant in her carrier, then watched as Mary Jo headed for her half of the duplex. Still leaning against the shovel handle, he studied her from behind and cursed himself for ever agreeing to this six-month engagement. He wanted to marry her.

Five minutes later, she reappeared with a glass of iced tea. Mack gratefully accepted it and drank the whole glass in one extended swallow.

"You *were* thirsty."

"I was," he said and noticed once again that she had a

hard time keeping her eyes off him. Good. He wanted her to feel this sense of deprivation as strongly as he did. Mack decided then and there to see if he could get her to reconsider. "Could we talk?"

"Sure," she said, backing away from him. "About anything in particular?"

Oh, yes, but Mack thought he'd approach the subject carefully. "Maybe we should discuss this inside."

"Fine." She picked up the baby carrier and led the way into her duplex.

Mack followed dutifully. He pulled out a chair at the small kitchen table and waited as she brought Noelle to her room. When she returned, she rinsed his glass and poured him another one.

"About our engagement," he finally said.

Mary Jo whirled around, her back against the kitchen counter and her hands behind her. "Yes—what about it?"

"I feel we might want to rethink—"

She bristled. "If you want to back out, I understand, really I do. You're under no obligation to marry me. I haven't heard from David in two weeks now, so maybe he's given up. But I appreciate how much you care about Noelle and—"

"Who said anything about backing out?" he asked, letting his irritation show.

She frowned. "I thought—you know…"

He shook his head. "I don't know."

"That…" she said, moistening her lips. "That you'd had a change of heart."

"I didn't."

"But you want to talk about the engagement?"

"Well, yes." The only thing Mack felt he could do was be honest. "Frankly, ever since we got engaged you've been avoiding me." *Some engagement,* he wanted to say.

"No, I haven't," she said swiftly. "*You* were the one who didn't want anything to do with me. You stopped coming over as soon as we got engaged!"

They could argue about it all night and it wouldn't settle anything. "If I gave you that impression, then I apologize," Mack said.

She offered him the merest hint of a smile. "I guess we've both been silly, haven't we?"

That was an understatement if he'd ever heard one.

"I know you weren't happy when I insisted on a six-month engagement."

"I can live with that," Mack said. "It was the fact that you didn't want me to touch you at all during that time."

Doubt flickered in her eyes. "I didn't say you couldn't *touch* me.... I just don't feel it's wise for us to be... intimate."

"Oh." Mack wondered if he'd misread the situation. But if she was interested in, say, a kiss or a hug, she might have given him some indication earlier.

The shyness was back. Mary Jo started to turn away and he caught her hand, stopping her. His fingers curled around hers. When she turned toward him, Mary Jo slid effortlessly into his embrace as if she'd been waiting her entire life for exactly this moment.

They kissed—two or three lengthy kisses. Not until they'd exchanged another heated kiss did he find the strength to ease his mouth from hers.

Mary Jo looked up at him, eyes wide. Slowly, ever so slowly, she smiled. "That was very nice."

"Yes, it was," Mack said. "Are you sure you want a six-month engagement?"

Staring up at him, she blinked, and then nodded. "I still think that would be best."

Mack could see it was going to be a very long six months.

Thirty-Two

Olivia warily eyed the horse, which was saddled and ready to ride. "I don't know about this," she said.

They stood just outside the barn. Grace walked over to the mare Cliff had chosen for her friend and ran her hand down the animal's long, sleek nose. "You don't have a thing to worry about," she assured Olivia.

Olivia tucked her hands in the back pockets of her jeans. "In case you weren't aware, I'm not a horse-riding type of person. I prefer picking wildflowers and sewing quilts. Riding never interested me. I didn't read *The Black Stallion* and all those horsey books when I was twelve."

"Me, neither, although I have since—when I took a course in children's literature. But that's not the point. I didn't think I was interested at first." Grace refused to listen to excuses. "It'll do us both good to get out in the fresh air."

"Grace, really, you and me horseback riding?" Olivia turned longingly toward the house.

"Yes—you and me." It was a mild, sunny Saturday afternoon and she wasn't going to let Olivia talk herself out of this. "There's a lovely path that meanders down to the beach. Trust me, you'll regret it if you don't at least try."

Olivia still didn't seem convinced. She cast a pleading glance in Grace's direction. "This horse has an evil look about her. How do you know she won't take the first opportunity to buck me off?"

"Sugarplum?"

"Her name is Sugarplum?"

Grace nodded.

"What does *that* prove? The camel that bit you was called Sleeping Beauty," Olivia said, referring to an unfortunate incident with one of the animals they'd housed for the church nativity scene.

"That's irrelevant. Anyway, you promised you'd do this."

Groaning in defeat, Olivia slowly edged her way back to Grace. "Oh, all right."

"You'll be glad," Grace said with an encouraging smile. She remembered the first time Cliff had talked her into getting on a horse. Like her friend, she'd balked and made up a bevy of excuses—really good ones, too. When she'd finally run out of ways to avoid the inevitable, she gave in. The short ride along their property line to the beach had been…wonderful. Afterward, Grace had no idea why it'd taken her so long to agree. She enjoyed horseback riding now and, given the opportunity, Olivia would, as well.

"You're used to this," Olivia said as she raised her leg and set her foot in the stirrup. She grabbed the pommel of the Western-style saddle, hanging on with both hands.

"Not at first, I wasn't. We all have to begin somewhere," Grace said, boosting her up.

"I don't understand why you're so insistent on this." It took Olivia three tries to heave herself into the saddle, even with Grace's help, but she managed. Olivia was breathless by the time she was firmly settled on the docile mare. "I hope you're happy."

"Ecstatic," Grace joked. "As to why I won't let you out of this, the truth is, I want you to feel alive again." After the chemotherapy and radiation treatments, Olivia had been spending her days holed up inside the house, with only rare treks into town. She ventured out to Justine's new restaurant once a week or so, and occasionally visited her brother's gallery, but that was about it. Even Charlotte had grown concerned.

Grace slid into the saddle with a bit more finesse, but then, as Olivia had said, she'd had more practice.

Now that she was on Sugarplum, Olivia glanced anxiously around. "Are we there yet?" she muttered in a weak attempt at a joke.

"We haven't started," Grace replied.

"I was afraid of that."

Olivia looked down, which was a mistake Grace had made early on herself.

"Just how high off the ground am I?" Olivia asked, her brow creased. "If Jack finds out about this…"

"He knows."

"Jack knows and he agreed I should do this?"

"Yes. Now let me show you the basics." She reviewed the lessons Cliff had given her in the beginning. When she'd finished speaking and demonstrating how to use the reins, Grace took the lead.

With a few grumbling words, Olivia followed. To Grace's surprise, once they were under way, her friend didn't seem to have the problems Grace had experienced as a beginner. For one thing, Sugarplum used to stop and graze whenever she felt like it, completely ignoring Grace's commands. She wasn't doing that now.

"Hey, you're a natural," she exclaimed, turning to look at Olivia.

Olivia didn't respond, concentrating on every move.

"You ready to go down the trail?"

"Sure." Olivia grinned sheepishly. "I guess Sugarplum isn't so evil, after all."

"Told you," Grace teased as she led the way at a slow, steady pace. She started toward the evergreen-lined path. Towering pines stretched up into the blue sky.

After a few hundred yards, Grace twisted around to look behind her again. "How're you doing, Calamity Jane?"

"So far, so good. Doesn't the sun feel nice? Especially on your head." Olivia wore a bandanna, tied gypsy-style at the nape.

"It feels great."

"Oh, look!" Olivia called a moment later, her voice animated. "There's an eagle. No, two of them!"

Shading her eyes, Grace peered up at the sky. The eagles were soaring high above them. Fascinated, she watched as they engaged in an elaborate mating ritual. One of the birds fell several hundred feet, and the second eagle swooped after it.

Eagles often landed on the beach off Lighthouse Road, so she knew Olivia saw them frequently. But this was different. More intimate somehow.

"I don't think I realized how fresh and green it smells in the woods," Olivia said after a short silence. "In fact, I didn't realize *green* was actually a smell."

"It reminds you of Christmas, doesn't it?"

"It does."

They continued to clop along, taking in the sights, sounds and smells of the forest. Soon they entered a clearing and the beach lay before them, scattered with driftwood. They could see Blake Island in the distance like an emerald set on an expanse of glittering blue.

"It's so peaceful," Olivia said quietly.

That had struck Grace on her first ride with Cliff. She remembered sitting with her husband on the pebbled beach, their backs against a piece of driftwood. She'd closed her eyes, and the sun had warmed her face as the sounds of nature hummed all around her. Grace had heard the gentle lapping of the water against the shore, birds chirping and the crunch of pebbles as the horses shifted their weight. The experience never failed to move her. It was what she wanted for her friend—this peace, this solace. The discovery of what it meant to be close to nature.

"Let's get down and walk for a while," Grace suggested. "If you feel up to it."

"I do," Olivia assured her. She slid down off Sugarplum and dropped to the ground, landing in pebbles. "Now all I have to do is figure out how to get back up there."

Holding the mares' reins, they strolled side by side. For a long time they didn't speak, content simply to be together. After fifty years—a half century!—of friendship, they were attuned to each other's moods and feelings.

"I've taken so much for granted in my life," Olivia said after a while.

"Don't we all?" Grace didn't think her friend should be hard on herself. She was just as guilty as Olivia of racing from one day to the next, barely taking time to appreciate what a gift life really was.

This second chance at happiness with Cliff had changed her. Her marriage to Dan had been good in its way; after all those years together, the two of them had grown comfortable, although Dan's troubles, the pain of war, had never left him. As much as possible, they'd adjusted and she'd done her best to deal with his mood swings. In the end, it'd all been too much for him.

Cliff had brought his own problems from his first marriage. They'd been patient with each other, though, and had survived misunderstandings and mistakes. Now she was happier than she'd ever expected to be.

"I'm thinking of retiring," Olivia announced out of the blue.

Grace had half suspected this was coming. "Are you sure you want to do that?"

"No," Olivia admitted. "But I'm enjoying these months at home. In the beginning I dreaded it. I was so certain I'd be bored."

"But you haven't been, have you?"

"Not at all. I didn't know how much I'd like quilting. Mom's always been the crafty one. I don't think there's anything domestic that my mother can't do and do well."

Grace nodded. Everything Charlotte attempted—from her special desserts to her knitting and sewing projects—was of the highest quality.

"Haven't you thought about retiring?" Olivia asked, looking steadily at Grace.

Grace had given it fleeting consideration. "I suppose I have," she said, "and yet I love what I do."

"I feel the same," Olivia murmured. "That's what makes this decision so difficult."

Slowly Grace shook her head. "I don't think I can yet. I have a lot I still want to accomplish at work. We're starting a new program at the library that excites me. I'm sure I've mentioned it."

"Teaching literacy by having kids read to dogs?"

"Yes," Grace said. "We've invited a trainer from Seattle to come in and work with us." She smiled. "I already have my first volunteers. Tanni Bliss is one of them."

"Tanni Bliss," Olivia repeated. "Why is that name familiar?"

"Tanni and her boyfriend discovered those remains in the cave. Remember?"

"Oh, yes." Olivia frowned slightly. "What an unusual case. I'm so glad it's been resolved."

"The press sure had a field day with that one, didn't they? That Seattle reporter made it sound as though Cedar Cove was a hotbed of criminal activity." She laughed. "Who would've guessed our sheriff was so good at spin? That press release said very little but somehow satisfied everyone."

"Nevertheless, it was a tragic story. That poor boy, frightened and all alone. I don't think we'll ever know what really happened." Grace had been touched that Cedar Cove's mayor had arranged for a proper burial. There'd been talk around town about his DUI, but that was over now. Jack had written an excellent article about it, with the mayor's full cooperation, which had no doubt subdued the gossip. Thankfully the sensationalism about those poor, forgotten bones had worn off, too.

"Tanni is Shirley Bliss's daughter," Olivia said as if the connection had suddenly clicked. "Will is dating Shirley."

"How's that going?"

"I don't know. My brother doesn't talk to me about his relationships."

Grace was naturally curious. She wanted to warn Shirley but didn't feel it was her place to speak to the other woman. If Will had changed—and there was reason to believe he had—she didn't want to do anything to ruin his chances. "I had my doubts when I learned Will was returning to Cedar Cove," she said.

Olivia gave her an assessing look. "I did, too. After

that…situation with you, I didn't feel I could trust my own brother." She slowed her steps. "I'm just relieved it didn't do any lasting damage."

She meant damage to Grace's relationship with Cliff. Ultimately it hadn't, but Will's interference—and Cliff's reaction to it—was one of the problems they'd needed to resolve.

Changing the subject, Grace asked, "What does Jack have to say about you stepping down from the bench?"

Olivia grinned. "Not much. He says he's fine with whatever I decide. But I feel that if I retired, he'd start thinking along those lines himself, and I'm not sure that's a good idea for Jack."

"Why not?"

Olivia was thoughtful for a moment. "Sometimes I think he's got ink running in his veins. Jack's a completely different person at the newspaper office. He comes alive when he's working to a deadline, and he has great instincts about stories. He might be tempted to hand over the reins, but I suspect he'd regret it after a few months."

Olivia had always had such empathy for others and such an unerring sense of what motivated them; it was one of the reasons she was so effective—and highly respected—as a judge.

"Look at Goldie," Grace said, smiling as she pictured their favorite waitress at the Pancake Palace. Goldie had been waiting tables at their longtime hangout from the first year Olivia and Grace were in high school. She had to be in her seventies and still worked three or four days a week.

"I doubt anyone would dare mention the word retirement to Goldie," Olivia said.

"Who'd serve us our coconut cream pie?"

"Exactly."

They strolled a little longer, and then Grace noticed that Olivia was slowing down. "Shall we sit for a while?" she said.

Olivia nodded, and they found a big log, tied the horses to a nearby tree and sat gazing out over Puget Sound. The Fauntleroy ferry, tiny in the distance, was steaming toward Vashon Island.

"I miss our aerobics class," Olivia said.

"What you miss is the coconut cream pie afterward."

Olivia chortled. "Perhaps you're right." Suddenly she slugged Grace in the shoulder.

"Hey, what was that for?" she said, rubbing her upper arm.

"Because you quit going."

"I need an exercise buddy," Grace protested. "You don't expect me to trudge down to the gym all by myself, do you?"

"I guess not. But we're going back, so don't get soft on me."

"Me?" Grace yelped. "I can run circles around you any day of the week."

"Wanna bet?"

Grace shook her head. "Maybe not."

At that they both smiled and lapsed into a companionable silence.

The year before, Grace had been terribly afraid she'd lose Olivia to cancer. She hadn't, and Olivia's prognosis was good. Her bout with cancer had taught both of them many lessons, but none as profound as the knowledge that nothing would ever stand between them. Their friendship was for life, in every sense of those words.

Thirty-Three

Megan was beginning to look pregnant, Troy thought. He'd stopped by the house after work on Wednesday afternoon because he had an important favor to ask.

"It won't be much longer before you'll need to wear maternity tops," he said when she let him into the house.

A sweet smile lit up her face. "Do you think so, Daddy?"

"I do." He felt a surge of excitement at the prospect of his first grandchild's birth.

"I noticed this morning that it's getting difficult to zip up my pants. Look." She turned sideways and placed one hand beneath the barely discernible roundness of her belly.

"Yup, you're pregnant, all right." How Troy wished Sandy had lived to hold this baby…

"I have a favor to ask you," he said, all business now.

"Anything, Daddy, you know that."

He followed Megan into the kitchen, where she'd just started dinner preparations. Craig, who worked as an engineer at the navy shipyard, wasn't home yet, but he would be soon. "I want Faith to spend the night with you."

His daughter didn't hesitate. "Of course. I love Faith." Then, frowning slightly, Megan said, "She can't stay with her son?"

"Scott's kids are on spring break and he took the family to Disneyland."

"Oh, heavens, you know Faith's always welcome."

This would be more than a simple visit. "Is the bed in your spare room made up?"

Megan nodded. "I hope you don't mind me asking why."

"I want her safe."

His daughter, who'd been stirring spaghetti sauce, instantly looked up. "Safe from what?"

Safe from *whom* was more accurate. "I'm going to spend the night at her house. I have cause to believe the intruder may come back tonight—if it's the person I think it is." He'd been giving the pattern of the break-ins a lot of thought. The man he'd become convinced was the intruder had been spotted in town by one of his deputies that afternoon. On at least one other occasion—the day Faith's tires were slashed—he'd been sighted at the biker bar on the edge of town.

"It's a long story."

"I've got time." Her eyes, so like Sandy's, sparkled with interest.

"Unfortunately, I don't. I'll explain everything later, okay?"

From the way she compressed her lips, Troy knew his daughter didn't like being kept in the dark, but there was nothing he could do about it now.

"Dad, I know you mean well, but I'm pretty sure Faith will insist on staying at her own home. Like I said, she's welcome at our place, but maybe it makes more sense if you stay there. With her."

Troy deliberated for a moment and decided Megan was probably right. "I haven't discussed this with Faith yet."

"Oh, Daddy, you should know better. No woman likes a man making decisions for her. Faith has a mind of her own." She shook her head. "I'm betting she won't agree to this. If I were her, I wouldn't."

He nodded slowly. What his daughter said made sense.

As they headed back into the living room and toward the front door, Troy heard her mutter something else under her breath.

"What?" he asked impatiently.

"Daddy," she said, "when are you going to ask Faith to marry you?"

"I—"

"You love her, don't you?"

"Well, yes, and I have every intention of—"

"What are you waiting for?"

Troy grinned. After all these months, his relationship with Faith was finally back on an even keel, and at last there was hope, real hope.

Once again, he acknowledged that Megan was right. He'd be a fool to squander this opportunity. Faith had been his first love, and while he'd loved Sandy with an intensity that couldn't be equaled, he'd never forgotten Faith. A man didn't forget his first love.

"Soon," he said. "I'll ask her soon."

"Good." His daughter hugged him as he left.

Once he got to Faith's house, Troy suggested she spend the night with Megan, and as his daughter had predicted, she was having none of it.

"I'm not leaving my home, Troy, so save your breath."

Troy shook his head wryly. "Megan told me as much.

But the truth is, you're more of a distraction than a help."

"Am I now?" The information appeared to please her.

"I don't want to put you in danger's way," he explained.

"Any more danger than I've already been in?"

Troy could only shrug.

"You can spend the night here," Faith said.

"The two of us, alone together?"

She raised her eyebrows. "Don't worry about being distracted. I'm not inviting you into my bed."

He chuckled. "That's a shame."

She smiled and looked away. "I can't say I'm not tempted, though."

"You're going to make this impossible," Troy groaned.

"I won't, I promise," she said in a serious voice.

"More's the pity."

"You won't even know I'm here," Faith told him. "You can settle in and make yourself at home. I'll go about my nightly routine, which is probably what this…person will be watching for. Agreed?"

Troy nodded. "Agreed."

"Good."

Troy leaned forward and kissed her with all the hunger and pent-up frustration that had plagued him since she'd moved back to Cedar Cove.

He couldn't speak for Faith, but Troy felt that kiss in every single cell. When they broke apart, she pressed her hand over her heart, gasping. "Oh, Troy…"

He brought her back into his arms. "Shall we do that again?"

Faith cleared her throat. "We'd better not."

"Maybe you're right. I need to concentrate. I've got

people to phone." His first call went to a couple of his best deputies.

"We're on," he said. Weaver and Johnson had parked a dark unmarked vehicle farther down Rosewood Lane and awaited Troy's instructions. His next phone call was to Megan.

"You were right. Faith will remain here with me."

"I hate to say I told you so."

"No, you don't," Troy said. "You love it." His daughter laughed.

After moving his own vehicle to the next street, Troy walked back to Faith's. With his deputies in place, Troy made himself comfortable, prepared to sit up all night, if necessary. He reclined in the chair in front of the television, while Faith sat across from him, knitting. It was a cozy domestic scene, one he hoped would be repeated many times once they were married.

He remembered Megan's words and wondered if he should ask her right then and there. He opened his mouth, but just as quickly closed it. He should at least give her a ring. He had to do this properly, but he didn't want to wait much longer. This weekend, he told himself.

At ten o'clock Faith yawned.

"You don't need to stay up on my account," he said.

"You're sure?"

"Positive. Go on to bed. Just promise me that if you hear a scuffle or any activity in this part of the house, you won't come rushing out of your bedroom."

"But—"

"Faith, please! This is important."

"All right," she agreed, although he could tell how worried she was.

It wasn't until after midnight that Troy's hunch proved

to be correct. He was sitting in the pitch-dark living room when he heard a slight commotion near the garage. Not wasting a moment, he contacted his deputies and had them surround the area.

"Troy?" Faith whispered from the hallway. "Did you hear that?"

Apparently she was a light sleeper or hadn't been to sleep at all.

"Go back to your room and stay put," he said, not hiding his annoyance. He enunciated each word as distinctly as he could, keeping his voice low.

She didn't respond.

"Did you hear me?" he asked more loudly.

"Fine, fine. I'm on my way," she muttered. "I never knew you were so bossy."

Maybe he was but Troy refused to take any chances with her safety. He was the one paid to take risks, not Faith.

A louder commotion broke out in the garage, and Deputy Weaver gave a shout. Troy ran for the back door and opened it just in time to see a man dressed completely in black dash across the side yard.

Troy was long past his physical prime, but, junk food aside, he kept in shape. Racing after the man, he tackled him, landing hard on the wet grass. Weaver, who was directly behind him, grabbed the intruder by the scruff of the neck and dragged him to his feet. Troy slapped on the handcuffs he'd kept attached to his belt.

Deputy Johnson shined a flashlight into their prisoner's face and Troy instantly recognized the man who'd been the source of all this trouble. He felt a sense of satisfaction.

"Take him to the station," Troy said after Deputy Johnson had read the perpetrator his legal rights.

The two deputies led him away while Troy brushed off his uniform. He was getting way too old to be chasing felons, but he wasn't about to let this one escape.

He returned to the house, turning on the kitchen light. "It's safe for you to come out now," he called.

Faith hurried in, wearing her housecoat. "Troy—oh, my goodness, what happened?" Without waiting for him to answer, she opened a drawer, retrieved a towel and dampened one corner. Standing close, she dabbed at his mouth.

"What?" He was surprised to realize he was bleeding. He hadn't felt a thing.

"You got him?" she asked.

Troy nodded. "Sure did."

Faith pulled out a chair and they both sat down. Her hands were trembling, and he reached for them, chafing warmth back into her cold skin.

"Did you recognize him?"

"I did."

"Who is it?" she asked. "And why does this person hate me so much?"

"His name is Mark Schaffer."

A puzzled look appeared on her face. "Who? I've never heard of him before. What could I possibly have done to make him target me?"

"This isn't about you, Faith. I should've seen that much sooner. This has absolutely nothing to do with you."

Faith stared at him in confusion. "I don't understand."

"I haven't got all the answers myself, but I'll tell you what I think happened and why."

"Please." Her eyes implored him to make sense of it all.

"Schaffer was a friend of Dale and Pam Smith, who were the tenants before you. While they were living here, my office received a number of complaints about them. I spoke to Schaffer personally on several occasions. He's involved with drugs and hangs out with a rough crowd."

"But…he eventually moved away."

"I don't think it was by choice. I can't say for sure exactly how they did it, but I believe Cliff Harding and Jack Griffin persuaded the Smiths and their gang, including Mark, to leave. They hadn't paid rent in months and they were bringing undesirables into the neighborhood. Grace was afraid that if she evicted them, they'd trash the house."

"And you figure Cliff and Jack convinced them to move?"

"True. But I don't know how." He gave her a half smile. "You'll have to ask Grace about that and, when you find out, don't tell me, okay?"

"Okay."

"My guess is that Mark, or one of his cronies, left a stash of drugs behind in their rush to vacate the premises. He's been coming back looking for that. Most likely drugs, but it could be money or something else of value. I assume it's hidden somewhere in the garage, seeing he's targeted that area."

"But he broke into the house first."

"Either he doesn't remember exactly where he hid his stash or whatever it is—or he was hoping to get you to move so he'd have time to search after you left. When you didn't turn tail and run, he had to take his chances, which is why he returned to the house. Then you got the alarm system and he was limited to the garage."

"It's over, then." The relief in her voice was evident.

"I believe so. Ironically, I think there's a good possibility that whatever was hidden inadvertently got tossed out when Grace and Cliff had the house cleaned and repainted."

Troy stood up to leave. The cut on his mouth had started to throb and he needed to get to the station to deal with Schaffer.

She walked him to the front door, but stopped him before he could open it.

"You're safe now," he assured her.

"I know," she whispered, then gently caressed his face.

He caught her hand and held it to his cheek. Every instinct he had told him to stay.

She smiled at him. Closing her eyes, she leaned forward and pressed her mouth to his, careful not to touch the injury. He could feel the swelling in his lip but it didn't impede their kiss.

Troy stepped back to keep himself from pulling her into his arms and kissing her the way he had earlier.

He released her, reluctant to let her go. "We need to talk. Soon."

"I agree." There was a warmth in her eyes, an openness in her expression.

As he walked away, he noticed that the pain he'd felt just moments earlier had disappeared.

Thirty-Four

Gloria Ashton sat in her patrol car with the radar gun in her hand. This spot on Harbor Street was notorious for speeders. Writing tickets was the least favorite aspect of her job, but a necessary one. As the most recently hired deputy, she had her dues to pay. She hoped it wouldn't be long before she had the opportunity to work directly with Sheriff Davis, the way Weaver and Johnson had on Wednesday night.

Mark Schaffer had been placed under arrest and was currently being held at the county jail. The *Cedar Cove Chronicle* had done a write-up on the incident. Needless to say, the entire Rosewood Lane neighborhood had heaved a collective sigh of relief.

She was on the last stretch of her seven-to-three shift. A car rounded the corner and, seeing her patrol vehicle, automatically slowed. Gloria didn't bother to check its speed. Whoever was driving hadn't gained enough momentum after clearing the corner to reach the legal limit. To her surprise, the car pulled in and parked behind hers.

She wondered if the driver was in some kind of trouble. She set the radar device aside and climbed out of her patrol car. When she recognized Dr. Chad Timmons, she stopped abruptly.

"Do you have a problem, Dr. Timmons?" she asked in her most professional voice.

He'd lowered his window. "Can I talk to you?"

"About what?" she asked, although she was pretty sure the subject matter wouldn't be to her liking.

"I'd rather do it over a coffee."

"I'm on duty."

"Afterward, then."

She shook her head.

Obviously frustrated, Chad sighed. "I'd like to clear the air between us."

"No. Our…encounter was a long time ago and, from my point of view, highly embarrassing. I prefer to forget it."

"Unfortunately, that isn't the case for me."

"It's over."

"Apparently it was over before it could even start," he said. "If you don't want to have coffee with me, then—"

"I don't."

"Okay, but give me a chance to settle this in my own mind. That's all I'm asking. Some closure, much as I hate the word."

Gloria sighed, unsure what to do.

"Ten minutes, fifteen," he said, no doubt sensing her indecision. "Is that too much to ask?"

"I don't see what purpose it would serve. From what I heard, you're dating Sarah Chesney now."

That she was aware he was seeing another woman appeared to please him immensely, because he broke into a wide grin. "Sarah and I are friends, nothing more. What's this I hear about you and Zack Birch?"

"Are you keeping tabs on me?" she demanded angrily.

"No more than you are on me," he countered.

She couldn't argue with that, so she said nothing.

"Ten minutes, Gloria. You name the time and place."

She glanced at her watch. "All right, meet me in two hours. That's when I get off."

He smiled in triumph and she wanted to wipe off his smug grin. "Where?"

She was going to suggest the Pancake Palace but changed her mind. Someone might overhear their conversation and she'd rather not risk that. "Meet me at the marina by the totem pole," she said. "Ten minutes. That's it."

"Fine. Do you want me to bring a stopwatch?"

Despite her irritation, she grinned. "That might not be a bad idea."

Two hours later, Gloria had changed out of her uniform and parked in the lot next to the library. The foot ferry from Bremerton was just getting in, and the first wave of shipyard workers disembarked. Her hands clenched the steering wheel. She couldn't shake the feeling that she'd regret this.

Waiting until the last possible moment, she left her vehicle and walked toward the marina. Chad was already there, waiting for her. She hadn't seen him in a couple of months and was struck, once again, by his classic good looks, which were precisely what had attracted her the first time they met. That night had been a disaster, one she had no intention of repeating.

Chad leaned against the railing, exuding confidence and poise. Where she'd once found that appealing, now it annoyed her.

As she approached, he handed her a coffee. Wordlessly she accepted it and looked at her watch. "Your ten minutes are ticking away."

To her surprise, he turned toward the railing, resting his arms on it as he held his coffee and watched the gently bobbing boats in the marina. "I never thought I'd enjoy living in a small town," he said. "You didn't either, did you?"

"Are you going to waste your ten minutes with chitchat?"

He went on as if she hadn't spoken. "I took this job at the clinic thinking I'd give it six months."

"And move on."

"Right."

"You should have." It would've been a relief to her if he had. Then she wouldn't risk seeing him—and remembering.

"I stayed because of you."

"Oh, please." She didn't hide her sarcasm. This was the last thing, the absolute last thing, she wanted to hear.

"I'm not making it up, Gloria." He paused. "How long has it been?"

"I forget." She hadn't, but she wasn't about to let him know that their night together still lingered in her mind.

"I can't stop thinking about you," he said quietly.

"Try harder," she advised.

"Do you suppose I haven't?"

"It was one night. I'd had too much to drink."

"No, you hadn't. You knew exactly what you were doing and so did I."

Gloria released her breath. He was right, and while she'd like an excuse for their brief interlude, there was no point in lying—to him or to herself. "Why can't you be like every other man? Notch your bedpost and go on to the next conquest?"

"Is that what you think of me?" He actually sounded hurt.

"I apologize. But apparently you read more into our…encounter than you should have." She *didn't* want to hurt him. Hurting anyone went against her nature; nevertheless it was best, as far as she was concerned, to forget this and move on.

He continued to look out over the water. "At first I thought your reluctance had to do with Linnette."

It had. Gloria had met Chad, and they'd spent that one night together. Then, through a fluke, she'd discovered that her sister had a crush on him.

Except that, at the time, Linnette hadn't known they were sisters. No one did.

After being adopted as an infant, Gloria had grown up in California, in a loving home with wonderful parents. Then, six years ago, she'd lost them in a plane crash. Her life had faltered until she managed to learn the names of her birth parents. It was a shock to discover that after they'd given her up for adoption, they'd gone on to marry and have two other children. These were Gloria's full siblings, her sister and brother. Hungry for the connection with family, she'd moved to Cedar Cove.

Then, as luck would have it, her sister had moved into the apartment next door. Her birth father, Roy, sometimes said that luck, good or bad, was all a matter of timing. In this case, the timing and the luck were both. Good *and* bad. Linnette, a physician assistant, had a huge crush on Dr. Chad Timmons, and Gloria had quickly bowed out of the relationship with Chad, preferring to step aside rather than risk destroying her chances with Linnette because they were both interested in the same man. She'd made so many mistakes, and sleeping with Chad was near the top of that list.

The night with Chad had been completely out of character. She felt embarrassed thinking about it. Even after Linnette had started dating Cal Washburn, she'd decided not to see Chad again. She'd convinced herself it was just easier that way. Less awkward.

"Linnette is out of the picture," he added gently. "She has been for quite a while."

Chad sipped his coffee. He still didn't look in her direction. "My point exactly."

"Why is it," Gloria demanded, "that you have such a hard time accepting the fact that I'm not interested?"

"Because I know it's a lie."

"You have a rather high opinion of your charms."

"Perhaps," he agreed readily. "However, I doubt it."

His remark amused her. "Really?"

"Yes, really." He turned to face her then, with his back to the railing. "I scare you to death because I'm the first man to get past your guard. You have your life carefully planned out and falling in love didn't fit those plans. Take a memo, Gloria: Life is full of surprises. Not everything happens according to schedule."

"Excuse me. I thought you were a family physician, not a psychologist."

He ignored that. "I don't mean to sound egotistical, but you're in love with me, and like I said, it scares you to death."

Her laugh was forced and high-pitched.

"If you want to laugh," he said in a bored voice, "go ahead, but we both know the truth."

In response, Gloria conspicuously checked her watch. "Your time is about up."

"I thought you'd be able to acknowledge your feelings and admit that what we shared was very, very good. I guess not."

"And you know all this about me, about us, after *one* night? One foolish, drunken night, I might add."

"No. It's taken me a while to figure it out."

For reasons she couldn't explain, a lump had formed in her throat.

"As you say, my time's about up. And I don't just mean my time with you now, this afternoon. I wanted you to know I've given my notice at the clinic, but before I left Cedar Cove I felt I should tell you how much I wish things were different between us."

An unexpected feeling of loss washed over her and she couldn't speak. She swallowed hard.

"I hope you find the happiness you're looking for," he said. "I just regret it wasn't with me." He looked directly into her eyes, smiled and threw his coffee container into a nearby trash bin. Without another word, he walked away.

Gloria remained rooted to the spot. After a moment, she closed her eyes and acknowledged that he was right. She'd carefully planned the reunion with her birth family, but nothing had worked out the way she'd hoped. She wanted to be close to her sister and brother, and that hadn't happened. Nothing had gone as she'd envisioned. She saw Mack once in a while, for a quick drink and some stilted conversation, and exchanged an occasional phone call with Linnette. It wasn't their fault; she'd counted on too much from them—too much too soon. They'd already established lives, with no firm place for her. Corrie was superficially warm and friendly, but Gloria felt she'd never got past her guilt over the adoption. Of all of them, she had the best relationship with Roy, a former cop himself.

Trembling, she leaned against the railing, watching as Chad walked toward the clinic. All these months, she'd been afraid of what would happen if she ever let him back into her life.

That night, that fateful night, he'd seemed to recognize her pain. When she didn't answer his questions, he'd whispered that she could tell him when she was ready. But she wasn't any more ready now than she'd been then.

After that one night with Chad, Gloria had felt vulnerable. He'd shaken her sense of self-preservation. Instinctively she'd fled, determined that what had happened could never be repeated. She didn't like being out of control. She couldn't risk getting emotionally involved with him, with anyone. Linnette's interest in him had been a convenient excuse, but that was all—an excuse. Especially when Linnette had fallen for Cal, when she was over her infatuation with Chad.

Although Gloria had rebuffed Chad several times, he hadn't given up and refused to accept that she didn't reciprocate his feelings. Only now did she admit what those feelings were, and only because he'd forced her to.

Now Chad was leaving and she had the strongest intuition that if she let him go, she'd be sorry for the rest of her life.

Gloria returned to her vehicle and sat there for several minutes, debating what to do. The safe response, she supposed, would be nothing. He could leave, and her life would be unchanged….

No, it wouldn't.

She couldn't lie to herself anymore. She cared about him, had cared for a very long time. Dropping her head to the steering wheel, she considered her next move. The lump in her throat hadn't gone away and she gave a shuddering sigh, trapped in her indecision.

Without any further deliberation, she got out of her car

and slammed the door. Anger vibrated through her. She wanted to kick, yell, scream, stamp her feet.

The medical clinic was close to the marina, and she walked there at a clipped pace, nearly breathless by the time she arrived.

The waiting room was crowded. She stepped up to the receptionist's desk and stood in line. "I need to see Dr. Timmons," she said when it was finally her turn. The woman started to ask her something, but Gloria broke in. "This is a personal matter."

For a moment she thought the receptionist was about to argue with her. Then she followed the woman's glance. Chad was speaking to a nurse in the background; he paused when he saw her, said a few words to the nurse and started toward the reception area.

Gloria met his eyes.

"Dr. Timmons," the receptionist said loudly, "this woman wants to see you on a *personal matter.*" Gloria cringed in embarrassment.

"That's all right, Micki." He directed his next comment to Gloria. "I'm on duty."

This was incredibly uncomfortable. In addition to the staff, the waiting room full of patients who studied them as if they were Hollywood celebrities indulging in a public spat.

"You wanted to see me?" he said coolly.

The least he could do was put her at ease. He didn't. She managed to nod, her mouth too dry to say anything at all.

"I have to get back to my patient," he said, looking quickly over his shoulder.

In other words, if she had something to say she'd better do it soon because he didn't have time to waste.

"What you said earlier..."

"I said a lot of things earlier."

She closed her eyes. "Don't leave," she blurted out.

"Are you saying you want me to stay in Cedar Cove?" he asked.

"Yes." She risked opening her eyes.

He was smiling.

Gloria heard someone call his name.

Chad reluctantly moved away. "We'll talk," he said.

Gloria nodded, turned and hurried away. Either she'd taken a huge step forward or she'd made the most foolish mistake of her life. No, the *second* most foolish mistake…

Thirty-Five

Mack rounded a corner of the high-school playing field during his five-mile run. His legs and his heart were pumping at their maximum. His thoughts kept pace as he contemplated his relationship with Mary Jo. Although they were engaged, it wasn't what he'd expected. Even now, Mack remained somewhat unsure of Mary Jo's feelings toward him. If she genuinely loved him, he saw little evidence of that. His own feelings, however, hadn't changed—he was crazy about her and Noelle.

Things had improved since their talk—and their kiss—but Mack sensed a reserve in her, a hesitation. In some ways their relationship had returned to what it had been before David's threatening visit. They had dinner together three or four nights a week and they'd resumed their card playing and television watching. That much was good. Most of the tension between them had abated, and for that Mack was grateful. Still, he was aware of her reluctance to become more involved and he didn't understand it.

They'd kissed that one time, which had been wonderful. However, their kisses since then were restrained. Perfunctory. Brief kisses at the end of the evening were the most he'd come to expect. Nothing too passionate or even playful. Mack wanted more, hungered for more, and always left her half of the duplex with an ache in his gut.

Five months ago if someone had told him he'd be engaged he might've been skeptical. Still, it would have been a possibility. But if anyone had predicted he'd be crazy in love with his fiancée, who was living in one side of a duplex with him on the other, and that they'd barely touch, he'd have laughed. Yet that was exactly what was happening and he felt helpless to do anything about it.

He didn't know what had possessed him to agree to her stipulation of a six-month engagement, in which they were to do nothing more than exchange quick kisses and hold hands. Unbelievable! They hadn't even been engaged a month. The thought of going an additional five seemed intolerable. Most engaged couples were in love and acted like it.

The harder he ran, the clearer things became. He should've realized it earlier. Mary Jo enjoyed his company and his protection, but she wasn't in love with him. If she was, she wouldn't have been able to maintain this hands-off policy. While he panted with longing, she kept a respectable distance.

What also became clear was that any feelings she had for him were clouded with appreciation for the help Mack had given her. She'd been desperate to get away from her brothers, to gain her independence.

In his eagerness to bring her and Noelle to Cedar Cove, he'd misjudged. She needed space and time to deal with her emotions and resolve the issues with David by herself—without him *or* her brothers meddling, making decisions for her.

Instead of recognizing Mary Jo's need to handle her

own life, her own affairs, and raise her daughter as she saw fit, Mack had been trying to play the role of hero. Hoping to smooth the way for her, he'd robbed Mary Jo of the opportunity to prove herself. When he'd moved her next door, he hadn't allowed her any genuine choice. He'd stacked the deck by renting the place to her so cheaply, without ever revealing the truth. He'd made it impossible for her to refuse. Mack had simply replaced Linc and become the big brother she both loved and resented.

What an idiot he'd been. Mack liked to think of himself as fairly intelligent and marveled that it'd taken him this long to see what he'd done. His emotions had blinded him to what should've been obvious. His love for Mary Jo and Noelle was suffocating her.

Even when he'd talked to Linnette, Mack had been so focused on himself and his needs that he hadn't given the slightest thought to Mary Jo's fears. No wonder she held him at arm's length.

Decisive action had to be taken. Difficult as it was, he had to step away, give Mary Jo the independence she needed and pretend he didn't care.

Depressed, Mack finished his run. He did some intermittent stretches, slowing to a trot to cool down. As he reached the duplex he came to a standstill.

Mary Jo was outside, sweeping the walkway; she often did light yard work on Sunday afternoons. She smiled when she saw him.

He made a point of looking away but not before he saw her frown in confusion. He'd planned to think about everything more thoroughly but since she was available to talk now, perhaps it would be best not to delay the inevitable. He walked toward her.

"How was your run?" she asked.

Consumed by his thoughts, Mack didn't reply. "Do you have a minute?" he asked, wanting to avoid chitchat.

"Uh, sure. Is something wrong?"

Hands on his hips, he flung his head back and stared up at a cloudless sky. He didn't offer any reassurances and gestured toward her side of the duplex instead.

He followed Mary Jo inside and into the kitchen. Knowing he liked iced tea, she kept a pitcher filled inside the refrigerator. Mack had taken it as a sign that she cared and realized now that she would've done it for her brother or a friend or anyone.

"Thanks," he said as she took a tall glass from her cupboard.

"What's up?" Mary Jo asked as she handed him the tea.

Mack took a deep swallow of the cold drink, savoring the liquid as it slid down his throat. He tried to compose his thoughts. When he'd drunk some of the tea, he set his glass on the kitchen counter. Mary Jo stood on one side of the room and he stayed on the other.

"I run for more than the exercise," he said. He had trouble meeting her eyes. "It gives me a chance to think."

She didn't comment.

"While I was out this afternoon, it occurred to me that I have a special bond with you."

Her responding smile was warm. "I know."

"That bond is Noelle."

Her gaze flickered, as if she was slow to comprehend his meaning.

"We both love Noelle." Finally, he looked directly at her. "You're her mother and I'm the one who delivered her. That baby girl captured my heart the moment she drew her first breath."

Mary Jo remained silent, watching, waiting for him to continue.

"I'm afraid my love for Noelle…confused me, and I assumed I'd fallen in love with you, too. While I was running this afternoon, I figured out that my emotions were all jumbled and that—well, that…my love for you isn't what I thought it was." He nearly choked on the words but somehow managed to maintain eye contact.

"I'm not sure what you're saying," she said after a strained pause.

"I guess I'm trying to explain that when I heard how David threatened to take Noelle from you, I panicked. Marrying you seemed like a viable solution and now…"

"It doesn't," she finished for him.

"Yes," he answered, grateful she'd said the words. Even now Mack wasn't convinced he would've been able to spit them out. Because he did love her and, more than anything in this world, wanted her as his wife.

"About Noelle…"

"Yes, Noelle. The engagement was for her protection. We both felt if we were engaged and then married, that would keep David from pestering you."

"But the only reason he's interested in Noelle is because he thinks he can manipulate his father into giving him money."

"Right." Mack nodded. "If you have any more problems with him, just let me know."

"What will you do?" she asked.

Mack didn't have an answer for that. "I'll sort it out when I have to. But rest assured, I'm not going to let anything happen to Noelle." Or to Mary Jo, either. "I'll help you whenever you need me to. You have my word on that."

She looked away and sighed. "And you realized you can help without the necessity of marrying me."

"Yes," he said. "Instinctively you knew that."

"What do you mean?" she asked, a slight edge to her voice.

"You wanted that six-month engagement," he reminded her. "Which was more of a probation period."

"Oh...yes." She did busywork in the kitchen, folding the *Cedar Cove Chronicle* and tossing it into the recycling bin, then smoothing out a towel that lay on the counter. "So what you're saying is you want out of the engagement?"

He hesitated and swallowed hard. "That might be for the best."

"Fine." She hung the towel on the oven door. "You said I knew marriage wasn't right for us, but you obviously did, too."

He frowned.

"You didn't tell your parents, remember? That must've been why."

Perhaps, but he doubted it. He took another long drink of his iced tea and set the empty glass aside. "Then we understand each other?" he asked.

She gestured weakly. "I'm sorry, I guess I don't. What *is* our relationship, Mack?"

Good question. He shrugged.

"We're neighbors," she began.

"Well, of course," he said. As well as landlord and tenant. He quickly decided this wasn't the appropriate time to divulge *that*. And it wasn't as though it was hurting him financially. Plus, he rationalized, the fact that he owned the duplex meant she'd been able to attain at least a degree of independence.

"Friends."

"I certainly hope so."

His response seemed to reassure her.

"But you'd like the freedom to…to see other women, wouldn't you?" she asked, her voice sharpening. "That's *really* what this is all about, isn't it?"

He stiffened. "If you're suggesting I've met someone else, then you're wrong." He didn't want her to think he was another David, a man who'd discard her without a care.

"But you want the freedom to see others," she said.

"That goes for you, too." Again the words nearly stuck in his throat. "You'd be free to date other men if you wished." He hoped that wasn't the case. It would be hell on earth to watch some other man stroll into her life, and stand idly by. Mack didn't know if he could do it.

She looked down at her bare hand. "I guess it's just as well we never got around to shopping for rings."

"Just as well," he repeated.

"Perhaps that was another instance of us both knowing that marriage wasn't right for us."

"Maybe so," he agreed.

They seemed to run out of things to say at the same time. But Mack couldn't bring himself to leave. In the pit of his stomach he knew that once he walked out the door, invitations to visit would be few and far between.

"Do you feel better?" Mary Jo asked after a lengthy silence. "I always do when I've finally told someone the truth."

"Yeah," he said and forced a smile at the irony of her statement. He started toward the door, then abruptly turned back. "If you need anything, don't hesitate to call, okay?"

"Okay."

"Promise me you won't let pride get in the way."

"I can't, not where Noelle's concerned," she said. "Anyway, I know how important she is to you, and I wouldn't keep you apart."

"I'm grateful."

She walked with him and held open the door. Head down, long hair hiding her face, she said, "I'm grateful, too—that you're my...friend."

Mack found he couldn't leave without kissing her. Slipping his finger beneath her chin, he raised her face and then, after a single heartbeat, lowered his mouth to hers. The kiss was slow and tender. When he lifted his head, Mack could hardly speak. "Friends and neighbors and...perhaps more." He wanted to be sure she understood that the possibility existed. What he hoped, what he needed, was some indication from Mary Jo that she wanted him as part of her life. Then and only then could they move forward.

Mary Jo closed the door after Mack, then sank onto the living room sofa, almost too stunned to think. She supposed Mack was right to break the engagement. She liked him a great deal and was already half in love with him—maybe all the way in love with him. So much had happened in the past year, so much she didn't fully understand. If her mother had been alive she could've talked things over with her. And there wasn't anyone else. She wouldn't dream of burdening Grace or Olivia.

Her life was completely different from what it had been a few months ago. She had little in common these days with even her closest friends. Yes, they chatted and stayed in touch, but Mary Jo had a baby and could no longer take off at a moment's notice to go to a movie or shop or do anything else. Her whole life, and therefore all her relationships, had changed since Noelle's birth.

In a relatively short time she'd become a mother, left her family home, moved to a new town, taken a new job. Now she had one more item to add to that list. She'd become engaged and unengaged within a month. But like everything else, she'd deal with that and with Mack's confused feelings for her.

He was right, of course; it was better to be honest, although she was still unsure exactly where their relationship stood. One thing she did feel sure about, though, was the fact that Mack would move heaven and earth to protect Noelle.

The baby stirred from her afternoon nap and Mary Jo went into her room. After changing Noelle's diaper and feeding her, she set her in her baby seat and began doing what she always did when she felt troubled. She cleaned house.

While she was hanging up her clothes in the bedroom closet, the nail from a loose board caught on the toe of her sock. It wasn't the first time she'd snagged a sock on that nail. Under other circumstances, she'd ask Mack to hammer it down for her, since he acted as the rental manager on behalf of his friend. But she couldn't go to him just now. Besides, she was fairly competent. All she really needed was something to pound the nail. A shoe with a solid heel would work equally well.

"Your mother is no dunce," she told Noelle as she knelt on the floor and found an appropriate shoe. Once down on all fours, Mary Jo saw that more than one board was loose. Retrieving a flashlight from her drawer, she aimed it at the closet floor, ready to pound away, when an object of some kind caught her attention.

"Noelle," she said, her voice rising. "There's something underneath this board."

The baby cooed from the other side of the bedroom.

Mary Jo used her fingers to wiggle the nail out, then managed to free the second one. Once the board was loose, she lifted it up and discovered, still partially hidden, what seemed to be a wooden box.

Mary Jo worked at the remaining floorboards in the closet until she could retrieve the box. Breathless, she sat on the floor, holding it in her lap. The wooden box was old; that much was apparent. It was larger than a cigar box and light. The writing on it had faded long ago to the point that it was unreadable.

"Shall I peek inside?" she asked Noelle.

The baby returned her look with wide-eyed wonder.

"I'm curious, too," Mary Jo said. Holding her breath, she raised the lid. There were letters inside, old letters. She picked up the first envelope and turned to Noelle. Reading the postmark, she said, "These are letters written in 1943 by…" The ink on the blue airmail envelope had faded. "Major Jacob Dennison." The letters were addressed to Miss Joan Manry, 1022 Evergreen Place, Cedar Cove, Washington.

"I'm going to read it," Mary Jo told her daughter. "I can't imagine why Joan would hide them like this." She carefully opened the flimsy paper.

The spidery handwriting was difficult to read. "It's written by Jacob—Jake—during the war," Mary Jo said. "He's in Europe…a pilot flying out of England, it looks like." She bit her lip. "It's a love letter. Oh, Noelle, he's about to go on a bombing mission over Germany and he's afraid he's going to die and he wants Joan to know that if he doesn't survive, he'll find a way to come to her…that he'll always love her."

For an hour or more, Mary Jo lost herself in the letters.

Sitting on the bedroom floor beside Noelle, she read one after another, her eyes often filling with tears.

She was startled into awareness by the ringing of her doorbell, followed by a knock. That signal immediately identified her visitor as Mack. Immersed as she was in the letters, she wiped her eyes and hurriedly got to her feet, excited about sharing her discovery with him.

She threw open the door.

"Mary Jo, listen, I think I might've given you the wrong impression."

"No, no, it's fine," she said. Grabbing his arm, she pulled him inside. "I found something I need to show you."

Mack frowned. "What?"

"There was this loose board in the closet and—"

"You should've told me. I would have taken care of it."

"That isn't important, Mack. The letters are." She couldn't contain her excitement. "I came across a box hidden in the closet. It has the most beautiful love letters, all written during World War II."

"You read them?"

"Well, of course. Anyone would have… You have to read them, too! Once I started I couldn't stop. They're so eloquent, so moving… I want to know what happened to Jake and Joan. I want to find out if Jacob Dennison returned from the war and if they married and had children. You need to talk to your friend right away."

"My friend?" Mack sounded confused and, little wonder, the way she'd dragged him into the room, talking nonstop.

"The man who owns the duplex," she elaborated. "They might be related to him. He'll want these letters—they're a treasure."

Mack shook his head. "That isn't possible. My…

friend, the owner, can't be related. He only recently purchased the place."

"Then maybe whoever he bought it from will know."

"I can find out, if you want."

Mary Jo nodded eagerly. "Please."

He grinned. "I'll see who might have owned the house during the war years."

"Thank you, Mack," she said.

Suddenly the uneasiness returned. "I apologize," Mary Jo said stiffly. "I didn't really give you a chance to explain why you came over."

Mack shrugged. "No reason. I just wanted to be sure everything's okay between us."

"It is," Mary Jo assured him.

Reading these letters had put everything in perspective—although she couldn't have said exactly how that had happened.

Thirty-Six

"Are you okay, Dad?" Megan asked, studying Troy closely. "You're pale."

Troy couldn't remember being this nervous about anything in his life. "It isn't every day a man asks a woman to be his wife."

"What's there to be nervous about?" Megan asked. As a child, she'd thought there wasn't anything her daddy couldn't do and she sometimes still seemed to believe it. "We both know Faith's going to say yes."

Troy wished he shared his daughter's confidence. He hoped and prayed Faith would accept his proposal, and yet he had doubts. On the one hand he felt optimistic, certain there'd been signs that she wanted him in her life. On the other…there'd been a few serious setbacks, and he wasn't assuming anything.

"Okay, Daddy, go out there and get your woman," Megan said, kissing his cheek. She steered him toward the front door. "You're sure Faith is home?"

Troy hadn't stopped to think that Faith would be anywhere else on a Friday night. They'd spoken a couple of times since the arrest, more than a week ago, but their conversations had been mostly related to that.

"I think so."

"Dad!" Megan's elbows jutted out as she put her hands on her hips. "You mean to say you didn't phone ahead?"

"Actually, no."

Without a word, Megan stalked over to the telephone and punched in Faith's number. She placed her hand over the receiver and looked up at him. "It'd serve you right if Faith's gone out for the evening."

That got his hackles up. "Who with?" If Faith was seeing another man, Will Jefferson, for example, he…he…

"No answer, Dad," Megan said, shaking her head. "I can't believe you didn't phone and say you wanted to talk to her. You aren't even married and you're already taking Faith for granted." Megan sounded more amused than annoyed.

"Who could she be with?" Troy wondered out loud.

"How am I supposed to know?"

Talk about taking the wind out of his sails. Troy left his daughter's house, calling himself every name for stupid that he could remember. He should've phoned, instead of assuming Faith had nothing better to do on a Friday night than sit home waiting for him.

He was back at his place and feeling miserable when Megan phoned.

"Don't ask me how I know, but Faith's at the movies with Olivia and Grace."

"Right now?"

"Yes, now!"

"Which movie?"

Megan told him and then with a smile in her voice,

asked, "Do you have a burning desire to see Clive Owen all of a sudden?"

"I sure do! Bye, sweetheart, and thanks."

"Good luck!"

Troy was out the door so fast he nearly ran to his car. The theater parking lot was full and he had to circle twice before he found an empty slot. He purchased his ticket; then, wanting it to look as if their meeting was accidental, he bought popcorn and a soda.

The movie had already started and the theater was so dark he couldn't see anything beyond his own two feet. He slipped into the first available seat and scanned the backs of people's heads, hoping to find Faith.

Although he squinted and leaned forward, nearly dumping his popcorn and his drink, he was unable to identify her. In fact, it wasn't until the credits scrolled across the screen and the lights came up that he saw Faith.

She was with Grace and Olivia, only about four rows ahead of him. If he waited for her to notice him, it might not happen, so he approached them.

"Faith, imagine seeing you here," he said, hoping that sounded less contrived than he suspected it did.

"Yes, imagine," Grace said, exchanging a meaningful glance with Olivia. Or was that a smirk?

"Megan phoned Jack," Olivia said under her breath. In other words, they knew he'd been looking for Faith.

"Hi, Troy," Faith said, ignoring her friends. Her smile was warm. "I'm glad we ran into you."

"Yeah, me, too..." While Grace and Olivia might enjoy embarrassing him, Faith had gone out of her way to make him feel comfortable.

By this time the theater had emptied out. One of the

teenagers from the concession stand started down the center aisle with a broom and dustpan, checking the rows for stray popcorn and assorted trash.

"Maybe we should talk outside," Troy suggested. He could hardly take his eyes off Faith. Suddenly realizing that Olivia and Grace were waiting, obviously interested in what he had to say, he added, "I'll drive you home, Faith."

"We were going to the Pancake Palace," Grace said. "Would you care to join us?"

Faith looked at him then, and everything else receded. The question finally registered when Grace repeated his name. "Oh…sure," he muttered absently.

"Great. We'll meet you there in fifteen minutes."

"Sure," he said again.

The two women left, and Troy and Faith walked slowly out of the theater.

"Did you speak to Megan?" he asked.

"On my cell." Faith nodded. "Just briefly."

"Did she say anything?" He hoped his daughter was sensitive enough to keep her mouth shut about his proposal.

Faith laughed. "All she said was that I should be gentle with you, whatever that means."

Troy frowned; they were halfway across the parking lot and he could feel sweat beading his upper lip. He'd rehearsed what he wanted to say in front of the mirror at least a dozen times. Megan had insisted he have a short speech ready. Now, for the life of him, he couldn't remember a single word.

As they reached the car, Troy licked his dry lips. "I think you know how much I love you," he mumbled as he opened the passenger door.

"I thought perhaps you did," she said.

Stepping back, Troy helped Faith inside and hurried to the driver's side. With his hands against the steering wheel, he said, "I was thinking, hoping, really—"

"Hoping?"

"Yes, you know, that you and I might…might get together."

"For dinner?"

"Not for dinner," he snapped. "For life."

His words were followed by a strained silence and then she asked, "Troy, are you asking me to marry you?"

"What else do you think this is about?"

"Well, there's no need to get huffy."

Tightening his grip on the steering wheel, he exhaled loudly. "Okay, I apologize."

"For proposing?"

"No, for blowing this." Troy doubted he could've made a bigger mess of it had he tried.

"Would you like my answer?" Faith asked him.

"No."

"No?"

"I didn't mean, no, I don't want your answer. I meant, no, I want to try again and do this right."

"Okay, then, I'll keep quiet and wait." Faith settled back in her seat.

Troy had no idea how to start over, let alone do this a little more elegantly. Then he grinned. "Do you remember the night we were at our old necking spot and one of my deputies caught us?"

"Oh, Troy, I was so embarrassed." She covered her face with both hands.

"You?" he muttered. "I was the one who had to look him in the eye the next morning and pretend nothing had happened."

The memory lightened his mood, which helped ease the tension from between his shoulder blades.

"I do love you, Troy," Faith whispered. She curved her fingers around his hand. "I loved you when we were teenagers and I love you now."

"I love you, too." His voice throbbed with the depth of his emotions. "I want to spend the rest of my life with you. I want to retire with you and travel with you and make our home here in Cedar Cove."

"I'd like that, too."

"Will you marry me, Faith Beckwith?"

She smiled tearfully. "I would like nothing better, Troy Davis."

Troy had the urge to roll down his window and shout at the top of his lungs. He didn't, in spite of his desire to let the whole world know that Faith had agreed to marry him.

"Are you going to kiss me now?" she asked.

"I would like nothing better," he said, echoing her response to his proposal.

They reached over the console, arms around each other. The kiss engulfed them both, fired by all the yearning of those long months apart. Those months of sorrow and misunderstanding....

"You know," Faith whispered, her head on his shoulder, "I'm almost grateful for that break-in."

"Me, too," Troy admitted and kissed the top of her head.

They kissed again, then Faith said, "We should go."

Troy started the engine. "I should phone Megan," he said.

"I need to tell Scott and Jay Lynn," she added. "Oh."

She flattened her palm against her chest. "When do we want to do this?"

Troy hadn't given the matter a thought. The hurdle had been convincing Faith to accept his proposal; anything beyond that was unimportant. "Next week?"

"Troy, be reasonable! I was thinking June, maybe July."

"In that case, I'd say June." The sooner, the better.

"Where will we live?"

"Well, together, of course."

"Yes, but where?"

"92 Pacific Boulevard."

"Okay," Faith said, looking thoughtful. "For now."

Troy nodded. He wasn't sure what *for now* meant—probably that eventually they'd find a new house with no history except what they created themselves, the two of them.

"Oh, my goodness, we have to tell Olivia and Grace. They're at the Pancake Palace, waiting for us."

Troy checked his rearview mirror and backed out of the parking space, giddy with excitement and relief. When they walked into the Palace, Troy saw that Jack and Cliff had joined the two women.

The two couples sat in the circular booth and glanced expectantly at Troy and Faith.

"Well?" Jack asked when no one spoke. "Am I going to have an announcement to make in Monday's edition?"

Troy placed his arm around Faith's waist. She leaned toward him. "I believe you will."

Grace and Olivia squealed with delight and clapped their hands.

"This is wonderful news," Grace said, beaming at them. "Just wonderful."

"What's all the racket out here?" Goldie asked,

coming toward them with a coffeepot in hand. "Much more of this, and I'll have to call the authorities."

They all laughed. "The authorities, in the form of our esteemed sheriff, are already here," Jack told her.

"Troy and Faith are engaged," Olivia announced, gesturing toward them.

Goldie shook her head. "Long overdue, if you ask me."

"Me, too," Troy whispered in Faith's ear.

Their friends squeezed closer together, and Faith and Troy slid into the booth. Everyone seemed to be talking at once, throwing questions at Faith, who did her best to address them all.

A few minutes later, Goldie delivered a tray filled with slices of coconut cream pie. "Seeing this is a celebration, it's on the house."

"That's so sweet," Faith said.

"Yeah, but we don't know what she's charging for the coffee," Cliff joked.

"For you, it's double," Goldie said, pointing a finger in his direction.

They chatted excitedly as they indulged in pie and coffee.

"Say," Jack said, licking the back of his fork. "Did any of you hear about the old letters found in that duplex on Evergreen Place?"

Everyone shrugged. "How'd you hear about it?" Grace asked.

"Mack McAfee was in this morning, wanting to read old issues of the *Chronicle*—from the 1940s. When I asked him why, he told me there was a box of letters hidden in one of the closets."

"Did you learn anything relevant from the papers?"

"Not really. He had me read a couple of the letters, though. Interesting stuff," Jack said.

"Evergreen Place?" Olivia repeated. "If anyone will remember, it'll be my mother."

Troy enthusiastically seconded that.

"I'll suggest Mack speak to Charlotte, then," Jack said.

With his free hand Troy reached for Faith's. It felt good to sit here with friends, people he'd known all his life, and—especially—to share this moment with the woman he loved. The woman who would soon be his wife.

Next September, come back to Cedar Cove and to
1022 EVERGREEN PLACE.
You'll want to find out how
Mack McAfee and Mary Jo Wyse are doing.
Will he tell her who her landlord really is? And will they get married? What about the World War II letters? Can they track down either the soldier or the recipient? And what's David Rhodes up to?

Then there's Lori and Linc. How do her parents feel about their marriage? Do you think Shirley will continue to warm toward Will? And Rachel's pregnant—although Bruce and Jolene don't know yet... What effect will that have on her family? These are only a few of the characters appearing in the next Cedar Cove book,
1022 EVERGREEN PLACE.

Don't miss it in September 2010!

And this September, don't forget to check out
DEBBIE MACOMBER'S
CEDAR COVE COOKBOOK!